I0769664

Content Notes can be found at the back of the book.

Copyright © 2025 by Katherine Silva

All rights reserved.

No part of this publication may be reproduced, distributed, or transmitted in any form or by any means, including photocopying, recording, or other electronic or mechanical methods, without the prior written permissions of the publisher, except as permitted by U.S. copyright law. For permission requests, contact trubornpress@gmail.com

The story, all names, characters, and incidents portrayed in this production are fictitious. No identification with actual persons (living or deceased), places, buildings, and products is intended or should be inferred.

Published by Truborn Press
Edited by Erin Al-Mehairi
Cover Art by Seanen Middleton
Cover/Interior Design by Truborn Design

ISBN 979-8-9915969-5-4 (Paperback)

FIRST EDITION

10 9 8 7 6 5 4 3 2 1

WHERE THE SOUL GOES

KATHERINE SILVA

EARLY PRAISE

"*Where the Soul Goes* is a unique and deeply poignant story, expertly taking readers on a fascinating journey through alternate history. The combination of an apocalyptic atmosphere and a lush culinary world fighting to survive make this book impossible to put down. Silva's gorgeous, moving prose, alongside a cast of complex characters and mysteries to be revealed, all work seamlessly together to provide a cinematic experience through this top-notch novel."

- Sara Tantlinger, Bram Stoker Award-winning author of *The Devil's Dreamland*

"*Where the Soul Goes* is a haunting, visceral journey through an apocalyptic wasteland where survival is measured not in days, but in moments of connection. Through the eyes of an ACE-identifying character, *Where the Soul Goes* explores the quiet, often overlooked struggles of love, intimacy, identity, and loss.

"As communities fracture and reform, food becomes more than sustenance—it's memory, ritual, and the last sacred thread binding the living to each other... and to whatever lies beyond. Blending introspective emotional depth with rich, sensory storytelling, *Where the Soul Goes* is a post-apocalyptic tale like no other—where the end of the world might just be the beginning of understanding."

- Amanda Headlee, author of *This is How a Villain is Made* and *Till We Become Monsters*

EARLY PRAISE

"*Where the Soul Goes* is a delicious feast. Beautifully written. Silva dazzles disparate elements into a rich literary meal that nourishes the soul. It is a love letter to good food, good people, and the power of hope."

- Chris DiLeo, author of *Empty Devils*

"This story shines a light on being Ace and the feelings of having to hide your sexuality and pretend. It felt so personal and raw. Katherine's writing style is elegant and flows so beautifully that I found myself rereading paragraphs just to let it digest and sink in. I made so many highlights of incredibly thought provoking quotes. I really didn't want the book to end."

- Paul Preston, Reviewer *(@pbanditp)*

"*Where the Soul Goes* takes you on a journey that is uplifting and beautiful while also exploring grief, regret, and radical acceptance. From culinary descriptions that will make your stomach rumble to an absolutely killer playlist in the chapter titles, this immersive sensory experience will gently take you by the heart, not letting go until you turn the very last page."

- Emma E. Murray, author of *Crushing Snails*

EARLY PRAISE

"As a writer, I seldom read a book where I'm like... I wish I had thought of that. Not because I wish I had written the book, but because the world within is so well-developed it feels like you could go there and be a part of it. Katherine's latest, a hefty tome, but worth every damn page, is a garden of rain-soaked culinary delights. As dreary as the story can be, there are these islands of pure, unapologetic humanity scattered within, popping with sumptuous details; these islands are the ties that hold the story together.

The characters are fantastic, well-developed, and sport an emotional range that had me connecting with all of them in some way. The main character's malaise, both emotional and disease-related, drives the story in a haunting manner that is as delicious as the foods described within. Eliot's condition is fascinating, and not something I've ever seen before, and I've seen and read a ton of horror. The character of Eliot reminded me of the chef in The Menu, but more relatable, and not a total psychopath.

There are so many fantastic scenes in here, that it's hard to highlight my favorites, from drippy swamps, BBQ joints surrounded by zombie-esque hordes, to a strange cult, there's a little bit of everything in this sprawling road trip tale of grief.

When I finished, it was all I could do to not go and ask permission to write a story in this world. And that's the highest praise I can give. Where does the soul go? In Katherine's case, on the page, obviously."

- Jacy Morris, author of *This Rotten World* and *The Taxidermied Man*

WHERE THE SOUL GOES

KATHERINE SILVA

TRUBORN PRESS LLC

ASCENT

FIRST OBSERVATION

A figure moves without seeing.
Feet heavy, plodding against wild tracts of earth—uphill, downhill.
Miles and miles of bitter sand churning and razing the flesh around
flaming eyes. Skin scarred by wind, reddened by heat, eclipsed by
water, blackened by an otherworldly absence of feeling. This is pain
without grasping *pain*. Consciousness drifting in the unknown, but
body grounded to earth. Always moving forward towards
something…

1
SEPARATE WAYS

Eliot pretends to ignore the swath of vile pictures on the news in the background as he prepares a family meal This is the last one he'll ever make. Some might be afraid of their reality changing: the daily ritual sloughing off like shedding skin in favor of whatever comes next. He is not. But he isn't ready for it either.

"...another seventeen patients relinquished into the Vast today after they fully succumbed to the Ash..."

He swirls linguine in a lemon cream sauce. This recipe isn't new—it's something he's had in his rolodex of memorized dishes since he was younger; something he knows his fellow cooks and servers will eat because he's made it for them hundreds of times. It's a Lamb family classic. Will he miss making it for them? He wants to say yes but can't be sure if it's an actual feeling or how he *should* feel. It's too late anyway.

"...heavy rain and fog in the forecast. We're looking at an accumulation of zero point four inches over the course of twelve hours..."

Over his shoulder, his cooks scrub the kitchen of its grease, spilt soups, and husked garlic and onion from their last dinner service.

The citrusy smell of degreaser hits his nose as he grabs a pair of tongs and plates their food.

Octave sits with Rose at the stainless-steel counter nearby. They've sorted the dining room and are now helping mix drinks for a toast to everyone for their hard work and for whatever comes next.

Meena sweeps the floor behind Eliot and gives him a casual bump in the shoulder with the head of the broom. A friendly gesture, or at least he hopes it is. They haven't talked much since he made the decision to close the restaurant; not like they used to. They *had* to talk in a kitchen to run a smooth operation: shouting of orders, communicating completed dishes, keeping track of order slips. But they haven't really *talked* since last Friday.

"...call 1-800-WEL-SUCK to book our services now! Flooded basements are our specialty!"

He's missing something. The pasta dish is acidic with the brightness of the lemon in the sauce. He grabs a block of parmesan and grates it over each bowl.

Octave calls to him. "Hey, El. Wanna grab me a lemon from the cooler?"

He obliges. He should joke, shouldn't he? Otherwise, he might seem off. "Suppose you'd like it sliced, too?"

"Is that too hard for you?" Octave's smile glints.

"I think I can handle it."

"...feeling tired? Losing your appetite? Numbness in your fingers and toes? Can't remember how to be happy? Caxaline is just what you need to take back your life..."

Back in the prep area, a knife finds its way into his hand. He slices the lemon and listens.

The team banters around him, ribbing each other, telling jokes. But the laughter is maudlin at best. It's a solemn end to the last service they'll ever give at Tempo, his restaurant. Everyone's disappointment is like a radiator steadily warming the room.

Judging by Octave's jocundity, he has another job lined up already. Maybe Justin has one, too. He didn't bother to show up for his last day, to go down with the proverbial sinking of the ship. *Move on, they tell you. Get started in a new routine.* Eliot knows Justin's mother's been sick off and on for a while. Poor kid can't afford to stop.

Rose is still looking. She called him last Saturday after service. It was around midnight, and he was waiting for the melatonin to kick in. It never did. She begged him not to close Tempo. Each hitch in her voice was like having someone squeeze staples into his back. Every time she tried to hold in her crying, it ratcheted up the helplessness in him. He wavered. For a millisecond, he *fucking* wavered. But, he couldn't do anything to help her; not then and not now. He can't do anything to help himself so what makes him think he can

"...called The Agave Tap in Getty. Reports confirm at least forty-three casualties. Everyone in the building, including customers and kitchen staff, is assumed to have died instantly."

His hand slips with the knife as he looks up at the TV. The picture on the screen is a blur of smoke and rubble.

God...

"El?" Meena sounds anxious but he can't look away.

His breath has left him. Movement seems impossible. They'd said The Agave Tap, hadn't they? He hadn't misheard that. And everyone is dead? *Dead.*

"...True Faith have claimed responsibility. Mayor North issued a statement from his home that he is working with local law enforcement on new initiatives to flush out members..."

"Tave, grab the med kit!"

They're showing footage of the blast, warning viewers of its graphic content. Eliot barely recognizes the Agave Tap: the blue doors are nothing but splinters, the graffitied yellow walls inside scored by explosion arcs and ash. Bits of charred meat and blood spot the wreckage and stripe the fallen plaster. The network has tried to filter it as much as they can, but the deed is done. Children will have nightmares from this. Parents will likely sue in spite of the caution.

Someone grabs his arm. There's sudden pressure around his fingers. "Jesus! It's deep."

For the first time, Eliot looks away and finds Meena clutching his hand, a rag wrapped around it. She's pinched two fingers together and that's when he finally notices the blood rolling down his palm.

Fuck. The rag is soaking through. His eyes drop on the knife, on the red-smeared lemon and the dark dribbles on the floor.

"What the hell happened? How did you not notice?" she asks.

He focuses on the lemons. He knows how. But he can't tell her. "I was distracted."

His mind skips back to the TV. *Maybe Alexis isn't working tonight. No. She's always there. It's her baby. Alexis is a workaholic. Can't keep herself away. Dinner service on a Saturday night? She had to be there.*

Octave plods over, rifling through the med kit from the wall by the back door. "Are we seriously out of bandages?" Items jostle in the plastic box. "And cotton pads?"

"It's not like we needed to refill it," Meena mutters under her breath. "It's fine. We'll just apply pressure. Rose, you want to call a doctor?"

They are all dead. Alexis is dead.

"A doctor? This late?" Rose pulls the phone off the hook but doesn't punch any numbers. "There's no way we'll get 'em to come down here at this hour, Meena."

She's not wrong. There are a number of traveling physicians in Getty but they all pack up after dark. If it's serious enough, people will find their way to hospitals or call an ambulance to venture into the bleak night.

Eliot takes Meena in. Her eyes are almost the size of dinner plates: conflicted, frustrated, confused. He knows she doesn't want to be here right now.

She shifts a stool over with her foot. "Sit."

All at once, he's been reduced to a child in her care. But that's Meena: the lost mother to everyone at the restaurant, even him. Being the eldest of four siblings would do that to you, he assumes. So, he lowers himself onto the stool.

Octave hands Meena another dish towel and she pulls the old one away. Eliot sees the tender flesh of his middle finger for a second before she clamps the new towel down over it. "What distracted you?" She's asking because she wants to fill the silence and divert him from the pain… What she thinks he must be feeling. He doesn't think she really cares.

"Holy shit," Octave says before he can answer. "Is that…a restaurant?"

Finally. They see.

Rose cups her hands around her mouth.

Meena finds the television next and there goes the maternal instinct. Now she's afraid. Her eyes are bigger now than they were before and there's a stiffness in her neck and shoulders. *God, it's almost like she's not moving at all. Not even breathing.* "Fuck," she finally lets out, the expression deflating her. "I thought they were only targeting art galleries, karaoke bars…"

Alexis is dead.

Now, Eliot can feel it: a dull throbbing in his finger but still no pain. It's as if he's looking at someone else's hand. Or maybe he's sensing Meena's heartbeat through her touch. But himself? Blank except—

Alexis.

Except—

Dead.

Meena's mouth hangs open. "Do we know which one?"

Tell her. "I missed it when I..."

You fucking coward.

"But it was in Getty?"

He nods.

Absolutely spineless. She'll find out sooner or later. He doesn't want to get into it right now. He can't even process his own physical pain let alone the fact that Alexis is gone.

"It was...them?" Rose asks, her voice quavering. She's hugging herself and eyeing the exits like she wants to run. They all know only one group could be responsible so Eliot doesn't respond and that's seems to be enough for her. All she says is "right."

"It's a good thing we're closed now." Eliot can't believe he's said the words and judging by Meena's expression, at the incredulity in Octave's and Rose's faces, they have similar thoughts.

If a younger version of him could hear himself now, he'd be so gutted. Even with that realization, Eliot keeps talking. "It isn't safe. That's why I closed Tempo. I didn't know how to tell you all."

If smoke could come out of someone's ears, it would be wafting from Meena's right now. He can almost smell it when he looks into her face; can almost see the heat coming off her cheeks when she regards him.

"Octave." Meena turns to him. "Why don't you take Rose out back for a moment? Get some fresh air."

The look they all exchange is one Eliot doesn't need to translate. He's in for it.

Even after the back door closes and they are alone, they steep in each other's silence for a while longer. Eliot listens to her breathing and tries to time his own with hers. How strange it is to ignore the basic function of breathing when not focusing on it but continue to do it anyway? Every breath out of Meena seems intentional like she's trying to keep it even. Part of him wants to ground himself to her. The other, the one steadily consuming him, is so removed it wouldn't care if his lungs stopped working right now.

"I wish I could believe you," she says suddenly.

"About what?"

"Your reasons for closing." She's staring at the floor between her feet, likely at the cracks in between the tiles. "How long have you known, El?"

He frowns. "I told you. I just heard it on the news."

"Not that." She lifts her eyes to meet his. "Did you think I couldn't tell?"

He doesn't like the way she's looking at him. "Meena, I—"

"You've always cooked a certain way, Eliot: with music in your movements. It's how you got your name in the business and it's how I've always seen you work. It's what made me want to work with you initially. But lately, that's been missing." She shakes her head. "I wanted to think you were depressed like me. With all this shit going on between the Ash and the weather and the bombings, it's hard to find the good in things. But then I saw it in your face when you told us you were closing the restaurant."

"What?"

"Nothing." She chuckles humorlessly. "There was just emptiness."

Hearing her say it feels like someone's taken an ice cream scoop to his chest. He should react. He should look and feel a certain way, but he can't—*for the life of him*—remember how he's supposed to. He can't even *react* to his friend telling him she knows his secret.

"We're not talking about this," he says as sternly as he can muster. "It's over. We're all going our separate ways."

"Did you go to a clinic?" Her grip on his injured finger gets a little firmer. "Did they officially diagnose you?"

The pressure should hurt, and he should be making it seem like it does. But the jig is up. Why did he think he could keep a secret from her? From Meena? The person who he spends most of his waking time with at the restaurant. The person who can usually read his face in two seconds and know exactly how he feels? *Damn it.* Even when her grip starts to become uncomfortably tight, he doesn't react.

"Meena, please."

Her eyes water as she stares into his. "Oh, God, Eliot. The tiger's eye. I can see it."

He puts a hand up to his face to shield it from her, but mostly so he doesn't have to look at her shock.

Her voice is barely above a whisper. "You don't have to go through this—

Alexis is dead.

"—by yourself."

Eliot carefully removes her fingers from his, holds them for a moment before letting go. "I won't be responsible for anyone else's pain but my own."

Meena slides her hand away. The smoothness of the action stuns him for a moment. She's usually not the one to give up so easily and part of him had expected her to keep at him, like a dog with a bone. Instead, she turns her back to him and walks to the back door. She collects her coat and pushes out into the rain where Octave and Rose wait. Words are exchanged on the other side of the door.

For a flicker of a moment, Eliot wants to call her name. But the feeling is gone as suddenly as it appeared. Why cling to them? This was the whole point of doing what he did, so he doesn't have to put anyone through the pain of seeing him die.

The voices are gone before he knows it. All he can hear is the steady pounding of the rain outside the back door, on the roof, and in his finger.

They're gone and he's alone with the tinny sound of the television once more.

"...that's 1-800-WEL-SUCK. Call now and we'll come dehumidify two basements for the price of one!

HUNGRY LIKE THE WOLF
1979

A greasy spoon. That's all he wants. He follows Clive down the narrow backstreet as rain sparks off their jackets. The coolness of it feels good after being in the kitchen all day. The night is young, barely eleven o'clock, and his appetite is ravenous. Clive knows Getty somehow better than Eliot does, so he lets himself be pulled along by the older chef's knowing hand, even if it leads him into a dark and crooked alley.

Clive darts down a set of stairs, his hand gliding along the shiny black paint of a metal banister and Eliot follows. Their footsteps plunk into echoes as they drop down. "Where are you taking me?" he asks. "Hell?"

Clive glances back at him, a curl of his salt and pepper hair dangling on his forehead. "Maybe. I heard they had good hot sauce."

At the bottom, they shimmy along brick, threading the prone bodies of the homeless, piled under cardboard and plastic to protect themselves from the elements, until they burst out into a square. Eliot has never been to this part of Getty in his year of living there, but his eyes drink it in as if it were a tall, gorgeous cocktail. "Where are we?"

"I think they call it Night Hawk Square. It's named after that famous painting because it looks just like it. You know?"

Eliot doesn't know. It sounds familiar but he isn't an art history buff like Clive. So, he shrugs and lets his sight narrow on a tiny food truck parked in the center of the square. A couple of rickety folding tables stand along with some plastic garden chairs out front. A tangle of warm white Christmas lights festoon the exterior of the silver tin can. A white sign on top decorated in permanent marker reads, "AGAVE."

"Is this it?" he asks, even as they saunter over to it, even as they eagerly scan the chalkboard menu, dotted with rain. It is divided into two: hot dogs on one side and burgers on the other—two of the best comfort foods to indulge in after a long dinner shift. After a full day of slinging soups, fettuccine, beet salads, and tiny fruit galettes, there is nothing more wonderful than the taste of meat patty or sausage on a toasted bun smothered in condiments.

"You wanted a hot dog," says Clive, his grin mischievous. "I'm giving you the best fucking hot dog you've ever had in your whole damn life. And the gal that works here? A sweetheart. You'll really dig her."

And no sooner does he say those words than does *she* appear: Alexis in her blue T-shirt with "Volunteer" in golden bubble letters across the front, dyed blonde hair clipped up in a chaotic mess of strands that stick this way and that. Sweat on her brow but excitement in her eyes and that electric smile kind of like a Jim Henson Muppet beaming as she swirls bottles of hot sauce, mustard, and barbecue in her hands like a mixologist in a classy uptown bar.

And true to Clive's promise, Alexis serves him the best damn hot dog he's ever had: an Andouille sausage roasted in hot sesame oil and tucked inside a homemade croissant hot dog bun with zha cai, Chinese-style hot mustard, and Char Siu barbecue sauce. The first bite is like being punched in the mouth, then hugged by a friend you haven't seen in years, then punched again, and then a feeling akin to melting into the floor.

"Fuck," he says.

"Fucking right?" Clive takes another mouthful of his hotdog.

"A croissant *bun*?" Eliot stares at the Frankensteined creation before him. "First of all, a French pastry, and then a French sausage, but *then* topped with Chinese pickled vegetables and condiments?"

Clive nods. "We *should* be outraged."

He hums in agreement. "But, I also don't give a fuck. This is so good that it makes me want to forget about every other bad hot dog I've ever had."

"Amen to that."

Eliot looks over his shoulder back at Alexis as she grins and scrubs at something on her counter. "Hey!" he calls. "You want to come work for me?"

She pauses, her eyes narrowing into thoughtful slits. "Depends. Do you make gourmet hot dogs?"

"Unfortunately, no."

"Then nah. But I appreciate the offer."

He nods. "Can't say I didn't try."

Clive chuckles. "You've gotta try harder than that!" He turns to Alexis. "Eliot is too nice to ask you again but believe me: you'd dig working in a kitchen like the one at Tempo."

She laughs. "Then where would you go for your after-hours food hangovers, Clive?"

Eliot tilts his head. "She makes a fantastic point." He browses the menu, his eyes sparkling with wonder. "I can't wait to try everything on here."

Clive takes a long pull from his amber brew. "We could do it all now."

Eliot frowns. "Now? Like in an hour? Or *now* now? How soon is *now,* Clive?"

Every culinary excursion with Clive he's ever been on feels like being launched into space. When Clive liked a place, really liked a place, he'd take them through the entire menu. He liked to see chef's sweat, liked to see how much they loved what they did. And while Eliot enjoyed these orbital gastronomical trips on occasion, he isn't sure his stomach can handle eight different kinds of hot dogs in one night, even with such an incredible assortment as the menu before him.

"Like tonight if Alexis is game." He's got that look in his eye. Once Clive has spoken, there's no going back.

Eliot nods. "Alright. We're going to need more beer."

In the low hum of the lights from the trailer, Eliot thinks Clive seems younger, a spitting image of the man he met when he finished culinary school. His first boss and best friend, waging the gastronomic war against bland food, concocting spiced potions of rubs and sauces, and making it all look like art.

"A flight of hot dogs?" Alexis laughs. That will become one of Eliot's favorite sounds. "Hell yeah. I'm down. Let's do this."

They eat hot dogs until one a.m., until the sounds of the city die around them and all that is left was the tinkling of rain on the table's umbrellas and the metal roof of Agave, until their voices are the only sign of humanity in that small, fog-cloaked corner of Getty.

"Okay, so where did you learn?" Eliot asks her. They are on their fourth round of beers or maybe it's their fifth? All he knows is that his stomach is full and Alexis is like someone he'd known his whole life.

"Gotta be CIA," Clive mutters as he takes a drag on his cigarette.

Alexis sips from her beer and wags her head. "Too rich for my blood."

"Walnut Hill?" Eliot muses. "They're private and fairly new. Seems like they'd be teaching some fusion experimentation."

"What if I told you that I'm not officially trained?" One of her eyebrows arches.

"Ooh, a renegade." Clive laughs.

Eliot props his hand on his chin and leans in. "Do tell us more, oh mysterious one."

Alexis leans in as well. Eliot starts to wonder if mischief powers the lights behind her because she emanates it with every look she gives them. "There's an Asian market on the bottom floor of my apartment building," she reveals. "I started fucking around with ingredients for fun, hit on a few combinations I liked, and decided to give it a try."

"Wait: investing in a food truck was just a fluke?"

"Sure." She gathers her hair together behind her head only to let it drop back down. Eliot doesn't understand why women do that. Is it going to go up and then they change their mind or is it some kind of memory loss that happens mid-ponytail gather? Fortunately, before he and the alcohol can ask, she keeps talking. "I had saved enough from working small jobs over the last ten years and dreamed of having my own little corner of Getty to myself. Agave is my first shot at that dream realized."

"Ah, so you're some kind of hot dog wunderkind?" Eliot says.

Clive finishes his beer. "The woman of my fantasies that I never figured would exist. You wouldn't happen to be a swimsuit model also, would you?"

She narrows her gaze at him. "I'm half your age, Clive."

"Also, part of my fantasy."

Eliot glares at him. "Stop talking, Clive, or she's going to ban you and me just for association."

Clive flips him off before standing up and glancing around the dark lot. "I'm going to find a corner to piss in. No one look."

Both Eliot and Alexis cringe as he stumbles off toward a far edge of the square.

"So," Alexis says, turning her attention to Eliot. "I've heard a lot of good things about Tempo. About you. Why the hell are you hanging around with that old sack?"

Eliot smirks. "That old sack taught me everything I know. He's here writing about my restaurant for his new book, and we filmed something for public access television."

"So, he's propping you up?"

"Well, any publicity from Clive Goodthin is good publicity. He's essentially a rockstar and I'm...well, not."

Alexis tips her head. "Not yet anyway."

"I meant it when I asked earlier, you know." The glass bottle scrapes on the table as Eliot pushes it away. "You've got skills, Alexis, even if this is just a hobby for you. I'd be willing to take you on as a trainee at Tempo, if you want."

From across the square, Clive sighs loudly.

Eliot closes his eyes, trying not to picture what was unfortunately very easy to picture.

"Like I said, I appreciate the offer. But I want to follow my own star for a while." Alexis clinks his beer bottle with hers and tips it back to finish it.

Her phrase puzzles him, but Eliot tries not to think on it too hard, knowing that four or five beers has him questioning silly hair behaviors.

"Hey!" Alexis perks up, her smile impish again. "Your nickname could be the 'Chef with the Treble Clef.' You know? Because of all the musical shit?"

Eliot opens his mouth to respond but was is interrupted by the boom of Clive's laughter as he returns from across the square. "That's brilliant!" he shouts. "Oh my God, Eliot. I'm going to call my editor right now and make sure that's the title for your chapter in the book."

Despite their unstated collective decision to stop drinking, they each have another.

2
DON'T YOU (FORGET ABOUT ME)

The cut in Eliot's finger has stopped bleeding by the time he's done cleaning the rest of the kitchen and a rawness has settled into it. He ought to go to an urgent care but it's late. He's tired. He can take care of it at home.

He dumps most of the family meal into the trash and saves his own in a Styrofoam takeout box. What a waste. But he can't take all of it. He removes his apron, folds it, and places it on the counter, then grabs his jacket from the hooks by the back door. The suede hugs his back and arms as he stares at the kitchen. So many years here at Tempo. So many lives lived. He wants to give this moment the gravity it deserves but doesn't know where to start.

The back alley calls to him, so he shuffles into its grip.

Getty's buildings are eclipsed in a dense teal fog as he wanders home. Silhouettes of people appear out of the darkness, huddled in phone booths, regarding directions beneath the icy lights of a bus stop shelter, walking their dogs. All of them exist in separate realities within their own minds. They don't wave. They don't tip their heads as they pass one another. They don't say hello. They go about their business with forward stares.

Eliot stuffs his hands deep in his coat pockets to fight off the evening chill. Dampness clings to his cheeks, tries to wrap itself around him as it has done with everything in this city for the better part of a decade. Two years ago, a whisper of sunlight crept through the cling and oozed over the tops of the skyscrapers during the daytime. If someone lived up near the top, they could catch a glimpse of it and bask in its warmth. Down here though, there's barely enough light to make one's way around.

There's rain and then there's more rain. The bricks on buildings always glisten and the asphalt gleams in the hazy lights. For a few days, they'll get a reprieve, and the fog will somehow thicken to absorb all that excess moisture as it presses into them. And then, it'll rain some more.

A streetlamp short circuits next to him and blinks out. The people walking by scuttle away from it like bugs to find the next closest ochre glow and Eliot does the same.

Being an electrician pays incredibly well in Getty or anywhere for that matter. Hell, if you are any kind of blue-collar worker: plumbing, HVAC, construction, auto-manufacturing, there's no end to the work you can do. The guys who run a dehumidifying business over on Alamy Square are backed up with appointments until the end of summer even though they still run their adverts on TV. Eliot had tried to get them to come out and do the basement of the restaurant but that was before he made his discovery, before he decided the restaurant would be better off closing.

His feet carry him toward what used to be the arts district, and he has to remind himself that his apartment isn't over there anymore. He pivots down an alley, the dumpsters and trashcans crowding around while the tall buildings loom over and watch. The arts district is now a war zone. Crumbled theaters, exhibition halls, and museums have become the field of combat for the city's law enforcement to push back against the True Faith.

Hard to believe two years ago now a siren going off in the middle of the night brought a mandatory evacuation: bring only the things you need. He took his cat, the clothes on his back, his knives... the next day, it was all gone. They suspected True Faith had a cell in the building; that they'd been planning something but couldn't be sure. There was also a reading club that had its weekly meeting every Tuesday, a knitting club every Thursday, a wine tasting and food pairing every Sunday afternoon and so many more beautiful things that were splintered in the wake of that.

Alexis had let him stay with her until he could find a place of his own. He'd had illusions they could grow close again, that it would be like old times for a little bit when Harvey…

No. He doesn't want to remember that name.

Shortly after he moved out, he found his current place out on the rim of the—

Eliot's foot teeters and suddenly he's staring down into a chasm of sickly green.

Someone throws their arm around his. "Careful!" they shout in his ear.

Eliot latches onto them, his hold on the takeout box lost as it plummets into the void.

A man with an umbrella wrestles him back against the building. "Nearly ended up on the other side of the world there like your supper."

Eliot's vision is sucked down into the blackness that the green eventually becomes. "Thanks," he says, and then turns it into a genuine, "Thank you."

"Hope you've got something else to eat besides that at home." His savior gives him a nod and keeps going on his way.

The fucking canals are one of the worst parts about the constant rainfall. The ground can't take all the saturation. Getty's chock full of shoddy construction and poorly maintained streets like several other parts of the country. The asphalt and the ground give way and drop into these depths.

He imagines versions of urban hunting pits down there, though instead of stakes, there are rusted car skeletons, mangled street signs, and mountains of trash floating in a sea of filth that would kill whoever made contact with it. People used to fall into canals all the time as they opened around the city and there were a handful of salvage operations that all ended without ever bringing anyone back. Now, it happens every so often and the city doesn't bother sending a rescue party anymore.

This one has been here for some time, and he knew it was at the end of the alley. But he is distracted by Alexis. She's nearly killed him for the second time today.

A quarter of a mile down, following the orange halos of lights from apartments above, Eliot sees his own. His building looks the same as all the others with the exception of some colorful graffiti art of two shapes, perhaps people, embracing just before his ladder. He climbs the skeletal structure of the fire-exit up until he reaches his kitchen window. He unlocks the padlock, climbs in, and seals the city out.

Even here, the apartment doesn't soften the tirade of sadness that crashes down on him. Out of nowhere, he's sinking down toward his kitchen floor forgetting how to breathe because the tears are coming so powerfully and so fast. An onslaught of memories assaults him too hard to stop and consider each one.

Alexis whisking eggs.

Alexis sipping from her cocktail straw.

Alexis dancing with herself around her living room.

Alexis resting her head on his shoulder.

Alexis crying.

Alexis threading her fingers in his.

Alexis.

Alexis.

Alexis…

Eliot inhales sharply, trying to take back some autonomy from the cascade of feelings. He's never had them come back this intensely before. Usually, it's like a tingling, like when your foot or your hand falls asleep but this time, it's someone turning off spigots, stopping the flow of blood and letting the pressure build. Suddenly his legs won't work and he's staggering onto his knees, then his arms. Pressure jabs at his lungs with a long needle, taunting him to see what he'll do next. He doesn't have control. He can't make himself get up and doesn't want to. He wants to curl his legs toward his chest and lie there between the kitchen counter and the fridge and just drown.

But a sound brings him out of it. The sound of a glass being set down on his coffee table in the living room. He stiffens there in the dark on the floor. Someone is in his apartment.

They know he's there, too. His crying wasn't quiet. He quickly gets to his feet and draws a butcher knife out of the block on his counter. He waits, his eyes glued to the kitchen door. Nothing makes a sound in the hall. From where he stands, he can see the faintest cast of light. His living room light has been turned on. Whoever the intruder is, they are waiting there.

The landline is in there, and by now, it's probably disconnected—either pulled from the wall or the receiver taken off the hook.

Eliot edges out the kitchen door and looks down the hall toward the living room. An elastic shadow stretches over the hardwood and up along the pictures in the hallway, bringing something up towards its face. A drink. The glass clinks onto the surface of his coffee table again. Cautiously, he sneaks down the narrow hall and pokes his head into the living room.

A woman is seated in the armchair across from the coffee table. Eliot's cat rests in her lap, curled with its ear tucked under its head, the white of its eye just barely showing as its paws twitch in dreamland. Apple was never a great judge of character but at least she isn't in any pain.

Her—

—spirals of brown hair with blonde highlights. Eyes like a peacock. A black dress swathing over her—

—body.

She smiles at him. It's a familiar one, one Eliot is haunted by because of how good it makes him feel inside. Good and sick at the same time. He misses it. He's calm and distressed all at once, like he has a swarm of bees flying back and forth inside his heart when he sees it.

Her body was in pieces.

"Hey, bitch," the woman says.

"Alexis?"

"That's not the line." She rolls her eyes. "Remember? You used to say it to each other every time."

A stray tear rolls down his cheek. Through the shock, he forces the words onto his tongue. "Hey, bitch."

"Bingo."

"You're alive?"

She doesn't nod, doesn't say yes. Her smile feels foreign now and her silence makes him sicker than ever.

"She's not, Eliot."

She's…not?

He squints. It's definitely her. Same eyes, same chin, same wild tendrils of hair spilling down her shoulders, same…everything.

She leans forward. The light beside them brings out all the shadows in her face. She says, "Come have a drink with me."

But she's dead.

He thinks he's hallucinating. That has to be what's going on. A side-effect of the Ash he hasn't heard of. But what if? What if the news was wrong and she did make it out? What if they were *wrong*?

Alexis gestures to the chair across from her. "Come on."

He can't turn her down, so he lowers himself cautiously into the seat.

Alexis eyes his hand. "What did you do there?"

"Cut myself. Agave blew up. You were dead."

She smirks. "So, you're saying it was my fault?"

Eliot thinks he wants to chuckle, but this feels *so* wrong. In fact, he hasn't stopped frowning since he first laid eyes on her. "How did you get into my living room, Alexis?"

"Maybe I can walk through walls."

…Maybe I was here the whole time.

He's heard her say this before. Now he knows he has to be hallucinating. He still reaches for the glass of whiskey waiting for him on the coffee table. He's not sure he wants to wake from this dream.

"It's not a dream," Alexis says.

"Did I say that out loud?" He knows he didn't, but he waits for her to confirm it.

"She's not coming back, Eliot." There's a sternness in Alexis's gaze that doesn't belong. She's never taken anything so seriously in all the years he's known her. And he knows now that there's something else under that skin that doesn't belong, something that makes goosebumps steadily percolate along his arms the longer he takes her in.

"Who the fuck are you?" He finally has the balls to ask.

She extends her hand toward him almost like she wants him to kiss it. Her bitten nails gleam under the low light from his floor lamp. "I'm Death."

"Oh." The word practically drops from his lips. "Is that all?"

Her mouth does this thing where it goes diagonal and she looks vaguely like a Muppet. Just like Alexis used to. Eliot always thought it was adorable in a goofy kind of way but right now, it feels like camouflage. The monster, Death, hiding its face behind one he used to know.

"So, where do you call home? The River Styx? Valhalla? St. Peter's pearly gates?" Maybe it's the Ash that makes him revert to humor instead of fear, but he can't close his fingers around the idea that any of this is actually happening. He takes a sip of his drink. The whiskey smacks the back of his mouth and reminds him once again that this might not be a dream.

She shakes her head. "I'm not an angel or a goddess or a skeleton in a cloak wielding a scythe."

Eliot nods. "Clearly. What's that dress, Versace?"

"I got an early peek at his unreleased collection." Her puppet smile gets even more crooked and her tone almost whispering like she's gotten away with something.

"Now I know you're not Alexis." He chuckles once he's taken another swallow of his drink. "She hated black. Always wore blue."

Her dress fades into the color of cornflowers. "Better?"

What the hell? The living room feels like a furnace.

His eyes drop on his telephone sitting on his rolltop desk. It has also assumed the same color, strangely. It isn't off the hook. It isn't unplugged. He could call someone. Maybe he should.

Am I dying? Is this what it feels like when your brain starts to—

"I'm just fucking with you," she says. In a blip of time between him looking at her and looking back, the phone is suddenly white again.

"Why are you here?" The words tumble out. "Why are you taunting me the night she died?"

The humor melts from her features. He's not sure if she's genuinely perplexed by his question or if she does care, does feel some shard of empathy. If this entire thing is his brain playing some horrible trick on him, it begs the question: is he capable of giving himself any grace? Does everything have to always be a joke for him to cope with things?

"I thought it was the best time to toss out a proposition," the thing that looks like Alexis says. "It's really now or never for you."

"Thanks for the reminder," he murmurs and downs the rest of the drink hoping it will do something to knock him out of this imaginary conversation. It doesn't. "But I'm not in the habit of doing favors for things that dress up like people I used to care about."

"I chose her because of what she means to you." Her gaze stabs him, and her words puncture straight after. "She never gave you an apology and you always wondered if maybe you'd made a mistake somehow. If it was really *your* fault your friendship ended."

Alexis crying.

Alexis shouting.

They are split-second memories that cleave through his thoughts like a knife. A swirl of emotions cling to them and follow after; a riptide trying to pull him out of his semi-comfortable warm puddle of nothing. He stands up and takes a few steps away from the table. "This isn't really happening…"

"I was there."

He looks over his shoulder at her.

There's an earnestness in the thing that looks like Alexis's face that he'd wished were there earlier. "I was there when she cowered in the kitchen, listening to the True Faith rant and rave in the dining room before they set off the explosion. I kissed her on the cheek as the blast tore her apart. And I know what her last thoughts were."

Eliot's jaw is locked but he finds the strength to say, "Fuck you."

She rubs the cat's ear. "I can tell you if you want to know."

He balls his hands into fists, tries to slow down his breaths. There is a pounding in his temples that wants to crash louder and louder when she talks. "Why her? Why Alexis? Why'd she have to die?"

"Because she was on my itinerary." Death finishes her drink. "It was nothing personal. It was just business."

"Business…" he spits the word as his chest swells. "That's cold."

Her gaze snaps back to him. "Four minutes ago, I walked into an apartment in San Jose and took a sweet old lady by the hand. Three minutes ago, I hugged a drowning high school graduate after he hit his head on the cement by his family's pool in Soho. Two minutes ago, I sang 'Sweet Jane' to a drug-addicted mother of three as she overdosed in Tampa. And as I've been telling you all of this, I rocked a child in my arms after he fell from the fourth-floor balcony of an apartment in Atlanta."

A feeling like ice water pours over him from his head to his toes as she talks and he realizes he's shaking.

She continues. "In each second between those deaths were more…hundreds at least. So, why do you think I'm here shooting the breeze with you?"

His throat feels like sandpaper as he utters, "Why?"

She licks her lips. "Because none of their deaths tasted as good as your cooking does."

Ah,

that moment when Death tells you that your cooking tastes
better than *dying people*.

3
LITTLE LIES

Food had saved Eliot's life, even if it was a token thing for chefs to say. It was almost synonymous with "I decided to start a little restaurant in my spare time" and "That has great mouthfeel." But that statement rattles around in his brain as he lies awake in bed Sunday night, with Apple curled up next to him, snoring softly. He wonders if it might save his life again.

He thinks about a certain family vacation in Italy. He thinks of a late spring-tinged sepia photograph come to life of him wandering the property of his grandmother's home in Florence, of tossing rocks at his uncle's empty wine bottles, of stealing cigarettes and smoking them up in the hills where the vegetation was so green it hurt his eyes. The summer he'd plucked olives from the neighbor's grove, tried his first sips of merlot, downed a raw oyster on the half-shell, and was plunked into a world of divine culinary splendor. He was nine and his older brother was fifteen, old enough to want to escape the pastoral existence in favor of the nearest town, in favor of chasing skirts and learning to drive.

Eliot spent most of his childhood alone. In that isolation, he discovered he couldn't and shouldn't depend on others. Even when he started as a dishwasher at a diner in Vegas where he'd met Clive when he was twenty-five, even when he worked his way up the ladder from line cook to sous chef, the basic understanding that he would always be on his own was like a tightened noose around his throat forever and always. No matter how close he grew to people, the rope yanked him back. It was safer on the edge. He'd be fine where there was no risk.

He was used to dipping into social circles, wading for a time before pulling himself out. No one saw him, really saw him. But they thought they knew, they thought they were in the company of one of the greatest chefs on the East Coast...or what was left of the East Coast. He let them think that.

Only Alexis had peeled back the foil to get a look at the raw, destitute him. She'd saved him almost as much as food had. In that respect he owed her, didn't he? But she had also almost destroyed him in equal measure.

The light barely changes, but before he knows it, it's Monday morning. The cat wakes and hobbles off down the hall in search of a breakfast that isn't there while he lies in bed and stares at the shadows in the corners of his room, wondering if Death's version of Alexis will materialize from them. When he is sure she won't, he rises, showers, and gets dressed. Normally, he'd go straight into a polo shirt and slacks. But he isn't working at Tempo today. The gravity sinks in as he paws at the mashed piles of clothes in his dresser.

He puts on jeans, then grabs an old band shirt from the bottom drawer that he hasn't worn in over three months; the soft kind that feels like it's been worn hundreds of times. He got that at a concert Alexis took him to a year ago with—

Nope. Still not doing it.

The concert was not his kind of music: Depeche Mode. The singers' faces are plastered on the front in black, the material an off-white cotton. It isn't about the band: it's just a comfortable shirt. And Alexis made him wear it to the point where it became one of his favorites.

He throws his suede jacket over it and regards himself in the mirror, the pang of loss rich in the base of his throat once more. *Fuck.* He feeds the cat, gives her a loving scratch behind the ears, and ventures out his kitchen window into the growing teal light.

...

You're going there.

You're actually going there.

His fists clench and unclench. He keeps his feet moving down the sidewalk even though his mind wants him to stop, wants him to turn back around and tuck his Goddamn tail between his Goddamn legs.

You don't even have to look, he tells himself. He doesn't have to remind himself that pieces of Alexis are still there under all that rubble across the street from where he'll be emptying his account.

Just.

Don't.

Look.

But as soon as he's through the tunnel, as soon as the streetlights catch his eyes, he's drawn to the excavation lights, the bulldozers trying to clear debris, and the twenty or so volunteers picking through rubble from the desolation that was the Agave Tap. Police cars set up a perimeter around what was once the building now crumbled, bricks like red dominoes in the roadway.

A crowd of onlookers loom around the yellow tape, curious fish puzzling at a new development that they've seen time and again in this part of Getty. There's a news crew of course: the over-confident news anchor trying to make it past the blockade over and over even with the cop right there. He's not letting her through, and the camera man is now getting in on it, his poncho over his barrel chest making him look bigger and more intimidating than the rookie cop before him.

Eliot zeroes in on his bank on the opposite side of the square: The Green Room Bank and Trust. The light over the doorway flickers in the early morning gloom as he crosses the intersection, meandering through the light traffic to reach it. A man saunters away from the ATM out front, his face scrunching up as he leaves the protective cover of the bank for the rain. Eliot pulls his wallet from his back pocket and digs around in it for his access card.

A young man guides an older woman around the corner nearby toward the bank door. It's the shoes that catch Eliot's attention: white Reebok Pumps with the tell-tale orange circle on the tongue. Two pieces of red tape have been striped over the back heel. He glances up at the glistening face and big ears of his ex-waiter Justin, as he clutches the woman's arm.

Justin's a skinny noodle of a young man in his early twenties. He graduated from the university in Getty a month ago and had been in desperate need of work. Only child with a sick mom, he'd said. Couldn't find anything else. Eliot had to hire him. He never would have forgiven himself and, at the time, it had made him feel mildly better about circumstances in his own life.

But he's confused why Justin is in this part of town. Eliot thought he lived on the other side of Getty closer to the water, where the housing was comprised of old salt boxes turned into apartments, one-story hipped-roof cottages barely holding together, and colonial capes battered by the storms that often clambered in off the water in late spring. It was a place where low-income families and those in dire financial straits lived. The arts district, or what was becoming left of it, wasn't where he suspected Justin would do his banking, even with a decent job.

"Justin?" Eliot asks.

Justin's eyes grow to the size of golf balls, a strange shade of white in the morning haze as he takes in his old boss. "El? What are you doing here?"

"This is my bank. Is this your mother?" Eliot cocks his head to look at Justin's mom, who is staring into space. A floppy, purple winter hat is scrunched down over her ears. He can only see the side of her face, but something seems off about it. "Is she okay?"

"She's fine," Justin answers quickly and tries to put himself between them.

But the presumed mother turns in Eliot's direction, and he sees it: the stark, slack expression that causes her mouth to hang open a little. Her eyes sing with the golden brightness of the tiger's eye which means only one thing.

She's got the Ash.

"Jesus, Justin," he murmurs.

Even now, Eliot notices her fingers up through her hands to her wrists have turned a charcoal color, her skin splitting, no…cracking like igneous rock in places and his stomach turns. What is *that*? He's never seen that before let alone heard of that as a symptom. But he's never seen anyone in such an advanced stage of the Ash either and this makes him want to crawl inside himself.

Justin's lip twitches as he looks back and forth between the bank and the police on the other side of the square. "You should go home, El," he says with a waver in his voice.

Eliot closes his eyes because he realizes Justin's anxiety now. He sees what was waiting for the young man at home day in and day out. How work must have felt so ordinary compared to facing your mother, your life-giver turning into…this. And then, Eliot took that normalcy away from him. But instead of apologizing, all he can say is "Justin, why didn't you tell me?"

Justin shakes his head. He bites his lower lip and takes a furious scrub at his left eye with his knuckle. "It doesn't matter anymore."

Eliot frowns. "What do you mean?"

"Go home!" Justin barks. He takes his mother's hand and Eliot watches as her fingers give way, crumbling onto the sidewalk like cigarette ash. Justin pushes her through the door into the bank without any notice.

Cold terror pins Eliot to the sidewalk where he stands. He can't stop staring at the little pile of smoldering cinder. He didn't know the name was literal. He assumed they called it Ash because of the way the tiger's eye consumes their whole eye like an inferno. That burns their brains up and leaves none of their former selves. But this…

He grunts, trying to get his breathing under control, trying to make himself move but can't. Fear has frozen him in place. His heart skips and the sides of his face tingle and gradually go numb.

That's going to happen to me. I'm going to turn into ash.

Horror has ensnared him completely. He can't focus. He can't slow down his own breaths. All he knows is he needs to get somewhere far away from here, somewhere private so he can think.

He's able to turn his head a little, to glimpse the ATM machine and his access card poking out waiting for him to input his code. He staggers toward it, and fumbles to pull the plastic out with stiff fingers, but something is gripping it from inside, locking it in place. His stomach is losing the war with his body. He needs to vomit now.

Inside the bank, there's a distant scream.

Eliot fumbles along the sidewalk. He uses his hands to brace himself along the building, to push off and go faster.

The boom is cataclysmic. Eliot isn't sure how he ends up on the ground, but a shroud of dust and smoke roils over him before he can get his bearings. Grittiness fills his eyes like glass, and he closes them, throwing a hand up over his face to shield it. There are things on top of him, he's not sure what but *heavy things.* Something wet trickles down his head.

...

"Get out."

His eyes open. Screams fill the air like bats or birds. The warbling of sirens and the roars of fire and rain compete as he tries to get his lungs to slow down. Air blasts out of his mouth in hurried gasps as he pushes himself up from his prone position. Chunks of plastic and bits of brick slide off him. As he gets to his hands and knees, something heavier stops his ascent. A telephone booth has collapsed. If it had fallen another foot, its jagged metal and broken glass would have impaled him.

Eliot crawls free of the mess and stands, coughing. Smoke is everywhere, its pungency flaring in his nostrils and bitterness stinging against his tongue. A whirl of red and blue light reaches him through the obscurity, and he staggers toward it.

Someone is yelling, but it's muffled. Moments later, a firefighter emerges from the thick black smoke right in front of him. They say something, but he can't understand it. They're a mile underwater. The firefighter scoops an arm around Eliot and guides him until the smoke turns to fog; until fresh air slashes through the mire and claws its way down his throat.

The camera man from earlier is hyperventilating in the back of an ambulance to his right. The news anchor is patting his shoulder and fretting, glancing between him and the carnage like she's missing out on the best buffet of her life.

More people emerge out of the fog: injured, shell-shocked with panic, crying… The fireman steers Eliot to another waiting ambulance. They've already got someone with a neck brace on who is buckled to a stretcher in the back. One of the paramedics immediately grabs some gauze from their bag and sits Eliot down on the tail end of their bumper. The gauze sinks against his skull and then…

Oh, the pain! Pain that grows brighter and brighter like white light and overtakes his senses in mere moments.

It's like the time Eliot unwrapped that horrible red sweater that a distant aunt gave him for Christmas. It's an all-consuming comet of horribleness or dumpster fire of distress and makes him want to fold in on himself. He passes out again.

A CHORUS

I beseech you, brothers and sisters, to listen and to lend me your ears: you have all been betrayed. That's the feeling, isn't it?

You can't help but grip at your hearts, and know that someone you thought you loved, someone you thought was your Lord and Savior would do something like this to you? How could a God so loving enact violence on our most loved ones? A violence that stores up its rage inside of them like a fire being stoked?

How you've cried with the doves.

How you've screamed.

How you've wailed at him for this atrocity.

But you have not lost anything.

Oh, no, in fact: you have gained more than you've lost. You've learned that your most beloved, the ones you have committed your lives to caring for, have been chosen.

They have been gifted a reluctant ending so that they may have new beginnings.

And who doesn't love a new beginning?

Say it with me now: redemption!

REDEMPTION!

4
FLY ON THE
WINDSCREEN

*"*G*ET OUT."*
He's treading water, churning in waves of disbelief. His eyes hurt from crying. His jaw is locked. His chest feels like it might cave at any moment. Is it possible for a human body to implode, to collapse into itself leaving a black hole, a vacuum in its wake? It would be like he never existed, which is what they want anyway. It would be better than living right now, better than feeling this…emptiness…

"…stabilizing."

The word is loud, so startling that Eliot jerks awake only to be held down by a firm hand on his chest.

"Easy," a nurse says, snatching up a light from her mobile kit next to her. "You've been in an accident."

Eliot's tension wavers. He lays on a bench in a bus shelter, the rain percussing on its roof like drums. Behind the nurse is a winnowing haze of smoke and lights and fire. He's on the other side of the square from the bank. Ambulances depart in a squeal of tires and shriek of sirens, making way for a cavalcade of new ones to arrive.

Firetrucks with revolving red lights block his view of the bank and its devastation.

"What's your name?" the nurse says as she shines the light directly into his right eye.

He flinches. "Eliot Lamb."

"Try to keep your eyes open. Follow the light." She tracks it back and forth from eye to eye. "Birthdate?"

"July 15, 1939."

"What city are we in?" The light pauses and she brings it closer to his left eye.

"Getty."

She clicks off the light and for the first time, he reads her face. Misery. Disappointment. Fear. "You've seen your tiger's eye, right?"

If he hadn't, this would have been an awful way to let him know. But he nods because he's too exhausted to wage a war on the semantics of bedside or even bench-side manner right now and his head *kills*.

"Your pupils aren't following the light as fast as I'd like. It might be because of the Ash but I can't tell. Might be a mild concussion. That cut on your head, while superficial, makes me a little more worried about the possibility."

The headache makes sense. The right side of his skull throbs like the beat of a Michael Jackson song. The lights in the bus stop shelter where he's triaged burn. He puts a hand up to the bridge of his nose and closes his eyes to relieve them. The faint humming noise around them cuts and he opens his eyes to see that the light has died.

His nurse blinks up at it. "Shit. I was hoping I could use this place for care since it's far enough away from the bank, but I guess I ran out of luck." She grabs his arm and helps him into a sitting position. "How do you feel?"

"My head hurts. But I'm sure there are other people who could use your attention more."

She gives him a look that he knows very well: relief. He's given her a reason to leave him. In the mind of almost every caregiver, it's only a matter of time before the Ash overtakes everything and renders a patient a moot point. Why bother to fix a concussion if that person is going to turn into a walking lump of coal two weeks later?

And then, he remembers Justin. He remembers Justin's mother. He remembers her fingers.

"Listen, I'm going to go check on the situation across the road. Wait here. I'll be back soon."

Eliot watches her dart back into the smoke. It's just as well. The likelihood of her coming back is nil at this point, not when she knows his secret. Eliot inspects the torn spot in the knee of his jeans, the dirt smudges on his clothes, at the spots of blood on his Depeche Mode shirt.

All at once, he imagines Death in Alexis's form gliding amongst the chaos of the square kissing and touching people only for them to die moments later. His hands shake and he makes himself get to his feet. Was this part of her itinerary as well? Was Justin a jotted note along with his mother and half the city block?

Before he knows what's happened, he's pushed inside the coffee shop behind him, the little bell dinging faintly. The place is mostly cleared out, save for a couple of people at a table in the back. One of the women there has a cup of ice chips that she's diligently sucking on while her husband mutters angrily into a phone. "We need an appointment now! No, we weren't in it. But we watched it happen… She's pregnant for God sakes!"

A bigger man with a short afro sits on a stool at the counter. His legs look as thick as logs, his shoulders squared and gut potbellied. Instead of looking at the carnage through the front window, he watches a television mounted up in the corner near the ceiling while he sips his coffee. A shaky shot of the bank roams to an anxious male reporter holding a microphone and looking side to side like he might be thrown out at any moment. Eliot can see the coffee shop in the background, if he glares enough, maybe himself?

Eliot sinks into a stool at the end of the counter. The lights are brighter here and their glare hurts more than the bus shelter had.

The middle-aged woman behind the counter pours a cup of black coffee and sets it in front of him. "You okay, hun?"

Was he okay?

He stares at the coffee's midnight surface.

Was.

He.

Okay?

"I don't know how to answer that question," he says truthfully as he accepts the mug. It's warm in his fingers. He goes to dig his wallet out of his pocket but realizes it's gone. It must have fallen when he was knocked out. He hangs his head.

"On the house. Don't worry about it." The woman moves away.

No wallet. No bank. No money.

His father had always told him never to put his money in banks. Harlow Lamb had died broke because he had never had much money to begin with but what he had saved was kept in these green bottles all around the garage, stuffed with random dollar bills and coins. His brother had sent them in a box with no note shortly after the old man's death. It had amounted to forty-seven dollars and twelve cents in total once Eliot had broken them all open and counted.

Should have hidden it in fucking bottles around my apartment, Eliot thinks. *There's no way I can get out of here now.*

The remainder of his conversation with Death the night before returns to him as he stares at the disastrous camera work of the bank.

...

SATURDAY NIGHT

"There it is," she says. "The panic."

There is zero warmth in the thing that looks like Alexis' eyes; just emptiness and that's when the fear cuts deep. It's been there the whole time like a specter watching over Eliot's shoulder but, oh God, right then, he feels its gravity. His legs turn to jelly as he shifts his gaze from one useless thing to another in his small, gray apartment.

His wavering hand grabs the back of the chair to steady himself. He is with a monster: a *monster*.

"Cat got your tongue?" she adds.

"Why shouldn't I panic?" His voice flitters: a bird trapped inside, beating against a window. "If you're who you say you are…*what* you say you are."

"Because I've just told you, I'm here to *offer* you something."

"A quick way out?"

Her eyes clear like storm clouds whisking away to show unburdened night skies. "No."

"Then what?"

Death nods toward his glass on the table. Was it that full before? No, he's finished it off. But there it is, full again with a different cocktail; this one's a fiery color with a strip of bacon balanced on a toothpick and orange rind that seemed to wave at him from the rim of the glass.

"Remember when you made that drink at Milliner's in Jackal, Missouri after a night of intense drinking," Death says. "It was morning. Nelly was asleep on the bar and Lucas had locked himself in the toilet. And Harvey…sweet, sweet Harvey."

He remembers. The mention of Harvey's name impales him with terror like the orange rind is impaled against the rim of the glass. The feeling makes him queasy and all he wants is to be alone right then. "I think you should leave." He gestures to the hall.

She remains where she is in the chair. "Don't you see? Inspiration *bloomed* in you. You lit a fire with that drink, with your food over the years, and that's gone into the bellies of countless people. But the fires are going out, Eliot. I taste their ash every moment I take a life."

The cat wakes in Death's lap and stretches its legs as it hops to the floor. Eliot hasn't fed Apple and all his concern and attention immediately falls on the old cat like a pile of blankets. He'd rather focus on her than on whatever fever dream is waging a war in his head. He picks her up and cradles her close to his body as he backs away from Death's chair. The cat's clunky purr rumbles against him. He suddenly doesn't feel so alone. It emboldens him to ask, "What are you saying?"

The thing that looks like Alexis shrugs. "People have lost something. They drift around like living ghosts haunting the places they used to care about. They need a wake-up call and you're going to help ring the alarm."

Eliot shakes his head. No. This is ludicrous. He *is* hallucinating. This is all the evidence he needs. A hero's journey scenario that his mother taught for years in her English classes? Of course, his mind has conjured this up. The Ash is pulling all kinds of bullshit out from the snarls of his subconscious. He turns his back on the figment of his imagination and walks into the hall toward the kitchen. "So, what do you need me for?" he says to himself as he chuckles uneasily. As he rounds the corner of the kitchen doorway, he jumps. "Jesus!" The cat growls and sinks its claws into his arm.

The thing that looked like Alexis sits on the counter in front of the window to the fire escape. "Sorry," she says, though the tone feels passive-aggressive.

"How am I supposed to accomplish this *world-changing endeavor*?" Eliot asks through gritted teeth as he sets Apple down on the floor and retrieves her bag of kibbles from the cabinet. He scoops the nuggets into her bowl with a loud tatting and watches her mow down, her teeth clacking on each one noisily. A small part of him falls into ease with the deed done.

"I need you to do the trip you were going to do before you found out about the Ash." She nods toward the refrigerator.

Eliot glances at the roadmap he's stuck there with bottle cap magnets. The course is as clear in his mind now as when he first drew it: a charted line of red marker from Getty to Las Vegas, meandering across the Midwest. He squints. "I can't."

Death hops down off the counter. With a quick fling, she yanks the map from the fridge, the magnets clattering to the floor.

The cat skitters off into the other room with ears pulled back.

"You can." She gives Eliot an encouraging smile.

"That was going to be a six-month trip," Eliot says. "I don't have six months left in me."

"Then you'll need to accelerate the process." She presses her finger to the route and glides it along the red line. "These are people you admire, people you've inspired in the past, people who've inspired you. You wanted to taste what they had to offer, check in with them, maybe have conversations that have needed to be said for years... They were going to benefit from the Chef with the Treble Clef. What could be a more fitting end to your life?"

He lets out a shaking breath. "I hate that fucking nickname."

Death smiles. "I think it's kind of cute."

"No. *Alexis* thought it was. It's *Alexis's* fault it stuck to me for so long." Eliot rubs his temples. "I wasn't supposed to go alone. I was going to take her with me."

A sincerity crosses Death's face. "It was going to be your apology to her. Even though you weren't the one who needed to apologize."

The whole idea had been a pipe dream: trying to find someone that would drive that trip was ludicrous and airline ticket prices had skyrocketed to thousands of dollars following the Ash's emergence and the horrible flooding. For all his supposed fame, even he doesn't have the funds to make that happen. Besides, he'd never gotten the courage to call her, especially not after his diagnosis.

"Hey," Alexis's voice slips through his thoughts. "You can *save* humanity. All you have to do is talk to four people and change their lives. Do you understand?"

Eliot clucks, more out of fear than out of disbelief. "What are you talking about? There's five billion people in the world. The Ash isn't going to kill them all."

The thing that looks like Alexis circles around the island toward him. Strange how the light seems to move to keep her mostly in shadow. "It might. Besides, the Ashen don't die."

They don't die. The sentence is like peanut butter on the roof of his mouth, like he is trying to figure out a way to unstick it, but the words glue themselves to his palette. For the love of God. They don't *die.* What does that mean? *Everything* dies. He always assumes when hospitals release the Ashen, they wander into the soup of the world until things start falling off them, until their bodies can no longer function. Sure, it is a miserable way to go but at least it *is* going…

Before he says anything, she continues. "What were your original plans? To rot in here until you completely lose your mind?"

"I'd thought about it." This, at least, is true. "You know, before when I thought there was an eventual end to it all."

"You've got probably…what? Two weeks left?" She moves toward him again. "It would be such a waste, Eliot."

He sidesteps her, not wanting to get trapped behind the kitchen island and the counter with nowhere to go. The fridge beckons and in it, the cold beer he's forgotten he has. He wraps his hand around it and its condensation blankets his palm.

She eyes the beer. "PBR? Really?"

"Don't fault a classic," he chides, cracking it open and taking a quick swig. Damn. He needed that.

"What about a facility?"

"What about it?" A slight tremor returns to his hand, but he takes another drink to mask it. "Doctors have better things to do with their time. Besides, I don't want someone taking care of me for the last month of my life."

Death curls her fingers toward the sky like she is summoning some storm. "Do *something*!"

Her tone and volume make him bump into the fridge.

She rounds the island toward him, eyes wild. "You humans spend so much time withering like dandelions, wishing you did the things you wanted to do but then let fate and circumstance decide everything for you as time picks your petals. It's *so fucking* annoying to watch day in and day out."

She stops so close, he thinks he smells perfume. Alexis never wore perfume. But Death has a light floral note like lilac coupled with the danger of wood smoke. She reaches out and takes his injured hand in her soft fingers. "The Ash is spreading. It will continue to ravage humanity, and it will swallow all in its impartial maw."

He squirms under her touch. Her fingers are soft, almost like peach fuzz but a metallic taste has blossomed in the back of his mouth as soon as she scoops up his hand.

"You can make a difference," Death says. "You can keep someone else from going through what you're about to endure. You could save ten people or a hundred."

He meets her gaze. "Or I could save no one."

She brings his hand up to her lips and kisses his cut. The metallic taste in his mouth takes over: like the copper in a dental amalgam or like holding batteries on his tongue. It swarms the roof of his mouth, his gums, his tongue, and the sudden urge to leap outside his kitchen window for fresh air hits him.

When she pulls away, the jagged knife cut through his finger has scarred over. "What's the harm in trying?" she says.

He touches the white mark there, frowning.

Death. Healer of shallow cuts. Nap location of old, ornery felines. Killer of friends.

"Why me? I still don't understand why it has to be me?"

Concern tugs lines in Death Alexis's face, and she whispers, "Why *not* you?"

5
CALL ME

Eliot takes his first sip of the coffee, and it drops down through him like hot tar. It's so strong that it pulls him out of his thoughts and sharpens the world around him. Reminds him where he is and what's happening. The bank gone. Justin gone. His mother gone.

Death expects him to carry through with her proposal but there's no way Eliot can get out of here now, no way he can delude himself with the idea of saving anyone's soul before his own. The thought of loafing around his apartment for two weeks as his body slowly crumbles away sends his mind into overdrive.

Pathetic.

He doesn't have enough to afford a plane ticket. He doesn't have enough to hire one of those ferrying services to take him across the country. If only he had enough for a bus ticket… even the buses were expensive these days.

"Anything else I can get you, hun?" the waitress asks.

"May I use your phone?"

She reaches under the counter and hefts the green block up onto the laminate with a soft clang.

"It's long distance. Is that okay?"

She seems a little more perturbed at this but gives him one more once over and nods.

He waits for her to depart before he dials the number, each punch of a button taking more from his shallow well of self-esteem.

"Hello?"

Thank God, Grady is home.

"Hello?"

"Hey. Hey, Grady, it's me."

"Eliot?" Does he detect immediate displeasure in his brother's voice?

"I need to ask a favor." The words are like kiwi fuzz on his tongue: uncomfortable, rough, stinging.

"A favor?" The disbelief in Grady's voice hits him with all the gentleness of a typhoon. "You expect me to do *you* a favor?"

"I know." Eliot props his elbow on the counter and tries to shield himself for some privacy. The other man at the counter now watches him. "I know you have no reason to want to. I wouldn't be calling unless it was an emergency."

"I told you when you moved out there that it was your own funeral, Eliot. You chose to head out to the coast even though it wasn't safe. And then you turned your back on me and on Mom when we needed you because you couldn't get over some bullshit that happened when you were a kid?"

Bullshit. The word is a reagent in Eliot's belly. It fuels and empties him at the same time and he's not sure whether to slam the receiver down or yell into it. He does neither one. "I need a loan, then I'll never talk to you again if that's what you want."

Grady inhales audibly. "You want money? Seriously?"

"Please."

"You know what? You can fuck off. You aren't my brother; haven't been for years. I just didn't see it until now." The line goes dead.

Eliot lets the receiver drop back into the cradle. Funny, he thought losing the last member of his family would hurt more. He thought it would be like losing an arm or a beloved pet. But all it feels like is eating the last cracker in a mostly empty sleeve and finding out it's stale. He's almost relieved because he isn't sure he can take one more gutting thing.

But he's still got no plan. No money. No way out of the city.

"Hey."

Eliot looks up.

The man across the counter is holding out a folded ten-dollar bill to him.

Throat closing, eyes stinging, Eliot stares at it. "I appreciate it but that's okay."

The guy doubles down, nodding. "Take it."

He accepts it, sliding it cautiously from the man's thick fingers and tucking it into one of his front jean pockets. "Thanks."

"No thanks needed," the man says. "I recognize that dejected expression. You just had a talk with your ex, didn't cha?"

Eliot shakes his head, the ghost of a laugh escaping. "My brother."

"Gotcha, gotcha." The man leaves his stool and scoots to a closer one. "My brother—well actually, he's my cousin but he's like a brother to me—he hasn't talked to me since I threw his pet rock in the lake when we were kids. Dude's clingy as all get out. I mean… a pet rock? Wonder if he's dated other minerals over the last thirty years."

That's funny, Eliot tells himself. *It's hilarious.* But he can't laugh. It's like he's forgotten how in that moment. *Don't you breathe in somehow and then…?*

The man puts out his hand. "Terry Boucher."

Eliot returns his name.

Terry touches his own head. "You need to go get that checked out?"

Eliot had almost forgotten about the injury. The pain had trickled into the background along with his emotions. He's not sure how violently it'll come back later and he's not looking forward to it. But he can't make himself go to a hospital either. He can't. He can't go *there*. So, he just squints and says, "Just a scrape. I'll be fine."

Terry's mouth forms a straight line. "You sure? You look kinda green, man."

"Well, my bank just exploded," he says slowly. "All my money is inaccessible. My wallet is gone. I think I may have also lost the key to my apartment…"

"Oh, you need someone to jimmy a lock? I can break down a door easy."

"It's a padlock on my window. No one's been able to use the front door of that place in years."

"I've got a set of bolt-cutters in my car." Terry smiles. "I'll give you a ride."

Jimmy a lock? Bolt-cutters? Eliot frowns. "That's really nice of you but we've just met, and I don't want to waste your time."

"Ain't nobody wasting my time, man. I was here fixing some stuff when that bank exploded. I've got all the time in the world. Let's go get you into your place."

Movement on the television screen behind Terry brings Eliot's eyes up to it and he forgets to breathe. Alexis stands on screen in place of the news reporter. She's nodding at him.

What the hell?

Eliot gives in, getting to his feet. "Okay. Thanks."

Terry drops money on the counter. "Susan, I'm giving you a bit more for this guy's coffee. Keep the change, okay?"

They exit into the rain. It's coming down harder now, which is probably a relief to the firemen battling the flames in the bank. There's only a slight glow coming from behind the smoke now but Eliot wonders if there's any use in trying to save the building.

"Damn it," says Terry, pulling the hood of his rain jacket up over his head. "Left my umbrella in the van. I just got this fresh cut. Damn hood's gonna mess it all up."

Eliot follows Terry down the sidewalk away from the wreckage toward the tunnel. There's a parking garage on the other side protected from the elements, its eerie, oily lights coating the concrete. He doesn't like the shallowness of the shadows. It's as if they could dart from one corner to another in the blink of an eye.

As they climb the steps up the levels, Terry looks back at him. "Were you in the bank?"

"Outside it."

"You see anything?"

Justin's mother appears in his head again: her eyes like twin flames, her crumbling fingers…

"Someone brought an Ashen inside the bank. Then everything…exploded."

"Shit. The Ashen fucking explode now?" Terry says under his breath.

He shakes his head. "I don't know."

"Something new every day." Terry clicks his tongue. "Fucking Soviet Union. Fucking Ashen. Fucking never-ending rain…"

They push out the heavy door into the third level of the garage. No one else is in sight. The odd car here and there sitting dark and empty.

Eliot begins to wonder why he let himself be convinced to follow a complete stranger, who boasts about having bolt-cutters and being able to jimmy locks, into a derelict garage. He assumed Alexis/Death was nodding at him to take the leap of faith with Terry but what if that wasn't what she meant at all? To her credit, Terry had seemed nice so far. But people can deceive. Eliot knows this all too well. So, he tenses, and his footsteps grow shorter as they make their gradual decent toward a row of vehicles.

"There she is," announces Terry, giving a quick wave toward a dark gray utility van with a ladder folded against the side. Thick metal panels concave in the front and back almost like a tank. The wheels are enormous with thick treads. The logo on the side reads: "Boucher Plumbing Inc."

A plumber, Eliot realizes. He lets out a relieved sigh.

Terry eyes him. "Something wrong?"

"No," Eliot chuckles. "The bolt-cutters make sense now."

"You think I was a criminal or something because I'm Black?" His eyes are so serious, Eliot is flooded with embarrassment immediately.

"N-no. That's not at all—"

"I'm just playing, man." Terry's smile returns. "You looked like you were going to shit a kitten."

He unlocks the driver's side door and climbs up into the seat. Reaching across, he pulls the lock up on the passenger side and opens the door.

Eliot climbs into the cab, his footing shaky. The van smells like chemicals, a fake vanilla and pine all coalescing together. A photo with curling edges is clipped to the underside of Terry's sun visor, showing a woman with an equally bright smile and a toddler in a striped shirt and pants. "Your family?" asks Eliot, trying to break the tension

"My sister and my nephew." Terry cocks his head as he turns the key.

The van rumbles to life and the dashboard lights ignite. There are so many buttons and switches, it almost looks like the controls of a space shuttle let alone a car. "What does all this stuff do?" Eliot asks.

"This lady has land and sea mode," Terry says. "Allows me to get to the most challenging places to work. Even those We-Suck assholes on TV don't have *this* sweet set up."

"You mean, 'Wel-Suck?'" Eliot laughs. "This floats, too?"

"Hell yeah. Spent a few thousand dollars upgrading her and it's paid off. Problem is, this city's got so many back allies and canals that this big ole girl can't fit into as many places. Besides, those Wel-Suck guys have kind of cornered the market in Getty."

The engine rumbles beneath them like the steady roar of an inferno. Terry backs out, deftly avoiding the other cars parked nearby in the limited space. Then shifting into gear, they descend to the bottom of the garage and out onto the road.

Eliot has never ridden in an amphibious automobile before but knows they have fast become a necessity with all the flooding over the last decade. The entire Getty Police Department converted their cruisers years ago. It is the vehicle of choice for taxis between coastal communities and every bus service he knows of has a fleet that can negotiate the odd lake, pond, or river along the highway if need be. But boy, are they expensive to make.

After twenty minutes of navigating streets, traffic and detours, Terry's van rumbles to a stop down on the street next to the alley that leads to Eliot's apartment. There's technically no parking there, but after the explosion in the square, no cop will be concerned with minor violations.

After Terry grabs his tools, they start down the alley toward the waiting canal. It seems wider and deeper today for some reason. Eliot's ears ring. He tries to ignore the blunt thud of his headache as he deftly sidesteps the drop and continues toward his apartment. When he doesn't hear footfalls behind him, he turns and finds Terry frozen at the end of the alley, his eyes locked on the canal.

"Terry?" he asks. "You okay?"

He looks up. A shaky smile shows off his teeth. "Yeah, man. I'm…I'm good." He scuttles after Eliot as though he's a mouse and not a six-foot tall man lugging a bag of tools. "You just didn't mention there was a canal."

Eliot frowns. "Yes, I did."

"Um… I just…" Terry continues to watch its depths. "I'm not a fan of 'em."

"Just stick close to the building. You've got more than enough space. You'll be okay," Eliot assures and continues.

They reach the apartment, and Eliot climbs the stairs first. After more placating, Terry follows, taking each step gingerly. The stairwell squeals under them as they come to Eliot's window. Terry pulls out his bolt cutters from his duffel, and with a quick clink, snaps the lock from the window. It bangs onto the metal beneath them.

Eliot slides open his window. His apartment feels cold, the inner blue vacant and quiet. "Want to come in?" he asks.

Terry peeks back down the fire escape toward the canal. Eliot isn't sure if the moisture on his forehead is from the fog or perspiration. After a moment, he says, "Yeah. Just for a minute though."

Eliot slithers through and snaps on the kitchen lights, banishing the shadows back to their corners. The light sears but it's better than the dark. It's almost as though the blackness has taken on a persona in the few days that have passed, ever since Death arrived wrapped in Alexis's skin. He doesn't want to be alone with it. He doesn't want it to consume the only space he treats as safe.

He gives Terry a hand through the window, the plumber's boot accidentally knocking a metal bowl to the floor which reverberates in the space like someone banging a cymbal. "Sorry man. Usually, I'm more agile than that." He straightens his rain jacket. "Like a cat. Or Axel F."

Almost as soon as he mutters the words, Apple appears from around the corner with a triumphant *prowww*. Eliot scoops her into his arms and sets her on the counter. His eyes fall on the map, the map that Death left there Saturday night.

He notices Terry looking at it. "Can I get you something?" he asks, hoping to deflect any questions. "Coffee?"

"Sure, man." Terry sinks onto a stool in front of the kitchen island and rubs the cat's ear. "You planning a road trip or something?"

Eliot brings the bag of coffee down from his cabinet and scoops the grounds into a new filter. "I was."

"You not doing it now because of the whole money thing?"

"I don't have enough to pay for a bus ticket. Definitely not enough to pay for a plane ticket." He grabs the pot from the machine and dumps the old coffee into the sink. "It wasn't meant to be."

"Shit man. I'm sorry. But at least you didn't get blown up today, right?"

An ironic smile crosses Eliot's face. "True."

"So, what are you gonna do?"

Eliot fills the carafe with water from the tap. It climbs against the tick marks on the side as he thinks. "I'm not sure."

Terry doesn't say anything more and Eliot is thankful. He knows what the alternative is: it's to sit here in this apartment and let the darkness overwhelm him gradually. Let the Ash take him bit by bit until he ends up like Justin's mother. He closes his eyes. No. He'll make sure *that* doesn't happen. He'll throw himself down that canal if he must to make sure it doesn't.

The cat trills and settles into a ball on the counter with Terry still stroking her fur. What about Apple? He couldn't leave her here. He needs to make sure she is taken care of. There was only one person he trusted her with and…well…Meena might not even talk to him if he calls her.

"You want a cat?" he asks softly.

Terry cocks his head. "Are you legit right now?"

He nods.

"Why the hell are you trying to give me your cat, man?"

The coffee dribbles into the carafe behind them. Eliot feels empty as he looks at his beautiful little friend's face, as he listens to her purr while she sleeps. "Because I'm not going to be around for much longer and I want to make sure she's safe."

Terry squints. "You dying or something?"

They don't die.

"Or something," Eliot answers.

"Fuck," Terry murmurs. "And this road-trip…this was like your last hurrah?"

"I suppose."

The floor warps beneath him and Eliot puts a hand on the counter to steady himself. He feels like he's falling while standing up. He's not even sure what's happening but before he knows it, he's gripping his own arm to keep his hand from shaking. He suppresses a grunt as he stumbles out of the kitchen and down the hall toward the bathroom. Terry's stool scrapes across the floor. "Hey! You okay?"

"Yeah." He's not sure he's even said the word at first, but Terry doesn't follow him into the hall. Eliot shuts himself in his tiny bathroom, making sure to flick the light switch first. It flickers before bathing the room in a pinkish glow.

"Fuck…" He grinds his teeth together and sinks down to the floor. The walls close in. Breathing becomes thin. His palms stick to the cold tile even as a sweat breaks out across him. The panic assaults him. He should have felt this during the explosion: a body's natural reaction to trauma and shock. But the Ash stuffed them in a room somewhere in the back of his head until they bucked free, broke down the door, and scratched their way out.

Cold skin touches the sides of his face. "Easy."

A tiny breath squeezes down his windpipe to his lungs. He gasps. "Fuck!" He is looking up into the thing that wears Alexis's face. She's cross-legged on the bathroom floor in front of him, holding onto him like she's giving him a mind-meld or is channeling his thoughts or who-the-hell knows what. He falls back on his butt and stares into the fluttering pink light overhead and breathes.

He sighs. "Why are you haunting me?"

"Are you asking the light or me?" Death answers.

"Guess."

"You're running out of options. Ride the rocket."

The statement is like drinking ice water. He's clear once again. The terror has receded. The bathroom is chilly, and goosebumps have risen over his arms. "Thanks, I—"

But she's gone. There is only the hum of the light.

Outside, there's a soft knock. "Yo, man. You all right in there?"

Eliot wipes away the lingering sweat from his brow. "Yeah."

"Good, 'cuz your cat is freaking the hell out."

He gets to his feet and opens the door.

True to Terry's word, Apple stands down the hall with all her fur on end, her tail doubled the size of its usual width, and ears flattened. Had she sensed Death in there with him? If so, her feelings had changed since Saturday night.

"Listen, man, I don't normally do this for anybody but…I'll do it for you if you want."

"Do what?"

Terry frowns. "Take you out there. Out into the Vast so you can do your bucket list."

Eliot's face slackens. "You don't even know me. Why would you do that?"

"Man, Getty is a sinking ship. This place used to be great to make a buck in, but it's gotten stale. You know what I'm saying?"

"That can't be the only reason. You wouldn't just drop your whole life here and decide to do this on a whim if it were."

Terry stares through him, and Eliot recognizes the look in his eye all too well. Pity. But there's something else there and it's the only thing that keeps him from telling Terry to leave right then and there.

Well. He wishes he was proud enough to do that.

Before he can ask, a banging on glass sets his teeth on edge. Eliot sidesteps Terry and marches into the kitchen. There's two people standing on the fire exit outside and a flashlight beam striking into the amber dusk of his apartment. He hears the radio static before he notices the badges being flashed. The cop on the left knocks on the window again.

Eliot reaches over the counter, unlocks the sash, and lifts the window. The flashlight beam hits him square in the eyes. The drumming headache resumes as he shields his face.

"Eliot Lamb?" the cop on the right asks. Rain courses through her short black hair and down her face, pooling on the extra material of her raincoat beneath her sharp chin.

"Yeah?"

"We have questions for you. Mind if we come in?"

He blinks. "Why?"

"You knew Justin Nguyen?"

The paramedic at the bombing. She'd seen his tiger's eye. She thought he was involved with what happened at the bank somehow. The police were clutching at straws and searching for someone to blame for this morning's attack. And they'd found a connection to grasp onto. Even *he* would have raised his eyebrows if he'd been in their shoes. He never should have left the scene.

Eliot nods. "He used to work for me at my restaurant."

"He blew up a bank this morning in the arts district!" the cop on the left shouts over the rain, louder than he needs to. He has squinty eyes and unlike his partner, he's spitting the rain out of his mouth with all the fury of a sprinkler. "But I'm sure you already knew that."

Eliot keeps his tone firm. "I saw him go into the bank, but I didn't know he was—"

"—a True Faith follower?" the cop on the right says.

"Mind if we come inside, Mr. Lamb?" Left Cop puts a hand on the windowsill.

Eliot hesitates, looking between the two cops, trying to read their faces. Left Cop was coming in no matter what. Right Cop held her cards closer to the vest, but he wouldn't be surprised if she was just as gung-ho about arresting him for something he very much didn't do. There was no way he could overpower them and why should he? He doesn't have anything incriminating to hide…nothing to do with True Faith anyway.

Eliot takes a step back and nods.

6
I RAN (SO FAR AWAY)

Left Cop wrenches the window as open as it can go and lets his partner go through first, all the while his hand hovering over the unclipped holster of his sidearm. Eliot's heart skips a beat as Right Cop climbs in. He offers a hand to help her, but she doesn't take it.

She studies his kitchen as Left Cop struggles to crouch through the opening. "Nice place. Hell of a stovetop you've got there."

He squints. "…Thanks?"

Left Cop fumbles and nearly goes down on the floor but catches himself on the corner of the kitchen island. He remains there a moment like a rickety human bridge between the two countertops before finding his footing.

The coffee machine beeps nearby, and Eliot suddenly remembers Terry. Where the hell had Terry gone? He spies the door to the hallway and wonders why the plumber never followed him into the kitchen after checking on him in the bathroom.

"What's the matter?" Right Cop asks. "You seem edgy."

Eliot clears his throat. "Of course I'm edgy. I barely survived a bombing this morning." He rounds the island and turns off the coffee maker. "Want any?"

Left shakes his head while Right nods. He pours her coffee into a white mug that Harvey picked out, and immediately, he scrubs the name from his head.

"Kind of a coincidence, don't you think?" Left's eyebrow is perked. It makes his forehead look less giant somehow when he does this but as soon as he scowls, it's there like a giant billboard again.

"Looks like you took a nasty bump to the head," Right adds. "There a reason you didn't stay and get properly cared for at the scene?"

Eliot sips from his own mug. "You know why I didn't."

"Because you're in league with the True Faith?" Left mutters under his breath and Right flashes him a contemptuous look.

"Because she knew I was dying. She saw my tiger's eye and she was triaging. I knew I wasn't among the most important people for her to take care of there."

"How noble of you," Right says.

"That wasn't the point," Eliot scoffs. "I didn't want to waste her time or mine."

"Did you know what Justin Nguyen had planned?" Left asks. He doesn't have a notepad out nor any kind of writing implement to take notes. This worries Eliot. They're not here to take his statement and leave him in peace. They're looking for conviction; for guilt.

Eliot sets the coffee down. He pulls his glasses off and rubs one of the lenses. "No. Justin didn't come into work yesterday. I assumed he'd gotten a new job since I was closing Tempo."

Something clicks in Right's face then. "Whoa."

"What?" Left asks.

"We're in the home of a celebrity." She smiles as she glances around the kitchen. "Chef Eliot Lamb. Thought I recognized the name. The Chef with the Treble Clef."

Left continues to stare at Right as if she's what she's said is completely gibberish.

"Which means the restaurant that got bombed yesterday, The Agave Tap, belonged to your rival Alexis Munro." Right steps toward him. "Isn't that…convenient?"

The start of her statement turns Eliot's body to water and then the next part to flame. Hearing Alexis's name mentioned is like a knife twisting in his gut. It takes a moment for the assertion of the statement to hit him, but when it does, he can barely contain his anger. "She was *never* my rival. Alexis was a friend."

"That's not what city papers said a couple months ago when she left your employ and started up Agave." Right's gaze narrows. "Could all of this violence be just because of one man's silly ego trip?"

"That's insane. You know how insane that is, right?" He glances back and forth between Right and Left. This had to be some kind of prank. They couldn't believe he would be capable of something like *this*? They didn't even know him.

"It wouldn't be the first time a man sacrificed human lives because he couldn't get over his own self-importance. Ever heard of Hitler? Stalin and the Great Purge? Idi Amin?"

Eliot stares at Right unblinking. "Are you accusing me of something, Officer?"

"Special Agent," Left answers for her. It's as if he's finally remembered he's a part of the conversation. "You're talking to the FBI; not Getty's fucking PD."

"I don't care what you call yourself." Eliot inhales deeply. "The fact that you could ever accuse me of being as awful as any of those people is…" He didn't have the words. He realized he was trembling with anger, with fear.

"I think you should come with us down to the precinct so we can get into the matter a bit further," Right probes. "Like you said before, we don't want to waste our time or yours. But we have to be thorough. And there are too many coincidences here to ignore."

"That's all they are," Eliot says. "Flukes. I would never do this to Getty. To anyone here. I love this city."

"We'll see," Left speaks up.

Before he realizes it, Right forces him against his own counter and head rams him into his cabinet doors as she wrenches his hands back. "Hey! Woah!" he shouts, hearing the handcuffs clinking as she pulls them from her belt.

Right reads him his Mirandas, tone unforgiving.

Eliot can't see Left, his face made to look toward his kitchen door. He's hearing his father's voice in his head; words he thought he'd buried deep and cemented over. They echo up like a heartbeat through the floor of his mind. *Always asking for trouble. It'll find you if you keep it up.*

A cat darts between the door and the island countertop like a flash. Left enters his vision, cocks his head, and says, "Hey there, little guy," as he stoops down and picks up the animal. Eliot frowns.

His cat, Apple, is a tabby.

This one is all black.

Terry thunders through the door at Eliot full charge like a bull, yelling at what seems to be the top of his lungs. He collides with Right, barreling her into the corner of the counter at the same time as he shoves Eliot in the opposite direction.

Eliot stumbles to the floor between the island and the counter, barely keeping himself upright.

Where the hell was Left?

Eliot whips his head toward where the cop last was, expecting to catch a bullet in the face. But Left is wrangling with the black cat as it tries to claw the skin from his face. Its wild yowling drives Eliot into the hall as Terry scrambles after him.

"Oh my God! Oh my Lord!" Terry shouts as they dash down the hall.

Eliot sees Apple crouched by the front door and tosses her to Terry with the order, "Hold her!" while he gets to work moving the side table from in front of the door.

"Hurry up!" Terry whines, juggling the unhappy cat in his arms.

"STOP!" Right yells from down the hall.

The side table tumbles to the floor as Eliot tears open the apartment door. He and Terry rumble out into the third-floor hall.

It's dark, the lights long burned out, the air dank and cold. Eliot hasn't set foot in these halls since he first moved in and knows, despite apartment building halls being communal meeting places, this one never was. People left by way of their windows. No one visited anyone else here unless they were bringing complaints to the manager in the apartment on the ground floor. Even their mail was delivered via window boxes.

He moves through instinct. Down the hall. His hip checks the corner where the banister turns to follow the stairwell. "We've got to go down," he urges Terry as he grips the rail.

"Can't see shit..." Terry mumbles. "I thought you said the front door didn't work."

"We're not going to the front door." He takes each step faster than he should. They're steeper than he remembers.

Above, the apartment door bangs open. "Freeze!" Right screams shortly before something shatters over Eliot's right shoulder: a wall sconce.

"Motherfucker!" Terry shouts. The cat yowls in the dark.

Eliot nearly trips over himself as he reaches the next floor. The lights work down there but dimly as if he's got a silk blind over his eyes. He hustles toward the end of the hall, Terry and the cat in tow.

"Where are we going?"

"Apartment at the end. It's vacant."

They thunder up to it, footfalls softened by the spongey rug. Eliot tries the door, but it doesn't budge.

Before he can ask, Terry unloads the cat into Eliot's arms, claws and all. After steadying himself, Terry jams into the door and it judders open. The apartment is darker than the hall but they all shuffle into it regardless and shut the door as best they can behind them. Eliot knows these apartments are all laid out the same, knows that directly in front of him is a long narrow hall with doors that branch off it. The one three spaces down will lead to the kitchen and to the fire escape.

"They think you bombed the bank?" Terry says behind him.

"Apparently." He cuts into the kitchen, recognizing the teal fog through the windows there. The kitchen is a mess—leftover food left on the counters, dirty dishes in the sink, a red stain on the floor by the small kitchen table…

He tries not to think about it as he hands the cat back over to Terry.

Terry waves him off and pushes the window open. The cool wet air hits them; the stench of rain. As Terry climbs up onto the counter and starts to slide out, Eliot hears the front door creak open.

He counts the seconds as Terry shimmies out onto the iron grating all the while murmuring swears. The moment he's out, Eliot hands him the cat. Apple squirms, with eyes huge, legs splayed.

The footfalls behind him make Eliot whirl around. Right stands in the kitchen doorway, gun aimed at him. "Don't fucking move," she orders.

"Eliot…" Terry hisses behind him.

"Go," he says defiantly, trying to block the windows as much as possible.

Right raises her radio to her mouth with one hand. "Suspect number two is on the fire escape. Repeat on the fire escape." When she doesn't get an answer, she adds, "You there? Goddamn it, answer me!"

"Let him go," Eliot says. "He was just at the wrong place at the wrong time."

Right frowns. "He attacked a federal agent. He's just as guilty as you are."

"I didn't *do* anything," Eliot snaps.

Right crosses the kitchen and spins him around to face the window. He watches Terry retreat down the iron stairs as the cuffs clink around his wrists behind his back. "Tell it to a judge," Right snarls. She nods toward the window. "Go on."

"I can't get up onto the counter without my hands," he protests.

"Figure it out."

Eliot spies the chair at the kitchen table and nods to it. Right rolls her eyes as she scrapes it out and over to the window, trailing it through the gore. The gun remains trained on him. He climbs onto its seat then steps onto the counter. He needs to sit to slide through the opening feet first.

From the stairwell, he can see down through the alley, down to the grotesque darkness of the canals, to the shapes of people making their way up and down the thin borders between them and the buildings. He searches for Terry, but he's gone. He doesn't even see him on the ground below, not that he could have gotten down there that fast.

Right seems to be agitated as well as she's sliding out beside him. "What the fuck?" She scans the stairwell below before raising her head to the landing above them; the landing for Eliot's apartment. "Hey!" she yells up.

"The window's closed up there," Eliot reminds her. "He probably can't hear you."

"Shut up!" she barks at him but doesn't turn her attention away from the top floor.

She isn't paying attention to the open window in front of them. She isn't paying attention to the shape of the black cat as it careens toward them like a lightning strike, as it soars up over the countertop and through the gap. It grapples onto her back and Right reacts by falling forward toward the railing and corkscrewing her body at the same time. And her foot catches on the barrier and sends her over…

Eliot springs forward to try and help but can't. His hands are cuffed behind his back.

Right hooks a leg around the iron bar, wraps her foot, and hangs perilously over the side, the entire structure croaking angrily with her movements. Her gun plummets into the canal below.

The cat has disappeared. He didn't see it fall but…where else could it have gone?

Right is billowing out breaths, trying to jerk her body into a sit up to get her fingers around the bar her leg is hooked on but can't. "Fuck!" she screams.

Eliot scans, searching for something to use to help her. Because, yes, he hates that he's being arrested for something he didn't do, but…Jesus…he's got to help her, right? She's a federal agent.

"Psst… Eliot!"

Terry waves to him from the first-floor catwalk. "Come on, man!"

Eliot staggers, unsure what to do. "But…"

"Let's get the fuck out of here!" Terry has Apple wrapped close to him inside his rain jacket. Eliot can see the cat's terrified wide eyes peeking out of the darkness beneath Terry's neck.

"Don't you fucking leave me," Right warns. Blood has begun rushing to her head.

Terry's waving frantically. "Come. ON!"

His compulsion is to apologize even as he finds himself skittering down the steps toward Terry, even as the cuffs around his wrists pinch with each movement. But he doesn't. He bites his tongue and follows Terry who seems much more motivated to get down from the fire escape than he had been to climb it.

On the ground once more, they scurry along the narrow lip of the canal. A strangled shout behind them makes Eliot whip around.

Right's body plummets, legs banging off the edge of the canal as she tumbles into the cavity below. The air dries from Eliot's lungs.

Holy shit. Holy shit.

He looks back up. Left has partially crawled out his apartment window with his hand outstretched and face frozen in shock.

"Oh my God," Terry's voice wobbles behind him. Eliot feels his hand on his shoulder. "Come on!"

Eliot focuses on the back of Terry's jacket until they find the alley. Every few seconds, Terry looks back at him as if he's making sure he hasn't been pulled into the vacuum as well. "The fuck have you gotten yourself into, Terry," he mutters to himself.

They reach the van, Terry opening the sliding back door to climb in first. He sets the cat down nearby and turns around to help Eliot up into the back before going to close the door.

A black cat hops up between the narrowing crack before it fully closes.

Terry turns on a flashlight in the back of the van, the white light blinds them both momentarily. "The Hell, man! You didn't tell me you had trained attack cats. What the hell are you? Some kind of lion tamer for domesticated felines?"

Eliot drops to his knees, preferring that over hunching over. He eyes the black cat as it rubs against his body. "It isn't my cat," he says.

Green eyes. They're piercing straight through him. Just like Alexis's had the night before.

As Terry shoves into the front of the van and plops down into the driver's seat, Eliot frowns and asks, "It's you, isn't it?"

"We've got to get the hell out of the city." Terry starts the van and it's like an earthquake has begun beneath them. "They're probably calling the entire bureau down to back them up right now."

Eliot turns his handcuffed hands toward Terry. "Any chance you could…?"

Terry buckles his seatbelt and shifts into first. He barely checks his sideview mirror before he's pulling out into traffic. "I'll do it once we're out of Getty. Besides, how do I know you're not going to sic that cat on me?"

Eliot rolls his eyes. The lurch of the van makes him fall onto his stomach. He stares at the animal as it lays down beside him. "You wouldn't, would you?"

The cat purrs and licks its lips.

DEVOTION
SECOND OBSERVATION

Is it mindlessness that propels these decaying bodies over the land? Or is it some extreme devotion toward the next chapter, whatever it may be in the human condition? While it's easy to point at the Ash and claim it as a natural abomination, as a disease that can be cured or a conundrum yet to be solved, it is wholly over-looked that it only affects mankind and therefore, might it be evolutionary? The Ash might be propelling these pitiful creatures toward a more pleasing environment, like birds or seafaring beasts seeking warmer climates. Or perhaps, we are more like insects seeking to become something more divine than our current selves.

7

REFUGEE

erry's first inclination is for them to get out of the city as quickly as possible, but Eliot convinces him to make one stop before they depart. The van slows in front of a brownstone on Nestle Street where the front doors are lit by rosy-orange lights. The rain is coming down harder now, drumming against the roof of the van loudly.

He persuades Terry to take the cat up the narrow front staircase to the apartment beside them and press the call button for Meena Hernandez's apartment. If Apple could be safe with anyone, it would be with her and Eliot doesn't want to worry about her being on the road with him, not like this.

"What about the other one?" Terry asks, nodding to the black cat.

Eliot frowns. "Something tells me it's not going to leave us."

Grumbling the entire time, Terry obliges, first removing all his tools from a leather tool bag and then plopping the angry cat inside to deliver her to the covered stoop before returning to the van.

"What did you say?" Eliot asks as Terry buckles his seatbelt. "Is she coming?"

Terry puts the van in Drive and pulls out onto the road, leaving the brownstone behind. "Oh, lawd, she's definitely coming. I didn't want to stay put and try to have to explain this shit."

Eliot blinks sorrowfully. He hadn't gotten to say a proper goodbye to the animal and the loss churns in his gut. He slumps against the wall of the back of the van and stares at the black cat that remains. "Look what you've done," he whispers. He isn't sure if he's talking to it or himself.

...

It doesn't take much time for the cityscape of Getty to slide away, like the skin of a fish being separated from meat with a sharp knife. Terry takes each street via the speed limit. No attracting attention. No one has identified him as the other culprit in Eliot's escape yet so why make it easier for them to be found?

The van rumbles down the wide avenues, until it hits the highway, which curls up and out over the ground on great stone stanchions that have sunk into the soft land. When they were originally built, one could still see down to the waist-high weeds, to the brackish water that carried the scent of the tide with it and herons that stood like statues in the mists waiting for salamanders or frogs.

Now, it's concealed by a haze; everything is always concealed by the deep teal mist.

Eliot wrestled his handcuffed hands down around his feet while laying down in the back of the van. There's not much room back there with all of Terry's plumbing tools, and with each pitch and turn, he's rolled around. Once he's got his hands out in front of him, he carefully makes his way to the front of the van and slips into the passenger seat with a sigh.

Terry gives him a side eye. "You think it's a good idea sitting up in front here?"

Eliot glances out the windshield at the foggy road ahead of them. "Visibility is shit. Besides, who the hell are we going to pass out here right now?"

"Those feds are going to have agents swooping down to find your ass," Terry bristles.

"Out here?" Eliot frowns. The fog has assumed a thickness that he immediately equates to being chowder-like. Opaque but with things that vaguely bob into existence off in the distance before melding into the vapor once more.

Terry shakes his head. "I bet that agent is already on the horn to Homeland Security about what went down. They'll have the army and the National Guard up here in like five minutes."

"They're not going to call off protecting the border from Soviet subs for this. Besides, everything they have to go on right now is circumstantial." Eliot looks down at the handcuffs. The skin around his wrists is red and chafed in places. "Would you mind taking these off, please?"

"Love how you just assume I know how to unlock a pair of handcuffs," Terry grumbles.

"Honestly, I figured you had plumbing tools that could saw them off or something," Eliot murmurs, feeling ashamed.

Terry takes a deep breath through his nose. "Not until we get south of the state line. We can't afford to stop."

Eliot knows Terry is correct but at the same time, he sees his new friend's hands trembling as he grips the wheel. "You didn't have to, you know?"

"Didn't have to what?"

"Run in. Knock that agent off me."

"I did though." Terry looks at him. "What she was doing wasn't right and…well…shit, this is going to sound weird. But I think I heard God telling me I had to help you."

The words jar Eliot into a state of ultimate discomfort. "What?"

"Like I said, sounds fucking crazy, man. But, when I was standing in the hallway listening to everything, I swear I heard a voice telling me I had to do something. Telling me that you were a good person and didn't deserve all that was happening to you." Terry bangs his palm against the steering wheel. "Starting to sound like my nutty Aunt Caroline."

Eliot doesn't understand. He is supposed to believe that *God* had spoken to Terry? *The* God? After everything that had happened in the last twenty-four hours, who was he to question it? But something needles him about the entire statement. The timing. The black cat.

"So, let me get this straight: you heard a voice telling you to help me: an almost total stranger… nd instead of questioning your sanity or anything really, you ran at an armed police figure and fought her off me?"

"I wouldn't have done it if that voice didn't sound exactly like my grandmama's," Terry says quietly. "And she's been dead and gone ten years. It sounded like she was saying it directly in my ear."

Eliot looks over his shoulder toward the black cat. It sits statuesque in the center of the back of the van behind them, leering at him with glowing green eyes in the low lights.

The route out of Getty transforms into what was once referred to as I-95. The interstate used to run all the way from Maine to Florida before much of the East Coast was swallowed back into the ocean following the near constant extratropical hurricanes. Since then, it's been patched in places, diverted from dropping cars down into the ocean. Switchbacks take cars out of their way nearly fifty to seventy miles before putting them back on what's now known as the Atlantic Spill Highway.

The state line is where one of these switchbacks resides and it pulls the van away from the highway further inland. The saltiness in the air fades away, the sound of water lapping departs as the van moves deeper into the countryside. Fields that once held corn are now mass graves of brittle stalks bent over as if bowing to a superior force of nature. The eldritch silhouettes of trees tower in the distance behind them.

All Eliot and Terry have to guide their way is the road, the intermittent streetlamps and the van's powerful headlights cleaving through the growing darkness.

Neon channel lettering emerges from the blue blackness on the roadside like a beacon. The gloom materializes beneath it into a long narrow trailer with a handful of cars parked out front; some models rusted, some glossy with new corrosion-resistant paint that gleams like crude oil. There's nothing else manmade around for miles save the telephone lines and streetlights.

Terry parks the van as far away from the lights as possible out of caution and, at Eliot's insistence, removes the handcuffs.

Eliot rubs his wrists. "Thank you."

"Thank my Swiss Army Knife." Terry grumbles. "Gonna have to get a new tweezer for it." He slides open the back door of the van into the gloom of the parking lot.

From inside, Eliot hears the plucky music of an old bluegrass song. He hasn't heard that song since he was a boy. His relief at being free turns to slight nausea. The sign above them reads "Bushel's."

"I'm not sure I like this, man," Terry says. "This is like *Oklahoma!* meets *Texas Chainsaw Massacre*, if you know what I'm saying."

Eliot shakes his head. "We need somewhere to stop and think. I haven't had anything to eat since before the bank this morning. And your stomach has been growling ever since we left Getty. We won't stay for long."

Terry glances down at his gut and winces. "Fine. But if these fools don't have sloppy joes, we might be hitting the road sooner rather than later, you feel me?" As he begins to slide the van door closed, the black cat slinks through and bounds off through the parking lot into the darkness.

Terry waves after it. "Good riddance."

Eliot watches its body vanish as he and his companion step up to the diner door and open it.

The clatter of dishware, the clinking of forks and knives, and a bubbling of low conversation welcomes them. The stratosphere of the long room is a concoction of mouth-watering aromas: fried oil, butter-soaked buns, and charred red meat. It's the hiss of the grill, the convivial but quiet manic of the dinner-time atmosphere that calms Eliot's nerves. This place feels like a hundred other diners he's set foot in over the course of his life.

A waitress in a blue smock waves at them from behind a long countertop and tells them to take any seat that's open. It's a small enough place that she's clearly the only one running tables no matter what the level of activity. Eliot and Terry sidle down the aisle and take seats at the counter toward the very end next to the old-fashioned jukebox. The music has switched to another downhome classic and that's fine by Eliot. Anything but that first song.

The plastic menu, covered in coffee rings and greasy finger prints, proports the typical diner-fare of a variety of burgers: with or without fries, with or without cheese, with or without—he squints—did that say, "fried green tomatoes?" There's Salisbury and chicken-fried steaks, Chicken a la King, and—

"Hallelujah." Terry gestures to the Father, Son, and Holy Ghost. As soon as the waitress arrives, he orders his sloppy joe and Eliot sticks to a cheeseburger, medium-well, lettuce, tomatoes, onions, and hell yes, to the fried green tomato.

"You still want to do your trip now that we're out on the road?" Terry asks him. "After everything that happened, I'd get it if you didn't."

"It's been a hell of a last twelve hours," Eliot agrees. "But what else is there? I can't go back home now."

"You remember all the places you were going to go? I can't remember exactly what your map said but I think it was like four or five?"

"Four."

A man a little way down the counter is eating mashed potatoes with the energy and fervor of a tortoise enjoying a leaf of lettuce. His lips barely move to accommodate the spoon each time. A spike of discomfort jabs Eliot in the ribs as he turns back to Terry.

"So, which one is first?"

"None of them are right near each other. But the cooks are exceptional or at least, they were. I'll admit it's been a year or so since I made that route on the map. I hope they're still working where they were when I made it."

"Why wouldn't they still be there?" Terry asks. "Seems like if they are as impressive as you say they are and they love what they do, they would have no reason to leave."

Eliot scoffs. "It's not always up to them. The restaurant industry is turbulent. Cooks move around all the time, kind of like pirates, I guess. They'll stay where something feels good for a while, but pretty soon, the wind is calling them somewhere else."

"Well, you ain't exactly Mary Poppins looking for some kids to babysit, are you.?" Terry chuckles, then loses his smile. "Suppose that makes me your umbrella or something for coming along." He gets up. "I'm going to find a restroom. Been damn near dying since we crossed state lines."

Terry saunters down the aisle they came in from and disappears through a light blue door with a gold bathroom sign.

Eliot focuses on the red marks around his wrists. It assaults him then like a sprinkler ticking on at an appointed time: he watched that agent fall to her death. He didn't help her—no— couldn't help her. But if he hadn't tried to escape her, hadn't tried to run, she might have still been alive, and he'd be...where? In a holding cell? In an interrogation room clipped to a metal table while Left and Right pummeled him with questions?

No. He *didn't* do anything wrong. This *wasn't* his fault.

Yet...

He feels so exposed. He notices one of the women at a booth down the way watching him surreptitiously. The man with the mashed potatoes slurps down another mouthful and raises his dead-looking eyes to meet his before Eliot can look away. He just wants to hide. This room is too warm and there's too many people. He wants to be somewhere *else*…

A cup of cola clonks down in front of him, ice-like buoys clatter in the dark waves and perspiration is slippery on the glass.

He looks up at the waitress. "I didn't order th—"

Alexis looks at him. "You're looking kind of flushed. I thought you could use a cold one."

He scans around him desperately and forgets to breathe. No one is moving. All human sounds have ground to a halt. Husbands and wives are locked in staring contests, mashed potatoes slide off the man's spoon back onto his plate with a pattering, and the one cook Eliot can see through the kitchen door watches a burger die on the fryer as he holds a spatula in mid-air above it.

"Don't worry," Death as Alexis says. "No one can see you now."

Simultaneously angry and relieved, Eliot sees Terry frozen in mid-stride on his way back from the bathroom to the stools, mouth scrunched in concern.

"Was that you at the apartment?" Eliot asks Death, returning his gaze to her. "The cat?"

Her smile brightens. "That was so fun, wasn't it?"

"Not for the agent who died, Lex!" He thinks better for using that nickname. It's not really *her*. "You've made me a fugitive."

Death shrugs. "They would have locked you up and thrown away the key, El. I can't afford to let that happen."

"So, this is all about you now? You and your little quest to reinspire humanity?" he snaps.

She plucks a straw from the container on the counter nearby and tears at its wrapper bit by bit. "This was never about me. It's always been about you. But you put so many obstacles in your own way that sometimes, I have to help."

"And what about God's voice in Terry's ear? Was that also you *helping*?"

Death shrugs as she puts the still mostly wrapped straw to her lips and blows. The wrapper flutters off and hits Eliot in the glasses. He doesn't flinch.

"You've manipulated him into helping me from the beginning, haven't you?" Eliot frowns. "He's just some poor guy trying to make a living and now you've shackled him to me with this ridiculous mission."

"If it would make you feel better to think that I basically closed my eyes and pointed to a random guy on the street and said, 'Yup. That one,' then sure, believe that." She pokes her straw into the glass and takes a sip of the soda. "Mmm, not diet. Got to love it."

"Glad you're enjoying yourself, you monster," Eliot whispers under his breath.

"Oh my God!" Death rolls her eyes. "You are such a stick in the mud, Eliot. What the fuck happened to you? Don't you remember when you and Clive pretended to be waiters at that catering gig I did for the aquarium?"

He did. God, he did. He remembered the two of them bumbling around the event in their suits, toting platters of hors d' oeuvres and flutes of Prosecco to feed hundreds of hungry gala-goers. They were very drunk. It was a ridiculous night.

"Don't you remember when you met Harvey that night?" Death adds.

He does. Despite the want to plummet down that vortex of reminiscence, the lure of familiarity and laughter in memory, he holds firm. "You're not her. And stop bringing up Harvey."

Death stands up straighter and nudges the glass closer toward him. "I'm just trying to help you hold onto what makes you *you*, Eliot."

The blaring of a smoke detector cuts off his next train of thought. The grill behind Death through the kitchen door is smoking, the burger reduced to a hockey puck of char. The cook snaps into action by leaping back from it while another quickly drops a stainless frying pan lid over the sprout of flames.

Everything erupts into movement. Every head turns toward the commotion in the kitchen. Even the man with the mashed potatoes who tries to eat from his now empty spoon and Terry who returns to his seat. "That doesn't bode well," he says.

Eliot tries to find Death, but she's vanished. The only one wearing a blue smock is the waitress from before who has rushed to the kitchen door to take in the damage.

"You okay?" Terry asks him. "You're sweating like you're in a hot house, man."

He feels his forehead and it comes away slick. Eliot grabs the still icy coke from in front of him and quickly drinks it down. The smack of high fructose corn syrup on the back of his palette feels artificial and the soda sits heavily in his stomach. In spite of that, it's the most refreshing thing he's ever had in his life in that moment. The sweetest thing, too.

"I think that might have been our dinner, Terry," he says, gasping after finishing the drink.

"Man, I knew I shouldn't have gotten my hopes up."

They sit for a moment in silence, watching the smoke as it wafts from the grill, as the cooks scrape the black meat from it and the head chef chews out the burger cook.

"Pardon me, gentlemen," a voice says from behind them.

They turn to the booth at their backs to see a man sitting at a table. He's older, probably in his sixties with a shaved head much like Eliot's. He wears a black priest's outfit with a white collar and is just setting down his finished glass of what Eliot assumes to have been milk. The white lactose still clings to the glass in places as it slips down toward the base.

"You're not from around these parts, are you?" he asks, his voice soft, friendly even. It reminds Eliot of a tough guy he used to know at a seafood restaurant in Jersey. Fisherman who delivered a fresh catch to their dockside kitchen every day. The kind of guy who smoked and put out the butt between his fingers. The kind of guy who it was told knocked out three men who were trying to drink him under the table to steal his cash. A man with a voice like smoke flowing across glass.

Eliot is tempted to ignore this man and catches Terry's eye cautiously before he answers, "No. We're just passing through."

"I'm afraid this is a regular occurrence here at Bushel's. Their stove tops are so old, there are smoke alarms going off for almost every service." The man chuckles. "Once that alarm goes off though, they have to wait until the fire department comes to make sure that everything is set before they can start cooking again."

Eliot frowns. "That doesn't make any sense. I've worked in restaurants all my life and one smoke alarm going off never shut down service before."

"Here in Adin, it's customary. Whole town nearly burned down in '82. Mayor instituted the ruling himself, and no one has thought to change it since." The man cocks his head a little, blue eyes piercing against his pasty skin. "Gonna be a while though. I think those boys at the department might be seeing to a fire out on the Briar Road right now."

"Let's get out of here, man," Terry growls. "I'm sure we can find something else down the road."

Eliot is inclined to agree though the heat hasn't dissipated like he hoped it would. Worse, the headache is back and a bit stronger this time.

"Why don't you all come down to my place for supper?" the priest offers. "I can rustle something up and you can stay the night if you'd like. Get back on your feet in the morning."

"That's…um…" Eliot isn't sure how to turn him down, but he knows he wants to. At the same time, he knows he's fading. "That's really kind of you." He stands up. "But we ought to be on our way. Come on, Terry."

Eliot follows the stained turquoise carpet toward the front door.

"Appreciate the offer. Sorry!" He hears Terry drop change on the counter before he scrambles after him. "Eliot, you sure you're alright?"

What casually started as a slight headache inside springs from the shadows the moment they make it outside, engulfing Eliot's skull within moments. He stumbles, losing his footing and drops into the dirt near a station wagon. His vision trails as he glances up at the sign from the diner, each letter leaving rivers of light across the coming darkness.

"Eliot!" One of Terry's hands drops on Eliot's shoulder, the other on his arm. "What's wrong?"

Eliot knows. His bump on the head. The paramedic had said it might be a concussion. But with the Ash suppressing things, it hadn't fully swept in until now. But every syllable that comes out of his mouth feels sluggish and there are no beginnings or endings. The ground is solid though. He wants to curl up on it and retreat inside himself.

"He all right?" a voice says.

"I don't know, man…"

"Get him in the back of my truck. Quickly!"

Movement happens. The air is cool and caresses Eliot's skin, and he revels in it for a moment before the pain hits him again tenfold. The smell of rust and old hay surrounds him before he realizes he's sitting on ridged metal, back leaning up against glass. A truck bed. Terry sits beside him, arm around his shoulders. "You're gonna be okay, man."

Eliot is reminded of the night at the aquarium, bent over the public toilets as he puked his guts out. Clive in the stall next to him doing the same. A familiar hand rubbing circles into his back. Then, blackness.

LEFT LOG #1

BITCHIN' CAMARO

It replays over and over in Left's head as he sits in the uncomfortable plastic chair. Right's face—that look of complete disbelief—as she fell before his very eyes. Blinked out of existence into the depths of the canal. No one would ever find her body. No one would ever see her again. He would never hear her voice again.

Left massages the knuckles on his right hand with his left and stares at the imperfect cracked tiles of the local police station floor. It's like a sewer here: the Getty's police precinct is underground in an old subway station, moved there temporarily after their old headquarters were bombed the spring prior. This whole city was going to Hell, and these sorry fucks were out of their depth.

Left and Right had worked the case for months, following the stroke of bad luck along what was left of the eastern seaboard from city to city. It was the same everywhere they went. True Faith was forming tiny collectives in barns outside of towns, switching off the lights at the local laundromat after hours to go over their little manifestos, sneaking into Ash Wards at the local hospitals, and stealing poor invalids away to sacrifice them.

He blinks and stands up, shoes squeaking on the tile. For what? For absolution? To drive the knife deeper? To toss salt in the ever-growing wound of America? Things were already horrible for everyone. Why not cause more bloodshed?

The tabloids were throwing around the phrase "domestic terrorism" now and he blew a raspberry at it every time it was uttered by some news anchor eager for a pay bump. The True Faith weren't planted Ruskis looking to cut up their country from inside. They were organized to some degree, sure. But they were sporadic, too. All a part of some bigger picture but operating in independent sects all over. One group was never like another.

Getty was the worst when it came to the blasts. These fuckers were all about destroying beautiful buildings. They'd gotten rid of museums, galleries, studios, and even a restaurant that specialized in gastronomy. Their efforts were about eradication and Right had posited a unique theory: they were trying to stifle artistic expression of the human soul.

It had sounded wacky. Left had let her know that repeatedly. But Right stuck to her theory. Even contacted a psychologist to bounce ideas around with because, after answering the phone half a dozen times in the early hours of the morning, Left had had it. It was bad enough that he couldn't fall asleep without sucking down a Blue Lagoon before bed and Curacao was not easy to find at his local market.

Right always made fun of his strange love for fruity cocktails. He didn't care. At least he wasn't married to his work like she had been.

Left paces, stares at the concaved bricks in the tunnel around him and the desks dragged around and sectioned off by room dividers for makeshift offices. Phones ring and echo in the cavernous space all around, and the alarm is like a pulsing nerve that thrums through the collective.

They have a suspect. The first real lead they've had in months: this fucking chef who'd given them the slip all because of an accomplice waiting to surprise them and a Goddamned cat. Left takes a moment to drag his thumb along the scratch that runs from his cheekbone down to his jaw. It's still puffy and it has a myriad of sister scratches that cover parts of his neck and the scalp beneath his hair.

The office door opens, and an ogre of a man steps out: large shouldered and long-torsoed but with a face that feels like someone let the air out of it accidentally. The Getty Police Chief waves him into his office and Left briskly pushes in, throwing himself down in the seat before the big kahuna's desk. "Well? Did we find them?"

The big man shakes his head. "Nothing so far. Not at the restaurant Lamb used to own. Not at the residence of his accomplice, Terrence Boucher. We're bringing in his old staff from the restaurant now to see if they give us anything."

"I bet every one of these guys is a part of it," Left snarls.

"You sure you don't want to pop over to the hospital and get those scratches looked at?" the captain asks.

"They're fucking cat scratches, not bullet wounds. I'll survive."

The captain sighs. "My brother got scratched once when he was working for the local shelter and it got wicked infected."

Left's lip drops. "Are we seriously going to sit on our hands right now?"

"No one's sitting on their hands. We're in limbo until we get people to interrogate. And excuse me if I don't want to take a risk and do it at their homes where they have the upper hand." The captain side-eyes him. "Or upper claw."

Left rolls his eyes and stands abruptly. "Fuck you, you fucking Clydesdale." He throws the door open and saunters out, eyes pinpointing the nearest cubicle. An officer is filing paperwork and barely has a moment to protest as Left squats against the corner of the desk and hefts the phone into his lap to call his superior.

He's just finishing dialing the number when the captain's meaty hand wrestles the phone out of his and hangs it up. "Get the hell out of my station."

Left scoffs, stands up, and saunters down the halls toward the stairs that lead him outside. From behind him, he can hear the words, "…fucking prick…"

On street level, it's raining. Of course it is. Left runs to his waiting Camaro. Well, Right's Camaro. He supposes it's his now. Right didn't have any family as far as he knew and he couldn't have gotten her to talk about them if he'd tried. Right talked about work, just work. She never loosened up. She never laughed. She didn't have a favorite song or food or even color, he was sure.

But he was pretty sure he had loved her.

And now she was gone.

Left inspects the dashboard of Right's car, his eyes following the mountains and valleys of every Post-it note that is stuck across the air vents, the radio controls, even down across the glovebox where his knees usually banged up against them. He'd always rode shotgun when it came to her car. Not anymore.

He finally finds what he's looking for: a telephone number scrawled hastily in pen on a sticky note stuck to the back of the passenger visor. No wonder he couldn't find it before: the psychologist's number. If there was anyone else he could exchange ideas with about Right's theories, it was them.

Running across the street to the closest payphone, he dials the number. It's after nine o'clock at night but he doesn't care. In the interest of National Security, the psychologist ought not to either.

She—of course it's a she—answers the phone and agrees to meet him. The problem? She's not in Getty. She's south along the Atlantic Spill Highway about a four-hour drive from him. He can't talk to her on the phone when it's pissing rain though. He needs her help and she, thankfully, seems to understand the urgency of the matter, especially once he tells her that Right is dead.

They agree to meet once he gets down there. Left hangs up and returns to the Camaro. Spread across the passenger seat is the map he took from the chef's apartment. Yes, he should have shown it to the Getty police. But what good would it do? Their jurisdiction was limited. He, however, could go wherever he wanted.

And go, he would.

As he drops his hand onto the soft leather of the gearshift, a knock at his window turns his head.

A young woman stands outside the car door, a yellow slicker pulled up over her head. Her soft face is framed by black curls. Keeping his hand on his holster, he rolls down the window a smidge. "Whaddaya want?"

"You're FBI right?" she asks. "The one looking for Eliot Lamb? I was his sous chef, Meena Hernandez."

Left's chest swells. "The police captain is inside. He's the one you want to talk to." He rolls the window back up.

She knocks on it again and he doesn't take the bait. This is a waste of time. No, he's got the map that Lamb left behind in his apartment and with every hour that passes, that son-of-a-bitch gets further and further away. He needs to stay focused.

Meena shouts something but the rain drowns it out. He side-eyes her.

Fuck it all.

He rolls down the window again. "What?" And then, he sees it.

"He gave me his cat." Burrowed in her coat, its head poking out the top of her rain jacket is a cat's head. It yowls in annoyance as rain spatters on its skull.

Fuck. He grits his teeth. *Fucking fuckity fuck.*

When he doesn't respond, she adds, "I'm afraid something's really wrong with him. Can we talk?"

"I'm on my way somewhere out of town," he says. "I'd suggest you go inside and tell the local police what you know."

She stares past him at the passenger seat, and he realizes she's seen the map—no—not just seen the map: recognized it.

Meena rounds the car and tugs on the passenger door handle. It opens.

He hadn't locked it. Probably because he didn't expect *this*.

She slides in, carefully lifting the map up out of the way and shuts the door behind her. Unbuttoning her coat, the cat peels out and stands on her lap.

"What did you bring the cat for? Who brings a fucking cat out in a fucking rain storm anyway?" he bristles, turning over the engine.

"I don't know! I panicked!" she said. "The police don't give a shit about Eliot. I know that. And you've got his map. You're the best chance I have of finding him and figuring out what's going on."

"Fine," he grunts, shifting into drive. They leave Getty for the road south.

EVERYBODY HAVE FUN TONIGHT
1981

After hours at the aquarium. It's the first time Eliot has set foot inside and he is still unsure about the soft pattering of his heart as it picks up speed. He grew up surrounded by undulating fields of grass, dirt, and sparse thickets that only seemed to congregate around rivers. He never saw the ocean up close until he came to the east coast to pursue a career in cooking and even then, has never gone out on a boat, paddled a canoe, or so much as taken a dip in the Atlantic.

The ocean. It feels insurmountable. Dark, vast, and impossible to frame in his mind. And all kinds of strange, huge things navigate its depths; things that he's read about in books such as *Moby Dick* and *Jaws* and *The Old Man and the Sea*. Clive dragged him to see the sequel to Spielberg's *Jaws* a few years ago and he'd been unable to keep the occasional nightmare at bay of a jagged-toothed beast swishing in the water around him as he flailed in it.

So, when Clive suggests they crash Alexis's catering gig that evening, Eliot is more than skeptical. The booze convinces him otherwise. They slip in through the front entrance, waving past the barely awake ticket-taker by stating that they are with the catering company. After all, Clive is basically a god in the food world. He is onto his seventh book and his following of cooks and patrons alike eagerly gobble up whatever he has to say next: whether it's about food, politics, music, or the industry. Clive goes wherever he wants and whoever tags along in his wake is often awarded similar treatment.

Eliot stares in awe at the lobby where two large columns, filled to the brim with sea water, surround the entrance to the central visitor arena. Tendrils of green underwater plants wave gently while technicolor fish skitter and shoot about. Larger ones lazily flap their fins and gaze out at him with wide, black eyes. His usual sight of fish is laid over ice at the local market waiting to be chosen for dinner service or through the fuzzy lens of his television set at home. He remembers catching tiny trout at the fishing hole back home with nothing but a stick and a worm; remembers their rainbow scales glistening in the fading evening light.

Clive brushes him along into the main atrium. What was once a large room dedicated to brochures, information placards, and stanchions to make lines for various exhibits has been cleared out to accommodate a series of white, linen-cloth covered tables. A pulpit has been placed at the head of the room next to a wide tank where catfish burble, flex their long whiskers, and sweep their lithe bodies around in the greenish lights.

It is an auction, a gala to benefit the aquarium by selling prized possessions, experiences, and more. The man up front is in the midst of describing an ocean cruise to watch bottle-nosed dolphins off the coast of what is left of Florida. Clive and Eliot skirt the outside edge of the room until they push through a set of double doors into the kitchen. The aquarium has a cafeteria, though Eliot assumes they aren't in the habit of making crudites and petit fours for their daily guests.

In the years that have passed since their initial meeting, Alexis has made quite the name for herself in Getty, mostly as a caterer. While she still occasionally brings her food truck around to special events, she's been invited to cater at a number of city events. The aquarium is her latest invite.

Alexis stands in the midst of a sea of platters. Each one is filled with a colorful array of hors d'oeuvres: banh mi sliders, cucumber slices topped with a maple bacon jam, a playful rendition of ants-on-a-log made with carefully cut celery slices, chili-infused peanut butter and honey-dipped dehydrated insects.

Clive picks one up and inspects it. "Look! A real ant on this one. Clever."

Alexis crosses the kitchen and slaps his hand playfully. "What the hell are you guys doing here?"

Eliot gives a meek smile. "It's Clive's fault."

"This is your third gig right?" Clive waves around. "We wanted to come and support you as two fellow culinary acquaintances and friends ought to."

Alexis eyes them both. "I'm supposed to believe that you two had nothing else going on tonight and you just happened to be passing by?"

"We never said that we were just 'passing by,' did we?" Eliot checks.

Clive shakes his head.

"No, it was all a very deliberate show of support."

Alexis squints. "Okayyyy…" She returns to her spot in the kitchen where the cooks under her supervision are hastily putting together each little amuse-bouche. "Since you came all this way, I have a job for you two."

Eliot salutes and says, "Aye, aye," while Clive giggles. At this point, whatever drinks they've ingested at the bar on South Street have completely overwhelmed them. Clive can hold his liquor better than most as a tall-statured, gangly giant but even now, his mask is slipping. Eliot had three martinis—or was it four?—and the effects of them are akin to his brain being blown around by hurricane force winds.

"I need wait staff. Two guys didn't show up and it really puts me in a shitty situation. If you could both run food out from the kitchen, pour drinks, and collect empty dishes, that would make this a little less of a clusterfuck," Alexis mumbles. "Can you guys handle that?"

"I'll be the best damn waiter you ever saw," says Clive, sliding a platter from the stainless-steel counter and starting to walk away.

Eliot chuckles. "There's nothing on that one!"

Clive quickly replaces it with a full tray of delicate finger sandwiches and promptly leaves the room, swaying a little as he navigates the push-open doors.

"Did you two get abducted by aliens or something?" Alexis whispers to Eliot. "You're acting like idiots."

"Well, the aliens that abducted him must have had a name that rhymes with 'Long Island Iced Tea.'"

Alexis rolls her eyes. "Fuck. And, you, too?"

Eliot tries to make the most serious face he can. It doesn't last as long as he hopes.

"Fuck it," Alexis laments. "I've had worse happen. As long as Clive doesn't solicit any of the guests and you both keep those charming smiles up, there's still a chance they'll invite me back next year."

She sends him out the door with another platter. He thinks he hears her say, "Help me, God" before he pushes through to the main room.

It takes approximately five minutes before things go to hell. In the beginning, Eliot focuses on dropping off new drinks and picking up empty glasses. And then forgetting he has a platter full of empty glasses, begins dropping those off at tables, much to various attendees' consternation.

Clive brings a couple platters out to the hors d'oeuvres counter before taking a seat at one of the attendee tables to talk to a lovely brunette there. Her partner is annoyed to say the least.

When someone shoves an empty champagne flute in his face, Eliot realizes his attention has strayed. Anxiety kicks up in him like sand in cloudy water, his vision twirling and pitching, colors blending into multicolored scarves of action before him. The water in the tanks surround him. He is suddenly inside of one of them struggling to breathe and that's when his stomach takes a violent turn.

Thankfully, someone grabs his elbow and tugs him toward a door next to the catfish aquarium. They push out into an empty cool blue hallway where aqueous light bathes them in rippled dances. Moments later, they navigate through a short maze into a tiled bathroom and the door to a stall magically opens for him. Eliot spills down onto his knees and empties his stomach.

His hearing has gone fuzzy; all his energy used to expel every single thing that has ever touched his stomach into the toilet. When feeling finally returns to him and the shrill whine in his ears dissipates, he hears similar sounds coming from the stall next to him. Moreover, he recognizes that someone is standing over him, gently massaging his back.

"Not exactly what you had planned for the evening, was it?" mutters Eliot, expecting Alexis to answer. After all, she is the only other one there who knows them and knows what kind of state they are in.

"Didn't expect this one, no," a deep British voice says. A man's voice.

Eliot manages to glance back over his shoulder. The man in question is crouched, leaning against the stall door frame, his suit jacket tossed to the side. His hair is parted to the left where a smooth dollop of chocolate bangs sweep over his forehead and barely hide his green eyes.

"Oh, come on," says Eliot, spitting more excess bile into the toilet. "I'm hallucinating, too."

"Are you?" the man asks.

"I mean, it doesn't make sense. I don't know you. And you're here kneeling on a dirty public bathroom floor with me." Another wave of nausea hits him, and he hurls into the bowl again.

"Didn't know we needed to be on a first name basis for a human to help another one in need," the man says. When Eliot looks back, he is smirking.

"Hey," Clive murmurs from the stall next door. "Are you impersonating Roger Moore or is there another person here?"

"I'm very real, guys," the man says. "At least last time I checked."

"Fuck," Eliot puts his forehead down on his arm. "Did we cross the ocean at some point? Is that why I feel seasick?"

The man continues rubbing circles into Eliot's back. "I live in Getty. As for being seasick, did you forget where you are?"

Eliot reaches a finger out and pokes him in the arm.

"Ow."

"He's quite real, Clive."

Eliot hears the sound of high heels growing louder, soon echoing in the small space. "Ah, shit," Alexis moans. She clicks over to Clive's door and opens it. "Double shit."

"I think I got them out of the room before anyone asked any questions," the man says to her.

"Thanks, Harvey. Do me a favor? Take them out the back door. Make sure they get home?"

He chuckles. "That's not exactly on the list of duties for 'event security,' Alexis."

"Neither is that."

Harvey's touch vanishes from Eliot's back.

"Listen, I'll give you a free dinner from Agave. Whatever you want." Alexis's voice softens. "Would you go call a cab please?"

Eliot watches Harvey climb to his feet. With a withering smile, he moves past Alexis and out the little crooked hall.

Alexis stands over Eliot, her eyebrows knit. She wears black that evening and it makes everything about her look harsh. The only time he remembers seeing her in black.

"Are you okay?" she asks, taking a few steps into the stall.

"I'm sorry, Alexis." His apology comes out weakly, mostly because of how weak he feels. He wants nothing more than to curl up in the corner of that stall and sleep off the thundering headache he knows is coming.

"Whatever Eliot said," adds Clive, and promptly vomits again.

Lines appear in Alexis' s forehead. "Look, Harvey's a *sensitive* guy. You know what I mean? He was just concerned."

Eliot frowns. He sees so many things in Alexis's eyes: frustration, anger, and exhaustion but fear is at the forefront now. Fear for what Eliot might say about a stranger's kindness, how it might be interpreted, how she thinks *he* might interpret it because she doesn't know…

Suddenly awash in shame and discomfort, he swallows hard. "I wasn't going to say anything, Alexis." He makes eye contact with her. "I wasn't."

She smirks. "I'd kiss you, Eliot, but you smell like puke." She starts to get up.

He tries to smile in return but can't. His memory is awash with reflections he sometimes catches in a mirror when his eyes look too much like his father's, or his smile too much like his mother's. He can feel himself backsliding into a dark pool of memories and reaches out suddenly, catching Alexis's hand. She flinches but brings her other hand forward to grab onto him. "Eliot?"

"I liked it," he says, his throat thickening. "At least I think I did."

Alexis gets down beside him, kneeling on the tile. "There's nothing wrong with that," she whispers, as if she can see the storm building behind his eyes.

Society thinks it's wrong. His father had thought it was wrong. Throughout his life, everything and everybody around him tiptoed around it because it was unpolite, it was troublesome, it was *unacceptable*. And it was easier to hide it than risk everything he'd worked decades for.

And now someone else knows. The water feels like it is receding from his dark room.

"Excuse me if I'm interrupting," says Clive, too loud, "But I thought I heard something about us being taken home?"

Eliot lets out a shaking breath. He doesn't know if Clive knows. His best friend and mentor. But if he's heard that admission…

"Your own private car, Clive," Alexis promises and puts her hand on Eliot's shoulder. Using her other hand, she crosses her finger over her heart and pretends to pull a zipper across her lips.

Eliot squeezes her hand.

8
DEVIL INSIDE

D ark room.

Dark water.

Eliot feels submerged and like he's burning up at the same time. But the memory of Alexis and her promise guides him to the surface and provides him with a much-needed breath. Except this breath smells like mothballs. He opens his eyes and finds himself horizontal in a bed. But not his own. This one was lumpy, but soft in all the wrong places.

A strange warm light caresses him from behind and only after pushing himself up and flipping over does he take in the strange scintillating glow. It's not the sun. It *can't* be the sun. The sun hasn't shown through the gloom and oppressive clouds for nearly ten years even out here in the Vast, away from the smog and light pollution. So, what is that insane bright beacon blinding him into thinking it's morning?

The ticking clock on the wall confirms it *is* morning, but early—just a bit after six o'clock. Getting to his feet, Eliot tries to remember what happened last.

The diner. Death stopped time. The man in the booth.

He'd had an episode. All the chaos of yesterday had caught up with him and took him down but he felt strangely better now, more like himself. The dream has left him melancholy, and he isn't eager to reminisce on its contents any more than he must.

He realizes that he's dressed in clothes that aren't his own: a set of striped pajamas. They're itchy, almost like a new set that's never been worn. Did someone redress him while he was unconscious? His skin crawls.

The room is decorated sparsely: a dresser, a chair, a bedside table along with the bed itself. A lone photo on the wall depicts a young man in naval uniform, perhaps twenty. There are knick-knacks alighting the bureau: metal toy cars, blocks, and a stuffed bear sits proudly next to a lamp. Eliot pulls open a drawer and finds a neatly folded plaid shirt that looks like it fits a five-year-old and slacks to match. The other drawers are filled with clothes that seem to get bigger.

Eliot notices his own clothes folded on the end of the bed, clean and ironed. He quickly redresses in them, feeling a modicum of ease return.

The door creaks when he unlatches it and pushes it forward, the light from the weird sun spreading out into the hall. He follows a narrow hallway around a low banister, passing watercolors that portray fields of flowers, restored travel trunks, and bookcases filled with titles he doesn't recognize.

There are two doorways upstairs: the one he came from and one at the opposite end of the hall, closed with only the sound of a rattling air-conditioner humming behind it. An acrid stench emanates from the other side of the door and Eliot backs away from it cautiously. It's something he's smelled before but can't place where.

As he draws closer to the stairs, the odor is overtaken by the mouth-watering aroma of food. He lets his nose guide him down to the first floor.

As he places his foot on the final step, Terry appears from somewhere on his left. "Whoa! You okay, Eliot?"

"What happened?" he asks. The floral wallpaper of the front hallway is yellowed, peeling in some places. An old radio plays religious hymns from the next room over near a flaming hearth. Funny. It looked like a HAM radio but he was sure those weren't supposed to play music. "Where are we?"

"It's cool. We're at Tom's place, just a little down the road from the diner."

Eliot glances out the window in the front door behind him, following the twisting dirt road into the dark. A small luminous sign from the diner glows in the distance. "Who's Tom?"

Before Terry can explain, the man from the booth behind them at the diner appears from a door at the other end of the hallway toting a large stoneware baking dish between his oven-mitt covered hands. "I see you're finally up," he says, joviality curtailed by a seemingly annoyed tone. "You want to give me a hand here, Terrence?"

Terry follows him into the next room, Eliot trailing along.

A dining table with three chairs sits in the center of the room. Terry nudges some plates aside and Tom sets the dish down on an array of knitted potholders and claps his hands together, the sound muffled by the mitts. "A hearty breakfast ought to get you boys straightened out. Hope you're hungry!"

"I'm starved, man," Terry says with a smile. "I'm sure whatever you made is a hundred times better than whatever that dincr would have made us, too."

Eliot frowns and his stomach grumbles in response. As much as he doesn't want to admit it, he could eat. But this place instantly reminds him of two things. One is when they visited his grandparents' house on his father's side. They'd lived forty-five minutes from where he grew up in a one-story ranch-style home. The meagerness of the walls, the worn rustic furniture, and the steady clinking of the off-balance ceiling fan in their living room matched the clanking of what he assumed was the air-conditioner in a room upstairs.

The second? The smell of dinner. Upstairs, it was welcome over whatever pungency was coming from behind the door of that room. Downstairs, nostalgia consumed him. While dinner with his mother's parents had been full of formative culinary delights, dinner with his father's had been more laidback: casseroles or things from cans and jars that could be thrown together in a Dutch oven and left to coalesce for hours while he and his brother played Monopoly or rode their bikes up and down the long dirt driveway, back and forth, back and forth...

It reminds him of humbleness. Of a time when his family had to make do with the little they could get ahold of. And then just his family itself.

Not to mention the fact that Tom was a priest or pastor or some minister of Christianity. While there aren't many paintings on the walls down here, there are several crosses hung here and there or displayed on the table. Questions of faith always make Eliot uncomfortable and more than anything, he doesn't want to get stuck in a conversation about them this morning.

But he's hungry. His body feels like it's been fished out of the sea and his equilibrium like it's still being tossed about on waves. He needs to be polite, eat the meal, and then get the fuck out of there with Terry's help.

"Come on over here, son," says Tom, patting the curved back of a wooden farmhouse dining chair. "You can sit right here."

He was on the far side of the table from the exit, the side with a door that presumably led to the kitchen.

As Eliot carefully makes his way over, he notices the old sepia photographs on the wall of men and women in pastoral outfits, babies and children. A faded color photo shows Tom with his arm around a woman, a grin rounding out her lovely face.

"That's my Cheryl," says Tom, when he catches Eliot looking. "Met her when I got back from the war. She was a fellow parishioner at my church, mourning her father who didn't make it out of France. Most beautiful creature I'd ever seen, even when she cried."

"I'm sorry for your loss," Eliot says. Maybe he was a little too hard on Tom. Perhaps the man was just lonely.

"Oh." Tom smiles. "Nah, she's still with us. Not as mobile as she once was but I take her out every day in her wheelchair. We watch the sun come up." He pulls out Eliot's chair for him.

Eliot stops and frowns. "The sun?"

Tom chuckles. "Probably saw it beaming right in your window this morning." He points out the window toward the barn and the celestially blinding quote unquote sun. "Had to weld together almost sixteen drop lights to make that damn thing but I do it all for her. Cheryl doesn't remember that we don't get to see the real sun anymore, so this is my paltry offering to her every morning."

Eliot sits in the chair, sadness striking him. "I'm sure it's appreciated effort."

Tom gives a tight smile. "You two dig in and I'll go get her. She wouldn't eat last night so maybe she will with some guests here." He disappears off through the kitchen door.

Eliot waits for his footfalls to soften before he turns to Terry. "Look, I'm not sure we should be here."

"You collapsed outside the diner, Eliot," Terry reminded him. "Didn't exactly leave me with a lot of options. Tom offered to take us up here when he saw you. Guy's just being decent."

"I know it seems decent. But we know nothing about him. And we've got the FBI looking for us, don't we?"

Terry's stare goes cold. "They're looking for *you*. Besides, he's a pastor! He might as well have a neon sign that says 'trust me' on it." Pulling back the foil on the dish, Terry dips a serving spoon in and scoops a healthy amount of casserole onto his plate.

Eliot winces as it glops onto the dishware.

Terry lifts the plate and sniffs it. "Might look like a chemical spill but it doesn't smell bad to me."

He was right. Even though the consistency leaves something to be desired, the casserole steams under the dim lights: cheese glistening over cubed potatoes, fluffy eggs, bits of green pepper, and slices of crisp ham. A fair amount of oil still languishes in the bottom of the dish in the empty spot where Terry scooped from, but Eliot doesn't think about it.

No. He's six and back in his grandparents' kitchen, watching as his grandmother pulls leftovers from the fridge, slices them up and gives them new life in her breakfast hoppel poppel. It was never the same recipe: always an inspired combination of whatever she and his grandpa had eaten recently, combined with fresh eggs from their neighbor's chickens and whatever vegetables were in season. The ghostly sensation of her hand patting the top of his head sent goosebumps rippling over his skin.

"Mmm, mmm, MMM!" Terry smacks his lips. "You *gotta* get in on this."

Eliot rolls his shoulders back as if trying to roll back the time-traveling his mind had just been on and indulges in a helping of the casserole. Tom's hoppel poppel isn't the same as his grandmother's, how could it be? But the taste makes him close his eyes regardless, makes him sigh at something finally being in his stomach.

Before he realizes it, he's finished off his plate and is going in for a second helping.

"Damn," Terry intones under his breath. "I thought I could eat."

As Eliot grabs a piece of toast and starts buttering it, the metallic rattle of something in the front hall stills him. No, not something. He knows the sound too well. It used to play in concert with the low sound of the washing machine, an empty tinkle of windchimes, and his father's hoarse cough.

Now, it comes with a squeaky wheel and heavy footsteps. The wheelchair rounds the corner from the front hall into the dining room, pushed by Tom who has a grin from ear to ear. But the similarities stop once Eliot sees the curled thing sitting in the chair and every bit of comfort is sucked straight from him like a vacuum.

"Cheryl, look! Not our usual visitors this time around, huh?" Tom pushes the wheelchair around Terry's side of the table.

Terry has frozen in place, a spoon handle poking out of his mouth. His eyes are as wide as can be and surveying Eliot as if he can explain the turn of events they've just witnessed.

But Eliot can't take his eyes off the wheelchair's occupant. A thing perhaps human once, but now barely anything other than a skeletal frame, skin charred and lifting from her forearms like bits of paper from a leftover fire. Her hair is only a few strands of gray, limp and like spiderwebs hanging from her splotchy head. The eyes, where eyes must have been once, is covered by a yellowed bit of cloth and their cavernous holes seem to gape at him from beyond the layer. Her mouth moves in slight utterances, only moans and grunts emanating from the toothless gap between where he assumed lips once were.

The sensation of being dropped cuts through him. Alone, falling, but mostly alone. He carefully sets the piece of toast down on his plate, the knife still shaking in his hand.

Tom situates the wheelchair at the end of the table and grabs the spoon from the casserole dish. As he digs the tip into the egg with a squish, he makes eye-contact with Eliot and says, "You're staring, Buck-o."

Eliot drops his eyes to his own plate of food, brain skipping with terror.

"Is she…um…" Terry falters. "Is…she all right, Tom?"

"Well, Christ, no, Terrance," Tom laughs. "Take one look at her and tell me she's all right."

Terry laughs nervously. Eliot is sure he can see sweat beading on his friend's brow.

"But," Tom says, dropping a couple spoons of casserole on Cheryl's plate. "We don't judge others based on what stage they are in on this mortal plane. If anything, my Cheryl is closer to God now than she ever was." He raises the spoon to Cheryl's mouth and slides the food from it against her bottom lip. Eliot sees it inside, barely clinging to the wafer-thin black skin. There is no effort to chew from the burnt woman.

Tom sidles back to his end of the table and fixes his own plate. "'…and give relief to you who are troubled, and to us as well. This will happen when the Lord Jesus is revealed from heaven in blazing fire with his powerful angels.' Thessalonians one: seven."

"But…" Eliot leans forward in his chair and huffs. "You know they explode, don't you? The Ashen?"

Tom's gaze narrows. "Are you tellin' me that my wife is going to explode, son?"

Eliot frowns. He doesn't like the patronizing tone of this man calling him "son." After all, he's probably what? Only ten years older than him? But there's a depth in Tom's wrinkles and in his eyes that speaks of living amongst the Vast for decades—of loss, of love, and of horror—and Eliot knows that age is only a number between them. Experience is quantifiably the thing that separates them.

Tom chuckles. "I wasn't born yesterday." He snaps up a piece of cinnamon raisin toast. He nods to the knife in Eliot's hand and Eliot hands it over, albeit hesitantly. "Only some of them explode. You can tell by how hot they get. They start getting volatile and their eyes look like flames in a boiler." He takes a bite of the toast. "If they don't melt out first."

Eliot forgets to breathe. It's what he saw with Justin's mother at the bank. He had just assumed that was how they all looked. The crease in his brow deepened as he considered his own tiger's eye. Did that mean he was one of the unlucky few destined to blow up?

"Nothing to be afraid of, son," Tom says, his fork spearing a potato on his plate. "The Lord is going to look after you. After all, he's chosen you, hasn't he? He's chosen you to be one of his Angels."

Eliot stiffens as discomfort sifts down through him.

Terry frowns at Eliot but says nothing.

Eliot straightens in his chair. "With all due respect, I'm an atheist, Tom." Saying the words brushes back the heat of arguments he thinks he's left far behind in his youth, arguments said between awkward stares over the dinner table, arguments that simmered in his father's fists or in his mother's nervous eyes. "Whatever it is that's happening to me, it's not God's doing or the Devil's."

The corners of Tom's mouth are upturned but he isn't smiling. Something simmers behind his gaze as he takes a long sip from his glass of milk. "Well, you seem like you have all the answers, don't you?"

Eliot blinks. "No, I don't. But that doesn't mean that the answer is automatically divine."

Terry's lips are drawn together in warning, his head cocked as if to say, "What the hell are you doing?"

But Eliot isn't going to do this anymore. He is tired of being pushed around, made to feel small, made to feel as if *he* is the problem. He is dying. *Dying.* He has to fight for his last right, to go out with the kind of bang he wants. Even if that bang is as small as telling a small-town preacher to keep his proselytizing to himself.

"So, what is it then, son?" asks Tom, his tone framed with a patronizing curiosity. "Is it science? Hard to believe there's any kind of virus out there that would make a person into an active volcano, isn't there? Is it environmental? Something about all this rain that makes the human body want to burn until it breaks apart? Naw, it doesn't make sense, son, unless you see it in the way our Lord and Savior intended. We are just drifting around down here like cattle, prodded by our own government—our senators, our congressmen, our judiciary—into believing every word they've had to say. They talked us into saving the wetlands in '85! You know how many wetlands there are now? The entire goldarn middle of this country is just one giant wetland, like the center of a tire sinking into a marsh… Everyone wants to rule the world, don't they?"

Tom takes a bite of his toast and chews while shaking his finger at Eliot. "The Ash is God's way of letting us know that we aren't listening to him. The rain is God's way of letting us know that we've prioritized the wrong things. We're ignoring the signs because of arrogance or narrow-mindedness or…" He squints at Eliot. "Socialism."

The air around Eliot burns warm for a second as he deflects the comment. "Says the man who was just complaining about the government."

Tom is laughing now, staring down at his plate as he saws through a large potato wedge with his knife. "You can't ignore Him and His will. Pretty soon, as you're lit up brighter than a roman candle, you'll finally see what he's got in store for you." He locked eyes with Eliot, then Terry. "A reckoning is coming."

Eliot senses the shift in the conversation and his anger fizzles out, bubbling into fear. The way the muscles of Tom's fingers clench around the knife as he holds it in his left while he stabs at potatoes with the right. His fork screeches on the plate when he misses one because he won't take his eyes off Eliot, not even to pay attention to where he's skewering prongs into soft objects. Eliot has half a mind to think that if he keeps rebelling, they'll end up in his chest.

"Sorry to butt in on this conversation," Terry intrudes. Discomfort has lodged a thick stone in his throat. It's the quietest voice he thinks he's ever heard from Terry. "But I was wondering if you had anymore coffee?"

Tom breaks his eye contact with Eliot to answer Terry, all smiles again. "Of course, Terrance. Let me just make another pot."

Clattering the chair back a little, he stands and edges around the table past Eliot toward the kitchen door. For a moment, Eliot swears that Tom pauses behind him and that moment splits into a thousand years of expectation.

A hand around his throat, a fork into his ear, a whisper of contempt—

Nothing happens. Tom steps into the kitchen out of sight and they are suddenly alone with breakfast and a wheezing lady made of charcoal.

Eliot is the first one to carefully slide his chair out, careful not to make any sound at all. Terry follows suit, each other's eyes locked on the kitchen door.

From within, they hear Tom whistling, hear the garbage can lid being wrestled open as something wet—the used coffee filter—is flung into it.

Eliot feels sweat on the back of his neck as he eases across the carpet of the living room toward the front hall, Terry at his heels, and curls his hand around the knob. The door sticks and in a moment of horror, he nudges it. The wood scrapes against the frame.

Terry's hands are now on the wood around him, shoving the door free into the cool rush of morning air. They thunder down the steps, shoes scrabbling in the dirt of the road as they run toward the beckoning glow of the diner, toward Terry's van.

In the rush of soft wind, the roar of his own breath, and the delicate tinkle of wind chimes, Eliot thinks he hears a creak on the top step of the front porch behind them, and every muscle in his body forces him into overdrive.

They are halfway down the road before he has the courage to look back and see the dark silhouette standing on the front porch, backlit by the infernal false sun. He doesn't look back again.

By the time they make it to the diner, Eliot's shirt is practically soaked and Terry is almost dry heaving. They climb into the van, gasping for air, start the engine and promptly lock the doors.

"Good-fucking-riddance," Terry grumbles as they pull back onto the road and leave the hamlet behind.

LEFT LOG #2

TAINTED LOVE

It's a haul: leaving Getty that late and embarking into the Vast. It occurs to Left shortly after they leave the city limits that he hasn't brought any snacks with him other than the half-drunk warm Sunkist bottle in the cupholder between him and Meena. It was Right's. That was her drink of choice whenever they were out on a case. As thirsty as he found himself, it felt *wrong* to drink it.

The road south along the Atlantic Spill Highway is pockmarked with the sight of endless orange traffic cones and concrete barriers. Construction is a persistent thing out in the Vast: the highways are always under duress from the elements, threatening to crumble and give way. Those who work in highway maintenance sometimes spend nine to ten months out of the year out here working non-stop. Their rain-lashed trailers line whatever level ground they come across along the way; dirt lots lit up by portable light towers, their generators buzzing into the night.

Hernandez doesn't say much. Left assumed she'd talk his ear off about the chef. After all, she'd barged into his car with a pissed off cat saying she had information. But all she's done since they started their little drive is look solemnly out the window and pet the feline which has curled into a ball on her lap.

Left sighs and turns on the radio but struggles to find a station that will come through clearly other than one playing classical music. It's not his thing. The only time he could tolerate it was at his daughter's ballet lessons and he barely paid much attention then. He was there for her and her attempts at pliés and arabesques; not to memorize the different acts of Swan Lake.

"Where are we going?" Hernandez finally asks.

Ah. The spell was broken.

"There's a psychologist my partner was working with out of Rust City. I'm bringing her on board as a specialist to help determine Lamb's next moves."

When he glances at her, he sees Hernandez glaring at him. "What do you need a psychologist for? I can tell you whatever you need to know about Eliot. Plus, you've got his map. If you think this is where he's headed, we shouldn't be wasting time. We should be heading after him."

Left's forehead crinkles in annoyance. "If you knew him so well, you'd have known what he was up to with the True Faith."

"Just because Justin was involved doesn't mean Eliot was." She stares down at the cat and rubs one of its ears. "He could never have coordinated all those atrocities. He's one of the nicest people I've ever known."

"Really?" Left rolls his shoulders back. "I can tell you all kinds of things about the nicest people others have ever known. In '84, we arrested a woman for peddling dope out of the school cafeteria in the Brisken Middle School. 'Sweetest old lady there ever was,' the principal told us. Had been working there for years.

"Three years ago, we had to call in SWAT for a man who had bludgeoned a family to death at the local bowling alley because they were taking too long to vacate the lane and he wanted to play. Guy was awarded the key to the city the year before through his work with the food pantry."

Hernandez stares at him, her eyebrows puckered. She's stopped petting the cat and he detects an unevenness to her breath.

He keeps going. "Last year, I got a call about a woman found bound and murdered off the Atlantic Spill Highway. Throat slit. The guy who did it was quiet, lived alone, and worked for the post office. Government job. Turns out he killed four others. He went after these women who came in to buy stamps or send out packages. No motive. Just did it because it was an itch he needed to scratch."

Hernandez closes her eyes and looks away and Left thinks he spots her wipe her eyes. "I'm not telling you this for shock value," he says. "I'm telling you because everyone thinks they know someone and when they don't, when you find out what's lurking below, it's *always* a surprise."

Contempt flashes in her dark eyes. "That doesn't mean he's guilty. It doesn't mean anything. You're jaded and that makes you suspicious. But Eliot is different. You know he took a chance on me? A girl who had barely graduated culinary school. Barely had a dollar to her name? A girl from immigrant parents who were never given the same opportunities that I was? He didn't have to but he knew I was in trouble, and he could see I had a gift. "

Left rolls his eyes. "Is that so?" The "he told me I'm special" card. All kinds of people who had been fooled played it; Hernandez is no different.

"I *know* Eliot." She falters here and Left picks up on it immediately.

"He kept something from you, didn't he?" he prods.

Hernandez strokes the cat. "He's dying. He has the Ash. But he didn't tell me."

"And why wouldn't he tell you? He considered you a friend, didn't he? Enough to leave his cat with you."

"Because he didn't want me to worry."

Left exhales. "He didn't want you *involved*."

She doesn't say anything, and he can tell he's right.

They drive a little longer, the only sound the squeak of the windshield wipers clearing the windshield in front of them.

"Eliot's always been private. Separates his food from his personal life. Then again, food *is* his life. Losing that restaurant, losing his ability to cook, is likely the most awful thing he's gone through. And losing Alexis…" Hernandez shakes her head. "God, I wish I'd known it was her restaurant Saturday night. I could have—"

"Lamb and Munro had a falling out." He'd read up on it while he sat and rotted at the police station earlier. His affiliate at the bureau didn't have much on Lamb but this at least was in the public archives. "You can't tell me her restaurant getting hit isn't suspicious."

Hernandez rounds on him, her anger thick. "Alexis was the one in the wrong. She tried to ruin Eliot's career. She's the reason they split, why *I* ended up in *her* job."

Left shakes his head. "That's what we call motive."

"Not him." She blinks. "Not Eliot."

Annoyed by the jaunty classical tune now playing, Left shuts off the radio. "Whatever you say, sweetheart."

…

Rust City is as forgettable as a lot of other cities along the Eastern Seaboard if not for one thing: the red lights. The roads in town used to all run on electric stop lights until the grid went wonky. No matter how many electricians tried to diagnose the problem, they could never get the lights off their red setting.

New lights only lasted for a couple days before they, too, would get stuck on red. The repairmen blamed ghosts in the systems: something wanting to bleed out that surpassed the wires and circuit-boards. Metal traffic signs litter the roads to make up for the malfunctioning electrical ones. Traffic is a nightmare, and Left suddenly finds his chest tightening at the prospect of spending any more time dying on the roads while waiting for someone to just *go*…

They park along an avenue where the red lights cast their glow against the gloom and dye everything in their wake a washed out vermillion. Left tells Hernandez to stay in the car and while she doesn't want to listen, she ultimately keeps put. She's probably still mad at him, he decides.

The Last Night is a seedy-looking place; the kind of place with no windows in the middle of a brick edifice that disappears into the gray sky as if it is never-ending. Inside, he descends a short staircase into a black lounge with a low ceiling. The coat checker tries to do his job, and Left interjects his badge before he can lay one finger on his jacket. He eases through a set of glass doors into the main room.

For a bar in Rust City at one a.m., Left figures there'd be more activity. But there's barely anyone still around. The bartender is scrubbing some glasses and gives him a surly nod. A pair of women finish off their cosmos and collect their purses while a guy in a jean jacket with a receding hairline watches from the other end of the bar. Just as he goes to get up, too, Left smacks his hand down on his shoulder and says, "Have another. It's on me. Those ladies don't need you hassling them tonight." He nods to the bartender and murmurs, "Whatever you want, barf bag."

Left notices a woman sitting at a booth in the back, her shaggy blonde hair hiding her face. *Must be her*, he decides. *There's no one else here.* He comes up behind her at the table and holds his badge out. "You the psychologist I talked to?"

The woman drags on a cigarette and tilts her head back. Sparkling lavender eyeshadow bruises her lids and makes her olive-green eyes pop. She pulls a straw up between her gloss-coated lips and sips at her clear drink. Could be seltzer water. Could be vodka. "You're late."

He gives her a once over. She's wearing a short dress, the naked curve of her butt barely visible. It's flashy and an odd choice for a meeting with a federal agent. But he finds himself sliding into the booth opposite her regardless. "Dressed like that in a place like this? Some might think you're asking for trouble."

She cocks her head. "Is that what you believe? That women dress purely with expectation of whether or not they'll invite trouble?"

This is definitely her, he decides. "When I asked you to meet me, I didn't mean we were going to go out for a dance."

The Psychologist smiles. "Again, here you are thinking that my outfit choice is based solely around you. Are you always so self-important?"

Left rolls his eyes. "You know what, never mind. I've got a suspect fleeing across the Vast right now and a woman in my car with a sleeping cat. I don't have time for this." He starts to get up.

She slides her hand over his on the table. Her skin is cool and soft and immediately makes him stop. "You've got questions. I've got answers, or at least, I can try to answer. After all your partner has done for me, I owe her that much."

A snapshot of Right falling slaps into Left's mind for a moment before he shoves it back into his tangled nest of thoughts and he sits down once more. The vinyl seat is slightly sticky in the humid bar and the lights inside flicker occasionally.

"Want a drink?" she asks.

He shouldn't. He's been driving for the last four hours and will likely drive another four once he leaves here. But he's parched and hasn't had anything to eat in hours. So, he orders a Blue Lagoon and whatever packaged bar snacks they have. The hulking bartender drops off his drink with a fuchsia umbrella poking out of its aqua concoction along with a packet of honey roasted peanuts.

The Psychologist eyes the drink. "Hmm."

He squints and a part of him desperately wants to crack into that "hmm" but veers back to the topic at hand. "Right gave you notes about the case. Said you discussed it together. Said you were working on a profile."

"It's a work in progress. But I've pieced together a few things that are irrevocably clear about your suspect. If he's the one coordinating all of this, that is."

"It's the guy," says Left, almost more to himself than to her. "There's too many coincidences."

"Sounds like you're trying to convince yourself in spite of that statement, Detective."

"Agent."

"Whatever."

Left takes a deep breath, lets it simmer through his lungs until they are at full capacity before blowing all the air out through the small slot he makes between his lips. "Well, what is it?"

The Psychologist leans further into the table.

Despite not wanting to, he finds himself doing the same.

"Your mastermind isn't a mastermind at all. He didn't have a plan. He didn't want any of this to happen. He simply adapted." She pulls a pack of Salems from somewhere (Left can't for the life of him figure out where they were hidden) and slides one out. It seems to take forever for it to clear the box. "In adapting, he became aware of a new idealism: that this world is broken but the Ashen are a part of how we put it back together. And now, he's devoted considerable amounts of his time to changing other people's minds to coincide with his."

"You mean he's started a cult," Left puts plainly. "This is stuff we already know. If you're going to waste my time…"

The Psychologist produces a lighter from the apparent pocket dimension in her fitted dress and flicks the flint wheel, sparks creating blisters of light in her eyes. "Cool it," she says, the cigarette between her teeth making her sound slightly muffled. "You can call it a cult. But that's not what he calls it."

Left squints. "I don't give two shits what he calls it. It's a cult and it's slowly burning up in city after city after city. We need to stop these guys, not have a philosophical debate about what this guy's favorite kind of eggs are."

She stops trying the lighter and cocks her head. "To catch him, you have to understand him. You drove four hours to get here just to snap at me about my choice of clothing and interrupt me at every turn. I had to cancel two appointments to sit down with you. You're wasting my time now, agent."

Appointments. The word lingers in Left's brain. What sort of appointments had he caused her to miss? Surely she wouldn't be meeting with clients for counseling meetings this late at night? Nevertheless, he says, "Sorry. Go on."

She brings the lighter back up to the cigarette. A flame ignites and she smolders the end of her cigarette in it before sucking on it and letting the smoke undulate like waves from her lips. "He doesn't call it a cult. To him, they are distant family. And this is a new religion."

New religion. So, they were dealing with someone who'd lost their Goddamn marbles. Left closes his eyes for a moment before dragging his drink closer to him and taking a long sip through the straw. The curacao hits him before the lemonade, floating on top of the ice like a chemical spill. He swallows hard.

A religious fanatic wasn't the last thing he'd expected her to say, and it wasn't necessarily groundbreaking evidence either. Lamb hadn't given off a bizarre ambiance when they'd interrogated him in his kitchen, but those zealots often didn't. They were all so cool and calm under pressure until they were "caught rapid" as Right had referred to it. She always had ridiculous euphemisms to throw out when it concerned tracking criminals down.

"So, he's not so much recruiting as he is growing the size of his flock," Left answers. "And his end goal is…?"

"What it is with all religions: to make the world a better place through conversion." Her next drag on the cigarette practically burned halfway up the paper.

"He's making it a better place by blowing up restaurants and art galleries?"

The Psychologist removes the cigarette from her mouth, the last of her smoke trailing toward the ceiling above them. "What do you know about the Ashen, agent? What do you know about the Ash itself? Had any experience with it firsthand?"

Left shakes his head. Sure, he'd seen them. Everyone did. In his line of work, they often appear at hospitals, confined to burn units, the entire wing stinking like charred flesh and creosote. More than a few times, he's glimpsed them from the Atlantic Spillway as he'd leered out the passenger window of Right's Camaro. They slogged through bogs or open fields, movements slow and aimless, eyes burning like fireflies in the darkness of day.

"To understand our killer, you must understand the core of his religion and that is the Ash." She abruptly stands up. "Let's go."

All Left can do is glance down at his still mostly full Blue Lagoon and then back up at her. "What the fuck?"

She rolls her eyes. "Obviously, I can't tell you my entire study on the Ashen here and now. It would take days, and I don't have all my notes here. Now, if you wouldn't mind giving me a ride back to my apartment, I can get my papers, and we can be on our way."

Left coughs. "Can't you paraphrase it? Just give me a summary of your notes so we can—"

"There's no summary that will cover it all. It's a lot of theory: jumbled and chaotic with lots of your partner's thoughts tossed in for good measure. And it's not a complete study. I honestly need more field notes to complete the report. Where better to do it than out there in the Vast?"

"Jesus." Left hangs his head. No other agent would ever degrade themselves to the point where they'd let a civilian and a cat hitch a ride looking for her old employer and now, he's going to have a psychologist practically wearing lingerie take up the backseat with all her folders, binders, and texts?

No one else would let this happen.

Right wouldn't.

But then again, Right had come to this Psychologist for help. Right had shared confidential files with her. She was already involved.

And the sous chef? She had invaluable information about Lamb. She'd worked under him for the last several years. Even if she wasn't ready to give up information on him quite yet, he knows she will inadvertently and probably once she hears what The Psychologist has to say about his behavior as a cult leader. He bets it will all line up perfectly.

But it will be hell until it does.

"Fuck," he snarls. Plucking the straw from the glass, he takes a deep drink of the Blue Lagoon. alcohol and lemonade swirling like a storm in his mouth before he swallows. Snatching the package of peanuts from the table, he gets up. "Rule number one: no one touches the Sunkist. Rule number two: I pick whatever plays on the radio."

They pay for their drinks and leave The Last Night for the deluge outside.

CONFLUENCE
THIRD OBSERVATION

They travel alone. Cast out into the Vast like refuse from our own crumbling societies, some have wandered days, weeks, months without coming across another like themselves. It's hard to judge if they find any pleasure or pain in this solitude. Beheld by spectators, the Ashen have stopped amid their treks, staring into the sky as if waiting for something…or longing for something, perhaps? It feels poetic to impart some ghost of thought onto these wretched creatures in hopes of making them like they used to be: human. But then, they continue as they did before, in the same amble.

Until…

A second one appeared out of the murk of night.

Without acknowledging one another,

they trudge onward,

going in the same direction…

HANDLE WITH CARE

It's seven o'clock sharp. Crickets sing, their pitches somehow sounding apocalyptic to Pastor O'Malley as he steps into the barn entrance and calmly shuts off his sun. With a clank, the lights fade, popping rhythmically as darkness rushes in to fill the void it leaves behind. Try with all his might, he just can't break a ritual he started months ago, a ritual he started to remind his darling Cheryl that there was still a night and a day, that time didn't circle on itself like some kind of serpent. And now that she doesn't have any eyes at all, he knows this is all just for him.

Leaving the barn, he stalks across the cool wet grass back to the old farmhouse and steps into the mudroom, the scent of dryer sheets and the tick of metal buttons in the machine welcoming him back from the outside.

It's been hours since Terence and Eliot left. It's been hours since he brought all the food to the local homeless shelter. Hours since he threw the plates into the garbage. Since he wheeled Cheryl back into her room upstairs and left her. There are just too many things to do on the farm, too many things to do at the rectory, too many things to do with his congregation, and yet…he can't seem to let her go.

But now…things have changed. He'd seen something in Eliot that day over breakfast that he couldn't identify at first, something that had caused him to go on the offense. That man was marked. The tiger's eye was relatively small, but it was there, glimmering and almost reaching out to Tom from the other side of the table. How could he not take that mark seriously? How could he just ignore the gift he'd been given?

Not only ignore…he'd insulted him. Insulted God himself! In the home of a pastor.

He's not sure but he also felt a shadow over Eliot that didn't seem to belong, something that he'd read about time and time again in the new and old testaments: a vile and pernicious thing that clung like a parasite to unfortunate folk, that used them and corrupted them. The work of the Devil.

And it was at home in Eliot, he was certain.

This was something he could not allow to invade the country he called home, these small towns, these small but genuine people he cared for. He had a calling and a purpose to serve, and Cheryl was no longer it.

Pastor O'Malley finds the box of matches by the wood stove and takes them up the creaking old stairs to the second floor where the hall still smells like homemade potpourri from Cheryl's old church craft parties she used to run, back in the days when there used to be people over to their house all the time. It was so quiet here now it drove him mad.

He stepped along the hallway, collected a lace runner from the top of a bookcase, and knocked on her door. He didn't need to, but he also couldn't help but picture her as she had been only a couple weeks ago before she'd first been diagnosed. Her flowing blonde hair, her radiant face, and her gorgeous smile… Just like Heaven.

None of that meets his gaze when he walks in. He's left her facing the wall which he never would have done under normal circumstances. Today was far from normal though. And oddly, he feels better that she's not facing him so he can do this while she can't witness him. Tom drapes the runner over her shoulder and down to the rug then lights a match. As he leans into her ear, he whispers, "May you fly like the angels, my darling."

He touches the match to the runner and her entire form ignites in a plume of flame.

Pastor O'Malley watches as she burns silently. No screaming. No flailing. No resistance. Only the most fitting death for his beautiful bride.

Tearing himself away, Pastor O'Malley leaves the room. Before he can descend the stairs, he pokes his head into the other bedroom upstairs, the one that Eliot stayed in, and takes the teddy bear inside. He's not ready to lose that yet. Not yet.

O'Malley goes downstairs, collects his hat and coat, and pushes out into the dark. The house's second story is already wreathed in fire as he climbs into his truck and pulls out onto the dirt road that leads down toward Bushel's. He spies concerned onlookers pointing their fingers at the flaming box in his rearview.

Onward, he tells himself. The Devil must be stopped.

SMALLTOWN BOY

1955

"I want you to imagine yourself in a box," says the voice, and so Eliot does. "Clear on all sides. Now, imagine the nozzle of a hose hanging over the top of the box where you can't reach."

Curiosity and dread immediately douse him.

"You're looking out into your bedroom. No one is home. It's just you in the box, the water, and my voice. Do you understand?"

Eliot nods. His throat feels tight with fear even though he knows this is imaginary, even though he knows he can open his eyes and be right back in that painfully bland office he'd entered only ten minutes ago, an office his father dropped him off at once a week for the last several months.

"I'm going to describe a set of scenarios to you and I want you to tell me the first word that comes to your mind when you hear them. Okay?"

He nods again.

"Good." He thinks he hears the shuffling of papers but is transfixed by the realization that, in this imaginary version of his room, his closet door was wide open and dark. Normally, it faces the windows that look out on the front of the house where sunlight streams in most hours of the day. That closet is never dark.

"There's a girl your age shopping for groceries in the supermarket with her parents. She has pretty dark hair and a demure smile. She winks at you and says hello. What do you think?"

"Sunday." The word is instantaneous. His mother often takes him shopping after they'd get out of church. He is always seeing other kids his age at the supermarket, but he's never thought anything more of it than that.

A hesitant scribbling of pen on paper and then: "You're at the lake. There's lots of people swimming and having a good time. You see a group of girls wearing swimsuits down by the water's edge. Your first thought?"

"Summer."

Eliot can't be sure, but he swears he sees movement in the darkness of the closet and his heart skips a beat.

"That's all?"

"I thought I was only supposed to share one word?"

"Of course. Of course." The pen scratched across paper again.

"You're in the locker room at school. You see a young man changing back into his uniform after gym class."

Something smolders in the base of Eliot's stomach with the words and suddenly, the temperature in his box skyrockets.

"He's wearing nothing but his briefs as he opens his locker to retrieve his clothes."

Eliot swallows and glances between the glass all around him and the open closet door.

"Your answer?"

"Hot."

Silence. There. Was that a sigh?

"I want you to imagine the hose at the top of your box turning on, Eliot."

Water splurged from the metal nozzle and Eliot shrunk against the side of the box. It was icy cold and surged across his skin, making goosebumps immediately rise. This is pretend. This is supposed to be pretend. But it's real: the cold, the wet, everything.

"The water in the box rises up to your ankles before the hose turns off." The voice narrates and like that, the hose slows to a drip-drop. "For every right answer, the water will recede a foot. For every wrong answer, the hose will turn back on, and it will increase a foot. Do you understand?"

He shakes his head, shivering.

"What don't you understand?"

"I don't know how I'm supposed to know what the right answers are."

"You know the right answers, Eliot," the voice says, dismissively. "You're surrounded by them every day in life. Now, next scenario: you meet a girl you know from school at a pharmacy for a soda. She's wearing a dress that shows off her legs and sandals. What's your answer?"

Eliot takes a deep breath. He doesn't want to say anything. If he doesn't say anything, he can't get it wrong. The water can't turn on.

"Eliot?"

"Flowers."

"I'm sorry?"

"Her dress has flowers on it."

Furious scribbling. "The water turns on and comes up to your knees."

Panic lances through him as the frigid water soaks him again. He bangs against the walls, his fists thudding dully. The walls are too thick. "Please stop! I don't know what I'm supposed to do!"

"A boy in your class from school drops a pencil on the floor. You pick it up and hand it back to him and your fingers touch."

"I don't want to do this anymore!"

"Word, please!"

Eliot gasps, sloshing around in the box in his head. Hadn't he had his eyes open not that long ago? Wasn't he in someone's office? But the more he tries to open his eyes, the clearer the room outside the walls becomes, the more he sees the shadows in his closet shifting…

"I don't know!" he shouts.

"This isn't a sensitivity test. Understand? This is an exercise to pinpoint the source of your confusion and see what we can do to change it."

The water gushes and soon, its chill laps at his stomach. He doesn't know what kind of confusion the voice is talking about except his confusion about this exercise. The glass walls fog up to the point where his fingers leave scratches though the clouded breaths he puffs at them. Through the streaks, he thinks he sees a face in his closet and terror fully grips him. "Let me out! Let me out!"

"Answer the prompts correctly. You have full control over this situation, Eliot. You can make the water go back down if you do the right thing." Words spill out again: he's on a date with someone and he's walking them home. When they get to his date's house, who is he looking at? Eliot immediately pictures Paul from his English glass. Paul who was quiet and knew Shakespeare's tragedies like the back of his hand. Paul who headed the school newspaper and talked about becoming a typesetter, who once partnered with him on an assignment and told him how easy he was to work with.

Eliot has never thought about asking Paul on a date. He's had dates with girls, girls who have asked him out. Girls who he is friends with but nothing more. He doesn't like the idea of dates. His brother goes on "dates." He brings a new girl home almost every week and they hang around the house like sloths, teasing one another, poking each other's soft places, kissing. The idea of kissing anyone ties his stomach in knots; even any of those girls he is friends with…even Paul.

"Eliot…answer the question."

"No one. No one!"

The rustling of paper slaps down somewhere in front of him. He struggles to tether his mind to it, because he knows this is all wrong and something else is happening outside the glass box. But the voice gets louder and closer and sets his skin alive with goosebumps.

"You think this is some kind of joke? That you can trick the test? The water's up to your neck now. Soon, it'll be over your head."

Eliot desperately gasps as the water climbs to his lips. In the darkness of the closet is a woman without a face, her long red hair dropping over her naked shoulders as his brother embraces her from behind. The carnal emptiness in Grady's eyes shoot fear down through his system.

"Stop!" he screams, hands treading water as he fights to stay above it. "Stop!"

"You're already in over your head as far as I'm concerned," the voice spits. "What happens when I tell your father how little progress we've made? All because you couldn't cooperate like a good—"

The squeal of a door opens nearby followed by a gasp. "What are you doing? Get the hell away from my son!"

Rustling. Something hollow clunks on the ground. Hands on Eliot's shoulders wrench him up. He screams as the box drops away, and the faceless girl and Grady and his bedroom and darkness floats up. His eyes snap open.

A wood paneled room. His father pushing him toward a door. An old woman in a pencil skirt crouches on the floor next to a bearded man holding his eye.

He is wet. His face is wet. His clothes are wet…

His father shouts behind him. "You send me a bill and I fucking call the police. You hear me? We're through!"

All Eliot can do is keep walking forward, following a hall he remembers and doesn't at the same time. It's a blur through the tears. Through a heavy door, they descend a flight of stairs. A man and woman are having a conversation at the bottom and stop to behold them as they go by.

"Mind your own business!" his father yells and puts a hand on the back of Eliot's neck to guide him out the next door. His father's familiar brown truck is parallel parked a few spaces away. The passenger door opens for him, and Eliot climbs into the truck. Its familiar smell creeps through the panic and the tremors in his hands gradually subside.

Soon enough, his father is in the driver's seat and the engine rumbles. They tear out onto the road moments later.

His father holds a death grip around the steering wheel, his lip moving like he wants to say something but can't. Are those tears in his eyes? Eliot has never seen his father cry and isn't sure that is what is happening.

"What's that?" his father asks.

All at once, Eliot realizes he'd been muttering the same words over and over. "I don't want to go back there. Please don't take me back there. Pl—"

His father puts a hand on his head and rubs his hair. "I won't. I promise."

Eliot blinks and as he stares down at his shoes, the sharp odor of urine hits him. He's peed in his pants. A sophomore in high school and he's peed his pants like a child. He tries to hold back fresh tears, but they slide out regardless.

Afternoon pales into twilight. A rosy hue overtakes the sky as the truck skates along the dirt county roads among the endless fields of corn. Their house appears over the next hill and his father parks the truck in the pot-hole riddled lot. They sit there in silence.

"Don't tell your mother."

Eliot swallows the lump in his throat. When he looked up at his father, he is staring at him, with a pleading in his eyes. "We don't need her to know. You understand me?"

He grinds his teeth and swallows again before nodding.

"I'll go in first, distract her. You go up to your room and get changed." His father pops open the truck door and hangs a leg out the side before glancing back at Eliot. "I was just trying to…" he starts and as if thinking better of it, climbs out and shuts the door behind him.

Eliot watches him trudge across the lot to the front door and open the screen before he follows. His legs slog heavily as he climbs the front porch steps and listens to the sounds of his parents conversing in the kitchen out of sight. Normal sounding. As if nothing had happened.

He sniffs as he walks inside and mounts the stairs up to his bedroom. The second floor is vacant now. His brother left the week before for his final year of college and the quiet ripples around Eliot like being inside a cavern. He stands outside the door to his own room, tremors returning to his body as he thinks about the box. The water. The people in the closet.

Turning the lights on, he steps inside and closes the door.

9
TALKING IN YOUR SLEEP

As Terry's van slides through the blue undulating landscape, Eliot sleeps and dreams about a time in his life that frightened him. Delving back into those memories is like sitting on a bed of needles, their points gently digging against his skin. One wrong move and they'll puncture him.

The tape deck clicks as the cassette switches sides and a burst of instruments rip Eliot from the mire of his memory. He glances at Terry as he shakes his shoulders back and forth in time with the music and quietly sings along. This is, if his memory is correct, at least the fifth time they've listened to this tape since they left the diner that morning. It isn't a bad sound, in fact, it is one that Eliot hasn't heard prior to this trip. But it is becoming old.

"You must really like this song," he murmurs, sitting up in his seat.

Terry beams. "I like to think of this as my get-up-and-go anthem. You ever heard of Enya?"

Eliot shakes his head.

"They're calling this style of music 'new age.' After all, we're on the brink of a new decade, baby. I've got a feelin' that 1990 is gonna be my year."

New age. Eliot isn't going to see the 90's. And it's hard for him to focus on the idea of anything drastically changing for the better with how things currently are. But Terry is smiling for the first time in several hours and he doesn't want to quash his enthusiasm, so he stays quiet, even as a seed of warmth sets his skin alight. And his eye... It burns, the same feeling as when he accidentally rubbed jalapeno in it as a young cook. He rolls down the window a tiny bit and heaves in the outside air. It's cool and welcome against the singe in his cheeks and forehead. "What's this song called?" he asks and closes his eye.

"Orinoco Flow."

"Sounds new agey," he scoffs, and Terry shares his chuckle.

The van passes a large green highway sign welcoming them into Tennessee. He remembered them entering West Virginia and had apparently slept away Kentucky entirely. The roads had been in decent shape for the most part as they'd passed various DOT work sites marred by cement traffic barriers, endless fields of orange cones, and diamond-shaped caution signs purporting work, so much work, still ahead. And as Eliot peered at each worker donned from head-to-toe in rain gear as they mindlessly traipsed through the sheets of hazy fog, he'd lost himself to the mire of sleep himself.

Until now. Until Tennessee.

And as soon as they are welcomed into its smoky pale pea soup landscape, a cavalcade of warning signs erupt along the roadside in quick succession.

"'Beware,' Eliot reads. "Leaving DOT Safe Construction Zone.'"

"'Beware: Animal Crossing,' Terry dictates.

"'Beware: Flooded Sections Ahead.'" Eliot's eyebrows raise. "At least you get to try out your van's propeller now."

"'Warning: Bog Conditions Ahead,'" Terry adds. "Uh oh."

"What do you mean, 'uh oh?'"

"'My lady can handle flooding, no problem. 'Bog conditions' present an entirely new situation altogether. You've got algae blooms, reeds, cat tails... things that can get stuck in a propeller very easily."

Eliot has only been in a boat a handful of times as a kid: fishing with friends, that one time in Italy as a child... but the idea of being stuck out on the water without a means of escape fills him with unease. "Does this thing have oars?"

Terry doesn't answer and squints through the fog at the next sign to emerge. "Looks like there's a Park and Ride up ahead. And boat rentals of some kind. I missed what it said. That print is way too small..."

"The place we're going to isn't too much further from here. Maybe we can make it by car and we won't even have to worry about renting anything."

"You might be willing to take that chance but I'm not." Terry slows the car and puts on his blinker as the Park and Ride lot approaches on their right. "We get stuck out there and your trip is done. My livelihood is done. You feel me?"

"Don't be so dramatic," says Eliot under his breath, even though the prospect worries him, too.

Terry parks the van in the paved lot in between an ancient-looking station wagon and a rusted-out Chevy truck. When he kills the engine, the air between them is consumed by the sound of water lapping and the creak of wood from the nearby docks. Large wooden racks full of dingy kayaks in once brilliant colors block Eliot's full view of the weathered sign over the dock. Jimbo's...something.

"What is this one anyway?" Terry asks. "Is it really that important?"

Eliot isn't sure anything is so important as needing to climb in a rickety kayak to cross a bog. The water looks silver and sits still like mud. He vaguely remembers a film that came out a few years ago with a scene in a sorrowful swamp where a character's horse died. Children and parents alike had been scarred by it. He'd gone to see it with Harvey but couldn't remember its name.

And all at once, his fear drops away along with his anxiety about remembering Harvey, about remembering how nice it used to feel to sleep next to him, about how he missed his smile. The gray of the swamp submerged his nostalgia. Surely it wouldn't be all that bad. This guy wouldn't be offering kayaks for rent if it was a dangerous trip, would he? That last thought melts away. No. He isn't afraid. Should he be?

"Eliot?"

He glances at Terry. "It's really important...I think."

"You think?"

He forces a thought through the fog in his head. "It's really important. This chef is like no one else."

Terry sighs. "Okay. Let's go see a man about a boat then."

They climb out of the van, lock the doors, and traipse across the lot toward the landing. A briny stench envelopes them as their shoes step onto the dock and the boards squeal beneath them. An old man in a long-sleeved, light blue shirt slumps on a stool next to a kiosk that faces into the void of the swamp, perhaps the eponymous Jimbo himself. The tiny radio next to him is playing a speech of some kind but he can't quite hear what it is, though for a moment the words *hymn* and *cross* leap out.

Jimbo watches their approach like a seagull watching for a discarded chip at the beach. Before they are even within ten feet of him, he's already on his feet shimmying toward his nearest boat track to unlock the metal cable there. "Day rental?" he asks, the congestion in his voice heavy.

Eliot wonders if it's a cold or a lifetime of working in this kind of business, close to the water, perpetually drenched. "How long would it take us to get to Flounder?"

The man cocks his head. "An hour. If you wait, there's a trawler coming back here in ten minutes. It'll tow you out there, so you don't have to paddle."

"That's perfect," Terry whispers.

Eliot realizes that Terry might not be much of a paddler and the idea of them losing themselves amongst the fog in search of a good bite to eat was more than he'd asked for when he agreed to help Eliot get back into his apartment. A great many things had probably been above what Terry was willing to do. Yet, he was still here, still helping Eliot. He cleared his throat as he tried to turn his attention back to the matter at hand.

"You got people frequently heading out in that direction?" he asked.

"Hell yeah. Dale Hollow Reservoir always gets a ton of people in the summer. The restaurant out there gets people flying and cruising in from miles around. Some foodie paradise, I guess. Can't afford that shit myself."

Eliot inspects the man's beaten-down and stained Topsiders, his calloused hands and his wild mustache. He isn't sure this guy can even afford a trip to the barber. Or maybe eating in an expensive restaurant just isn't worth it to him. "So, the restaurant is thriving then?"

"Last I knew. Had a couple people come back from a trip yesterday saying it was unexpectedly closed though. They paid a shit ton to get out there. Talked about suing. Silly stuff if you ask me. I'm sure Diablo just didn't want to serve such uppity pricks."

Eliot recognizes the name: the chef he was hoping to visit.

The man hefts a kayak from the middle rack with apparent ease as though he's lifting an empty cardboard box. "I'll just get these in the water for you. If you could just sign the forms there."

Terry does so. While Eliot is fairly certain the FBI isn't going to be searching every boat launch in every state for them, he doesn't want to take the chance by putting his name on anything causing them to be found during their trip. He watches the man lug their kayaks down to the water's edge and drop them into the water, ripples edging out amongst the lily pads and reeds. "Is it always this thick out here? How does anyone ever find their way in this fog?"

The man chuckles. "How does anyone find their way anywhere, man?" He slides two paddles from the barrel at the end of the dock and tucks them into each kayak alongside the seats. "Almost forgot." He returns to his kiosk and collects Terry's signed forms before dropping a couple crusty-looking compasses onto the counter. "Just in case."

They don lifejackets. The one Eliot puts on stinks of sulfur and low tide, but he imagines Terry's is just as bad. As he clips the front closed, an image of a box filled with water snaps forward in his head and he inhales reflexively at it.

Back. Shove it back. It's not real.

In a few more minutes, the fishing trawler appears out of the smog like a puttering ghost, its paint-chipped exterior reminding Eliot of a lost houseboat from the bayou, the kind of ancient thing that someone spent their lifesavings on and watched wither away along with themselves as the years went by. The men running it are like skeletons themselves: their oversized waders gaping like mouths around their skinny arms and legs. They fling a ratty rope toward the docks, and the man grabs it, helping pull them in.

They talk quietly for a few minutes, and the renter jabs a thumb over his shoulder toward Eliot and Terry. The two fishermen share a glance and Eliot senses something that doesn't stick. There's already something inside of him fluttering to be free and he's not sure he should let it out.

Terry, however, leans over toward him and says, "Did you see that look? I'm not sure we should be doing this, man. That boat looks like it's straight out of a horror movie or something'."

"There's no other way out to Flounder other than this," Eliot says. "Besides, we'll be in our own kayaks. Autonomous. Safe."

Terry glances back over Eliot's shoulder toward the van. "Maybe I should wait here for you?"

The man and the fisherman wave to them and Eliot steps over to climb down into his kayak. The man holds it steady as he drops his foot down in, the boat bobbing back and forth before he finds his equilibrium and can sit. Then, the man helps Terry into his.

Down at water level, Eliot realizes just how close he is to it and another needle pricks at his psyche before the Ash drowns it out.

Keep it down. You're safe.

After he finishes tying off the dingy ropes to the fronts of their kayaks, the man spins a finger in a circle around his head and the trawler's motor putters to a start. Slowly, they edge away from the dock and Eliot feels the gentle tug as his boat is yanked after them.

"Use the paddles to steer," the man yells after them. "Make sure you don't hit any logs or rocks or anything."

"Great," Terry mutters from across the water. His boat is tied to a stern cleat on the opposite corner from his. They're rusted and seem to jiggle and click as the boat pulls them along.

The dock fades into white mist behind them and the man's silhouette with it.

Eliot wonders what used to be here before the rain came. He wonders how much more highway is below them, lost amidst the endless black-looking water for what seems to be miles and miles around them. As soon as they fall away from land, the boat ahead of them chugging along, the tops of trees appear from the water around them, branches leafless like fingers reaching out from sculptures.

A subconscious chill blasts down through him and his cheeks feel hot. He closes his eyes.

"Not too much longer now."

He opens them to Alexis sitting on the prow of his kayak, her legs crossed and her dress flitting in the light breeze. A thought sinks into him like a hook, slowly—how is she staying put so well? Won't she fall in?—before he remembers that it's not really Alexis. It's Death. And Death might as well be a figment of his imagination at this point.

"Are you afraid?" she adds.

"I'm not," he says. "Oddly."

"That's the Ash talking for you." Ever so slightly, Death presses her hand to one side of his kayak. It teeters in the water.

His breath falters. "Don't do that. Why would you do that?"

"Because I'm trying to wake you up. The more you try to bottle it up, the more space it claims inside you."

"So, you want me to have a full-blown panic attack right now? Is that it?"

Death rolls her eyes. "I didn't say that."

Eliot glances through the fog towards where Terry's boat glides through the water, wondering if he can see or hear his conversation. What would he say to seeing a woman sitting on his kayak like an incubus on a sleeping person?

"Don't worry; he can't hear us."

"Why shouldn't he? After all, you manipulated him into this. He should know that God or his grandmother or whoever he thought you were didn't ask this of him. Shouldn't he?" Because as he's saying the words, he suddenly realizes that he hasn't asked Terry much about himself at all. He never bothered to ask him about his grandmother, about his fear of canals, about why hearing a disembodied celestial voice would push him to go to the ends of the earth with a perfect stranger and not assume that he was hallucinating, suffering a medical event or something else. He should be ashamed. But he feels nothing.

"Terry needs this just as much as you do," she says, a soft smile shaping her lips. "It's not like his life was boring or anything? But it was getting…stale? Stale is just as dangerous as repetitive…as dangerous as boring. He needed to be shaken up. You're helping him. Just like you're going to help humanity defeat the Ash."

Defeat. The word sounds like it belongs in a fantasy book, like one of those books he used to read at the local library while crouching in a corner for hours while his mother volunteered. It didn't belong here.

The boat ahead of them revs a little and he hears chatter from the bow. Can't tell what they are saying. The sound of a nearby "bloop" drops into his ears. The sound of something in the water. A fish splashing. Or something bigger maybe?

"It's so bold of them to let people come out here on their own," Death says.

"Why is that?"

"You remember the Everglades?" she poises and uncrosses her legs to plant her feet in front of her, knees hugged up to her chest.

He nods. "Used to be a national park before they took over the entire southeast coast…" They didn't need any protection anymore as it turned out, even though activists still lobbied for increased defense of its many species of flora and fauna.

Something large catches his attention and from out of the mist, a large sign appears, the neon no longer working as its giant metal arrow protrudes from the water. The letters D and I are visible and the top of what he assumes is an N. A tip from a roof juts out just behind it.

Melancholy washes over him like a storm and he inhales to try and keep its effects at bay. All he can think of are submerged vinyl seat cushions, stacks of plates and diner mugs coated in growing algae, a left behind newspaper floating in midair over the counter…a solitary apron hanging from a hook by the back door to the kitchen. Everything left behind. Everything drowned.

"Whoops," Death says under her breath and her voice pulls him back from the brink. She's glancing out at the water to his right, towards where Terry is.

Or was.

Eliot can't see his form any longer through the mist.

"Where's Terry?" he asks.

"I think…" Death cocks her head. "Nope. I know what happened. I put a bubble around us. Not only could Terry not hear us, we can't hear him. Sometimes, that bubble extends to include the things I'm connected to…like the trawler."

Eliot whips his head over his shoulder. That sound. That thing dropping in the water…

He notices the stern cleat on the opposite side of the boat is now gone.

"Fuck! Hey! Hey, guys!" Eliot tries to yell.

But his resolve is buckling. He has made it so far into the bog letting the Ash consume his fear all so that a submerged diner plucks his courage from him in one fell swoop. His voice barely comes out as he feels the mist closing in around him, the water darkening and deepening somehow at the same time.

"You've got this, Eliot."

He looks up at Death. "Don't tell me I've got this. I definitely *don't* have this." His vision narrows on her hand and the knife suddenly in it. She has it raised over the kayak tow line. "Don't you fucking dare."

She wags the blade at him. "You're just going to leave Terry in the middle of the swamp? Some friend you are."

Breaths ripple in and out of him in a frenzy as he looks between the fog behind him and the boat before him. "Damn it. God damn it." He gestures to her. "Fine. Cut it."

Death holds the knife up and slices it down against the tow rope. The blade bounces off it and she frowns. "Shit." She saws at it.

"Hurry up before I change my mind." Eliot grits his teeth.

"Seemed like it was going to go right through," Death mutters. She shears the last bit of rope, and the remaining tow line slips beneath the water.

Eliot's boat slows to a stop, and he watches the trawler putter off into the mist.

10
CRUEL SUMMER

Water. It's everywhere. And all that's between Eliot and it is a thin plastic layer of a battered kayak. All that's keeping him afloat is this stinky puffed life vest that probably saved countless individuals before him. What if it ended its streak here?

Don't panic. He tells himself. *Don't...panic.*

"Your paddle is right there." Death points to it, tucked into the kayak by his feet. "I can see Terry. He's only a short way back."

Eliot grips the hard plastic shaft and finds the foam where his hands are supposed to rest. He flips the paddle so it's right-side up and the blades scoop away from him. He dips one side in the water and pulls hard, turning the boat around steadily.

"Just watch out for the wildlife," Death whispers, and he swears she's hovering somewhere over his shoulder as she says it. He looks and sees nothing. She's gone.

Eliot glances at the water around him, hyper focusing at the sound of the fading engine of the trawler, at the sounds of peepers and his own paddle clunking against the plastic of the boat.

Trust me. I've got you. You're safe.

Eliot slips his paddle back into the murky water, then the other side. The words infuse him momentarily. They hurt and the memory behind the voice in his head hurts more but Eliot binds his attention to their truth and to the momentary relief he felt when he first heard Harvey say them.

Their first date nearly a year after they'd met, after they'd awkwardly seen each other at various parties Alexis had held or concerts where she had unknowingly invited the two of them to join her and no one else. At the time, he had known she was trying to set them up but chose to go with the flow, especially because he liked how Harvey spoke, liked the smell of his cologne, even the smell of the tobacco he smoked.

But the Aquarium after hours, which was meant to be a sweet gesture on Harvey's part had only brought on a fright the longer they walked the halls and admired the fish. Pretty soon, Eliot was hugging himself in front of the window to the jellyfish tank trying not to cry as images of the dark box filled with water slammed into his psyche over and over again.

Harvey's cool hand had found his. They'd sat on the bench in the near darkness with only the blue aqueous light caressing their faces and Harvey had asked him innocently what was wrong. And Eliot had told him all of it. The first person he'd ever told in his life.

The kayak glides faster now and soon enough, the submerged diner has vanished once more into the mist behind him.

Harvey had been his therapy, his mere presence pushing that horrible trauma into a smaller, harder to open box in the back of his brain. And now that he was gone, it was peeking out with wide eyes from a crack in the lid, watching him.

In the quiet before him, he thinks he hears panicked muttering and the splish splash of something in the water.

"Terry?" Eliot calls into the fog.

"Eliot!" Terry's voice emanates over the water somewhere off to his far left. "Thank God! I've been yelling and no one's said anything back. I thought I was going to get lost out here..."

"Stay where you are and keep talking. I'm coming to you." Eliot rows harder, his arms burning as he forces his paddles in and out of the water rhythmically. Lily pads and muck cling to the blades with each slice. After another minute of rowing and Terry monologuing about how he's never been a water-sports person, Eliot glimpses the red smear of Terry's kayak as it emerges out of the mist. He pulls up alongside it and grabs hold of the cockpit edge.

Terry reaches out and grabs his. Their kayaks bump together. Sweat drips from Terry's forehead and the moisture from the fog has soaked through most of his shirt.

"Thought I was going to fucking die out here, man," says Terry, and Eliot thinks he detects a fleck of embarrassment in the words.

"You could have turned around. Paddled back to the docks."

"I can't! The tow rope is caught on something down below. I can't get it free. That and...I lost my paddle."

Eliot glances at the rope from Terry's kayak pulled taut beneath the surface of the black water. Using his hands to pull his kayak up to the front of Terry's, he grips the line and heaves. Sure enough, it holds firm to something below.

"Must be the stern cleat. It pulled right off the boat," Terry adds.

"Hang on, I'll untie it." Eliot fiddles with the knot, his own fingers slipping and nails digging against the loops until it pulls free and the rope sinks out of sight.

"What are we going to do now?" Terry asks.

"I'm sure they'll notice we've come loose, and they'll be back to find us." This plan sounds logical, but Eliot wonders how committed these fishermen are to towing tourists back and forth between the dock and Willow Grove every day, not to mention the vastness of the wetlands around them. What if they'd drifted off course enough that the fishing trawler missed them coming back through?

As if on cue, Terry asks, "And if they don't?"

Eliot takes a deep breath. "Come on." He flips his paddles around and backs his kayak up so that the bow is close to Terry's cockpit. "Untie the rope from my bungee."

Terry scrambles to do so. "My fingers are too big for these tiny knots. I can't get it."

There are no deck lines on these kayaks in either the fronts or the backs, stripped down to the basics. Hell, maybe they'd had them at one time, but after years of use, these things looked banged up and worse for wear. A part of Eliot's courage withers. "Then, I'll have to tie onto the back of your kayak, and you'll have to tow me."

"How the hell are you going to reach that?"

The tow rope is still tied to the bow of Eliot's kayak though Death hacked off a considerable chunk of it. From the cockpit to the bungee, he estimates it's another three and a half feet to reach it and probably another foot more to secure it onto Terry's kayak. He swallows as he stares at the water.

"This is stupid," Terry growls. "I should have never come out here. Should have just let you do this on your own and stayed in the van."

Eliot winces as he navigates his boat toward the back of Terry's. As he passes the cockpit, he passes Terry his paddle. Then, guiding his hands along the rotomolded plastic, he reaches the stern and stretches himself across the front of his boat toward the tow loop. The kayak bobs perilously beneath him as he inches along, forcing himself to take breaths, because otherwise, he wouldn't.

Trust me. He can almost feel Harvey's hand on his own. *"You've got this. You're absolutely f—*

"What the *fuck* was that? What the fuck was *that?*" Terry blurts.

Eliot hugs the deck of his kayak, his chin pressed against the slick plastic, as his eyes wildly search through dense fog around them. Nothing. He sees nothing. "What?"

"I swear to God, I just saw something out there. But I'm not sure. I think this mist is fucking with me, man."

Eliot's fingers curl, the tips of them digging at the boat as he cautiously pulls himself out of the cockpit. The life vest bows up around his shoulders. Part of him wishes he didn't have it on and the larger part of him is glad he does. While it's slick against the plastic beneath him, he knows it would be worse if he fell in without it. Reaching the tow line, he dips his hand over the lip of the kayak and finds the slimy shorn end of it in the water. Then, he stretches his hand out toward the tow loop on Terry's stern and curls the rope through it.

Every second feels like a millennium. He ties a clove hitch knot to secure it, and steadily, he finds Harvey's voice replaced by that of his father's.

By the time he finishes it and scrambles back into his own cockpit, he's shuddering. "Okay," he says, forcing the words to leave his body. "Let's go."

Terry starts to paddle.

. . .

Eliot isn't sure how much time has gone by. He thinks maybe twenty minutes, but it could be forty. It could be close to an hour. Or it could be five minutes.

Everything feels the same out here on the water; looks the same. The black tangles of shapes that once were trees, their skeletal branches looming over their boats like outstretched fingers, the steeples of churches like medieval-looking spires jutting out of the swamp with shingles peeled and once brilliant stained-glass dulled by mud and age. At one point, they pass something that might have once been a warehouse, the various smokestacks like slaloms for them to maneuver around before they, too, are left behind.

More than anything, Eliot wants not to feel right then. He wants the Ash to come back and take away all of it, leave him an apathetic husk if only for the rest of their duration in the boats. But it won't. Instead, shame crowds in on him and a lingering sense of guilt. A picture of his father that he can't part with from the last time he'd seen him: his skin pulled taut over lean arms and strangely drooping around his eyes and ears. The once intimidating portrait of his father reduced to the prison of old age, of regretful nostalgia and somehow, self-justification.

Why did that have to be the last memory of the mighty Harlow Lamb: staring at him with a recalcitrant glare, as if he never amounted to anything? As if he never made him proud? As if he hadn't sacrificed anything for the Lamb family image...

"You see that? Eliot? Eliot, man, pay attention!"

Terry's voice is cannon-fire in his mind.

He reluctantly opens his eyes and sees Terry trying to look back over his shoulder at him. "What?"

The plumber has stopped paddling. "There's something out here with us."

What had Death whispered in his ear again?

"Just watch out for the wildlife."

His gaze drops to the water. What would they need to watch out for out here?

"Keep going," he says.

"I'm not even sure *where* I'm going," Terry answers, dipping a blade in the water.

"We have to hit land at some point. We're not on the ocean: it's a reservoir."

"Says the guy who doesn't have to paddle." The words are filled with frustration.

His father's eyes boring holes into his own. The image nearly rips the air from Eliot's lungs. He exhales through his nose and focuses on Terry. "Just for the record, I'm glad you came."

Terry pauses before he resumes paddling. "Well…I couldn't let you come out here all by yourself."

"When you were telling me about hearing your grandmother's voice yesterday… What did you hear her say exactly?"

"Why do you want to know?"

"Because I've dragged you all the way out to the middle of a swamp and I figure whatever she said must have been pretty convincing."

Terry sighs. "My grandmama was a lady of few words. Took me and my sister in when our mom split. Our father was trying to make ends meet with three jobs and didn't have time to look out for us. So, Grandmama Jean made her home our home."

Eliot leans back in his seat. "She sounds like a remarkable woman."

"She'd take that," Terry chuckles. "She had to put up with us for twenty years, helped put me through trade school, helped put Rosanna through college. The year she graduated, Grandmama Jean wanted to take her out for a dinner celebration. I was in town, so we all walked over to this place a few blocks from her house, a place we always used to go growing up. They had the best sloppy joes, man. And their coleslaw? Phenomenal."

Eliot could hear the smile on Terry's face even if he couldn't see it.

"But…we didn't get there. Just before the turn passed her street, the road gave out. A canal opened right underneath her and Grandmama Jean just…fell. Didn't even have time to scream. And we just sat there for hours. The fire department didn't send a truck. No ambulance got dispatched. A cop stopped by out of curiosity but as soon as he heard what happened, he turned tail and left."

"Fuck," Eliot says. "I'm sorry, Terry."

Terry's strokes through the water remain strong. He doesn't look back. "I ain't talked to my sister in a long time. She blames me, I think. Thinks I should have done more. That picture in my car of her and my nephew is almost ten years old now."

Water ripples somewhere on Eliot's distant right. Could be just a turtle or a fish. "What did you hear her say, Terry?"

He clears his throat and sniffs. Damn it. He's crying.

"She said 'That man makes a mean coleslaw, Terrance.'"

Eliot frowns. "That's…it?"

Terry shifts to look behind him. "I mean, she wasn't lying, was she?"

He scoffs. "No. I make a great coleslaw."

"Then it's all worth it."

A sudden explosion of water erupts next to Terry's kayak. Eliot shuts his eyes instinctually and when he opens them, Terry is gone. The kayak is overturned, bobbing in the swells of muddy water still rippling away from it.

"Terry!" he yells.

Moments later, Terry's head surfaces, his hair limp and plastered to his skull. "Shit!" he shrieks. "It's a gator, man!"

Scanning the water, Eliot reaches out. "Grab my hand!"

Within moments, Terry latches onto him. "Don't let go! I don't want to be gator food!"

"I can't pull you up; I don't have enough room," Eliot cautions. "We need to flip your kayak. What happened to the paddle?"

He scans the surface and sees the tip of the blade just as it vanishes underwater.

"Shit!"

"Get me the fuck out of here," Terry begs, clinging to the cockpit of Eliot's kayak, his arm draping over up to the elbow.

"We need to get to your kayak. Don't kick a bunch. You'll just attract its attention."

But Terry is pulling on the kayak hard and in a panic, and Eliot feels the entire world pivot moments before he's suddenly immersed in brackish warm water. The shadow of the kayak folds down on top of him and all Eliot can do is claw at the water as he fights to surface. He comes up under his kayak in the small bubble of air provided by his cockpit. His brain is assaulted by glimpses of the box full of water, of the feeling of staring into the dark closet, of the faceless woman, of his own horror…

Something brushes against his leg below and it yanks him back into the here and now. He dips back down beneath the surface and comes up on the other side of his overturned kayak. The air is bitterly cold around him.

Heaving, he whips his head around. "Terry? Terry!"

How had he gotten so far away? Eliot knew. Terry was in full panic mode, swimming as fast and as hard as he could toward a partially exposed tree about ten yards away from their overturned boats. Eliot held his breath, trying to stay calm as he waited for his friend's head to get pulled under water with each second that passed.

Terry reaches the tree and hefts himself up into its branches, coughing and spasming with each tiresome movement.

The box.

The water.

The box.

The water.

Eliot forces shallow breaths in his mouth and out his nose, trying to remember Harvey's guidance. Something tickles against his leg. A fish? Branches from a tree? A monster? He can't look down. He *won't* look down.

His heartbeat ramps up in his chest and fills his head as he thinks about his father.

Fuck.

Fuck.

Fuck.

Had he failed? Had his whole life been a failure? Was this it?

The guttering of his heart is so loud, it vibrates his entire body and when something closes on his shoulder, he nearly screams.

Fingers. A human hand. It jerks back in response to him, and Eliot practically bangs his head into the kayak when he realizes there's a large fan boat gliding just a foot away from him. The man holding his shoulder has the other hand outstretched. "Grab on!" he orders, and Eliot does so, his fingers, hand, and forearm locked in an embrace that thrusts him out of the water and onto the flat deck of the fan boat moments before the water beneath him explodes with the thrashing of reptilian violence.

Spilled onto the deck, Eliot turns around in time to see his savior thrust a pole down at the behemoth gator a few times with expert precision. The creature hisses and slips back beneath the water into the darkness.

Still trying to catch his breath, Eliot takes in the man before him: a broad-shouldered stout Native American, his long hair grayed and tied up out of his face. His cheeks seem hollower than Eliot remembers from the article he saw in Cuisine a year and a half ago, and his eyes have that same vacancy for only a moment before something fills them. All the photos in the magazine had made Diablo Onofre seem statuesque and imposing but, Eliot realizes, he's probably only about the same height as him—in the range of five foot seven or eight.

Diablo steps over to him. "I know you. What the hell are you doing all the way out here?"

"I was looking for you, actually," Eliot says. "Had a bit of boat trouble."

Diablo's eyebrows perk. "I can see that." He nods to a skinny Black man operating the fan to try and help overturn the boats. At this point, he spots Terry waving wildly from his tree of refuge. "Is he with you?"

"Yup."

"You're lucky I'm out here fishing. You two would have missed the landing for Willow Grove by at least a half a mile if you'd kept going."

Luck. Eliot wants to believe it's as simple as luck. But, with Death presiding over his every move, he knows somehow, she's had a hand in making sure they get where they are going.

The deckhand ties the kayaks onto the side rail of the boat and then maneuvers the fan boat over toward the tree to pick up Terry who practically dances on board the vessel, shivering with all the vigor of a seal who's avoided a killer whale.

"Let's get you back to Flounder. Wasn't having much luck out here anyway," Diablo adds more to himself than to them. The fan bursts to life, filling the swamp with a high-powered drone as they sweep toward land.

AUGMENTATION
FOURTH OBSERVATION

There is no such thing as the perfect organism. The perfect existence. Separation. It's all been altered: gone are the confusing array of emotions to distract them from their basic biology. They've been augmented for a higher calling, one that beckons them across the land to its messianic purpose. The wandering body does not evaluate the terrain they shuffle through. They don't complain about its murky depths or its arid dunes. There is only the call now, clicking away in the caverns of their mind in bitter summons.

11
APACHE

The Cuisine article comes back to Eliot in flashes as they ride the air boat through the murky swamp. He remembers reading it late at night in the restaurant, when everyone had gone home and he was trying out a twist on a traditional Italian Christmas cookie for his seasonal menu. He was waiting for his third batch to come out of the oven. He'd already prepared the crushed nuts for the topping, and the warm icing he'd just stirred clung to the spoon like frosted milk and smelled of warm sage and orange zest. He'd sat at the counter with a Negroni and peeled through the week-old magazine, and there—he'd found Diablo Onofre or as the columnist had referred to him, the only Apache chef this side of the Mississippi.

The article wasn't written particularly well, and Eliot had a feeling that Diablo hated that title as much as Eliot did, for it spoke in definitives and, once he'd read the article, he thought Diablo seemed like the kind of person who didn't care to be lauded for his ethnicity and what geography he lived in. The journalist hadn't bothered to interrogate Diablo about his upbringing, but instead had focused on a single aspect of his culinary practice that separated him from other Apache cooks: he cooked with fish.

As part of an understanding within the Apache and several other southwestern desert tribes, it was a taboo to eat anything from the water, even waterfowl. Not only did Diablo specialize his menu in fish-centric dishes, he caught them himself in the waters surrounding Flounder. It had caused an outcry. It had caused a separation from his home, as those he had lived with and loved now refused to recognize him as a member of their nation.

As Eliot had read, he glimpsed the glossy photos of prepared dishes: a pan-fried small-mouth bass over a bed of fennel with diced potatoes and squash, a grilled walleye with agave Tennessee barbecue sauce with a creamy wild onion potato salad nestled up beside it, and something that had stayed with him, something he had been wanting to put in his mouth for years: Diablo's take on the classic Nashville hot chicken—hot fish—breaded and fried and colored fiery red from the mouth-tingling cayenne pepper and paprika sauce. The fish sat atop a rustic hunk of bread, yellowish in color, and off to the side sat a heap of fried pickles. More pictures showed Diablo standing in front of the wooden butcher block in his kitchen at Flounder, staring not at the photographer but off at a place perhaps just over his or her left shoulder. There was something in his expression that had impacted Eliot then; a certain come-at-me he'd seen in seasoned chefs and newbie cooks alike.

This one harbored the indifference of opinion that the novice lacked and more.

When Eliot looks at Diablo now, all he sees is exasperation. Maybe the Diablo of years ago was no longer the Diablo of today. Had the Ash and the flooding and the war changed everything that Eliot had expected to find here?

The boat cuts power and they drift in toward the dock that pokes out of the clearing fog before them. Diablo and his co-pilot, Tyrone, paddle to make sure they stay on course. Once they reach the dock, they throw a loop over one of the posts there to anchor and everyone climbs off the boat. Diablo lifts two large coolers from the swamp boat into Tyrone's waiting hands and the man practically hops up a steep hill to a waiting Jeep as deftly as a mountain goat. Once the rest of them scale the climb and are safely buckled inside the car, they rumble down a dirt road through weeds and soupy fog.

"Why were you looking for me anyway?" Diablo decides to ask Eliot at this point, which pulls him out of his reverie like a straw being yanked out of a thick milkshake. "Thought you'd have your hands full with your restaurant up north?"

As vast as the restaurant sphere was, it somehow manages to get smaller once chefs are amongst one another. In the back of dark bars and huddling over tables in late night eateries, chefs comb through the various encounters they have with such and such chef here or there. These are the mere kindling for wildfire tales that spread like embers caught on the wind. Soon enough, everyone knows everyone else's business; everyone knows how someone acts in their kitchens to their staff or behind closed doors at home or after they've had a few beers or a snort of some coke.

Eliot, for all his faults, skirted the drugs and the rock and roll lifestyle that some chefs clambered into in favor of darkness. He didn't want them to know his life outside of the kitchen. His circle was tight: if he visited anyone else's restaurant, he kept his lips tight, his nerves taut like steel cables. Nothing slipped. His personal life might as well have been someone else's, and it never entered the limelight.

Until, one day, it did.

"I promise when we get you to Flounder, I'll get you into some new clothes. Then, we can talk," Diablo adds. Eliot isn't sure if the chef assumes he's too cold to talk, but he's grateful for the breath to get his thoughts in order.

Plastic covered greenhouses appear out of the gray like cows in the fields: first only a few, then dozens, sporadically placed here and there and surrounded by wheat, by wild onions, by ever-reaching sprouts of mint mingling with dark leaves from rhubarb and spinach. Workers gather crops into wheelbarrows and wooden crates in the back of tractors. Eliot watches one of the steel behemoths steadily roll away from the bountiful fields, tires rumbling over mud and engine flaring.

Shacks appear next. A variety of places that Eliot would have expected to see on the coast of some small tropical island or on a beach somewhere. Each one is only large enough for one or two rooms inside and a small front porch, decorated by little flags or flowerpots, one with a dingy blue bicycle in front, another with a moped, and another with what looks like an unmanned child's lemonade stand.

And then, Flounder emerges from out of the fog: a two-story log building connected to an old barn. Hanging dried herbs decorate the wrap around front porch, while a set of lacquered steps lead up to a heavy glass door. A sign bearing the restaurant's name in all caps is lit by a dusky lantern at the end of the drive. It reminds Eliot of something from a children's storybook—the world hugged by mist and the building rising out of the untamed land as if from the magic of a witch.

The Jeep parks in the circular drive and they all climb out. Diablo is quick to pass off his newfound guests to a small woman with what seem like the muscles of a professional boxer. "Anna will get you cleaned up. Meet me at the barn when you're ready!" he calls at them over his shoulder as he disappears carrying the other cooler behind Tyrone.

Anna leads them around the restaurant to a wooden boardwalk that ambles over marsh flats toward a cottage-style home on the edge of the trees. She tells them to kick off their shoes at the entrance and directs them toward the one bathroom down the hall while she searches for some clean clothes. Eliot lets Terry take his turn first. Terry hasn't said much since they were picked up by Diablo's boat and a lingering fear presses in on Eliot that, once they're back on the other side of the marsh, they might go their separate ways.

As he listens to the shower turn on behind the closed door, he tries to distract himself by glancing around the hall he's standing in. Lit by only a small table side lamp, he stares at framed photographs lining the walls: smiling pictures of Diablo and Anna on their wedding night (he hadn't realized they were married but it makes sense), pictures of children running down the boardwalk, fishing with their father, and photos of a younger Diablo hugging an older man that shared his discerning eyes and nose. The more he looks, the more he thinks about the lack of such photos in his old apartment back in Getty.

The photo albums hiding in that cabinet he'd taken from his mother's and he hadn't looked at them since she'd died. No, they were safer locked away just like the rest of his memories.

Anna shuffles down the hall with two stacks of clothes and chuckles. The outfit she'd found for Eliot was from their oldest son's room as they were closer in stature. He thanks her and she excuses herself to go check on the kids.

The shower head turns off and Eliot knocks after a moment, offering up some of the clothing that Anna brought. Terry accepts it through a crack in the door with little but a small "thanks."

After a few more minutes, the door opens again and Terry sidles out, now wearing a navy-blue Nike T-shirt with a bright orange swoosh across the front and heavy-duty work pants.

They say nothing to one another as Eliot takes his turn.

In the privacy of the small yellow bathroom, he undresses and steps beneath the torrent of hot water, massaging his face with his hands. They'd nearly died because of this insane trip. The next time Death decides to show her smug face, he will make sure she knows this is the last stop on th—

"Don't tell me you're getting cold feet?" Alexis's voice asks from outside the shower.

He pulls his hands away from his face to see her body silhouetted against the curtain.

He manages to keep his tone level. "You nearly got us killed back there. I'm not going to do this to Terry again. He doesn't deserve it, no matter how good my coleslaw is."

Death scoffs. "Aw, come on. Don't be like that. You know I wouldn't let you get hurt out there, right?"

"Doesn't keeping us alive go against your very nature? You're not here to just give us a thrill."

"Isn't that what Death is?" she poises the question. "The very idea of me used to *be* a thrill. I used to invigorate people, used to motivate them to get their shit done. Now, it feels like I've lost my edge. It's like people are just waiting for me to show up like I'm late to the party or something."

He peels back the curtain, mouth agape. "Don't tell me this little stunt is all about reinflating your ego?"

Her face sours. "The point of it is to fix what's wrong and what's wrong is you: you and the rest of humanity. You've lost your nerves."

"Humans can't change what the Ash does to us!" Eliot can't help but bark. "This is going to kill me! This fucking thing has already taken so much from me and I don't know how much longer I can hold on. But I won't to be responsible for anyone else's death just because I'm trying to feel something again. Just because you're a prima donna."

Her expression doesn't change as she pinches the curtain with two fingers and says, "You're wasting hot water, big shot." She pulls the shower curtain closed between them.

12
A COUNTRY BOY
CAN SURVIVE

Dressed in a pair of worn jeans that were just a smidge too big and rolling up the sleeves of the gray plaid shirt with a Vans patch over the right bicep, Eliot leaves the bathroom and joins Terry in the living room.

Anna appears from another room; her hands and lower arms covered in streaks of muted paint. Terry points out a dab of green that made it to her neck. Painting with the youngest daughter, she explains. They've just started making a jungle scene on her bedroom wall.

"Diablo is up at the barn. Are you good making your way back up there without me?" Anna asks. "Getting out of this jungle is a little tough right now."

Eliot nods and he and Terry leave.

Terry keeps pace with Eliot and, under his breath, says, "I'm sorry, man. I should have known. I mean… I should have guessed."

Eliot frowns. "What?"

"I heard you talking to yourself in the bathroom…"

Eliot slows. Death: that bitch. Talking to himself? She must have masked her voice or something. Clearly *something*. She could do whatever she wanted, it seemed.

"The Ash... All the clues were there."

"Listen, Terry, I don't know what you heard but—"

"Hey, Eliot, I made my own decisions, okay? Whether or not I heard my grandmama's voice telling me something, I made the choice to help you out, to get you where you need to go. It's not as fun as I expected it to be, you know what I'm saying, but I'm in it for the long haul, man."

The admission makes the back of Eliot's throat tingle, and he clears it. He gives Terry a pat on the back. "Thanks."

Following along the backside of Flounder, they walk through a rock garden, meandering across flat stones dribbled on by the ever-present rain, around bursts of fragrant sage and lemon balm. As they cross the lawn, Eliot realizes it's not a lawn at all, but just millions of tiny thyme plants and each footstep kicks up their pungent sweet aroma.

The barn doors have been heaved open and just inside, they find Diablo standing next to Tyrone at a conveyor belt, picking through bundles of asparagus. He nods to Eliot's shirt with a grin. "You feelin' 'Off the Wall,' yet, Chef Lamb?"

He chuckles. "This is about as gnarly as I'll ever look."

"Now that you're all gussied up, you want to take a tour?"

"Sure."

Perhaps sensing the privacy of the conversation ahead, Terry announces that he'll return to the house and help paint the rest of the jungle. "I never got to do this with my nephew. Plus, I need something calm to focus on after all that business in the swamp."

Diablo and Eliot walk further into the barn. What were once stalls for livestock have been converted into produce storage—crates of sweet potatoes, cucumbers, and butternut squash sit across from a stall filled with okra, cantaloupe, and eggplant. In a separate corner, someone plucks poblano peppers from a recent harvest while in another corner, another person shells butter beans.

"This is quite the operation," Eliot remarks.

"Everyone that works here lives on the island," Diablo explains. "They make their livings here helping with the produce. I figure if I can create a community that can give back as much as it rakes in, it's worth it. It's all worth it."

The statement tinges Eliot's thoughts. "Otherwise, it's not?"

Diablo shrugs. "Still trying to figure that out, I guess."

They continue out the other side of the barn and stare across the marsh at the retreating form Terry on the boardwalk. Diablo puts his hands on his hips and takes a deep breath. "I heard the news. Hard to believe you'd ever shut down Tempo. Place seemed like it was going strong."

"It was," Eliot confirms, brows furrowing. "I'm not though."

"You sick?"

"It's…" Eliot starts.

It only takes a moment for Diablo to look into his face, really look, before his eyes close and he's shaking his own head. "Fuck."

"I'm not like a sea captain. I can't go down with the ship," Eliot adds. "It was better to just put her out of her misery, you know?"

Diablo sighs. "I'd like to think that if that ever happened to me, someone would keep Flounder going, but…I guess I don't know any better, do I?"

The two men turn and step back through the barn and toward the building that houses Flounder. A pumpkin orange door brings them in through the back to the kitchen and its gleaming, white-tiled walls, the shimmering metal countertops, and already prepped stoves. Cooks bustle around ladling soups, tasting reductions, and scooping delicate fish from pans onto platters.

There's an energy and a musicality to the movement that makes Eliot feel right at home. God, he misses cooking. He misses being in the kitchen. This is the longest he's been away from one in years. And the kitchen at Flounder reminds him of a time when he first discovered the cadence in cooking for himself, guided by Clive's theories of dropping all the bullshit and just letting things flow. He felt that here: a bullshit-less kitchen not executing dishes so much as letting them pour out like water from a tap.

"You've got tourists coming in tonight?" he says.

"Yeah. I closed the restaurant yesterday because…" he trails off. "Anyway, I had to reschedule some dinners. We've got extra seatings tonight. They're finishing up some new appetizer options to offer as an extra bonus to our disgruntled diners tonight."

"I thought you'd be overseeing this more." Eliot glances at a young cook as she flips scallops in a cast iron, the rich smell of butter reaching out to him.

"I do. Normally, I do. But this part, I want them to have fun with, you know? I want to encourage play first and technicality second."

They continue toward the doors to the dining room.

"Most chefs I know would say you've got those two things in the wrong order," Eliot added.

Diablo laughs. "Guess I would have said that, too, before I had kids." He pushes through the double doors into the dining room.

They settle at the bar which glows with soft peach light behind its impressive array of liquor bottles; Eliot on a stool and Diablo standing behind it. He makes them sazeracs and they drink them while chatting about nothing and everything. When the sazeracs are gone they make more, only stiffer. It's during this second round that the taste leaves Eliot's mouth. He almost doesn't notice it at first. But when he knocks back the rest of his drink and it doesn't kick him like it should, he sets the glass down gently on the bar and frowns. Normally, two drinks in, he'd feel something. He wouldn't be wasted or even buzzed, but he'd *feel*…something. But sobriety encases him in that moment, and he realizes that he's completely forgotten what they were talking about. Had they been laughing?

"You okay?" Diablo asks.

"I can't taste the drink."

"Didn't make it strong enough for you?"

"That's not it. It's the Ash. It comes in waves. One moment, everything is fine and then the next… I know I'm missing something. I know I should be able to taste it, but my brain just gets zilch."

Diablo finishes his drink and solemnly joins Eliot on the stool next to him as they gaze out at the empty restaurant. "What's it like?"

Eliot swallows. "Like I'm lost. All the time. These memories that I have associated with certain foods—how they feel, how they smell, how they should taste—they don't kick in. My whole career has been about getting to know these ingredients. I don't feel connected anymore."

Diablo stares at the floor. "Sounds fucking horrible."

"It's only sometimes." Eliot cocks his head. "But it's happening more and more. I've probably got another few weeks left until everything goes. At least, I hope I have that left."

"So, you came down here because I was on your bucket list?" Diablo smirks.

"Yeah. Someone told me that I needed to 'invigorate' people like me, that it would make a difference, maybe slow down the Ash more. But when I look around here, it seems like you've already got things figured out."

Diablo sets his jaw and stands up. "The typical white guy move. Try to show others how it's done when everything is working just fine as it is?"

Eliot exhales. "I can't feel the humiliation from that statement like I should, but if you saw what it was like up north…"

"It's the same up north as it is down here, man." Diablo walks to the nearest window and glances out. "This island and Flounder…there's no one else out here doing what we do. The casual diner is so concerned with speed versus quality nowadays that it's not about the experience anymore, it's about basic sustenance. It's about getting from work to daycare to pick up the kids and then to the nearest fast food fuckcan to shove it all down before getting home for Night Court."

"But Flounder isn't…floundering?"

"I can't believe you went there…"

"Forgive me."

"No." Diablo sauntered back to the bar and poured himself a straight whiskey. "It's not. As weird as this place is to the typical Nashville vacationers, they seem to like it. It's not their usual steak and fries, but they don't seem to care."

Eliot nods but is caught by the distant look in Diablo's eye. "But?"

"But I don't think that food is really going to make much of a difference against the Ash and, as much as I hate to say it, the industry won't give a guy like me much of a chance to let it either."

Eliot frowned. Open mindedness in the restaurant trade was designed for the few proud veteran chefs who broke the molds: Alice Waters, Jonathan Waxman, Ken Frank, Wolfgang Puck, Jimmy Schmidt, Clive Goodthin. They were the ones who created the movement of chefs in the seventies—something more than just a faceless cook who made the same old dishes in the same old ways over and over. But that turning tide, while popular in some of the big cities, was still slow to happen in most parts of the country. And if one didn't travel around to witness it, it might as well not be happening. With the flooding as horrible as it was now, too, there were lots of people going nowhere.

Not to mention those making headlines were mostly straight and white.

The only reason Eliot had made it anywhere, in his mind, was because he'd clung to Clive's coattails and had hidden the things about himself that made him different. Wearing the mask had grown tiresome and, in the end, had done nothing but delayed the inevitable blowback he'd worried about for so long.

Diablo's head lolls back as he grins. "We're such alarmists. Fast food isn't the end of the world. And look at us, acting like it is."

"It's not fast food that's the end of the world. It's our lack of passion. Our lack of passion to make food, to enjoy it. To savor it." He nods to the whiskey. "Pour me another."

"Why? You can't taste it."

"When all my feeling comes back, I want to make sure I'm properly blitzed so I can keep up with you."

He pours and they drink.

...

The sky darkens toward nighttime. Diablo, several drinks in, uproots himself from the bar and turns to the kitchen to oversee food preparation while Eliot follows like a floating ghost behind him. Feeling has not returned. He suspects it won't for quite some time.

Along the wooden countertop, the various cooks have set out their individual dishes they've experimented with in Diablo's absence and now stand back to stare upon them with the same fervors of artists admiring their own creations.

In the line-up is a young man who resembles Diablo: a seventeen or eighteen-year-old with a curly mop of black hair, a hooked nose, and a smile that Eliot recognizes from photos in the Onofre home. "Keeping it in the family, eh?" Eliot tries to put on a smile and somehow manages it. He's gotten good at pretending over the last few weeks.

Diablo's face does not share the same enthusiasm as Eliot's or his son's. "I thought you were going to work on your applications?" he asks his younger doppelgänger.

The young man's smile wavers. "I saw that you'd brought in some panfish and I—"

"So, you didn't do them?"

"What's the point in doing them if I know I already want to be a—"

"I'm serious," says Diablo, and he looks it. Gone is the sparkling playtime joviality he'd displayed in the dining room, and the wistfulness along with it. He's an upset father now, taking tones that Eliot remembers all too well from his own youth. "I want you back at the house working on them. Go."

The young man's lip twitches as he tears off his apron and tosses it onto a nearby counter before sprinting off.

Diablo tastes the rest of the dishes and gives feedback as though he's a teacher grading poetry, and Eliot can't tear his thoughts away from what he's just witnessed.

Before he can bring it up with Diablo, the chef flings on his son's discarded apron and starts walking to the cooler. "You gonna cook or just watch?"

Eliot can't cook when he's like this. He can make his body go through the static motions of slicing and dicing, of frying and flipping. But to move like he does when he's really feeling things…he needs to be able to hear the rhythm of the sizzling and the chopping, touch the textures of the food on his fingers and taste everything. So, he shakes his head. "I'll watch for now."

"Tell me then, what does Chef Eliot Lamb want?"

"The hot fish."

He remains on the edge while Diablo Onofre skates around the kitchen, gathering ingredients. "You're not even going to try it?" Eliot nods toward Diablo's son's dish.

"Don't have to," he mutters, hefting a bag of flour down onto the counter. When Eliot doesn't respond, he continues. "I know it's good. That's not the point though. He shouldn't be wasting his time here when he can be doing other things."

Eliot suspects there's more information he's missing but doesn't want to disrupt Diablo any further, not as he's about to make the very thing he's waited years to see, so he keeps his mouth closed.

…

Diablo prepares his cutting board first. Scrubbing it down with soap and allowing it to soak in before washing it off again. He explains it's important as a precautionary measure and it makes things easier to clean after the entire deed is done.

The glistening, iced catfish drops on the counter; this whiskered monster of the swamp with slick brown skin and a mouth better suited to a television talk show host. This one is at least five pounds, and Diablo is quick to locate a tapered filet knife and a glove for his other hand before he slices from the dorsal to the pelvic fin. Diablo's arm muscles flex as he pushes on the knife and pivots smoothly, gliding the knife along the spine and stopping an inch or so before the tail.

He flips the creature and finishes separating the meat from the skin carefully. His cuts are precise and measured, with each discarded bit being tossed in a nearby bucket. Soon, he's slicing the ribs free from his filets.

The process is a cautious one, and Eliot watches every bit of it while nursing his remaining whiskey from the doorway. Behind him, he hears the sounds of children laughing and catches a glimpse of a hot pink frisbee being tossed between a couple of them outside in the garden. The rain has backed off and he swears he can see a glimmer of purple on the horizon beyond the oil lamps at the edges of the property.

When the fish is properly cleaned and skinned and he's removed the head, Diablo washes each piece of meat in the nearest sink. The blood runs in rivulets down his fingers and into the drain and something sparks in Eliot with the sight of it; something that makes him squirm in his spot momentarily.

The cutting board is cleaned again and the fish laid out on ice until it's ready for the next step. The fish head goes onto the ice after it's cleaned as well. *It'll make a nice soup*, Eliot thinks as Diablo moves onto the next step. He prepares a pan with milk and lays the yellow catfish filet into it— a known method for reducing the overt fishiness of the catfish. "I love how muddy they are," Diablo explains, "but some of the diners can't handle it. They want something that's closer to haddock."

"Something that doesn't remind them they're eating fish, right?" Eliot jokes.

"Exactly."

The flour that Diablo heaps into a bowl with his fingers appears darker and nuttier than the typical all-purpose. Wheat flour. Stone ground there on the island and mixed with a healthy scoop of cornmeal.

A rainbow of red powders is tossed into the same bowl around the edges—various peppers, salts, and spices, some of which he recognizes at a distance and some he could only guess at. Diablo whisks them together into a fiery dust, dips his pinky in to taste, and adds more paprika, more cayenne…in another bowl, he mixes milk and something red from a skinny bottle.

"Hot sauce?" Eliot probes.

Diablo grins. "You could say that." It takes more nagging from Eliot to get that its base is from agave. As far as other individual ingredients go, Diablo stays quiet. He swirls the two liquids together until the milk is creamy orange and then returns to the fish. He cuts it into portions and slips each one into the spices before dunking it in the milk and hot agave sauce. Then, they're dredged again in the spices before all ending up in sizzling oil at a nearby fryer.

As Eliot watches, he asks a question that he's been curious about ever since he read the Cuisine article years ago. "Why Tennessee?"

"That wasn't the plan originally," answers Diablo, scooping the spider skimmer into the oil and turning pieces as needed. "At first, I just wanted to get away from home. My plan was to hit the east coast. Maybe the Carolinas. But I ran out of money in Nashville and needed work. I ended up at a fried chicken place. And I fell in love."

"With Anna?"

"No. With the food." He pulls the first pieces of fish from the frier and their deep red skin scratches against the skimmer as he places them on a paper towel-lined plate and adds more fish to the oil, all the while checking temperature to make sure it's maintained. "Hot chicken from Prince's became my new religion. I hadn't thought about a career based in food before that, but it became my everything."

More agave hot sauce is painted on each piece of fish, by brush dipped in an old coffee can filled with the stuff, before another fine mist of the dry powder is added. Diablo plates the chicken with plain white bread, some quick deep fried pickle slices, and a squirt of Dijon.

Eliot stares at it and begs with every ounce of his being for his taste to come rocketing back. He wants to feel inspired. He wants there to be something reaching down into this submersed *nothing* blanketing him that can grab hold and wrench him to the surface. It's there. The thing he's been wanting to try for years.

Nothing.

He shakes his head and wishes only that he could feel the sting of disappointment from his new friend's face as if it were jellyfish tendrils wrapping around him. He deserved that.

Instead, Diablo gives him a small smile. "Try it. Believe me. The taste will linger."

Eliot hesitantly picks up a piece of fried fish, the sauce oozing down the pad of his finger, and takes a giant bite. He chews, and as his molars grind into the soft flesh of the fish and crunch through the breaded crust, a miracle occurs. Hurtling up through his body like being lost in the rush of an incoming wave against the shore, flavor explodes onto his palate and fizzles like saltwater against him. Salty, sweet, and hot—so unbelievably hot—it spikes his temperature and the walls glow as he takes a step back from the plate.

"See?" Diablo has a hand in front of his mouth, eyes squinting trying to hold back laughter. "Dude, you should see your face! You're sweating!"

And just like the tide once more, the flavor recedes lapped away from his mouth, his mind only to come slamming back in full force. Although this time, it isn't the heat from the fish, it's the alcohol.

Eliot doubles over and just barely holds it together as he laughs. "Oh my God! The fucking whiskey…" His head drums in a cacophony as he quickly grabs another piece of fish and eats it, hoping it'll distract him. It does—the briny, full heat and the tang of mustard and pickle brightening on his tongue.

"Right." Diablo knocks back the rest of his whiskey and calls to the rest of his chefs out the back door of the restaurant. "Let's make some food, y'all!"

13
CARRY ON

There's steam. There's the near electrical excitement that buzzes on the skin of every cook when they are alive in the kitchen. They feel the heat. They feel the pulse of the time ticking away as fish sparkles beneath oil in the fryer, as they dice potatoes, chop the various veggies, and arrange for plating.

Eliot is enthralled and falls into the groove. Diablo's sous chef shoves a handful of crystallized ginger into the pocket of his donned apron and then a knife. He isn't sure why they think it's best he carries a sharp object when he's two sheets to the wind and can barely feel his face, but Diablo doesn't seem to care. He's anchored inside the routine; his forehead dripping, eyes focused on whatever his fingers touch. He calls times to the kitchen, and they answer methodically, but Eliot can almost sense that there's something offbeat about tonight's dinner and it's not him.

Even as he busies himself with chewing the ginger and chopping the onions—something he can do with his eyes closed, drunk or not—he can see that the rhythm with which Diablo had executed his hot chicken sandwich alone was not the same now. It was as if he was one cog and the rest of his kitchen were another, and while they kept a steady, smooth action, he spun faster. Was it fear that made him pull spoons out of his cooks' hands and taste what they were doing mid-stir? Had the alcohol sunk in and turned him into a discordant whirling dervish dashing about the kitchen trying to put his hands into everything?

Eliot chops his onions. He feels the beating in his head and the gyration of his stomach as he chews on the ginger and lets its spice coat his tongue and gums. He focuses on it until someone takes the onions away and replaces his knife with a clean one. A bunch of bananas appear before him. "For dessert," one of the cooks explains. Mindy, he later learned was her name.

He wants to ask if Diablo is always like this during his services but doesn't trust his own lips to open without the contents of his stomach coming soon after.

"It's cool you're here," she says. "It's almost like you knew or something."

"Knew what?"

"Diablo's father passed away. He got the call yesterday morning." Mindy returns to her station.

As Eliot peels and cuts bananas, he thinks of his own father. He thinks of banana pudding sitting in a pale pink plastic bowl on the food tray of his hospital room. He thinks of the smell of antiseptic and watching his father shuffle to the bathroom with a nurse guiding him and rolling the IV cart after. He thinks of staring out at the painted blue sky on the mural in the hallway and how much he missed Getty; how much he missed Harvey and wanted to be home.

And before he knows it, he sliced all the bananas.

…

Servers take out the dinner to eager diners in the restaurant. Diablo sits on the back step, lights up a cigarette and watches the curl of its smoke as it rises against the dim light.

"I heard, you know," prompts Eliot, speech still a tad slurred.

"Ah," says Diablo, under his breath. He offers a cigarette and Eliot declines.

He can't tell if Diablo's annoyed or doesn't care, but he feels it's safe to ask another question. "Did you come out here to Tennessee because of him?"

"That man…" Diablo takes a long drag. "I think I thought it was him at the time. I was close to the old man when I was younger. But, as a teen, I had the same urges as a lot of young kids on the reservation do: they want to get out and see the world. They want a taste of something new. And at the time, it was only supposed to be a trip to see the Atlantic." He chuckles. "Never did actually see it."

"You don't have to. It's practically in your backyard now," Eliot scoffs.

Diablo's laughter hisses out like steam escaping. "You know they still have desert over there? In spite of all this fucking rain?"

"No kidding?"

"I dream about it sometimes. Miss it a lot. Wonder what would have happened if I'd ended up back there instead of here."

There are cheers from somewhere far off in the dining room. It sounds like a birthday celebration: people singing and a few cascading claps resounding over the murmur of the boiling water and sizzling of the fryer.

"You regret this?" Eliot asks.

"No. Just wonder what the next conversation with the old man might have been."

Diablo puts out the cigarette on the bottom of his boot and tosses it into a nearby overfull ashtray and heads back in to finish service.

...

It's late. There's a hotel on the far side of the island that the diners are ferried to by way of battered jeeps, so they don't have to make the perilous trip back through the swamps in the dark. Once they've all left and the cleaning of the kitchen is finished, Diablo guides Eliot to a nearby shack that's been kept vacant for the occasional visiting cook or farmer's family.

They sit in the small kitchenette of the shack and take shots of Jack Daniels No. 7 and talk more. Eliot misses this. He feels like he hasn't talked to another chef in such a long time. In truth, he misses when he used to be able to do it with Meena and Octave at Tempo. He misses his late-night jaunts into the underbelly of Getty with Clive so many years ago.

And he misses Alexis. God. He misses her so much.

He thinks about all their after-dinner service heart to hearts. All the parties in her apartment, catering to her friends, all their hungover late breakfasts drowning themselves with fancy coffees and shoveling down eggs, blood sausages, and fried potatoes.

Diablo speaks of haunting dive bars in Nashville with his closest friend and now sous chef, Enrique. The bleary black lights and old Christmas strands over battered pool tables and tilted tables, allowing progressive country music like Flying Burrito Brothers, J.J. Cale, and Johnny Cash to seep with the emerging Memphis soul of Wilson Pickett and Booker T. And The M.G.'s. And then, there was the food. Dry rub BBQ ribs with a bark that would crackle in their teeth, sweet potato fries and hushpuppies, and moist cornbread that practically melted in the mouth. He'd been forever changed.

Diablo told a story about how in the early days, he and Enrique had gone down to the city to pick up their first order of kitchen utensils for the restaurant, various tools and appliances notwithstanding. They ended up getting lost and found a hole in the wall bakery with the best (and perhaps only) Drunken Hummingbird cake either one had ever tried. They ended up stopping and making sure they picked up the baking essentials to try their hand at it before going home.

"Turns out the Drunken Hummingbird cake wasn't actually a thing. The baker just got really fucked up that morning after a breakup and substituted almost all the liquids in the recipe with bourbon. We had to take a couple walks around the block before we felt good enough to drive again," said Diablo, doubling over laughing with his sixth or maybe seventh shot.

Eliot had slowed down, mostly because he was still nursing a hangover from all the drinking they'd done earlier, and two, because he wanted to remember this, all the sensory things that came with this moment: from the smell of the fields carried on the wind to the sound of thunder rolling in the clouds above and the low timbre of Diablo's voice which sometimes wasn't loud enough to scratch it.

"You can't tell me you'd rather have stayed home versus coming here and starting Flounder…marrying Anna."

Diablo's laughter dries but he nods. "I can't. But I know that's a complicated answer, too. I don't know who my wife would have been if I stayed home or if I'd even have one. Who my kids would have become if I had any there?"

"Are you afraid of who they'll become here?" Eliot cocks his head. "Kind of seems like it judging by how you reacted to your son in the kitchen."

Diablo closes his eyes and hangs his head a little. The smoke from his nearly spent cigarette drifts into Eliot's eyes. "He's got a gift in the kitchen. He likes to experiment, and a lot of his experiments are pretty damn good. But he's seventeen. I didn't know what I wanted to do when I was his age. And there's so many opportunities out there for him if only he'd just open his fucking eyes and look at them." He takes the shot.

Eliot thinks of a telephone call he received, expecting a certain voice on the other end and hearing a different one. He thinks of the letter he sat reading at his kitchen table a week after getting home from visiting his father in the hospital and how he had just sat there staring at it, looking through it as the words morphed together with the aid of tears. He clears his throat before he says, "Is that what you're worried about? That your son will change his mind? That he'll blame you?"

He can see the wheels turning behind Diablo's face as lines grow across his forehead. "Anna calls him my twin. Looks like me, loves all the same stuff as I do…" Here he leans in. "Except for the cigarettes. Gods knows if he started smoking, she'd kick me out of the house so fast…"

"But he's not you," Eliot answers. "And maybe this is what he really wants to do. Maybe he's made up his mind?"

"How can he when he doesn't know what he's missing?" Diablo glances off to their right. "He has no idea how big the world is and how much he could gain from exploring it."

Eliot nods. After all, if his family hadn't taken that trip to Italy when he was a child, he wouldn't have had the exposure to new tastes and a new culture either.

"You know I didn't grow up on the East Coast?" he says instead, sipping his shot and savoring the burn at the back of his throat.

"Nah."

"I grew up in the Midwest. Didn't leave until I was eighteen. I started in the back washing dishes just like every chef does, got enough money from odd jobs to go to the culinary institute and then met Clive working at a kitchen in Vegas."

"Goodthin? Yeah. I heard you two were like this." He crosses his fingers.

"Clive is my mentor. He gave me a chance to work under him, to learn from him and, I know it's going to sound soppy, but he became like a dad to me. Like the one I needed and not the one that didn't want to understand me."

"Fuck man." Diablo's eyes glisten. "You're right, that does sound soppy."

They laugh.

"My point," continues Eliot, setting the shot glass down and threading his fingers. "So, what if your son changes his mind? He knows what he wants right now. And he's got the best mentor for a father. Right?"

Diablo pours himself another shot and fills Eliot's to the brim again. "Yeah. I think losing the old man really knocked me. We didn't resolve anything." He glances at Eliot. "Back home, when someone dies, we immediately bury the person and burn their belongings. Sometimes, families even move house just to get away from the spot where someone dies. I can see my mom already talking with a realtor.

"From a young age, we're all taught that Death is something to be afraid of; that it's considered an enemy. If you had come to my door and I was still living with the rest of my family out west, I'd have turned you away. You're dying. They'd have seen you as one foot in the grave."

"One more reason I'm glad for your hospitality," says Eliot, his vision lost out in the darkness of the grass in the fields.

"Just because my family renounced me doesn't mean I don't still worry about death…or fear it. Sometimes I think it's here with us all the time ticking down the minutes."

In the field, a figure stands up against the glinting lightning in the clouds beyond and Eliot forgets to breathe for a moment.

Alexis.

Death.

Whatever *it* is.

The increasing breeze pulls at her hair and the long dress she wears billows in the gusts like a sheet left out on the line to dry.

"Anyway," Diablo continues. "Everything I have left of the old man is in here." He taps his temple. "And I don't know how to sort these feelings I still have toward him."

"I haven't," says Eliot, his eyes locked on Alexis's figure. "I've been trying to sort my feelings out toward my father for almost a decade. Eventually, I just got to a point where I chose not to give them my time and attention. Couldn't afford to. And it's not worth wondering what if he'd had a different perception of the person I became. I like the person I am."

The fingertip grazing the back of his shoulder sends knives of terror down through him as Alexis's voice whispers into his ear, "*Mostly.*"

"'Mostly,'" he echoes, closing his eyes.

The two men finish their drinks. Diablo finally gets up, his weight making the steps squeal. He offers a hand to Eliot, and they shake. "I'll get you and your friend back to the mainland tomorrow. Sweet dreams, man."

Diablo's figure wobbles over the small dirt path back toward the restaurant as the wind picks up around him and ran sparks the ground harder. Diablo runs and Eliot shuffles back inside to his lonely shack, closing the door. Finding the bed in the dark, he rolls onto it and exhales, watching the flecks of lightning ignite the windowpane a few feet away.

"I'm proud of you, you know," Alexis's voice is soft in the darkness behind him. Soon enough, he feels one of her arms wrap around his torso, cupping under his arm, her hand on his chest.

He freezes. "What for? I just told the truth."

"That's what he needed. Someone to put it in perspective."

Eliot shivers. It was the first time in a long time he's felt cool. Usually, the Ash keeps him hot to the point where he sleeps with windows open and air conditioners going but now…every bit of Alexis's skin against him is like being basked in cool river water. It feels *so* good.

Remember the last time we did this? he wanted to ask her. Both of them had been alone. Both had needed comfort, not in the sexual way but in the human one—a friend to hold, to be held by.

"She showed up drunk at your apartment," Death says anyway. "Your friendship probably could have survived if either of you had reached out after that." She scoffs. "She was too proud. And you were too afraid. Fear really ruined your life, Eliot."

Eliot squeezes his eyes shut. "Please stop talking."

"I forgot, you're not into 'what if' scenarios," she whispers. "Could have saved a lot of your relationships if you had been."

Eliot grabs Death's hand and peels it off him. "I did what you wanted. Now leave me alone."

Thunder rumbles followed by silence.

Uninterrupted silence.

A PROCLAMATION

Have you heard the latest from our Lord?

Surely, you've seen the headlines, brothers and sisters. There is music orchestrated by the Messiah's hand and wrought by the Ash to show you, to show all of us, the next cycle. To show you he's been remade on Earth time and time again.

This Ash, denounced by modern medicine as a blight on our world, is how we are transformed. We are so close to divinity, and have become so blind, that we can't even see it! The unbelievers are afraid. They are terrified that this is the end and they have given up all hope of trying to understand.

But we are turning the tide.

God is telling us to focus and forget our own self-indulgences. We have begun to treat ourselves as though we are a higher power unto ourselves: celebrities deified for performance, for fashioning visual and audible and consumable art that is meant to *distract* us from His Truth.

He is metamorphosing us. He is making us anew with holy fire and we *must* spread the word.

LEFT LOG #3

SHE DRIVES ME CRAZY

They're too late.

Left spends in inordinate amount of time swearing at the top of his lungs into the mist-soaked air, stomping his feet and kicking pebbles on what's left of the pavement before the road turns to dirt and opens into a park and ride. Nearby, Hernandez and the Psychologist sit in the car, the former cradling the cat as always, and they watch him. Far off to his right on a dock, an older man shakes his head and scrubs down a battered-looking kayak.

They'd missed the chef and his plumber accomplice by a matter of hours. *Hours*... The word circles in Left's head like soap circling in the sink before the drain takes it. Right would have told him they were close; to stop whining and get back in the car. They could catch up. They would catch him. They would get their man.

But Left isn't sure he can spend any more time in the car with these two and that cat...that *blasted* cat. The cat that needed to be taken out for a poop break every few hours it seemed. The cat that they needed to feed, not in a car whilst chasing a suspect, but stopped in a dim gas station slash truck stop as they all wolfed down greasy burgers chased with nuclear colored soft drinks. Every stop they made wasted time.

They'd complained throughout the hours that they were tired, their backs hurt, they just wanted to sleep in a bed. "So, what did you get in the damn car for?" he'd ask them because, as he remembered, they had both volunteered themselves for this and clearly hadn't thought about his intentions at all. Left didn't mind pulling long hours, driving in the nighttime, in the gloom, playing radio tag. It was the only time he got to himself or well…he'd used to do it all the time with Right but she'd been used to it just like he had.

But these two… it was like being in the car with his daughter. Sure, she was fine for short trips: going to school, going to ballet, going to the community center. But heaven forbid he try and take her somewhere more than an hour away. It wasn't her fault, he knew. She was antsy. She was nine. She was the kind of kid who needed space like a greyhound. She needed to be out running around, enjoying whatever vast space he could find for her in their neighborhood. But he also wanted to show her other things, too. Things that weren't just in a ten-block radius from home.

She would get sick to her stomach if he tried to give her something to read. She'd kick the back of his seat until he put on music she liked. She'd cry if he didn't talk to her *constantly*…

"Hey!" Hernandez shouts from the car and Left's head bolts up from staring at the line between pavement and dirt. He returns to the car, gets in, and buckles his seatbelt without a word. They're back on the road heading north again in moments.

...

Left had asked for the bureau to update him if they could with any information they learned about Eliot Lamb or Terrence Boucher. He'd expected to get calls on the car phone, something that Right had had installed a couple years before since they were often on the road more than they were sitting at their desks. But the blasted thing hadn't gone off, not even once.

"Probably because we're out in the sticks," the Psychologist told him at one point when he'd been staring daggers at it. "Reception is terrible out here. Not to mention all the storms..."

Eventually, a city crept up on the horizon and Left made a deal with his anxious passengers: they'd stop for the night at a motel and get some sleep if they shut up and let him make a call there. They'd agreed though the looks they gave him were as full of spite as they were exhaustion.

Headlee wasn't a city he was familiar with but there were lots of those. It came out of the mist like a lot of the others did but it lacked something he couldn't put his finger on, and until they were within its billboard-laden brick buildings, he didn't know what. Then, he noticed the rubble on the streets, the collapsed walls, rotating blue and red lights, and realized that most of the buildings here were devoid of lights.

Where normally the sidewalks would be crowded with people, Left barely noticed anyone. The few cars they passed were packed full of belongings, suitcases strapped to the roofs and piled with families. They were all heading out of the city.

A building was smoldering on the edge of the next block, fire trucks surrounding it, hoses blasting the inferno. Left pulls the car to the side of the road next to a police officer, putting a white sawhorse in place to secure the scene.

Left rolls down his window and flashes his badge. "What the hell happened here?"

"True Faith. Took down the city theater a few hours ago," the cop shouts to compete with the sound of the blaze. "Two days ago, it was the Crichton Gallery on 11th Street. A week ago, it was Artist's Square. The whole city is in a panic."

"Thanks." He rolls up his window. "Shit."

They drive through the next several streets of battered buildings, shops with "going out of business" signs taped in the windows, and the charred remains of what might have once been a dance hall or a painting studio but was now a blackened scar on the cityscape.

"He wouldn't do this," says Hernandez, under her breath as if reading Left's mind.

Left scoffs. "He probably came through here and instructed his little cronies on exactly what places to hit. This is all part of his farewell tour."

The Psychologist is jotting something down in her myriad of notes that have overtaken the backseat. Left wonders how she keeps track of it all. She's wearing more normal attire now instead of her barely-there outfit from the night before, though her hat made him scratch his head. "Is that a pink beret?"

"Raspberry," she answered without looking up from her papers.

"None of this is in line with Eliot's personality at all." Hernandez shakes her head. "Eliot *loves* art. *Loves* music. *Loves* cooking. To destroy any place that introduces people to them is insane."

"Well," the Psychologist says, "He's losing his mind and his body. It's not out of the question for him to take out his frustrations on the things he used to enjoy."

"What?" Hernandez turns her head; her expression scrunched up in disgust. "Don't tell me you're now a party to his hair-brained theories?"

"I'm merely trying to explain what the reason would be if Mr. Lamb were a point of interest in this case so that it fit with the agent's narrative. I personally don't think it does though."

Left whips his head toward her. "What?"

"There are too many inconsistencies for the suspect to be Lamb. For one, True Faith is a pro-God religion with Christian roots. Lamb is an atheist according to whatever files you were able to rustle up. Our suspect was most definitely connected to his religion prior to some traumatic event that sent him off in this new direction."

There's nothing more that Left wants to do than argue but sitting here next to an exploded city theater isn't the place to do it.

They've been going almost twelve hours in the car now and he's exhausted. All he wants is to get out, eat something that doesn't contain sugar, and sleep. As he pulls away from the curb, he grumbles, "Un-fucking-believable."

The first motel they come across is a dingy, single floor motel on the north side of Headlee. Left pays for two rooms even though his finances are hurting. He needs privacy. He wants to get away from them if only for a few hours.

He leaves the women to their own devices in their hotel room and goes in search of something to bring back. Every diner he stopped at had the strangest list of menu items including things like Burgoo, something called a Hot Brown, Spoonbread, and rolled oysters. As soon as he found a place with burgers, he immediately ordered four and brought them back to the hotel.

They all ate in silence in his room, the cat even getting her own burger. It was the frozen patty kind of burger with American cheese and mushy tomatoes plus pickles on the bun. The same as every other cheap burger being slung in fast food chains across the country. Nothing special but good enough to fill his stomach.

"Did you even search for any real food?" comments Hernandez, after only taking one bite.

"Some people can't afford even this," he replies. "Besides, I'm not taking you on a culinary tour of Kentucky."

Hernandez shakes her head.

"It was pretty rough," The Psychologist comments giving him a look.

"Oh my God!" He puts his hands up to his skull and scrapes his fingers through his hair. "Are you all trying to make me lose my Goddamn mind? Is that it? And what the hell was that about not believing Lamb is the suspect. His parents have a history with the Catholic church in Idaho. You know his father had dealings with this crazy Christian conversion therapist in Diller's Creek back in the fifties? That guy apparently got arrested for some hypnotism bullshit he was pulling. Someone sued after former patients started committing suicide."

Meena's face slides into shock, then into horror. "What?"

Fuck. It was classified information. He wasn't supposed to drop it like it was gossip and certainly not in front of his closest link to the suspect. He opens his mouth. "Listen—"

"I didn't say that Lamb's life wasn't filled with trauma." The Psychologist cuts in. "I just said he doesn't fit the profile."

Meena retreats from the room, slamming the door behind her.

Rage takes flight in Left's body as he turns back to the Psychologist. "And what exactly is that? Because after all the miles we've logged you still haven't explained why you and my former partner think there's a link between lack of creativity and the Ash?"

The Psychologist clicks off the television and turns toward him. "Simple. It isn't about what we believe. It's about what *he* believes, and he believes that the Ash is caused by an instance where a person's ability to channel their inspiration is negatively impacted. This most often occurs due to a singular event where in a subject has lost the will and desire to produce creatively. In fewer cases, it's due to a solid decline in energy or enthusiasm."

"Jesus, you could sell drugs on the radio with those descriptions," he groans.

"Ha ha ha," she says without humor. "Now what does that mean for our guy?"

"It means that by destroying these places that showcase creativity such as theaters, galleries, restaurants, music halls, etc., they're limiting the number of places where people can connect with other people's creativity."

"Therefore…"

"They're slowly breaking us down."

"Exactly." The Psychologist finishes the rest of her burger and then takes a sip of her beer. "The more people they can push toward the Ash, the more people they consider converted."

"It's fucking sick," he comments.

"They don't think it is. We just have to figure out why they don't. Clearly, they see something in the Ash that we don't. They think it's godly or divine or something. Once we figure it out, we'll be closer to figuring him out." The Psychologist stands up and gathers her bag.

"That's it?" he asks standing to throw away his fast-food wrappers.

"It's been a long day, yeah?"

It has. He's exhausted. He's been looking forward to sleep ever since they pulled in yet… their conversation has unnerved him.

All he can imagine is his daughter's pink ballerina tutu in flames, the mirrors of her studio awash with fire as he stares through a window watching.

"Agent?"

"How did you know her?" he asks so suddenly, even he's surprised by it. "My partner? You're too young to have been in class together at college. She never went out anywhere. Never talked about her day to day. Never shared a Godamn thing."

"Maybe because it wasn't any of your business, agent."

The defensiveness in the statement smacks him. "It's my business as far as this investigation is concerned. Why pick you? There must be dozens of other candidates studying Ashen she could have chosen from."

The Psychologist narrows her gaze at him. "Are you just going to tip toe around it or are you going to ask?"

"Were you two in a relationship?"

The Psychologist crosses her arms in front of her chest. "And if we were?"

He slumps down onto the bed in disbelief. "Holy fuck."

"Does that vastly change your opinion about her? About me?"

He shakes his head. Frustration sends up smoke signals from his brain. He can't do this right now. "No, you're right. Sleep would probably be good right now."

She crosses her arms. "Sure. Avoiding the subject ought to make it all better."

Left glares at her. "Never thought she would be a dyke," he mutters to himself. "I mean… I thought she was thorny because of the job."

"She *was* thorny because of the job," the Psychologist says offhandedly. "Doesn't mean you need to consider her less than a person now that you know what her preferences were."

"Stop…" He waves at her. "Stop putting words in my mouth."

"You just called her a 'dyke,'" the Psychologist growls. "And by extension: me."

Left bolts to his feet and paces. "Sorry. I just…I thought she… I thought we—"

"You thought you had a connection?"

The humor in her tone is minimal but it's there and it sends Left's mind into an embarrassed fury. "Fuck you."

"Yeah. You were partners. That was your connection. And anything else you thought there might have been is likely just mixed-up attraction on your part."

He stopped pacing. He could feel his heartbeat through his temples as he tried and failed to keep his fury under control. "Mixed-up attraction? Who the fuck do you think you are? You don't know anything."

"Judging by your reaction, I think I can guess."

"No. There was something there. She was there for me when Brooke…"

The name is like cannon-fire in his brain. He had said his daughter's name out loud. He hasn't let it rise to the surface of his mind in almost a year and now he's blathered it out in front of this stranger. Just like he'd blathered Lamb's traumatic history to Hernandez. He was losing his grip.

"Agent?" There's a touch of concern in her tone, the first he's heard from her ever on this trip. "Should I stay or should I—"

"Leave." Anger bristles under his tone as he manages to say the word.

The Psychologist doesn't give him another one of her obnoxious sentiments, likely noticing the change in his behavior, and leaves closing the door behind her.

Left doesn't sleep a wink that night.

14
EYE OF THE TIGER

There is something ominous about driving in the nighttime and being the only car out on the road. Eliot embarked on road trips all the time back when he was a younger chef, back when the media had eaten up the novelty of his brand. How he danced as he cooked; how he found the song within the dish and the rhythm required to perfect it. He had spent long hours on the interstates—on and off ramps, handing bills and coins to rain-saturated toll booth workers, and stopping to spend the night in gas station parking lots cramped in whatever rental car he was given.

He isn't as young as he used to be. And the road is a lot emptier than it was back in those days. Now, anyone that travels out here only does so in long commuter buses made to withstand the elements, ones with propellers and reinforced siding to get through any mires if they come across them, vehicles made with bulging tires and aggressive tread to handle even the most formidable of obstacles. And if they can't, then there was always DOT in their military grade Humvees to swoop in to assist.

But here, crossing the border between Illinois and Missouri, there is darkness. There is the low rush of a static-like sound from the van's tires on the road. There is the percussion of rain on metal above him. And there is him alone with his thoughts.

Terry insisted he could stay awake until they got to St. Louis, saying he wasn't tired at all. But the fact of the matter was that since they'd left Getty, Terry had been behind the wheel doing all the driving and that hadn't seemed fair to Eliot. That and he was tired of sitting in the passenger seat staring out at the same blue darkness every hour. He needed to *do* something. Being back in Dante's kitchen had given him the cooking itch again. He'd enjoyed having something for his hands to do, something methodical, something like routine. And now that they'd left, he was going outside of his mind wanting to be back doing it again.

So, he'd volunteered to take the wheel. And while Terry was at first apprehensive with statements about the van's temperament such as "she's not so easy to handle" and "I'm the only one who knows how to drive her," Eliot cajoled him into letting him "learn the controls" so that should Terry ever actually feel tired, he could take over. After a simple run down of the various switches and buttons on the dash, Eliot noted that his teacher had grown awful quiet and found that Terry was already dozing, the passenger seat even reclined.

As the distant glow of the city brightened the darkness on the horizon, Eliot reminisced on his last time in a car out on the open road. Harvey had been there. Toto's *Africa* was playing on the radio as they laughed about something—he couldn't remember what, but he guessed it might have been a terrible joke Harvey told, or they'd reacted to something they heard on the radio.

Usually, Eliot did these trips alone. But Harvey had convinced him he could come along, that he wouldn't get in the way of any of his business. "I can find plenty to do to amuse myself while you're tasting food and being a rockstar," he'd said, winking. "Besides, you came back from the last one in such a funk. Wouldn't you be so much happier with someone waiting for you in the hotel?"

It was true. He would.

These trips were always to new places, always with the idea of networking—expanding his own tastes, bringing new ideas and new flavors home to the restaurant, making connections with up-and-comers. Invariably, it was always the same routine: he'd go to the restaurant, they'd drink, he'd tour the kitchen, he'd try the food, they'd go out and find a hole in the wall place that served something beautiful and messy and hard to come by like oxtail stew or roasted bone marrow and drink the heavy stuff and complain about people and the industry and other cooks until he stumbled back to his apartment bleary-eyed in the quiet of three a.m. He'd make it back only to find a too cold room overlooking the fast food-clogged main artery of town, an unpacked suitcase, and the soft distant sirens of police cars. He'd cover himself up fully dressed in the spacious bed and let the emptiness engulf him with its most merciless spell: insomnia.

But having Harvey along on that trip changed things. Those very reflective car rides he'd sometimes enjoyed, sometimes hated on his own, became mirthful with his partner's bright grin in the passenger seat in his periphery. Returning to the hotel was often not as late or early as it had been in other cities, with the promise of knowing there was someone waiting for him to steal his attention away from his job momentarily. They were replaced with his clothes hanging in a closet, the cool rush of air wafting in from the open balcony, an ice bucket with a chilling bottle, and Harvey.

Considering this trip, the last time he'd done a drive to the Midwest, they'd stopped at a gas station just outside of St. Louis so that Harvey could use the bathroom and pick them up some drinks. As Eliot had studied the map, he'd let his eyes pop up for only a moment to glimpse sunlight glinting off a flash of red as Harvey returned to the car, a shiny star-shaped balloon dangling from the top of a glistening ribbon.

"What the hell is that?" he'd asked.

"I got you something." Harvey's eyebrows perked.

Eliot shook his head, as a slightly stifled noise edged out of his throat.

"Oh, come on!" Harvey laughed. "Just because we're out on the road doesn't mean we can't celebrate your birthday, right?"

"With a tacky gas station balloon that says, 'It's your lucky day' on it?"

Harvey pointed at him. "Maybe it *is* your lucky day."

The small squirrel of panic that Eliot often had when Harvey did something like this hit him then, stared into his psyche like the animal that just couldn't flee or act as a car hurtled toward it. Had the attendant seen who he was buying the balloon for? Had Harvey told him? Was anyone watching them?

Harvey had perhaps, no *definitely* sensed, the change in his demeanor because he blinked and let the balloon go in the back seat of the car, his smile meek. "You're right. We'll celebrate when we get back, okay?"

The words had been like being stabbed with something hollow, something that not only impaled him but also sucked at him. Like a straw. He was the Goddamn plastic lid on a Goddamn soda drink, everything fizzing and turbulent underneath as he realized how his reaction had hurt the person he cared about most.

He reached a hand over and took Harvey's in his. "Thank you. I don't deserve it but I'm going to make a wish on the balloon as if it were a real star, okay?"

"That's the spirit," chuckled Harvey, and squeezed his hand back.

In the here and now, Eliot drives past the spot where he remembers the service station being and is instead gifted with the sight of a derelict building, the doors bolted and windows covered over with wooden sheathing. Even the lights in the pothole-ridden lot blink in and out like his memory of that day.

He drives past and there's a sound like the squeak of plastic and air rushing from behind him before the shine of something grabs his attention in the rearview mirror. He glances over his shoulder for a moment and nearly swerves the van.

A red star-shaped balloon hovers in the back, bouncing against the ceiling, string dangling down.

Trying to calm his own breathing, he murmurs, "You've got a fucking horrible sense of humor, you know that?"

"You don't let yourself think about him. About the one you loved." The voice that returns is dry, as if it hasn't been used in thousands of years, the kind of voice that he imagines belongs to an old man with blackened lungs, or perhaps the warm air of a deep desert night. Whatever voice Death is trying to emulate, it doesn't belong *here*.

"That's what we humans do," responds Eliot, under his breath, refocusing on the bleary world ahead. "We stuff the memories of our mistakes down, even when we know it isn't good for us…until we get complexes."

"Harvey wasn't the mistake," the voice answers.

"I never said he was."

"You can still forgive yourself." The last word hissed out and his shoulders prickle as the balloon turns to reveal the jaunty ebullient scribble of "It's Your Lucky Day!" on the opposite side.

Eliot can't help the sardonic smile from crossing his cheeks. "No, I can't."

There is no forgiveness for the kind of mistakes he'd made. There is no telling Harvey he is sorry. He'd been given so many opportunities to change what he was doing and he'd wasted every single one of them in favor of furthering his career.

He deserved to be alone in the end.

"The self-flagellation isn't noble, you know." It is Alexis' voice again, but try as he might, he can't see her anywhere. The balloon remains, now drifting into the shadows at the back of the van. "There's no one sitting around calculating human morality and dignity on a scorecard for every human. There's too fucking many of you for that."

"I'm not doing any of this for heavenly bonus points. None of that exists."

"You think it's a whole big ball of nothing after we die?"

"I'd rather not think about it."

Alexis laughs. "So that's how you want to leap into death? With blissful ignorance?"

"I don't want to leap into death at all!" A nervous laugh ripples through him. "I don't want to do any of this!"

Terry shifts in his seat and Eliot worries for a moment his hysteria awoke his friend. When the snoring resumes, he whispers, "I'm only doing this because I need to put something back into the world. I took enough out of it. *Quid pro quo.*"

"Oh, baloney!" Alexis mutters. "Cut the equilibrium crap. You know what I wish people would do more when they know they're going to die? Just give themselves some fucking humility. Just accept the biology that you are a flawed and imperfect being and you made mistakes. You didn't kill him. You didn't stifle his voice. Didn't take his ability to make choices for himself…"

"I still caused him pain," he says. It's raining harder now, and he clicks the wipers up to the next level to keep up with the deluge. "I cared about myself before I cared about the people I loved. And those wrong things, even if I was imperfect and flawed as a human for making them, still have consequences. Saying sorry to a vase full of ashes isn't going to heal those wounds."

"How do you know?" she asks.

"Because it wouldn't be enough for me."

The balloon drifts back into view from the back of the van. Funny; it seems more deflated now, hovering a few feet off the ground. "You wouldn't be the first person to choose money and fame over love, Eliot. You sadly will be far from the last."

The statement cut him. All he can remember are the tears, the shouting, the slamming of doors. All he can remember is voice after voice after voice saying, "GET OUT!"

He doesn't answer her. He pulls the van onto the next off ramp and looks for the nearest lit sign for a hotel. It's a Nitelite Inn; budget hotels located around the country in almost every major city. Two stars but no bedbugs or domestic disturbances, and often, you can find a room last minute without a reservation. He's stayed in a handful of them over the years.

He pulls into an empty spot in the front and goes in to book a room, giving them Clive's name. He hates doing this. But once he caught up with Clive after their next stop, he'll explain everything. After all, they just need a place for the rest of the night.

After getting the room number and key, he returns to the van and shakes Terry awake. His friend stretches and glances around the bare parking lot. "We made it?"

"Not quite. I need to sleep, Terry. I'm not feeling too good." It was an understatement. His body was on fire, sweat collecting on his brow and in every crevice. He wanted a cold shower and to lay down.

Terry doesn't argue. He turns in his seat to unbuckle his belt and stops to regard the balloon. "When did you stop to get that?"

"While you were asleep. Felt like a laugh," he lies.

The two of them drag themselves into the room. Two twin beds with ugly floral-patterned duvets greet them. The walls are a weird pale green and are hung with scenic prints in an art style that Eliot loathes—people whose faces seem too small for their heads running as they fly kites in a park and another of a horse galloping in an open field. Fauvism. Clive had taught him that style as they'd sat in a museum eating sticky toffee pudding from paper food trays. They weren't supposed to have food in there, but Clive was never one to bow to conventionalism.

Terry slumps onto the bed closest to the windows and grabs a remote control from the buffet nearby. Turning on the television, he diligently thumbs through the various channels until he excitedly exclaims, "They have HBO!"

The scene on screen is of a mummified corpse puppet speaking to the viewer inside a decrepit looking room. "Oh, I've heard about this. *Tales from the Crypt*, I think was the name. Supposed to be some real spooky shit."

Eliot gives a timid smile, remembering the airy voice from the van's back seat and dips into the bathroom to take his shower.

The cold water is a balm, dowsing the inferno and bringing his temperature back down. When he gets out, he's shivering but with a smile on his face. Grabbing a towel from the rack, he realizes that his skin is already drying as if doing so from beneath. He wraps the towel around his waist, and walks up to the mirror. He stares his reflection down, and freezes.

No.

Denial is pointless. He knows this. It was going to happen sooner or later, he'd just hoped for much, much later. After all, they'd said he'd had two weeks, hadn't they? But when was that? A week ago? Was this how it happened for everyone, or did people degenerate at different speeds? He wished he'd asked more questions at the clinic, wished he'd been more than a husk then. He'd stared at a chart on the wall of the doctor's office, which showed the different parts of the human skull. A bit morbid for the layperson who might have been getting their final diagnosis like he'd been.

His entire left iris is golden. Leaning in, he notes how it seems iridescent in the ultra-white lights over the mirror, how something inside it seems to twist and roll like fire.

But that's not what he's afraid of.

It's the hint of that same fire now in his right eye.

He turns on the water full blast and splashes it into his face, its iciness pricking his cheeks and forehead, going into his nostrils by accident and against the corners of his eyes. He turns the torrent back a little and lets it run as he holds his head underneath it, letting it pour into his eye. *It'll put out the fire*, he reasons insanely to himself. *I'm just tired. It's not there. It's* not *there.*

But when he opens his eyes again, when he dries his face, it's still there.

Without thinking, he grabs the box of bar soap from the counter and throws it as hard as he can against the shower wall. He hears Terry yell in surprise outside the bathroom, but the noise is drowned in his own panic, in his anger. He pulls back and slams his knuckles into the mirror. It doesn't break but his hand explodes in white hot pain. He recoils and curls his hand toward his body.

Moments later, there's banging on the bathroom door. "Eliot!" Terry yells.

The anger recedes as pain takes hold and shame washes into him, surround him. Groaning, he unlocks the door and Terry sweeps in not a moment later.

"Eliot, man, are you okay?" He does a once over of his friend: half-naked, swearing, and cradling his hand to his chest before he loses his cool. "Jesus! What the hell you doing in here?"

"I tried to punch the mirror," Eliot coughs.

"You do realize there's a solid wall behind it, right?" Terry growls. "You're going to get us thrown out. Here, let me look." He grabs Eliot's hand, and as he makes momentary eye contact, his anger fades. "Oh. Fuck."

Eliot looks away, his face contorted in sadness. "I know. I know."

They stand there in silence for a moment before Terry grabs the bathrobe off the back of the door and hands it to him. He examines Eliot's hand closer. "Does it hurt to flex it?"

Eliot hums but adds, "I don't think its broken though."

"Okay. I'll wait out here, okay?"

The door shuts.

Eliot wraps himself in the bathrobe's fluffy embrace, forgetting about the scorching heat within him. He wants to disappear inside of it. He wants to be unseen.

Tying off the belt on the bathrobe, he leaves the bathroom behind. In the room, Terry has muted the television and is nowhere to be seen. On the screen is a man staring up at the viewer from inside a coffin. Eliot averts his eyes quickly.

The door to the room opens a few minutes later and Terry walks in with a full ice bucket, and two bottles of beer sitting inside, while he tugs the haunted balloon along by its string in the other hand. Terry packs a fistful of ice into one of the empty plastic trash bags, twists the top, and hands it to Eliot who crushes it against his knuckles.

The beers hiss open moments later as Terry uncaps them, one off the other and then the second on the door strike. The two men sit on their respective beds and drink from their beers. On the other side of the wall, someone is listening to music and its softness barely ruptures their silence.

Terry holds out the balloon. "You want to tell me what the story is with this?"

"It's a reminder," says Eliot, against his better judgement. "I pushed someone away that I shouldn't have. It's something I can't leave behind. Though," he chuckles. "I'll be leaving it behind sooner than I thought."

"Someone you loved?" Terry asks carefully.

Eliot thinks about the word. Had he actually loved Harvey? Or had he just liked having him around? What exactly was love when two people didn't have the same concept of what it should mean? Had Harvey thought less of Eliot because of what had happened between them? "What is love?" he spits out before he realizes he's said it out loud. He closes his eyes. "I mean…yeah, Terry."

"You're really hard on yourself, you know that?" When Eliot looks up he sees Terry has let the balloon go and is shaking his head. "You're gonna die, Eliot. You've gotta forgive yourself, man."

Eliot stares at the balloon as it bobs against the ceiling, at the curl of the string floating between them. "I'm trying."

Terry nods. "How much further do we have to drive to get to your next stop?"

"Jackal is between Columbia and Kansas City just off I-70. Two or three hours at most."

"And then from there?"

"Clive's flagship restaurant is in Vegas. Depending on how the roads are that's another three days…maybe."

"And how long until you go…" He struggles to find the words. "…kablooey?"

"I don't know." Eliot stares at the ceiling, at the sprinkler over his head, and wonders if any part of the room would actually remain if he went 'kablooey' here. He glances over at Terry and sees that he's thinking something and not saying it. He thinks he knows what it is, so he says, "It's fine if you want to back out, you know. I'm not going to put you in a position where you might find yourself being barbecued by my spontaneously burning body."

Terry smirks. "Never thought I'd hear those words in a sentence before, but I appreciate the thought, man." He shakes his head. "That's not what I was thinking. I just can't wrap my head around how this thing is killing us. How any of this is happening. I think about it a lot sometimes. It feels kind of like I'm living a fantasy, you know? Like none of this is real?"

"Yeah," Eliot says.

"And I've gotten through it before by just putting my head down and doing my job. Taking solace in what I'm doing being helpful. That it's making things better in this whole fucked up world. If I feel like I'm pushing back against all the bad, then I'm doing good. I'm not just surviving; I'm thriving. I'm doing my thing. I'm getting mine and giving it back. It makes me feel like things are all happening for a reason and it's not all just crazy happenstance."

When Eliot doesn't say anything, Terry cocks his head. "I'm not leaving you, El. We're going to get you there, no matter what." He gets up and heads into the bathroom, closing the door.

Maybe he's right. Maybe there is a plan after all. Maybe Death was lying and this is all meant to be. She'd been puppeteering things from the beginning, setting this all in motion, playing with reality in order to get what she wanted, which was him, barreling down the highway with Terry toward culinary perfection and appeasement. Or maybe it was bullshit. Maybe this was the actions of two desperate people hallucinating as they try to grasp what little meaning is still left in their lives. Maybe he'd fed Terry the fantasy by telling him of his death, by making him feel like he was making a difference in this ludicrous cross-country quest.

He fell asleep thinking about it, not even realizing that the balloon was hovering just to his left between the bed and the wall, as if watching him.

15

LAND OF CONFUSION

In the morning, Eliot wakes up with sore knuckles and the balloon floating over him. He stuffs it inside the room's closet and shuts the door without a word.

Waking Terry, they get back on the road, stopping to find breakfast at a small, decades-old bakery on their way out of town. The doughnuts are crisp on the outside but soft through the middle, spilling fluffy whipped pumpkin filling and raspberry jelly into their eager mouths with every bite.

The road, as ever, is doused in the gloom of late morning, which resembles the gloom of early morning, and even the gloom of afternoon—always in shades of somber blue. The interstate crosses through what was once flat farmland, eroded by the soft soil, the roadways crumbling around the edges. Detours keep them on the road longer: places where the entire highway has cracked through and given way, places where the DOT shuffles around in the rain miserably as they do their work.

The detour becomes nothing but a dirt road turned to mud, and for a frightening few minutes of being stuck, they are able to get free with the help of a passing farmer, who tows them out with his tractor.

They hit a stretch of Lost Highway when they have to turn around due to the roads crumbling into the expanse of a wide canal below. As they are carefully turning the van around, Eliot spies something in his sideview mirror. "Stop."

Terry halts the van and Eliot squints to try and see what the shape is through the darkness and the rain but can't quite make it out. It almost looks like a…cross?

He climbs out of the van, asks Terry to hand him a flashlight, and once it's in his hand, he pivots its beam up toward a spot beneath the overpass on the other side of the canal.

Horror engulfs him. He drops the light on the pavement, and it flutters out.

"What the hell?" Terry calls to him from inside the van. "That's my only good light, Eliot. Be careful."

Scraping it up off the pavement, he shakes it, and it lights again, so he directs the beam toward what he saw, what he thought he saw…

A charred body stares down at him, flesh still pink in places, and the shimmer of bone and slick muscle glistening against the rain. It's tied onto an iron grate about six feet high by six feet wide with a silver cross welded onto the back of it. A lump of ash and burned down logs litters the road beneath it.

Someone had been burned alive out here.

Eliot practically throws himself back into the van and snaps off the light and tells Terry to, "Drive, just fucking drive."

...

Jackal appears out of the cerulean afternoon; its town mere shambling corroded structures. Gone were the assembly of French Colonial architectures mixed with ambling brick edifices of the usual downtowns. Jackal's buildings creep out of the darkness like phantoms. White-washed old churches with broken windows, one old schoolhouse with a steeple in the front, and their van's headlights illuminating the waves in the old glass windows eerily.

"Didn't you say the next restaurant was in Jackal?" asks Terry, his grip tightening on the steering wheel. "This place looks like a ghost town."

"That's because it is. Or was," Eliot confirms. "Used to be a town until it was bought out and used as a military outpost in World War II, like Bloodland. Residents were forced to evacuate. As of late, there's been talk of turning it into a museum if not for the...other problem."

"What other problem?" Terry asks.

Eliot pointed into the dark off the road. "Them."

They were always there. Like headstones or fence posts or inanimate things that people chose not to notice because to do so and ignore them was like losing a piece of one's humanity. They had been human beings once; arguably they still were. They just didn't act like the rest of society. And as the van lazily drove down what was once the main road through town, they watch the always walking, stumbling, ambling bodies continuing through the overgrown grass off the roads, around the skeletal buildings, and down the broken sidewalks in the same direction.

Eliot can't tear his eyes away. This is what awaited him. Mindlessness, moving in the wet and the dark, people turning their heads away in shame. His throat closes at the thought.

"Seems like there's a lot more here, for some reason..." Terry mutters and breaks Eliot's concentration.

He clears his throat. "It's a convergence point," he answers. "At least, that's what I think it is. There's a few of them across the country. For some reason, it's a spot where Ashen come to from lots of different places. They all come to Jackal and then leave going in the same direction."

"It's a little fucking weird, right?" Terry says. He's driving the van slower now, though not slow enough to keep in step with any of the Ashen.

"Yeah. It's fucking weird."

"Does anyone know where they all end up?"

Eliot shakes his head. "I've never wanted to find out."

Terry steps his foot on the gas, and they leave the Ashen and the pieces of old Jackal behind. "So, why would someone want to put a restaurant out here in the middle of a ghost town? Who would even come to it?"

Eliot smiles. "It's not just any old restaurant. The building was once a saloon: Milliner's. And while the bar was a memorable part of the town, it was Louise Athemy's Burnt Ends and Pork Steaks that brought patrons in for meal after meal. Because it was outside Kansas City, it never got the same glitz and fervor as Bryant's did as a barbecue joint and didn't have the chance to when the military came in and pushed everyone out. But Nelly wanted to bring it back to its roots. So, she got Milliner's up and running again."

"Burnt Ends?" The corner of Terry's lip curls. "Doesn't sound like anything worth traveling to the middle of nowhere for."

"Trust me," Eliot says. "You'll think so when we get there."

Milliner's is a bright pink neon explosion culminating out of the darkness in a bare stretch of land ahead of them.

"What…the…?" Terry starts to say but the rest of his words drift into silence the closer they get.

Eliot can't help but grin ear to ear, a small laugh escaping him. It hadn't been this bright last time he came but he didn't put it past Nelly to have opted for as many bells and whistles as she could to make Milliner's stand out. And stand out, it did.

It reminds him of the lights at The Strand in Getty. The burst of excitement and glamor on the marquee for whatever new show was in town, the giddiness of excited guests waiting to claim their tickets at the box office, the aroma of buttered popcorn, and the entire sidewalk blooming gold to cut into the swath of darkness that held its closed fist over the city.

He missed those days before the theater was destroyed by the True Faith.

Milliner's doesn't quite have the same polished art deco accents that the Strand had, but it does have every bit the glitz and pop that spills down over its white-washed bricks like pink paint. It seeps into the wind tumbled grass that surrounds the place; a trick candle against the rain, a symbol of gumption in a town filled with spirits of the other variety. That night, there is even a crowd with cars packed around the nearside of the building like fries in a carton.

But, as they close in, Eliot's smile fades.

What he assumed were the figures of hungry patrons ready for Milliner's barbecue delights are revealed to be hundreds upon hundreds of Ashen, their limbs crumbling smoke gray beneath shredded flannel and cotton and gleaming like a herd of deers' eyes against the shine of their oncoming headlights. They are all crowded around the perimeter of Milliner's, their eyes fastened to the electric glow above like moths to porch lights.

Terry stops the van at the nearest spot he can, and they both climb out. Eliot inspects the closest truck, then the next sedan over. All the cars in the lot are a shroud: several busted in and all empty. "What happened here?" Terry asks at the same time that Eliot thinks it.

"Oh no you don't!" someone shouts from the direction of Milliner's shortly before an enormous boom erupts into the air and the windshield of the truck shatters.

Eliot throws himself down into the dirt of the parking lot shortly followed by Terry.

"Don't!" he screams. "Don't shoot!"

"You've got ten seconds to climb back in your van and take your Ashen with you!" the voice shouts back followed by the pop of a rifle being opened…being reloaded.

Eliot scrambles, his fingers digging in the dirt as he leaps up to his feet. "Nelly! Stop!"

"Fat chance!" Rifle casings tinkle off a hard surface. He can see her short dark hair just barely over the sea of cars in front of him. She's standing on the roof of the restaurant.

"It's me! It's Eliot!"

Her head shoots up from where it had been bending over the rifle, her black curls bobbing. "El?"

"Yeah," he calls, a frightened laugh skirting along at the end of it. "Yeah, it's me."

Nelly vanishes from sight; the sound of a door slamming echoes into the night.

Eliot helps Terry up from the ground. "You didn't tell me she was crazy," he said under his breath, brushing off his clothing.

A moment later, they hear the squeak of a door opening followed by Nelly appearing from the back of the building. She waves at them. "Over here! Quick!"

The two men skirt around the parked cars up until they hit the throng of Ashen. The stench is atrocious. Eliot feels like he's back at the scene of the explosion in Getty, his entire head wreathed with the acrid tang of smoke, of burnt flesh now mixed with the sourness of rot. One of them, a woman with long, pleated blonde hair stares through Eliot as he sidesteps her. He notes the sallowness of her skin and how the flesh has begun to tear away to reveal bone on her forehead and on her cheeks...

"Hurry up!" Terry grabs hold of Eliot and pulls him along through the mass until they reach the back door. They file inside past Nelly, and she shuts the heavy metal door behind them, sealing them in the kitchen.

Nelly stares at Eliot, her expression a void.

He cocks his head. "I'm sorry I haven't visited."

She sets the rifle down against the wall nearby and grabs him, pulling him into an enormous hug. He can hear the hitching of her breath as he holds onto her.

"I thought I saw the shine of a tiger's eye from upstairs. I thought it was just another one of those Kansas City assholes looking to dump their unwanted Ashen patients off." She pulls away and stares into his face, resting a hand on his cheek. "I never thought… I mean… You of all people…"

He bows his head. "I know."

She glances at Terry out of the corner of her eyes. "Who's this?"

"Terry. He's giving me a ride across the country." Terry nods and eyes the rifle.

"A ride?" She frowns. "You're at death's door and you're going on a joyride?" She chuckles. "Sounds like you're the same old you."

"I came out here to see you." Eliot glances around the kitchen of Milliner's. He remembers its grills, sinks, and counters as if it were yesterday. After a busy day of cooking, they'd all gathered on the roof with bourbon and applejack for Missouri Mules and laugh about food, about music, about everything until the horizon glowed pink with morning. Him, Harvey, and Nelly and her husband, Lucas.

"Where's Lucas?" he asks, glancing around the empty kitchen.

Nelly's lip trembles. "I don't know."

He frowns. "What do you mean?"

"I mean 'I don't know!'" she shouts back at him, and he takes a step back reflexively. After a moment, she deflates, and grabs hold of his arm. "Come on in here. I'll explain."

The three of them push through the saloon-style kitchen doors out to the dining area and the bar. Nelly pours them mezcal on the rocks and picks up a half-smoked cigarette from the ashtray to finish. The room is huge: an iron spiral staircase ascending to a second floor full of more tables and chairs overhead. The walls are streaked with painted murals of wolves in stripes of blacks and grays with yellow running through their fur; an abstract style he'd never seen before but enjoyed. But the silence devoured all in its wake. The way the ice in their glasses clinked seemed to echo on for eternity.

"Place looks great," Eliot says. "Kind of surprised you don't have any music playing though."

"It brings them closer." Nelly flashes a glance at the windows outside where the Ashen have gathered. "It's like Romero's *Night of the Living Dead* for God's sake." She makes eye contact with Eliot and mutters, "Sorry."

"I'm not one of them yet," he answers. "I've never heard of them stopping like this before though. I mean they pass around cities all the time. Why don't they ever stop and stare at the lights or the sounds?"

"Those gates you've been seeing around most cities? Those are for keeping out the Ashen." She sighed. "Small towns have other means of getting rid of their Ashen: usually driving them out to the middle of nowhere and leaving them like strays. Which is what I thought you were doing when you drove up. Jackal has become kind of rampant for that as of the last several months. With the uptick in drop-offs, instead of leaving, they've just been hanging out. It's like they're gathering for something."

Eliot glanced out the window. Every Ashen was gazing upon the lights as if they were the coming of Jesus or something holy, the fuchsia reflected against their gold eyes.

"Why don't you just unplug the lights?" Terry asks.

"We can't. It's the only way anyone finds us out here." Nelly sips her mezcal. "Milliners was an institution back in the day. And now that we've brought it back, it's the only thing that's really keeping Jackal on the map. Business has been better every year. We put these lights in two years ago in May and we had a record summer and fall last year, a record spring this one… We lose the lights and we might as well put out the closed sign."

"Doesn't look like you're patronizing anyone now, Nel," says Eliot, glancing around the empty room.

"It's Tuesday. We're normally closed."

"And Wednesday?"

"Open. If people can stomach the crowd."

Eliot cringes.

Terry's eyebrows perk. "Your customers better have some strong stomachs. Some of those folks out there are ripe as hell."

Nelly chuckles. "I thought about getting the hose out to give them a wash down but I'm not sure some of them could stand up to it."

"You haven't explained where Lucas went yet," Eliot reminds her.

She finishes the mezcal and rounds the bar to join them. "It started with the cars. Lucas made a deal with a salvage yard in Nile. We thought if we built a kind of wall with them, we could keep them from getting too close and that worked for a while but… A windstorm knocked it down. They got in.

"After a couple weeks of losing business, Lucas had an idea on how we might get them to move on. There's an old radio station about halfway between Jackal and Acceptance. That's the next town over. They have speakers mounted on the outside of the tower. The whole thing shut down with everything else decades ago, but we thought, if we could get it running again, we might be able to lure them away. They seem to like music just as much as they enjoy the light show."

"When did he leave?" Eliot asks.

"Yesterday. He said he finally found someone that might have a key to the place, and an electrician who might be able to get things running again." He was supposed to be back last night. I don't want to leave the restaurant. I figure it's only a matter of time before the Ashen start trying to get inside. After all, we'll have to make food again soon. We'll have to turn on the music and invite patrons in again…"

"Seems like an awful lot of trouble just to keep this place going, sister," Terry says. "Wouldn't it just make more sense for you to start over in a place that isn't a convergence point? I'm sure there's all kinds of abandoned saloons out here that can be turned over and fixed up."

"Starting over isn't an option," Nelly says fiercely. "Milliner's isn't going to get canned by these things. It isn't going to get forgotten out here. I won't let it."

Eliot sighs and takes hold of Nelly's hands in his own. "You know as well as I do that all restaurants don't make it. And it's not the fault of the owner. Sometimes, it's just the world around us changing."

Her face scrunched up in surprise. "Nuh uh. The Eliot I knew never would have said something like that. He never would have let Tempo get lost in obscurity. So why should I let it happen to my restaurant?"

"I closed it, Nelly."

She cocks her head. "Come again?"

"Tempo's closed. The Agave Tap was blown up a few days ago. Alexis was killed. And I'm…" He takes a shaking breath. "I can't do it anymore."

Nelly stands from her stool, her hands sliding out of his. "You *can't* do it? Or you don't want to try?"

Before he knows what's happening, she lashes out a hand and slaps him. His cheek burns for a moment before going numb—before *everything goes numb*.

He reaches a hand up to his face slowly and has a tiny sensation in his fingers that he's touching his own skin, though it tingles like an arm that's fallen asleep.

"Whoa, whoa!" Terry leaps in between them. "What the hell is that for?"

"He's giving up!" Nelly shouts. "You don't *give up*. It's the first thing they tell you when you're diagnosed with the Ash. You keep fighting. You keep beating your fist against it and *feel*…try to keep *feeling*."

"How do you know what they say about the Ash?" Terry asks.

"There ain't one person in this world who doesn't know someone who got the Ash, or whose family has an Ashen or who's seen a news story or commercial spouting off about prescription drugs for it. We've all seen it happen to someone and if you haven't, you're about to," she snapped, glancing between him and Eliot. "The Ash preys on our emotions. It steals our ambition. It coddles our fear and nurtures doubt."

She looks past Terry to Eliot. "When I met you, you were untouchable. You had goals, Eliot Lamb, and you jumped whatever hurdles got in your way to meet them. Death? You'd have stared down its nose and spit right in its eye. Where is *that* man?"

Eliot swallowed, his hand still plastered to his cheek. "I honestly haven't seen him in a while," he answered blankly.

"You let me know when you find him." She walked across the room toward a door on the opposite side of the room. "Until then, I'll be waiting here." She went through the door and slammed it behind her.

Terry hums lowly. "That lady has got to get her priorities in order."

"I don't really know what to say," Eliot answers. "I know what I probably should say, I think?"

Terry nods. "We should find her husband."

"At the very least."

16
COME UNDONE

They leave Milliner's. Terry almost has to guide Eliot the entire way to the van. His equilibrium is off, and he can't seem to get his balance. Even in the passenger seat, everything sloshes around as if he's on a boat at sea. It makes him sick to his stomach.

They drive through the emptiness beyond Jackal, passing old farmhouses with barn doors that have crept open, a gentle breeze rolling through the seas of wet grass beyond them, rusted out farm equipment left in the fields to become sculpture art of a pastoral era.

"Kind of wish we'd asked for directions or something," Terry says. "What if we drive right by it?"

Eliot clears his throat and tries to say something, but his tongue has gone numb as well. A panic sets in at the idea that he can't speak, can't even open his mouth to ask for help. No. He isn't an invalid. He isn't gone yet. He closes his eyes and focuses, grunts as he drags his tongue forward across his teeth, forming each word in his head. "Th-there," he stammers, jutting his jaw forward.

Terry sees what he's trying to gesture toward: a red blinking light. A black silhouette of a radio tower emerging from the trees on the horizon. "Got it," Terry answers before he touches a few dials on the dashboard. "You cold? Kind of sounded like it. I turned up the temperature. You should feel it soon."

Eliot strains to speak again and it comes out a little easier. "Thanks, T-Terry."

Dozens of dirt roads split off from the one they're on and vanish into the darkness in the direction of the radio tower. It takes more than a few tries of guessing the wrong one before they follow the correct lane down to a squat one-story building made of brown brick. It sits on a concrete pad surrounded by trees. There's a car outside the station but no one is inside of it.

Terry climbs out. "Wait here," he says to Eliot. "I'm going to have a look around."

Eliot nods: it's all he can do at the moment. The smallest feeling has begun to drift back into his fingertips and toes, but everything still feels heavy, still feels like it's been shot full of Novocain, and he knows even if he could move, he'd probably get sick almost immediately.

Eliot is left in the dark.

He's so tired.

He's sore.

He's been sitting in this seat almost the whole damn day and now, he can't move to get out of it.

He waits for Terry to come back, listening for his footfalls, and drifts to sleep without meaning to.

. . .

1985

"Don't you ever want more?" Harvey's voice cracks. "I mean, sometimes I wonder if you even do want me here. It's hard to tell with you."

Eliot feels like he's being torn in half with each word. They are standing in the kitchen of Harvey's old apartment. Eliot has just made them dinner: a carbonara, something he'd spent hours on perfecting for the menu of the restaurant, something he wanted Harvey to try because he knew he'd get an honest answer.

But things had shifted somehow to…this.

"Of course I want you here." He puts his hand on his forehead. "I don't know how to explain…"

"You're telling me you don't enjoy sex?" His partner winces. "How am I not supposed to take that personally? The fact that you don't want to have it with me, I mean…"

"It's not you. It's never been you. You're just the first person that's really mattered, Harvey." His lungs are tight. Every muscle is tense. Even his jaw hurts. "It matters to me that you know that it doesn't matter to me. That it's not how I want to show you that I love you."

Harvey's crying. "I don't understand."

"I don't know." Eliot is, too. "I've never liked it. I've always tried to tell myself I was wrong for not liking it. For not understanding it. But I don't think I am…wrong, I mean."

"You're telling me that you've had sex with other people before and faked liking it every time. Even with me?"

Eliot hates himself. He hates every part of him that he doesn't understand and that he's spent years trying to understand even as the words fall from his lips. "I was trying to convince myself that I did. I thought for a long time that something was wrong with me. But…there are others who feel like this. So maybe it's not just me?"

He hadn't heard the term *asexual* until a few years ago, never knew it was even a concept for someone to not feel sexually attracted to his or her partner. But it's hard to convince someone of this revelation when you've had sex before, sex that left Eliot lying awake in bed, wondering why he didn't feel gratified, why he didn't enjoy it. Sex because he was drunk and he thought whoever he was with expected it. Not just with Harvey, who he deeply cared for, but with past romances as well.

"Get out."

At first, he isn't sure he's heard right. "What?" The word drops from his lips, and he realizes the gravity of Harvey's words seconds before they are repeated again: stronger, angrier.

"GET OUT."

Eliot goes numb. He shuts down, under pressure, water pulling him under. He finds his jacket slung over a couch. He shoves on his shoes. He snaps up his keys and his wallet and all but runs out the door of the apartment. Are there bubbles of air rising from his drowning body as he navigates the narrow halls, as he finds the elevator? It's a solitary ride down to the bottom floor and he's trembling the whole way, swallowing back the guilt and the shame. By the time he's reached the front door, he can't keep his breathing under control.

You never should have said anything. You should have kept on pretending.

The voice chips away at him. He's vaguely aware of where he's walking, of the looks he's getting from passers-by as he cries and pushes his way through the streets, through the traffic and the heavy snow falling.

He's outside of Alexis's apartment moments later, not sure how he got there but buzzing her name on the call sheet, nonetheless. When she responds, he isn't sure what to say and after he doesn't answer for several moments, she tells him she's coming down.

Should have kept it inside. Should never have said anything.

He sits down on the steps in the wet inch of snow that's accumulated and gives in to the sadness. He's sobbing, hugging himself in the cold, and vaguely hears the door open behind him. He barely registers Alexis's arms folding around him, her gentle voice in his ear. "El. Eliot, talk to me. What's happening?"

He can't say. Not right then when the world feels like it's imploding. Everything that he's ever felt that he's kept to himself for years, that he tried to share with the person he cared about... the weight was gone and somehow replaced tenfold. He couldn't get out from under it. He couldn't breathe.

Alexis held him, didn't ask any more questions, and let him cry.

He remembers going up to her apartment with her later, remembers the warmth of her space as she wrapped him in the comforter from her bed and told him to sit on her couch. As she made him tea. He remembers the light from her fake Christmas tree in the living room, from the glittering tinsel and the smell of her balsam candle burning nearby. He remembers the feeling of wanting to escape reality right then and there because he felt safe, momentarily. And he was terrified because he wondered if maybe Harvey would also reach out to Alexis for comfort. After all, they'd known each other longer. Why shouldn't he? Would he explain what had happened and turn her against him?

Was it always and forever going to be his fault?

…

"Wake up, El."

The voice is Alexis's. It's a whisper, the lick of candle flame against a finger. He stirs and tries to discern his surroundings. Not the darkness of her holiday decorated apartment, no, but dark, yes. But there is a glow coating his body in its pink and green radiance.

His eyes open more. An aurora.

He stares up at it, at the clarity of the sky beyond. Stars. How long has it been since he's seen stars? Constellations he doesn't remember, the formations expanding over him and—light! So much gorgeous strange light!

He's pinned beneath its alienness and can't look away from it. No one saw the night sky anymore. The storm clouds, the light pollution, the chemicals in the atmosphere made it next to impossible… This was probably the first time he'd seen it in over ten years and the first time he'd seen the Northern Lights ever.

Something gave way inside of him, and the sadness that clunked around in his head lifted as if trying to reach out to those colors in the sky, as if trying to tear itself out of the cage that was his body.

"El."

Alexis's voice again.

He glances behind him but there's no one there. And he's not sitting in the van anymore. He's standing next to a white building with an enormous plastic cheeseburger pinned to the roof like an olive in a martini. The paint on the tomato and parts of the bun is wearing off. The fluorescent lights are off, and the distant hum of streetlights nearby seems to be the only other source of sound out here. He's in a fast-food drive thru.

He spins, searching for the van, searching for signs of Terry but there are none. His pant legs are wet, and his shoes coated in mud. Had he sleepwalked there without realizing it?

"You did."

Again, he looks behind him but there's no one there. "Where are you?" he asks.

Alexis clears her throat and the sound of it seems tinny and garbled by static. He focuses on the drive thru speaker a few feet away. It's shaped like a box, but has two cartoon bubble eyes that poke up from the top as well as two arms with gloved hands that stick out from its sides. It has legs with red boots on either side of the stand that holds it in the ground. "You've got to be kidding me," he grumbles.

"You were out of it. I tried to get you to go back to the van, but I couldn't. Not until the lights came out anyway. They stopped you in your tracks."

The revelation fills him with dread. "Where am I?"

"It's a Lucky Link's just outside of Acceptance. You cleared about two thirds of a mile in your sleep."

The information makes him feel weak in the knees. He'd gone under—the Ash forcing him into its weird near zombie-like state as it made him meander across the county. He glances down at his hands and arms and notices the scratches and scrapes, likely from scrub brush. He pulls a tiny thorn out from his wrist and discards it as he starts walking. "I've got to get back to Terry."

They need to get Lucas back to Nelly. Get the radio up and running. Get the Ashen away from the restaurant so that he doesn't take up anymore of Nelly's precious time.

"You're mad at her?" asks Alexis from the speaker.

"How perceptive of you," he jeers, still walking away.

"Why?"

He whirls around. "Because she expects me to be the same person I was years ago and that's a ridiculous standard to hold someone to. Especially given everything that's happened."

"She doesn't know what you've been through. And that works the other way around, too."

"I didn't come here expecting anything from Nelly. I just came out here because you told me she needed my help and that's what I'm doing, helping."

"What a crock of shit, Eliot Lamb."

He glares at the speaker. "*You're* the crock of shit. Death? The almighty and powerful Death can't stop *this*?!" He gestures at himself fervently. "This fucking end of humanity that's happening to us that you have no control over? And you've got nothing better to do than poke at me? Pretend to be a fucking balloon or a Lucky Link drive thru speaker? Seriously?"

The speaker sits silently. Is it his imagination or does it seem like the smile on the Lucky Link's face is getting broader somehow?

"You know what? Forget it!" Eliot laughs. "Of course you've got the time. How silly of me. You're able to zoom around and kill people willy-nilly and still have time to torment me. It's all fun and games for you."

"Way to make me sound like a psychopath," Alexis drones.

"You *are* a psychopath. You're using the voice of my dead friend to goad me across the country to do you a favor." He sits on the curb next to the speaker and glances up at the aurora again.

"What happened to helping Nelly? Helping Diablo?" She almost sounds sympathetic now.

"You framed it well; I'll give you that much. 'Help out your friends before you go nuclear.' 'Do something with the time you have left.' I just wanted to stay in my apartment. I just wanted to not get involved. I wanted these last weeks to be mine."

"That's not who you are."

"How the fuck do you know who I am?" He scoffs at the speaker. "Who are you to tell me who I am? I know who I am. It's my life! I've had to spend my whole Goddamn life figuring it out, but I know now exactly who I am."

"And who is that?"

"Someone who should have just kept his mouth shut. It would have been better for everyone." He rubs the back of his head.

"You'd have been unhappy," Death says.

"What's the difference? I'm unhappy now."

"Hiding away who you are for the sake of other people's comfort isn't you. The people who matter, the people you've surrounded yourself with who love you for who you are—they are the only ones whose opinions should matter."

Eliot hangs his head. "I lost Harvey. And I lost Alexis because of Harvey."

"You lost Harvey because you were afraid of how he saw you once you told him the truth. You lost him because you never trusted that he could get to know you—the *real* you. You gave up on him. And Alexis lost *you* as a friend, not the other way around. She made her own choices. She wanted to climb the ladder and saw you as her next rung."

Hearing Death say that in Alexis's voice brought a chill to him. He hadn't wanted to believe that she had done what she'd done out of a need to outgrow him. He could take her being angry with him. He could understand her doing it out of rage or as a reaction. But ambition… He'd never suspected.

"Likewise, you haven't lost Nelly yet," Death continues. "Nelly isn't angry with you because of change, Eliot. You haven't changed. You've hidden. As someone who inspired chefs to dance to the beat their own drum, you refusing to hear the music is why she's mad. Where would she be without you?"

"She'd have made it." He nods.

"You were her *mentor*," Alexis snaps. "She sees herself in you. And right now, you are a man giving up. You think she hasn't thought about it? After what she and Lucas have had to endure with this place?"

Eliot tightens his hands into fists.

"You aren't here to tell her to close. She doesn't need that. She needs a reason to stay open. You need a reason to *keep going*. You need to give one more rebel yell against the dark, Eliot."

He closes his eyes. It would be so easy to lay down and not move from this spot, so easy to let it all go. But Death's words… They strike like a clock in his psyche. The flares from the aurora above meander over him as they begin to fade.

It was *too* easy to let go.

"All right." He stands up. "I was never about things being easy anyway."

"That's my guy," Death says the same way that Alexis used to say it and it fills him as he begins the long walk back toward Jackal.

17
JUKE BOX HERO

Eliot is only ten minutes down the road when he sees the headlights of Terry's van emerging over a hill. He slows and steps to the side of the lane as the van stops and his friend rolls down the window. "Eliot, what the hell man? Where did you go?"

"I went for a walk," he lies.

"Well, get in. We've got problems."

Eliot rounds the van and climbs into the passenger seat. "Did you find Lucas?"

Terry turns the wheel and executes a U-Turn. "He was in the radio station with a couple other guys trying to get things up and running. Sounds like there were some electrical problems which kept him there longer than he meant to be. But we succeeded!"

Eliot smiles. "The radio is up and running?"

Terry nods. "Problem is those speakers that used to be on the outsides of the tower aren't there anymore, so it's not going to help us with trying to lure any of the Ashen away."

"Hmm…" Eliot frowns. "Where's Lucas now?"

"On his way back to Milliner's to break the news to Nelly. I was going to follow him when I noticed you were gone. Left the door open, too…"

"I'm sorry," Eliot says. "I really needed to clear my head. But we should get back."

"Yeah. I've got a feeling Lucas will be sleeping on the roof tonight if you catch my drift." Terry turns on the radio and finds the local station. Foreigner hums out of the speakers on either side of them.

Soon enough, they see the pink glare of the lights from Milliner's, the lot, and all the battered vehicles in the lot surrounding it.

It clicks then. "Terry, I've got an idea."

"What?"

"Let's get inside."

They pull up as close as they can to the back entrance of the restaurant and get out. Terry tries to make as much of a path through the bodies as he can and Eliot follows in his wake. Inside, they're greeted by the sounds of soft voices talking beyond the kitchen door.

"So that's it?" Nelly asks. "There's no other way?"

"Unless we can find someone who knows how to install new speakers out there, then no. There isn't."

They push through the doors into the main room, Eliot taking the lead.

"Eliot," Lucas greets him, hesitance keeping him from going in for his handshake. He gives him a once over. "Where did you—"

"I've got a plan. Maybe," he interrupts. "The cars. The ones you used for a blockade outside. Are any of them still drivable?"

"A few," Lucas says. "I asked for whatever I could get from the salvage yard. But I know he drove a few of them here instead of putting them on the flatbed."

"Got the keys?"

Lucas walks to a drawer behind the bar and opens it, fishing out several sets of dingy looking car keys.

"Come on." He waves everyone toward the back doors. "We're going to move some."

...

It takes a bit of coordination. Eliot directs Terry and Lucas to drive each busted up car a little further down the road while Nelly watches and gives the okay from the roof of Milliner's. Only six of the cars still had any gas in them. Once they are all laid out in a line that stretches from the road in front of Milliner's all the way to the top of the hill a half mile out, Eliot reveals his next step: tune all the radios to the same station, leave the engines running, and turn up the volume starting with the car closest to the restaurant.

Lucas leans into the open driver's side door of the old coupe and finds the right station. It's playing Quiet Riot's *Cum On Feel the Noize*, the intensity growing as he jams his thumb onto the top side of the volume button.

The Ashen don't react from atop the hill.

"Louder," Eliot remarks from the roadside.

Lucas presses his finger on the button and the sound bursts from the old speakers in the car, echoing up the hill and into the night.

An Ashen turns its head, swaying to one side as it plants a boot in the grass, taking one step, now two as another peels away from the restaurant. Then another. Then several more.

"Yes!" Terry cheers from the driver's seat.

"It's working!" Lucas skitters out of the car and jumps back into the passenger seat.

"Get to the next one!" Eliot waves his arm.

The van rumbles along the dirt road to the next car: the truck with the windshield that Nelly had blasted out earlier in the night. Lucas dutifully jumps out; tunes the music in the truck to the same station and cranks up the volume dial until the entire vehicle vibrates.

A stream of Ashen tromp down across the wet lawn of Milliner's toward the road and the car. With the eruption from the second car, they continue past the first one, chasing the music and the increasing volume.

Lucas and Terry repeat the steps with the following three cars before Lucas climbs in the last one, sets the radio, and begins driving slowly down the road away from the other cars. As the Ashen make their way down the road away from Milliners, Eliot jumps into the first car and cuts the engine, shutting off the sound. Terry meets him at the second car with the van, and they turn that one off as well.

Quiet Riot fades into the distance as they shut off each car, and soon after, the Ashen in their slow methodical dirge, vanish along with the song.

The low hum of the lights above Milliner's are the only sound left in the area. Terry and Eliot return to the restaurant where Nelly greets them inside with tears in her eyes. "You smart son of a bitch," she says, giving Eliot a soft punch in the arm.

"You're going to have to keep doing it," he says. "You know that right?"

"We can get gas for the cars," she answers. "It's not as easy as it would have been if the tower still had its speakers, but…" She shrugs. "Who likes easy?"

Headlights shining out the window indicate Lucas's return. Once he's inside, they fire up the ovens, open the fridge, and pull out two slabs of pork ribs.

"You people are crazy," Terry says. "It's nearly three o'clock in the morning and y'all are going to start cooking ribs?"

Lucas laughs. "They should be ready in time for breakfast."

Terry shakes his head and looks at Eliot. "If you'll excuse me, I need my beauty sleep, thank you very much."

"There's a sofa in the office outback," Nelly offers. "May be lumpy but I've slept on it and survived plenty of nights."

Terry acquiesces and vanishes into the dark office around the corner.

Nelly rolls up her sleeves. "You ready?" she asks Eliot.

He does the same. "You need to know that I might get lost, Nelly."

She stares at him.

"I lose my senses and can't keep up."

Her gaze softens. "I've got you. You'll be all right."

They get started.

Lucas stokes the fire on the patio grill, the smoke wafting into the trailing night as clouds once again move in. The meat is all pre-cut, the pigs butchered the day before from a local farm. Lucas has gone in and trimmed the fat and the bone back to form beautiful racks of thick fat sluiced spareribs. The pale pink flesh glistens under the hot kitchen lights as Nelly rubs it with her own blend of spices: black pepper and cayenne, even some celery salt and dried mustard. Eliot adds alder wood kindling to the fire for added flavor.

They add four racks of meat to the iron grid once the coals turn white. The sizzle of it is music to their ears, the fat popping and crackling in almost no time. Nelly throws one of her mix tapes into her boombox in the kitchen, turns the speakers down so as not to wake Terry (or bring back their unwanted Ashen guests), and they let the rhythm of Tone Loc's *Wild Thing* infuse their movements.

Eliot closes his eyes, and lets the noise take over, lets the jam pump him up into a rhythm where every step he takes is on time. While Lucas monitors the meat on the fire, he and Nelly set about the kitchen to cook up sides. Nelly gives him direction as needed. A warm Panamanian Pink Potato Salad, baked beans with marbled cuts of bacon and wild rice, moist cornbread, collard greens, and hand cut sweet potato fries.

It's in the middle of mixing the potato salad that Eliot's right eye begins to sear. At first, he tries to power through it. He doesn't want it to stop him. He won't let it stop him.

But it overwhelms him, the whole right side of his face soon throbbing with the pain, enough that he stumbles to find the bathroom and barely makes it to the toilet before throwing up. He claws at the toilet paper roll and wipes his mouth on it, keeping his eyes closed against the torment assaulting his head.

Nelly's hand rolls over his shoulder. "Your eye?"

He nods, ramming the heel of his hand against his forehead. "Just hit me out of nowhere."

"Come on." She guides him out of the bathroom, finds him a bag of peas from their freezer, and tells him to hold it up against his face. He does so, the bag sagging in his grip. He knows the heat from his body will thaw it within a few minutes.

"What's next, El?" she asks. She's trying to keep him focused, trying to keep him from thinking about the pain.

"Salt and pepper."

She salts and peppers the potato salad and tastes it before adding a little more salt. She spoons a little into his mouth.

It's like someone feeding him warm plaster. He can't taste anything. In spite of it, he nods.

"Good."

When he tries to open his eyes again, everything is doused in brilliant scarlet. Almost immediately, he loses all his strength. "I need to sit down," he tells her as his legs buckle.

"Whoa," she tries to grab him, but they end up on the floor together, Eliot barely catching himself with one hand on the ground.

"Lucas! Get your butt in here!" Nelly calls.

Her husband appears a moment later, sweating, still holding the metal tongs in his hand. "Shit! What the hell happened?"

"The Ash."

Lucas picks up the exhausted Eliot and brings him into the darkened office.

Terry stirs from the couch at the sound. "What's going on?"

"We're tagging you in," Lucas says. "El needs to rest."

Terry unquestioningly gives up his spot and Lucas rolls the barely conscious Eliot onto the couch.

Nelly snaps on a light moments later and tells Lucas to go back out to the fire and watch the ribs. She crouches down in front of Eliot. He flinches when she puts a hand on his cheek. "It's okay. I know it hurts but just trust me." She cautiously peels back his eyelid. "Fuck," she mutters.

"What does that mean?" he murmurs through gritted teeth.

"Nothing," she answers quickly.

Nervously, "Terry, what does it mean?"

"It's—" he starts but Nelly clears her throat.

"What?" Eliot prompts.

"It's nothing, man."

Eliot groans. "It's *not* nothing. It feels like I've been shot in the face."

"You got ibuprofen or anything like that?" Terry asks Nelly.

Nelly vanishes for a moment before coming back with aspirin. She gives Eliot a couple along with a tall glass of water. He isn't sure but he swears he hears the hiss of something in his throat when he drinks.

"You just rest now," Nelly says. "We'll wake you when it's ready, okay?"

He nods because he doesn't want her to see how much it hurts. He doesn't want her to see the fact that he's suppressing the urge to scream against it. It's as if there's something in both eyes now, burrowing its way further down into his corneas.

He hears Nelly say something to the effect of, "I could really use your help out here," to Terry before she's gone from the room and it's just him and Eliot once more.

"Are you going to be okay if I leave you?"

Eliot nods though deep down, he's not sure. The pain is so intense, he isn't sure he is going to be able to see when he opens his eyes again. Is this it? Is this the last time he will ever see anything?

"You didn't just leave the van tonight, did you?" Terry asks him after a few minutes.

"No." He buries his head in the crooks of his arms. "Can you turn out the light? It hurts."

Terry cuts it and the room plunges into darkness.

It's an hour before sleep takes Eliot, and with every moment, he wishes he would go numb again just so he won't feel the pain. But it stays with him the entire time, twisting and burning in his head until the aspirin finally kicks in and dulls it a little, enough for him to pass out.

When he awakens, he's in the back office alone and the entire room smells like barbecue. His empty stomach pulls him up from the couch and into the doorway. The counter tops are full of magic: beautifully charred slabs of ribs gleaming with Nelly's homemade barbecue sauce, pink fluffy potato salad, homemade cornbread, and more delicacies, lots of it wrapped in tin foil, more scooped into stoneware dishes or left in frying pans to sizzle and keep warm with radiant heat.

The Pixies are softly emanating from the boombox which has been dragged out toward the flagstone patio, and he can hear distant giggling and murmured discussion. He scuffs to the door and sees Lucas, Nelly, and Terry all doubled over in laughter. The sight makes him smile.

"Does it make you feel better? Seeing their happiness?" Alexis asks from behind him.

"Yes," he answers hesitantly.

"That tone doesn't convince me."

He glances back at her. She's standing at the other end of the kitchen, wearing that fluffy alpaca sweater she wore the night he came to her apartment, the night she took care of him.

"The Ash is getting worse," he says, looking at his hands. It might be the poor lighting, but he swears he can see the tips of his fingers reddened as if in prelude to frostbite. "It's almost like it's killing me faster."

Death doesn't say anything, though there's a gleam in her green eyes that catches his attention.

"You know why."

"You're still giving in. In spite of all the good you're doing. You're letting it in. So, it keeps coming."

He blinks. "I don't have much time left, do I?"

He wants to believe it's Alexis reaching out for him, her fingers curling around his, her carved concern staring into his face. "It's taking you down faster than I thought it would."

"I still have two more stops to make," he says. "Las Vegas and then Montana. I just need to hold out for a little longer—"

"Eliot?"

He turns around to glance at the sound, and Alexis's touch vaporizes. Nelly stands in the doorway from the patio. "You okay?"

When he turns back, Death is gone.

"No."

She crosses the kitchen and sees her face drop a little when she takes him in. "Your eyes…" She pulls him into the bathroom and points to him in the mirror.

Eliot's skin grows cold. Both of his eyes are sparking in gold, fully lit and gleaming. He touches the skin under his left.

"Does it still hurt?" Nelly asks.

He nods. "Not as bad as before. Feels like there's chlorine in them or something. Like they're just really tired."

They exit the bathroom, and she takes his hand in hers. "I'm sorry."

He's quick to keep speaking. "What's that quote from Virginia Woolf? 'I am hungry, so I'll be okay.'"

She knits her brows. "'So long as you have food in your mouth, you have solved all questions for the time being.'"

"That's basically what I said."

Nelly calls out to Terry and Lucas as she guides Eliot toward the counter of food. "Let's dig in, guys!"

The ribs are heaven. Eliot can slip the bones out cleanly with his fingers and every forkful of the flakey meat melts in his mouth, the barbecue sauce tanging in his cheeks. There are places where he'll crackle into the bark and it's a welcome change in texture: smokey and more bitter. The corn bread is light, moist and sweet, sopping up the left behind barbecue sauce and dropped fat perfectly.

Forty-five minutes later, they've eaten their fill, stomachs rumbling in happy coalescence as they sip black coffee and discuss what's next in the timeline for Eliot's and Terry's drive. Las Vegas. Clive's restaurant, Les Contemplations, was there amidst the glitz and glamor of the strip, the hotels and the casinos.

"They'll have gates," Nelly warns them. "They'll be looking to make sure no one with the Ash gets in. Vegas already has an Ashen problem in the valley and the last thing they want is to have more coming into their upscale neighborhoods."

"I'm basically like a lit-up Christmas tree now," Eliot murmurs. "They'll take one look at me and know I'm turning."

Nelly stands up. "I have something I think might help." She vanishes into the kitchen and then into the back office for a moment before she comes back with a pair of sunglasses in her hand.

"Didn't think anyone really wore these anymore," Terry chuckles. "Unless your blind, I guess. We don't exactly get much sun anymore."

"I kept them from the old days," she says, fitting the Wayfarer Aviators over Eliot's eyes, their golden accents gleaming. "There. You look like a rock star now."

He huffs. "I feel like one, too. All strung out on drugs, body parts failing left and right..."

"Since you don't have any other visual symptoms that call you out as an Ashen yet, you should be able to get into the city," Nelly says. "And once you're in, Clive can take care of you."

Eliot nods as a bubble of anxiety rises in him. It's been years since he and Clive talked, years since the scandal that Alexis ignited to try and destroy his career, since Clive cut ties to shield his own.

Will Clive even let him in? Will Clive want to keep his distance even knowing that Eliot is on his last legs?

The group say their last goodbyes as Terry and Eliot pack up their van. Nelly puts together a small picnic for them for the road and Lucas gives them a few hundred bucks to stay at a motel if they need to, for food, for clothes and gas.

Eliot hugs Nelly and she holds onto him tightly. "I'll never get to tell you it again," she says. "So, you need to know how much you've meant to me, Eliot Lamb. Milliner's wouldn't exist without you. I just wish you could see how much you matter for yourself."

He doesn't know how to react to her last sentence. He wants to say something witty and deflecting but knows this is it: the last time he'll ever see Nelly again, the last time he'll behold her beautiful smile, hear her assertive tone and taste her food. So, he just closes his eyes, holds her closer and says, "Thank you."

With his sunglasses on and the entire van smelling like the tang and charcoal of barbecue, Eliot and Terry leave Milliner's behind.

IMPEDIMENT

FIFTH OBSERVATION

Not all the Ashen can survive here in the Vast. It's basic math. There are too many dangerous impediments for them to come across and, in their mindlessness, they lack the wherewithal to even understand that they are stuck or doomed.

Such is the case with this one: it's hung up on a fence in what was once a cow pasture. The grass is overgrown but also lost in at least a foot of murky water in the low spots. The Ashen pushes against the wire to the point where its barbs are shredding cloth, shredding skin…
This is how some things die. Not die, but cease to be. It's going to tear itself apart like an octopus self-mutilating. Like love does to two unsuspecting people.

But…
A truck has driven up on the side of the road, headlights blasting through the fog. A man gets out in rubber bibs and tall boots and sloshes down the embankment to the caught Ashen. He nips all four wires and stands clear as the Ashen stumbles through, catching itself

in the tangle of discarded metal momentarily before they free themselves, clothes ripping in the process. They resume their trudge up the small hill to the road and then beyond.

"Wouldn't you free a trapped animal if you saw it?" the man tells me.

"It's not an animal," I argue.

"Wouldn't you try to free anything that's trapped?" he answers. "Especially if it can't help itself?"

Do the Ashen deserve our pity or our ambivalence?

Are we interfering with nature's will if we save them or are we merely prolonging a process that, in time, will do more damage than good?

LEFT LOG #4

TAKE WARNING

Headlee is a smear in the fog behind them along with countless other cities as they continue their drive across the Midwestern sprawl. For much of the journey, it feels like time has stood still, the light barely changing and the little Camaro effused with the spirit of a dreary march onward in dogged pursuit of something. Left feels alone, his own thoughts about Lamb's guilt beginning to turn with the pieces of the Psychologist's convincing argument steadily ticking into place.

Perhaps it was all just coincidence that had put Lamb in the path of those bombings in Getty? Perhaps Justin Nguyen had had some prior beef with Munroe that had caused him to target her. Or maybe Nguyen wasn't even involved in Munroe's bombing. The bank had seemed an incredibly odd choice to Left for some time as it didn't fit in with the Psychologist's and Right's carefully considered story about creative expression being destroyed by True Faith.

"You know they were hosting art, right?" the Psychologist says at one point during their drive as he lists the inaccuracies out loud. "While we were stopped in St. Louis, I checked with my source at the Getty Tribune. She said they ran a story back in April about accepting a batch of paintings by some local artist to put on display there. So, it does fit."

Left takes the longest and deepest breath he can muster and holds it as he continues to drive them along.

The next location that Lamb had marked on his map was devoid of most life with exception of a barbecue joint that is open and thriving when they arrive, and later on down the road, a horde of Ashen making their way lazily toward, again…something. The owners of the barbecue joint, Nelly and Lucas Fricasse, don't give anything away, insisting they haven't seen Lamb in years, but Left is sure they're lying. He notes a photo that's set up in Fricasse's office depicting a younger Eliot and both of them and another man drinking. It's not dusty like most everything else.

It's another day before they are through the rest of Missouri and into Kansas. The open roads, flat fields, and never-shifting telephone poles begin to grate on him the further they drive. There was *nothing* out here. Why the hell was Lamb doing this when he was about to die? Some kind of insane bucket list? Or was he motivating True Faith with every little town he pushed through, nudging them toward further carnage?

They stop at a rest area somewhere between Soloman and Trenton and the weary travelers unload and splinter to do their requisite business: pee, find food, and take a break from each other for however long they can before they have to climb in the car again.

Left finds himself standing in line at the convenience store with a few packages of corn chips in his hand and a bottle of Sunkist.

He's not sure why he's grabbed it. Maybe because it reminds him of what he's doing all this for. It's been almost a week since he last heard Right's voice. The memory that sticks in his head is her complaining about traffic. About some car on I-90 that had nearly caused an accident. He remembered how her lips moved, how he watched the cupid's bow of her mouth pronounce and vanish with each thought spoken aloud. He thought about her short, bristly dark hair and how he wished he had been able to brush his hand through it just once.

And he thinks about what he learned from the Psychologist. That she and Right were playing tonsil tennis during the course of her involvement on the case. He hadn't bothered to ask at the time because he was so stunned and maybe because he didn't care but… had their relationship been deeper than sex? Was that why the Psychologist had implied those things about him not really loving Right?

By the time he's checked out and is standing back in the middle of the rest area, he isn't sure he wants to get back in the car with either the Psychologist or Meena. Maybe he could leave them behind and finish the journey with the cat. At least she had settled down over the last twenty-four hours of travel, sleeping on the floor of the backseat for most of the ride without a care in the world.

A hand touches his arm, and he nearly jumps out of his skin before he sees Meena's face painted in an equal amount of shock. He silently curses.

"Where is the Psychologist?" Meena asks.

"No idea." He searches the area. There's a bus full of summer school kids all standing in lines for various fast-food eateries and dozens of couples and families all milling about the food court center of the rest stop, taking photos, playing on arcade games, whining, screaming, laughing…

Meena shrugs. "Maybe she's still in the bathroom."

Left yawns and checks his watch. "It's already three o'clock. We're wasting daylight here."

"Do you have a take-it-easy setting?" she asked.

"'Scuse me?"

"You've been going at a solid eleven ever since we left Getty. You're going to burn yourself out if you don't give yourself a break."

Burn out: the word strikes him like a sharp stick sticking in him and he's suddenly uncomfortable. He frowns at her. "I don't need your mothering, Ms. Hernandez. I'm perfectly capable of handling myself."

"Really?" Her brown eyes grow serious. "Tell me, agent, what do you do in your off time when you're not hunting down delusional killers with religious agendas. I'd love to know."

"I sit around waiting for someone like you to tell me how to behave."

She glares at him. "Smart mouth."

"At least some part of me is," he jeers.

"Why are you always so comfortable with derision?" Meena asks. "Just seems like an awful lot of effort to go through to convince people that the broken pieces aren't actually broken."

His eyebrows rise. "Listen, I never asked for either you to tag along and now every time I tell you to pick up the pace, one of you tries to psychoanalyze me like I'm the one with the problem. It's obnoxious."

"She's right."

The Psychologist's voice is right beside him and it sends spears of fright through him. "Definitely some classic burnt out behavior." she says softly.

"Just stop it," he orders. "Both of you."

Meena cocks her head at him, and the Psychologist scratches her forehead.

They leave the rest area, Left walking slightly faster than the two women. When they get to the car, he frowns. The cat, who had been soundly asleep in the back seat is now gone. The Psychologist had left the back window down.

"Oh, no!" Meena shouts. She drops onto her hands and knees and looks under the car. "Here, Apple. Here, kitty kitty."

"For fucks sake…" he grumbles.

They spread out in search of the cat. Left walks into the wooded area next to the car, allowing himself to enjoy the rustle of the wind in the trees as he checks beneath benches and picnic tables for the frightened feline.

He remembers doing this with Brooke after her dog ran away once. They drove the length of their street back and forth, back and forth, as she cried and he prayed to some higher power that a car hadn't hit the poor pup. They'd found him in the park eventually, splashing around in the fountain with his tongue lolling happily.

"Hey!" someone shouts. He looks across the green toward a family using one of the municipal barbecues and focuses on the cat, Apple, being fed by one of the children there. The father is trying to frantically shoo it away.

Left jogs to the group and quickly picks up the feline. "Sorry."

"Who the hell takes a cat on a road trip?" the dad mutters to his wife as Left walks away.

"Thank God," says Meena, when he returns to the car and dumps the cat in her lap. She coos to the animal while he glances around, searching for the Psychologist. She's exploring across the lot, hasn't seen that he's found the feline. He waves to her to get her attention.

Meena puts a hand on his arm and it catches him off guard. "Thanks. Really."

He shakes his head. "Don't mention it."

There are tears in her eyes and all at once, Left's stomach drops. He scuffs his shoe against the pavement and adds, "I'm sorry about what I said back in Headlee. That was classified information about Lamb. I shouldn't have let it slip."

Hernandez exhales, the curls framing her face bouncing with the burst of air. "I always thought there was something. Eliot is such a giving person, but there was always this pain in him. I had no idea it was that. That he felt he couldn't love who he wanted to love publicly. I don't think I ever saw him with anyone in that way, let alone another man. He never showed any signs."

Left stays silent. He knows better than to speak his thoughts out loud at this point because it will only start another argument. But the fact that Lamb kept his homosexuality a secret, even from those close to him meant he was capable of keeping secrets, perhaps darker ones than this. Could he still be the one they were after?

The Psychologist returned to the car, apologetic about letting the cat out and promised she'd be more careful the rest of their drive. They get back on the road.

18

I WEAR MY SUNGLASSES AT NIGHT

1986

"What the hell has happened to this town?" Clive asks Eliot as they stare out from the balcony of Eliot's old apartment, sipping Old Fashioneds. Clive's only been back in the city for a few days but Eliot senses a pessimism in his mentor. Clive always carries a cynicism around with him that he seems to play internal tetherball with: slapping it back to give compliments and hopeful sentiments to new and upcoming venues, cooks, and ideas only for him to strike it the other way a few months later with derision and snide commentary about how things are changing for the worse. Eliot can't figure out where the seemingly violent alternating comes from, or what spurs it, but it gives him pause. He always knows to be cautious around Clive when he is in *this* particular mood.

But this question about Getty unnerves Eliot. The thought that Clive would take issue with the place where he lives, where he had helped to motivate a culinary movement. He takes it more personally than he should. "What do you mean?" he asks.

"I mean, you used to be able to walk down some of these alleys and get that sting of adrenaline on the back of your tongue," answers Clive, taking a slug of his drink. "I mean, there were all kinds of places with unsavory people around here, but they were institutions! History *happened* there. And now it's replaced with these obnoxious touristy joints. Everyone wants the authentic Getty taste as long as it looks exactly the same as everyone else's and they don't have to search in the dark alleys for it."

Eliot shakes his head. "I can't tell what you're more upset about: that your favorite eateries have fewer holes in their walls or that there's nowhere to park your car on the main strip?"

"It's not just redevelopment, my friend," asserts Clive, finishing his drink. "It's gentrification! The old and the good being pushed out by the rich and the pompous. And we started the movement because we're two self-important white guys with dreams of seeing ourselves in glowing reviews and hearing our names mentioned favorably in food critic's columns."

Eliot turns and walks back into his apartment. "So, what do you want to do about it?" His apartment building overlooks the arts district, the golden glow of a part of Getty subsumed by folly and laughter and wonder. Tempo stands just at its edge as if a welcoming pillar to the beauty that visiting people would find there in Getty.

"There's nothing that can be *done*..." Clive says.

"So, you just want to complain?"

"Yeah! I want to complain. And then I want to go out and get wasted and forget about it for a bit." Clive sets his empty glass on the bar cart in the living room and follows Eliot inside. "Where is that friend of yours? Harvey? Why don't you give him a call? Give Alexis a call. We can all go out and get some pizza, find a place to hole up in for a while?"

Eliot clears his throat. "Why don't we just go out, huh? The two of us?"

"I told you. I've gotta leave town tomorrow. I've got that early meeting with the publisher in Chicago." Clive grabs his jacket from where it's hung on hooks by the front door. "Besides, I haven't seen Alexis in a long time. I want to know how she's holding up under your brutalist regime. I hope you're not pissing her off, man. And that Harvey guy? Last time I was out here, you two were practically inseparable."

Harvey's face flashes through Eliot's mind for only a moment. "Maybe I'll stay here then."

Clive freezes, shooting him a 'what-the-fuck' expression.

"I've got some stuff to do. You guys will have more fun without me."

"What do you mean you've 'got stuff to do?'" Clive sasses. "You're working too hard, Eliot. Come on, give yourself a break."

"Harvey and I aren't really talking, Clive," he finally says. "And yeah, I've got *stuff*." Eliot walks into the living room, pours himself another drink, and tries to ignore the look of derision he knows his mentor is giving him at that moment.

"What the hell does that mean? 'Not really talking?'" Clive slides around the couch and slumps onto it. "Was it a fight? Did he and Alexis hook up or something?"

The insinuation is enough to burn down Eliot's already withered wick to the bottom of his proverbial candle. Nervous laughter erupts out of his mouth moments before he can stop it. "Jesus Christ," he mutters through it, unable to stop, and retreats to the kitchen nearby.

"You're acting fucking weird," Clive says. "Stop walking away from me and tell me what the fuck is going on."

"Really? Seriously?" Eliot yells over his shoulder as he sets the glass down on the counter and turns back around. "He's gay, Clive! And he's not fucking Alexis."

"But he was fucking *you*," answers Clive, and catching Eliot's raised eyebrows continues, "Don't give me that look. I've known you were gay ever since that time I saw you sing *I Will Survive* at karaoke."

Eliot glares. "Ha…ha," he grumbles. "And to your point: no. We weren't. That was the whole problem."

Clive stalks up to the countertop that separates the living room from the kitchen and throws one of his long legs over a bar stool there to sit. "What? You weren't into him like that? Seems like this wouldn't be so complicated if you *had* just fucked him."

Closing his eyes, Eliot opens a porcelain dish on the counter and grabs bulbs of garlic out of it. "Not all of us are so cavalier about our romantic encounters, Clive."

"Are you worried about AIDS or something?"

"*Of course,* I am." Eliot stares at Clive, his brows furrowing. "But that's not why."

"Then what?"

"Sex isn't important to me," says Eliot, squashing the garlic clove under the flat of a chef's knife. "It's not why I was attracted to Harvey in the first place. But he doesn't understand it. And he won't. Just like you won't."

Clive puts both of his palms down on the counter between them. "You're right; I don't understand it. But if you want to be celibate, then fine! Find yourself another good-looking fag and then move on!"

Eliot cringes. "Don't say that word, please."

"What? Celibate?"

"You know which one."

Clive pushes off against the counter and stands.

"Where are you going?"

"I'm going out like you wanted me to," says Clive, moving toward the front door. "You're going to stay here and brood like you normally do."

"Fine. Go." Eliot shakes his head and gives the chef's knife a wave. "It's not like you were really listening to me anyway."

"Listening to you isn't my job. Go call up your next conquest for that, seeing as how that's all you need them for." The door slams behind him.

· · ·

They see the lights of Las Vegas from almost fifty miles out. The days since they left Jackal have been especially rough on Eliot and poor Terry has taken the brunt of the driving responsibility because of it.

The pain behind Eliot's eyes is always there. Sometimes it's so bad that he finds himself reclined in the passenger seat, curled in a fetal position as he tries and fails to keep from whimpering. In the moments it's not so bad, something else is. There is a whole hour period where he thought things were fine and stared out the window at the hazy landscape in complete awe before he realized that Terry had been talking to him and he hadn't heard a word of it. He hadn't heard a thing: not the movement of the van's tires over the landscape, not the rain spatting against the metal or the windshield, not even his own internal breaths. And when the sound came back, it rushed in like a windstorm, assaulting him with a loud fury that made him shrink in his seat.

There is also a scratching in his throat now. It began as a little tingling early in the second morning and had developed into something of a persistent cough by that afternoon, and now, this. Terry had stopped for cough drops at one point and Eliot is now on his fifth one, everything tasting and somehow smelling like metallic cherries.

But Vegas! It is so close now and its closeness brings relief as much as it brings trepidation. It has been three years. Three *years*. What can Eliot do to Clive except ask for an apology and apologize in return? After all, Clive has a chain of restaurants, several cookbooks, a television show in the works, and dozens of accolades and awards to boot. He doesn't need anything from Eliot.

Maybe he *wants* something?

"We're almost there," Terry says. He practically says the words in a sigh, and it makes Eliot wish he could do something to help. This was exactly why he hadn't wanted to go to a care facility. It was exactly why he had wanted to stay in his apartment until the end. He wouldn't be making anyone fuss over him. He wouldn't be a burden.

"You hearing me, man?"

"I did this time. Yeah."

"What do you want to do once we get into the city? Are we going to find a place to crash? Do you want to go straight to Clive's place?"

He hears the exhaustion in Terry's voice at the latter sentence and quickly shakes his head. "No. Let's find a hotel. I'll call Clive and see if we can meet up for lunch tomorrow. It's late now and if he's not three sheets to the wind with his head in between a girl's legs, then it's probably an off night for him."

"Oooh, all right," Terry hoots. "I'm detecting some bitterness maybe."

Eliot catches the small smile on Terry's face and scoffs. "He and I had a bit of a falling out."

"He was your mentor, right? Figured you'd be on good terms with him. Are we going to have to sneak you in with a disguise or something?"

"No." Eliot laughs and coughs. "Not unless I show up with something from Benjamin Schott's restaurant in a bag anyway."

"Ooh, I like him!" Terry turns the van off from the overpass onto an off-ramp. "He had that show on PBS, didn't he? He does those cooking competitions in different states? *Beat Benjamin Schott*?"

"Yeah," Eliot chuckles. "Novel idea. I'm sure everyone will have a show like that come out sooner or later."

"They will."

The voice comes from somewhere in the back of the van and it makes all the hair on Eliot's arms prickle.

Terry continues as if he hasn't heard anything. "Imagine hating someone like Benjamin Schott. Seems like a pretty nice guy to me."

"We all seem like nice guys, Terry," Eliot says. "Just wait until we have a knife in our hand and we're barking orders."

"Hard to imagine you barking anything," Terry answers. "You just don't seem like the type. You or Benjamin Schott."

Terry takes the van through various roundabouts, passing under dark bridges and overpasses, through tunnels and along construction clogged routes. The city doesn't so much as smash itself over their heads with a hammer as it does leap out from behind a very dark, very boring section of industrial looking buildings. But there it is: the lights. The traffic swallows them, engulfing them in wide lanes hedged by giddy blinking neon lights of every shade, rustling palm trees, horns honking, police sirens shrieking, and a variety of music emanating from every street vendor stand, every hotel door, every impromptu and strangely themed wedding chapel they passed by.

Eliot sees at least three with Elvis themes, two with extraterrestrial aliens out front, and one with a dog theme? He isn't going to question it.

Terry pulls them into the first motel block he can find: a place with two floors of rooms tucked just off the strip. The doors are all the same shade of off maroon, the walls between each one a swimming pool blue and lit by flickering fluorescents that seem to have barely survived their inception in the forties. Terry goes to take care of the room while Eliot stays in the car and glances around the place.

It is a full house that night, packed with cars visiting from various states: Idaho, Wyoming, Texas, California. There was even one from Alabama.

Terry gets back in the car. "Fucker is gonna get his ass kicked if he turns up his radio any louder."

Eliot frowns. "What?"

"Guy at the front desk is listening to some religious propaganda shit. In this town? Seems like he's in the wrong place to me."

Eliot nods.

Their room has two single beds. A color TV with a decent selection of cable channels. A telephone. A yellowed shower and tub in the bathroom gives Eliot pause. Harvey would have called it "scody".

Terry goes in search of dinner, not promising any profound culinarian gastronomies.

While he's gone, Eliot calls Clive's restaurant in the off chance he still might be there. There is no phone book in the room, so he walks across the magenta-highlighted parking lot to the front desk. The attendant sits in his weathered vinyl seat behind the counter, while watching an episode of Wheel of Fortune on the dingy little TV mounted in the upper left corner. He has on a worn jean jacket and slacks, his hair balding but shaggy toward the back. Nearby, an old radio blares, the station drowning out the sounds of the television with its static-filled rendition of "How Great Thou Art."

Eliot asks for the phone book and the attendant plops one up on the counter after a moment. When Eliot tries to slide it away, he slaps a hand down on it. "It's the only one I've got. So, make sure you bring it back."

Eliot promises and walks stiffly back to his room with the beat-up and dog-eared book. He finds the number for Les Contemplations and dials it. The answering machine picks it up. He doesn't bother leaving a message. It's almost eleven o'clock. Dinner service is over. If Clive is still there, he'll be helping clean up the kitchen and likely won't be answering the phone. He'll try again tomorrow.

He copies the number down on the room's one notepad and then diligently brings the phone book back. As he enters the tepid little office once more, he hears a voice speaking on the radio.

"…emancipation from our own fleshy prisons. We are cast in his likeness, yet our souls search for freedom, search for a release that only He can give us. He is calling us home, children. Some of us have heard the call. We have to help those chosen to find their way…"

"The phone book?"

Eliot gasps when he notices the attendant standing with his hand out toward him. He hands over the book and turns to leave.

"Strange," says the attendant, and Eliot glances halfway back over his shoulder.

"What?"

"Wearing sunglasses at night." The attendant cocks his head.

Eliot quickly returns to his hotel room.

Terry returns, having found them some take-out food for dinner of five-dollar steaks which are nearly impossible to cut through but don't taste half bad, French fries, and slushies from a nearby convenience store.

They eat quietly while watching *Seinfeld*. Eliot is only able to eat some of his dinner before his taste vanishes again and his eyes start stinging. He pulls the covers up over him and somehow finds sleep.

In the middle of the morning, he wakes up. Sweat covers his skin; the sheets soaked through. His breathing is heavy, throat burning as he struggles to figure out what was happening. The room is *so* hot. Why is everything *so hot*?

Clambering out of bed, he staggers to the bathroom and closes the door. Spinning the faucet wildly in the tub, a torrent of water pours out from the spout. He strips and climbs in, the cold an instant relief. So cold it was almost chilly. *Almost.*

. . .

1986

The phone call comes as he is getting ready for brunch service. It's Mother's Day and one of the only times of the year he opens Tempo up earlier in the day. He's done this brunch for four years and counting now, having the routine down well enough that it doesn't feel new or strange anymore. This Mother's Day, the menu revolves around the tomato, an idea he's conceived because of the historical significance of mothers and grandmothers in cooking of traditional Italian food.

He thinks about his own mother off and on, about the last time he saw her years ago when she called him out of the blue and told him to come home. His father was in the hospital. He needed to be there, she'd told him. And he'd gone, like a son was expected to. He'd watched his father lay on life support and tell him how he wished Eliot would have done something with his life. How he wished that those sessions with the doctor back when he was a child would have done some good.

Any remorse his father had felt for putting him in those conversion sessions was immediately revoked and with it, Eliot felt his own lingering respect for the man dither. Before he'd left, he'd told his mother everything.

One week later, they were both dead. He wasn't sure if it was because of what he'd said but he felt it was true. He'd been the one to cut both of their lives short. His mother had died of heartbreak and his father had died being ratted out. His brother's call was a soundtrack of hatred before and after Eliot refused to visit for the joint funeral although he'd helped pay for it. When he refused to go back home and help his brother go through his parents' belongings. In the end, Grady had sent whatever hadn't fit in storage, or his own house which ended up being several boxes from the basement and the attic, the pieces of his parents' lives that they'd shed like skins to become who they were when he grew up.

But that was all years ago. Every Mother's Day, he thinks of his mother and how he cruelly snuffed out her life because of his own pain. He makes tomatoes four ways in her honor: oven roasted with oregano and mozzarella, mashed into a rustic Bolognese sauce with gnocchi, baked into an heirloom tomato pie, and pureed into a delicate gazpacho. Each is a recipe she perfected and served via family parties and get togethers in his youth. Each is a tribute to someone who had done nothing wrong other than not open her eyes to what was happening behind her back.

This phone call isn't about her.

But, like others he's taken, Death plays her part in ensuring he receives it.

It is a nurse calling from a hospital in Pittsburgh. They've had a patient die in urgent care who has left a letter for him.

"I don't understand. Who was the patient?" he asks, balancing a wooden spoon between his index and ring finger of his unoccupied hand.

"Harvey Denman."

His cheeks flush. "That can't be right." He drops the spoon, and it clatters across the floor away from him. "You have to be wrong."

But they aren't. And as the nurse reassures him it is the correct name, Eliot stares through his paper of cook times for each dish coordinated between each station. The operations. The cogs behind the beauty on the plate. Each part broken apart from the whole. Eliot thinks about Harvey lying broken on a hospital bed before he died.

"How did he die?"

"We're not at liberty to say."

"What?"

"Unless you're next of kin, we can't tell you what happened."

"But, he was my…" The sentence is gone. He'd let Harvey go. They weren't together, hadn't been together in several months. He wasn't even sure where Harvey had gone but now…he knew.

The nurses ask for his address to send the letter, and he gave it to them before hanging up.

Alexis passes through the hallway to the back office, her apron on, eyes intense. "You ready to go?" she asks him as he slumps in the chair, watching the dropped spoon.

"Yeah." The word is distant, not in the same room as them. It drifts up and out as if it belongs somewhere only the wind can take it.

She kneels and picks up the wooden spoon. "You okay? What was that phone call ab—"

"I'm fine," he cuts her off. "I'll see you out there."

Giving a nod, she continues on her way.

And still, somehow, the world doesn't fall apart. Eliot stares and stares and stares into his shoes and the floor and whatever dust and dirt lies past them as if trying to discern it with X-ray vision. When he finally stands up, he is measured, composed: the same old Eliot. He meets Alexis in the kitchen with the rest of the cooks, lays out the plan, and they execute it flawlessly. Every time he thinks he is straying, he pinches himself to stay in the moment.

They have a record Mother's Day. They'll need to prepare dinner service, but are out of a few essentials and he is in charge of family meal that night. He is out of lemons. So, he leaves for the farmer's market, manages about a block, and breaks down in an alley between buildings sobbing uncontrollably. When he returns, he makes sure he looks like nothing has happened.

Family meal and dinner service go off without a hitch.

19

IT'S A SIN

"**E**liot!"

The name jars him awake.

It's cold. It's *so* cold.

He shivers, and as he tries to move, water thrashes around him. Terry leans over him.

"You left the water on," Terry whispers. "The people in the room downstairs noticed it coming through their ceiling and called that mook at the front office."

Eliot sits up and crosses his arms. "I was so hot... I just needed to do something to—"

"Is he all right in there?" A woman shouts from somewhere outside the bathroom and it makes Eliot clam up immediately.

"Yeah. You can go on now," Terry calls to them.

"Our bathroom is so fucked up," Eliot hears someone say to the woman as their hotel room door closes. He looks at Terry. "I'll get out. Just give me some privacy."

Terry leaves. Eliot can tell by the lighting that it's morning which he's thankful for. He gets out and puts back on his boxers and the white tank top he'd had on last night. Both feel grimy.

As he rounds the corner, Terry is sitting on his bed expectantly, fingers threaded together. With one look at Eliot, he stands up and begins pacing. "Listen, El. Someone's got to be the one that says this and since I signed myself up for this crazy ass ride across the country, it's going to be me. We should think about getting you somewhere where someone can properly care for you."

Eliot stands there, jeans in hand, and immediately feels like less than himself. He exhales. "I knew it was only a matter of time."

"What?" Terry asks.

"I know this whole thing was crazy," he says, with an ironic smile on his face. "Trust me. I *do* know."

Terry's eyes grow serious. "I'm not saying this just to try and weasel my way out."

"You have every right, Terry." Eliot puts his jeans on and zips the fly, then grabs the navy-blue shirt nearby. "I'm not taking it personally."

Terry's bottom lip curls in as he cocks his head. "See! That's just the thing, you are!"

He puts the shirt on. "I'm not."

"Usually, I'm not the worrying type," Terry adds. "But when you disappeared out of the van in Jackal... You passing out with the water on like this... What if you'd drowned in your sleep? It's too much and I don't want to be the one to have let it happen to you."

Eliot sits on his bed opposite Terry. He knows Terry leapt into this with the fantasy that he was helping, that he was doing good for a dying man, that he was helping a dream come true. But he hadn't realized the cost. He hadn't understood just how much responsibility he was taking on. And Eliot realizes now he hadn't been ready for all of it, for any of it.

"Whatever happens to me, it's not your obligation—understand?" Eliot tells him.

"Obligation?" Terry frowns. "*Obligation*? I'm your friend, Eliot. I'm not saying any of this because I want to hightail it out of here. I'm saying it because I'm afraid of what could happen next when I'm not paying attention."

"Which is why I'm going to go to a clinic after I talk to Clive." Eliot stares down at his shoes as he puts them on. "The pain is worse than I imagined it would be. If I lose my marbles there, at least it'll be with veins full of opioids."

They shared glances with one another, then the inanimate objects of the small awkward hotel room, then themselves once more. "I'll see if I can get through to Clive. Odds are he's already at the restaurant getting prepped for a big night," he adds.

"Okay," Terry whispers. "I'm going to go get the van ready. I think we should get the fuck out of here before that hotel attendant decides to charge us for any damages." He scoots out the door and shuts it behind him.

Alone in the musty room, Eliot sinks down onto his bed and closes his eyes for a moment. They hurt so much, especially in the bright light from the lamp on his bedside table. He clicks it off and picks up the phone, dials the number for Les Contemplations. It rings once, twice, and is in the middle of a third when someone picks up the phone. Not Clive.

"Hello, I'm calling for Clive, please."

"You people just keep on calling…" the man on the other end grumbles. "I've said no comment, and I mean no comment! There's no story here—"

"Whoa, whoa!" Eliot frowns. "I'm not a reporter. I'm an old friend of his. I just wanted to talk with him."

"Oh," the man gasps. "I'm surprised you haven't heard anything yet. I'm sorry to have to be the one to tell you this but Clive passed away."

All the air in Eliot's lungs evaporates. His jaw locks even as he tries to say, "Wait. What?"

"I'm so sorry." The man sounds like it, too, and Eliot has a tangent thought about how many times he's had to deliver this news.

"When did it happen?" he asks.

"A few days ago. He overdosed."

Eliot pinches his nose beneath his glasses to keep the tears back and sniffs. "God…"

"I haven't heard any plans for a burial yet. When I do, I can let you know. Do you have a telephone number I can reach you at?"

He swallows hard, says, "No. It's okay" and hangs up.

Movement seems impossible. The only motion he can make is putting the phone back in its cradle and then staring blankly at the wall. Everything feels heavy, a sponge sopping full of moisture, pulling him down. He topples sideways onto the bed as all sensation creeps away from him, as if he's been blown out by a strong gust.

Clive is gone.

Clive is *dead*.

You lied to me, he thinks as he pictures Death wrapping her hands around him in Alexis's form a few days ago.

"What good would lying do?"

A tall, lean shadow falls over him. The voice would have sent chills through him if he could feel them. Something spurs deep in his chest, and he wants to get up, he wants to turn his head and see the shadow's owner standing on the other side of the bed because he knows it'll be Clive or at least, something that looks like him anyway.

He grunts as he tries to make sounds into words and force them out of his mouth, but it's garbled. He can't move. He can't talk. Panic skips across his brain as he thinks each word: *You killed him and still brought me all the way out here...*

Not-Clive laughs. God, how he *misses* that sound. "I didn't bring you out here for *him*, dummy."

Then why?

"That's for you to find out."

The shadow rotates and he watches it vanish slowly back across the floor, then the bed, until it dissipates.

He exhales and feels residual tears begin to fall, the tickle of them sliding down over the bridge of his nose and across his face. He tries to move again, the strain centered in his chest as he forces, forces, *forces*...but nothing moves. All he can do is lay there and make awkward noises that barely emanate from his closed mouth. He can't even scream.

Pretty soon his neck begins to hurt. Then his lower back.

It feels like eons pass in only a few minutes as he fights to win back autonomy and flails mentally in the misery of losing Clive.

The door eventually opens and the swath of light peels in before the lights come on. Eliot knows by the steps that it's Terry, even before his friend says his name and appears at the edge of his vision. "I was waiting in the van for you and…" He trails off. "Shit, are you okay?"

Eliot moans.

"Oh my God."

Terry springs into action, rounding the bed and grabbing hold of Eliot's torso to try and help him up. Eliot's head lolls as he heaves with the effort. It doesn't take long for Terry to lose his grasp and for Eliot to flop back the way he was, the extra weight popping muscles in his left hip and intensifying the pain. Terry grabs his legs instead and hauls them up onto the bed so that he's prone. Then, he crouches down in front of him. "I'm going to go borrow the phone book from the front desk so I can call a clinic, okay?"

No. He doesn't want this. Not yet. He's not ready yet. But he can't move his tongue and every sound that comes out of him sounds the same: painful, horrible, bestial.

"Be right back." Terry leaves him again.

Alone.

Again.

Time is infinite.

He can hear the sounds of the television set in the room next to them blaring. Something with a lot of squealing tires and guns shooting and terrible yelling. Or maybe it was the people staying in the room who were yelling at one another. Screaming.

He closes his eyes to it and Clive is there in the darkness. The friend he wishes he hadn't lost. Another person he never got to settle things with. His mentor. His best friend.

Footfalls on the stairs send trepidation skipping through his brain shortly before he hears Terry's voice in the parking lot far below. "No! Get off me!"

Someone had him. Police? Someone was—

"He's not up there!" Terry yells.

Why would Terry say that? Unless—

Instinct plummets like a meteor shower through Eliot's body as he tries to roll and does so with surprising efficiency, tumbling off the bed to the floor between it and the wall. Grunting, he shimmies under his bed as best he can.

The door to the hotel room squeals open.

Eliot can barely see anything under the bed skirt as he tilts his head in that direction.

The shadow falls over the room. Then a second.

"Fuck, he's not here…" someone growls.

"Larry said he was up here. Said he didn't see him leave after he returned the phone book," the other man argues.

Pressure on the bed above him makes the springs squeal and Eliot closes his eyes as the mattress bows down toward him.

"It's still warm," the first guy says.

"We must have just missed him. Come on!"

The door squeaks as the two of them leave.

Eliot exhales, not realizing he'd been holding his breath the whole time. He stays hidden, listening to the noises outside the room and trying to predict where the men went. A moment later, he hears the door peel open again and someone say, "Yeah, he's not here" before the footsteps retreat down toward the stairs back down to the parking lot.

Shuffling out from under the bed, Eliot sneaks to the window and looks out. Four men are putting Terry in the back of a large, brown van while another talks to Larry, the front desk clerk.

A family of four is watching everything as they pack their car across the lot, their faces carved in concern. Another man stands outside his hotel room staring at the scene.

"Too much attention here," the man talking to Larry says. "Meet us later?"

Larry nods, and the men take their leave without him, the van rumbling out of the lot with Terry in it.

Eliot's skin vibrates with terror. Even as he questions who these men are and why they are so interested in him and Terry, he knows he can't leave his room until Larry makes his exit. Terry's van keys glisten from the nightstand where he left them.

He'll have to stay put.

The prospect fills him with dread but there's nothing else he can do.

He hunkers into the most comfortable position he can and waits.

...

It is late. The apartment still smells like the Chinese Take-Out he ordered from one of his favorite little places in Chinatown: a pork and liver stir-fry that pulls at the cobwebs in his brain. Sleep is elusive that night, the same as it has been almost every other night since the phone call about Harvey. He tries to tuck in at eight, knowing he needs to be at the restaurant early the next day but ends up lying awake in bed, wondering about the letter Harvey left for him.

It hasn't arrived yet. He spirals and wonders if it's lost somehow, the final scribblings of Harvey's lovely hand slipped into the cracks of some mailing facility, or down a gutter, or ruined by rain.

Food would calm him. Food always calmed him.

He opens the fridge and pulls out the white cardstock box by the little metal handle, and just as the door closes, his apartment speaker buzzes. It's almost midnight. Whoever it is must be drunk, must be trying all the buzzers, because they forgot their key... but whoever it is, they are insistent. They keep buzzing. Impatiently.

Who can it be now? He drops the takeout on his bar and walks to the intercom, toggling to the speaker. "Yes?"

"El?" The voice is unmistakably Alexis. "I really need to talk to you. Can you let me in?"

Her frantic tone pushes him toward fear. She'd shown up in the middle of the night before—after having too much to drink, or needing a place to stay after a one night stand she'd crept away from, or needed him to pretend to be her boyfriend when a date had gone bad. But this doesn't sound like any of those. She sounds desperate. She sounds wounded.

"Yeah, come on up." He buzzes her in and opens his liquor cabinet. Something is wrong. When Alexis needed to talk, she could go on for a whole hour and that meant at least a two-hour talking-down session with something to steady her nerves will be in store. He opts for the whiskey and finds two glasses from the cupboard.

Just as he is cracking the ice tray, she knocks on the door. He opens it, barely having time to be stunned as she pushes past him into his apartment. Trail-marks of tears pull mascara and eyeliner down onto her cheeks and her nose and eyes are red.

"Hey!" He shuts the door and follows her into his kitchen. "What the heck is going on? Are you okay?"

"Tell me you didn't know," she whimpers, her bottom lip shaking.

"Didn't know what?" But he already has an idea of what this is about and that edge of fear skulks into his voice.

"Harvey. Harvey's dead."

He frowns, trying not to give anything away.

And she deflates into one of his kitchen chairs and shakes her head. "You *did* know. I knew it. I just fucking knew it."

"Alexis…" he starts.

"Don't," she snaps, standing up again. "It was that phone call you took on Mother's Day, wasn't it? And you couldn't even tell me? You couldn't even let me know?"

"I didn't know how to tell you," he answers softly and he means it. He hadn't known how to break that kind of news to her. To Alexis: the invincible woman, the one who had time and time again picked him up after shit had hit the fan in his life, the one who never gave anything away with her incorrigible smile and devilish green eyes.

Because he knew it would hurt her. Because he knew *he* would have dealt a blow to that invincible woman.

"So, you didn't say anything at all?" Her voice squeaks before dropping an octave. "For a whole fucking week?"

"I didn't mean—" he tries to say, and she immediately cuts him off.

"Did you know they burned him?"

The sentence almost doesn't register and when it finally does, Eliot's stomach turns. "They did what?"

"They burned him because they couldn't find any next of kin. No one to pay for a funeral service. No one to be there to say goodbye…"

Eliot coughs, tears stinging his eyes as his brain works to process her words. "B-but...they didn't ask me. They didn't ask me..."

"It was AIDS, Eliot." She narrows her gaze at him. "But you already knew that, didn't you? It's why you didn't tell me. It's why you didn't offer to do anything for him, even though you two were ludicrously happy a few months ago, even though you knew he had no family over here."

"I just said they didn't ask me, Lex! They didn't ask me!" he yells. The scratch on tile pulls his attention to Apple whose tail vanishes around the corner toward the hallway.

"Were you embarrassed?" Alexis spits. "Did you think if you paid for some out gay man's funeral, tabloids would start talking? Were you afraid of someone thinking you might have it, too?"

"Stop," he asks her, trying to stay calm, realizing things are escalating out of his control. "Just stop."

"It's always about you, Eliot." Alexis pushes past him, her shoulder hitting him roughly as she moves toward the door. "It's always about your name. Your image. You."

Anger sours into pain at her words. "That's not fair, Alexis. I've been here for you whenever you've needed me. You know that Tempo isn't just about me, it's about us. We're a team."

"I'm not talking about *us*!" she screams back at him. "Harvey was my friend. He was your other half for three years. You know how much you meant to him."

"And we broke up, Alexis!" he shouts. "It happens. People move on. People's relationships change. Eventually, they end."

"He was burned to ash, Eliot," she cries, losing her volume, the tears streaming harder and faster. "They treated him like he was less than human. They treated him like some diseased indigent rather than who he was. And he's probably sitting on some shelf in a fucking box instead of being honored by the people he loved."

Eliot's lip quivers as he tries and fails to hold back tears. "I thought he'd found someone else… I thought he was happier with someone el—"

"I'm going down there." Alexis rips open the door and steps out. "You can stay here and hide behind your precious façade and make fancy pasta and pretend. See if I fucking care." She stalked down the hall to the elevator.

Eliot knows he should go after her. He knows that if he lets her leave, there will be little to no chance of resolution, of working anything out between them. Yet, the pain of her words keeps him glued to the floor. That she thinks that about him. That she assumes he wouldn't have tried to do something if only he'd known…

So, he stays put. He doesn't even watch her get on the elevator. Instead, he closes his apartment door. He steps back inside the kitchen and stares at the melting ice in the tray. He picks it up and flings it in the sink, the ice clattering out. Pouring himself a whiskey neat, he slugs it back, the alcohol burning as it shoots down into his stomach. There are stars in his vision as he tries to pour another, and his hands tremble. More whiskey ends up on the bar top rather than in the glass. He sets the bottle down and lets the sobs hitch in his shoulders.

He isn't a monster.

He isn't a—

Alexis's words haunt him, ignite the rage, reignite the visions of Harvey lying dead in some hospital bed, of his body being delivered into waiting flames…

Eliot grips the counter and cries.

LEFT LOG #5

TAKE ON ME

The next town they stop in is called Morning Sun and nothing could be further from the truth. The place is miserable, just like every other bad town they've been through on this insane road trip. Left is on the brink of delusion, his hours behind the wheel pushing him toward dreaming while awake. He imagines the cars around him swirling in pirouettes as they hydroplane on the wet roads, the sound of "Claire De Lune" providing a serenity to the chaos at hand. He's lost control of the car and is careening around alongside them, Brooke pinned to the passenger seat in fear. He'll never forget her eyes, how much like her mother's they'd been. He remembered how empty they'd been as he'd watched them left behind, as they'd pulled him from the car wreck. The last time he'd seen them before everything went up in flames…

"Watch it!"

The voice is Hernandez and Left blinks as he sees the blur of oncoming headlights and swerves the car back into his lane.

In the back, the Psychologist is jolted awake. "What the fuck?"

"We need to stop," Hernandez says. "You need sleep. We all do."

Taking a sharp breath, Left nods and pulls them into the next motel he can find. It's a Western-themed motor inn, The Rifle Ranch. If he were more awake, he'd hate its downhome dixie bullshit with the wagon wheels and fake cardboard cactuses everywhere. But he's exhausted and the images from his waking nightmares are the only thing keeping him awake.

He pays for the rooms and before either of his passengers can say anything, he shuts them out. In the bathroom, he takes a long, hot shower that leaves him on sleep's precipice. He'll feel better with a good night's rest, he convinces himself seconds before there's a knock on his door.

He doesn't say anything, hoping they'll think he's gone to bed, but the knocking persists.

"What?" he yells finally.

"Can I talk to you?" It's Hernandez.

"Can it wait? I'm trying to sleep."

"I'll be quick."

Blowing out a hot breath, he quickly throws on his pants and a T-shirt before letting her in. She's holding a takeout container in her hand and offers it to him.

The thought of food makes his stomach roll over. "No thanks."

"All I've seen you eat today was that donut and some coffee. It's no wonder why you're crashing now," she says setting the container down on the nightstand. She turns to leave.

"Thanks," he says hesitantly. "I'm—not great with being taken care of. You should know that. But I appreciate the thought."

She nods and turns back around to lean on the doorway. In the soft light from the porch light, her black hair glows and softens all her features. She asks, "Who's Brooke?"

His whole body goes rigid. "What?"

"You were saying her name in the car…before you woke up."

Shit. He closes his eyes, hangs his head before opening them again. Maybe it's the tire, maybe it's the fact that Hernandez has been slowly wearing him down this entire trip, maybe it's because he's just too tired of avoiding it anymore. He says, "She was my daughter."

And all at once, Hernandez's face changes. Understanding transforms her features completely, the aloofness she's had in her eyes since they met is suddenly gone, replaced with compassion. She nods. "I'm sorry. I'm so sorry."

"Yeah. Everyone always is," he mutters.

Taking the hint, Hernandez grabs his door handle and starts to pull it closed. "You know," she says slowly. "I'm here for Eliot. I'm here because he was the first person who ever took a chance on me, who wanted to hear my voice and see me express myself. After I lost my third job in a month, I lost my dad. My dad was the one who encouraged me to work in the food industry, to follow my love for it. He told me I was too much of a mother bear for my siblings and that

I needed to spread my wings." She laughs and he can feel the pain in it.

Left wants to show he cares. He wants to be the kind of person that reaches across the door frame and gives her a hug because that's what a normal person would do. Wouldn't they? But he doesn't move. He's not sure he knows what love is or if he wants to know. He can't quite make the sound of his own daughter's laugh go away as he listens.

"Tempo was the first place that felt like home to me. Eliot made it that way. He made everyone that worked in his kitchen feel like they were listened to and that they had a rhythm unlike anyone else's. That their food story was unique and needed to be told. We all need someone like that. I might be saying this because we've been stuck in the car together for almost a week now, but I truly hope you have someone like that, agent. And if not, I want you to know I'll listen."

He doesn't say anything. What can he say to that? His defensive sarcasm wants to leap in and get the last word, but he keeps his mouth shut and forces a nod.

"Good night." She shuts the door.

That night, Left doesn't dream, lost to the nexus of enervation that not so much guides someone to sleep as much as it yanks them down its elevator shaft.

The phone in the room rings with such brilliance that when he bolts out of bed, he's not sure where he is or what day it is. He answers it after the next ring, rubbing his temples.

The voice on the other end is from headquarters and what they say makes him practically leap out of bed. They know where Eliot Lamb is. And he's surrendering.

20
MAJOR TOM

It's evening by the time that Larry, the motel front desk attendant, leaves. Eliot has spent what feels like an eternity crouched in his little corner of the hotel room creeping through the blinds at him. He realizes vaguely that Larry was probably under orders to wait and see if he returned and, with nothing to report, is being called back.

Eliot nearly falls asleep, as he imagines lying on a metal slate inside of a stone lined furnace, flames licking at either side of him. He wants to beat his fists against the stone but can't move them. He wants to scream and can't open his mouth.

He wakes to the office door closing and watches the frumpy man leave the office behind as he vanishes into the portable restroom next to it. Eliot immediately takes his leave of the room. His entire body shakes in fatigue as he clambers down the staircase to the parking lot and quickly climbs into Terry's van, making sure to close the driver's door as quietly as he can.

The plastic door to the toilet bangs open and Eliot reclines the seat to stay out of sight. He hears Larry's shoes scuffing across the sand in the lot shortly before his car door creaks open and then slams.

Eliot hazards a glance up at the clerk's car as he rumbles into reverse and then starts out of the lot.

Moments later, when the car is down at the entrance and far enough away, Eliot starts the van's engine, backs out, and follows.

The Vegas lights constantly demand his attention the further down the strip they drive— blinking, radiating out, and blasting his vision with neon bursts of reds and whites. He forces himself to focus on the taillights of the 80' Impala sedan in front of him and to try and ignore the lingering sadness about Clive and the fear about how he'll find Terry when he gets to wherever they are going.

What do they want? Is he just heading into a trap?

The Impala leads him away from the Strip, through the neighborhoods of Henderson and southwest toward the valleys, the night sky reigning supreme beside the endless expanse of rock fields and herds of cattle. Eliot slows down considerably as traffic drops off; he doesn't want to alert Larry of his presence.

Eventually, Larry turns off onto a dirt road and Eliot slows to a stop at its entrance, noticing the old farmhouse and barn that await at the end of the lane. There are lights on and a myriad of vehicles gathered outside.

So. This is the place.

Eliot looks around the van. He wishes he'd called for help before leaving the room at the hotel but then isn't sure who exactly he would have called anyway.

A shout echoes out over the hills. The hair on Eliot's arms prickle as he recognizes it.

Terry.

He needs to get to Terry.

Turning off the headlights on the van, Eliot rolls down the lane and parks the van behind the barn for cover. Pain ebbs from his attention as his adrenaline kicks in. He climbs out leaving the door slightly ajar and slides through a back door into the old barn.

The lofts above are darkened, spiderwebs billowing in the warm night air while the rusty skeletons of old farm tools hang on the walls like trophies of a bygone era. He glances around for a weapon here: something with a sharp edge or heavy enough with a blunt one and finds a sickle with a bent blade. The inside edge still seems sharp to the touch. Gripping the handle, he thinks about the need to use it. He'd only been in a handful of fights through out his life and often as the one trying to break them up. The idea of swinging this thing at someone makes him ill.

Again, a distant shout. Terry crying out "No!"

Eliot tries to reel back his terror as he gets low and maneuvers toward the barn doors. He can see through the gaps in the wood: an empty yard, an old tree with a tire swing teetering in the breeze, a flowerbed of ground up mulch, an old plastic swimming pool filled with greenish water. There's a white farmhouse about a hundred feet away, the lights a milky yellow on the ground floor and black above. He can see shapes in the windows— arms gesticulating, people walking in front of it.

He cautiously opens the barn door, and it whines as it peels back. He slips out and shuts it again behind him. His legs feel stiff. It's hard to bend his knees, hard to feel the soft ground beneath the soles of his shoes. Everything tingles, and the things that don't tingle, hurt.

Focus, he tells himself and quickly crosses the backyard toward the house.

Movement on the porch catches his eye and he ducks behind the tire swing tree moments before someone emerges from the backdoor with a cigarette in hand and a lighter. They light it and puff smoke into the wind, their form painted in slashes of blue and black by the shadows. It's Larry.

Eliot trembles as he peeks out. There's no way for him to get past the front desk clerk in order to get into the house. Larry probably won't move until he finishes his cigarette.

Where the hell are you when I need you? he thinks, picturing Death in Alexis's form.

"You rang?"

He turns his head and there she is, standing right in front of him in what should be full view of everyone from the house. But he knows they won't see her; not until she wants them to.

"Help me," he mouths not wanting to make a sound for fear of being heard.

"I've already interfered with your path more than I should have," she answers and there's something that edges into her tone like annoyance, as if someone has told her she can't scribble on the wall anymore with crayon, or that she can't knock hapless detectives into voids anymore or freeze time in order to burn perfectly good burgers.

"Bullshit," he whispers. "You owe me this. For not telling me about Clive sooner. You owe me for Alexis. For Harvey. For all the people you've taken from me before I was ready—"

"Is that how this works?" She squints at him. "Is it that Death can only collect souls when you're ready now?"

Funny. He'd never heard her speak about herself in the third person. He peeks out behind the tree at Larry who hasn't moved before turning back to Death. He's putting more weight on his left leg to stay crouched out of sight and now it's wobbling with fatigue. "Please."

"Are you ordering me or asking me, Eliot Lamb?"

"Asking. I'm asking you to please help me save Terry. He doesn't deserve this." This time he reaches out and grabs her and she jolts with surprise. "Please."

Her tone is empty. "No one *deserves* death. It doesn't stop it from happening."

Third person again. Was she distancing herself from this? Was she going to kill Terry? He grits his teeth as a bolt of anger soars through him. "I don't have time to debate morality with you right now," Eliot hisses. "Are you going to help or not?"

She stares at him and steps backward out of his reach.

His lungs deflate. "Fine." He turns his back on her and notices that Larry is turned toward whatever is happening through the window, fingers to his cigarette. Eliot sidles around the tree and pads across the grass to the porch steps. He knows they'll make noise when he climbs them, and if they don't, a board on the deck probably will. He moves quickly.

The third step squeals and he is already within four feet of Larry as he's turning, the sickle pulled back and ready to swing forward.

He doesn't see the second man emerge from the shadows on the other end of the porch. Eliot's sickle arm is wrenched back, and a boot takes him out at the back of his weak knee. He's down before he realizes what's happening; his whole body folding like a card table against the soft deck.

Desperate, he kicks out his leg at the first thing he can and feels the heel of his shoe slam into something that gives, something that pops before Larry's body spirals down next to him, howling. His arm is free. Slicing in a wide arc, Eliot feels the point of the sickle stick. He shrinks when he sees it embedded in Larry's cheek, the rusted silver glimmering inside his mouth as blood spatters out in black sparks.

Fingers scrunch into the neck of his shirt and hoist him up from the deck before throwing him against the nearby door. Sharp metal jabs him in the back of his ribs as he careens into it and lands in a heap beneath. Something wet trickles down his back and cold slices into him where it shouldn't. He's able to reach a hand around himself and feel the tear in his shirt. When he looks, his fingers are slick with blood and something more: ash.

The second man looms over him, the toes of his work boots poking into Eliot as he laughs. "For an angel of God, you sure are a fucking devil." He grabs Eliot's arm, roughly yanking him to his feet. "The Priest will be happy to see you're up and in fighting spirit."

Eliot barely has a moment to ponder who the Priest is before his arm is forced behind his back. His muscles strain, then shriek.

Something with the force of a car crash slams into them both. Eliot is thrown clear, tumbling across the deck. Dazed, back on fire, he glances behind him and frowns. A rusted bicycle lays on top of his attacker, one of the tires bent in a hard right angle. The guy is out cold; the glass window on the door shattered.

He looks out into the grass and sees what looks like the tree with the tire-swing rippling back into its upright position. The limbs twist into gnarled shapes and the ground undulates as the roots settle.

Footfalls gather. Eliot sees the abandoned shotgun on the deck between he and his previous assailant and scrapes it up seconds before the door opens. Still on his back, he points the muzzle up at the first man who appears through the broken glass.

The man ducks seconds before Eliot squeezes the trigger. Glass explodes, wooden splinters rain down over him and the butt of the shotgun slams into his chest, effectively knocking the wind out of him. He drops the gun, coughing frantically.

The man scrambles out from behind the door and breaks for him. Out from his left, a rubber tractor tire careens into his attacker's figure, knocking him down before it's yo-yoed back out past the deck by the old rope that connects it to the tree branch.

Gasping, Eliot feels the air punching through him, and subsequently, his lungs constrict. He curls into a ball, hugging himself as the pain latches onto him once more.

He's in a box.

He's treading water.

He's *fucked*.

He's not sure how he grabs onto the gun once more, how he uses it as a prop to get to his feet but he's on them, teetering as he points the weapon ahead of him and enters the house through the busted door.

Barely inside, he's assaulted by the smell of familiar cooking—garlic bread, tomato sauce... The sight of green checkerboard dish towels and gray decorative pottery plates hung on the walls, Naugahyde leather furnishings, and rough-hewn coffee tables. The strong aroma of coffee smacks him in the face as he passes through the kitchen and heads for the front hallway.

A wall phone catches his attention. It's impossible to hear the dial tone through the ringing in his ears as he hooks his finger into the rotary dial and picks each number: 9-1-1.

The operator picks up, her voice cutting through the whine.

"I'm Eliot Lamb. The FBI is looking for me. This is where they can find me." He leaves the phone off the hook and moves toward the stairs without waiting for an answer.

From the darkness upstairs, he swears he hears someone say, "Don't. Let him come up," but doesn't process it until he's nearly at the top of the stairs. There's a hall with three open doors ahead of him, one with the lights on. He edges into it with the shotgun poised, letting the lingering spell of adrenaline guide him.

Terry sits in a chair tilted back near an open window, tears streaming down his cheeks. Eliot's mind bristles as he imagines what they had been doing up there: threatening to drop him out. His friend is sweating like Eliot has only seen a couple times before, once when they were running from the FBI in Getty, and second, when they were running from Tom's house. Terry's eyes ping-pong back and forth between Eliot and the men only a few feet in front of him.

Each of the other five men in the room is clothed in what he imagines are their Sunday finest: clean button downs, slacks and suspenders, even shiny shoes…except one: a man in black. One man that when he turns around, Eliot withers in place because the face that stares back makes him realize: of course.

"Good to see you again," Tom says to him, smiling.

Eliot levels the shotgun with Tom's face. Or at least he tries to. He's shaking all over. The pain is winning, his energy slipping away.

Hold on, he tells himself. *Just a little longer.*

"Let him go," he says out loud, voice firm.

"Aw, Terrance and I were just having a little chat, weren't we?" Tom gives Terry a pat on the shoulder and Terry shrinks away from his touch. "You know, I can forgive you two taking advantage of my hospitality back in Adin. But, what I can't forget is how you insulted our Lord right in front of my wife. Shortly after our exchange,

God chose to grant her wings. Commit her to her next life. It was a sign, boys. A sign that I needed to help you realize your destiny. So, I made sure the flock kept an eye on you."

Eliot shudders, remembering the HAM radio in Tom's house, remembering the man with the kayak stand listening to proclamations as he leant them boats, various people in various towns who he felt had watched him and Terry just a little too closely, and of course, Larry.

Tom was a True Faith follower. Perhaps *the* True Faith priest.

"Are you the one organizing everything?" he asks. "Getting people to bomb places? Destroying cities?"

Tom shakes his head. "No. I'm sure it would make you feel better to think that, but I'm just one of many traveling salesmen, spreading the word from state to state about the resurgence of Angels."

Eliot frowns. "What?"

"The Ash is God's way of transforming us into his most supreme entities. Those who will go forth and guide humanity back from its wicked ways. You've been chosen, Eliot. You are being cleansed of your sins and remade to guide others towards the light and the fire. There's no running away from that anymore."

"Get out of here, El," Terry urges from his seat as he pants heavily. "Don't let them—"

Two of the men tip the seat back toward the open window and Terry screams as he starts to go upside down.

"Stop!" Eliot shouts, staggering forward, the muzzle of the shotgun now only a few inches away from Tom's face. "Let him go or I'll send you up to meet your fucking maker next."

Tom doesn't look stunned, doesn't appear nervous or uncomfortable in the slightest. He raises a hand and flicks it before saying, "Let Terrance go."

The men bring the chair back down on all four legs and untie Terry's hands from behind him.

As Eliot watches, the tendrils of pain begin to wrap him up. The cut in his back sears, his knee pounds from where it was kicked, and his lungs ache. Not to mention his eyes. His whole head feels like it's a ball of flame, the room's temperature spiking.

Just hold on, he hears Alexis' voice somewhere. *Hold on.*

Terry stands up and scuttles to his side of the room. He winces at Eliot. "Your bleeding…"

"Are you okay?" asks Eliot, turning the focus away from himself and examining Terry closer. A few bruises. What looks like the beginnings of a fat lip.

Terry nods. "I'll survive."

Eliot takes one step backward toward the stairs. "Come on. We're leaving."

"How far do you think you'll make it before your body gives out?" Tom asks. "Do you think you'll even get out of the house? Let's say you somehow do. It's a half an hour drive back to the city and the nearest neighbor is ten miles away. We'll catch you."

Sweat drips down the side of Eliot's head as he pants. He doesn't want to admit it, but Tom is right. His knee is wobbling. His eyes hurt and his vision has gone wonky in the few moments that have passed.

"Take the gun, Terry," he says under his breath.

"What?"

"Terry. Take the gun. Now."

Terry's hand enters Eliot's vision and grips underneath the barrel, gliding it out of Eliot's hands. He immediately puts a hand on his thigh, trying to keep himself straight. He's going down. There's no time left.

"Let Terry go, and I'll do whatever you want," he says.

Tom perks up an eyebrow.

"No, Eliot," Terry takes a step forward to put himself in line with him. "We can get out of here…together. Come on."

"I won't make it, but you can. The van is out behind the barn. Keys are in my pocket."

"That's not how this works," argues Terry, even as he collects the car keys. "We're going together. We—"

Eliot turns his head toward him. "I've got nothing left," he rasps and shakes his head desperately. "You need to go. Get out. Get help."

Terry's face is carved in anguish. He rests the shotgun under his arm, keeping his finger on the trigger and puts a hand on Eliot's shoulder. "I love you, man." And then, he backs away.

Eliot eyes Tom's lackeys as he listens to Terry's fading footfalls on the steps. As one starts to move forward, Tom puts a hand on his shoulder. "Let him go."

Down below, a screen door yawns open and then snaps closed.

Eliot's knee gives out and he collapses on his side, wheezing. Exhaustion threatens to drag him under, and his body is full of tumbling, gyrating pain.

"Sacrifice," Tom murmurs crouching down over him. He puts a hand on his head. "Giving one's life for another. You have sinned but even now, you are embracing the righteous path of becoming one of them: an Angel."

Eliot bats his hand away with his own which feels heavier than it should.

"Take him to the rack," Tom orders.

As two heft men rush in, their hands and fingers scrabbling over Eliot's weak limbs, the priest adds, "Gently, please."

21
TRUE FAITH

They all pile into a brown Ford Astro. Tom's religious nuts have hands on Eliot the whole time, not that he can move much on his own, but now, there's absolutely no way as he's surrounded on both sides. All he can hope for is some kind of roadside accident, and briefly does before realizing that none of them are buckled in and they'd all suffer if the van crashed. The vehicle leaves the farm via dirt roads before bumping up onto smooth asphalt. They travel what feels like only a couple minutes before they stop and everyone gets out once more.

Night blue engulfs his vision. A vast stretch of highway stands lonely around them surrounded by curled, browned landscape, the hewn crags of rocks, and—Eliot gasps. A road crumbles into darkness ahead of them, pieces of asphalt barely holding onto twisted rebar. A band of fifteen or so people await them on the other side of the canal close to its edge as they hold small statues with wings.

He squints. Angels. They're holding angels.

An overpass looms over them collapsed through the middle, the metal guard rails curling like falling water off the drop. A section of Lost Highway. They existed all over the United States, ever since the flooding began, ever since it became impossible to keep up with the demands of roadway maintenance. It was just easier to shut some sections down than it was to rebuild them. And when canals opened, it was beyond much of the DOT's control to make them safely passable again.

The men half walk, half drag him from the van up to a contraption that immediately sets his nerves alight. He recognizes it immediately: a somewhat rusted metal rack with a cross forged in the center and four horizontal iron bars behind it. He remembers the twisted form of the burned corpse he'd seen when he'd gotten lost with Terry.

Two men hold Eliot up against it as he fights to break free, though he's no match for their strength. They secure him to the iron bars using rope to wrap his shoulders and under his arms, loop his extremities onto it before adding final bands of it around his chest.

Tom stands with his back to him the entire time, addressing the flock of onlookers: men, women, and children alike, all gazing onward in a horrible, inhuman awe as if they've come for dinner and a show. Cars and trucks are strewn about every which way on the road behind them, as if these people were called from near and far to some weird crossroads in the middle of the Nevada desert.

Tom eventually turns around and joins his men just as they are securing the last knot around Eliot's torso. "You ready to become a true believer? A saint amongst the Vast?"

Eliot grinds his teeth. "This is torture," he says. "This isn't heavenly or sacred."

"'Suffering reminds us of our dependence upon the Lord.'" He smiles. "It's the only way we can know him, truly know him. Pain is his purest language. It's the true faith."

When the words hit Eliot, a full panic breaks out over him. He grits his teeth as he struggles harder. He can't move a thing.

Tom puts a hand on Eliot's arm. "It'll all be over soon, son."

"Why pain?" he asks so suddenly, it startles him as much as it does Tom.

"Excuse me?"

"Why does pain have to be the cornerstone of your faith? Why not love? Why not joy?"

Tom blinks. "If you'd stayed for the rest of that breakfast in Adin, I could have shown you photos of my son. All Tommy ever wanted was to fly. To see space. To touch the stars. Every Christmas, we bought him an angel ornament. He believed they were the most fascinating of God's creatures."

"And he died?" Eliot answers. "Didn't he?"

"My son was one of seven astronauts on the Challenger Space Shuttle." Tom's eyes dimmed. "So, no. He didn't so much as die as he did explode. As much as he took to the sky. Became an Angel."

Eliot closed his eyes.

"We were watching it live on television. There is nothing so horrible in this world as hearing your son's mother scream as she watches him die. As watching someone you've cherished and protected be lit up in televised particles of fire and ash. It changes you. It makes you a whole new person. It lights a holy fire inside of yourself."

"I'm so sorry, Tom," says Eliot, trying to keep his voice calm. "But you need help. Nothing you're doing is going to help anyone. All you're spreading is fear."

"My son and my wife are transformed. They are with God now. And every single one of you that we reunite with the Lord bring us a step closer to accepting our own fates that He has in store for us."

Eliot knows there's nothing he can say that will change Tom's mind. How many other people had bargained for their lives and had died without an ounce of mercy? Worse: he knows that Terry is likely miles away, driving through endless stretches of cornfield searching for help. He's alone. He's going to die alone.

"There's no reason to be sad," Tom says. "You're about to be changed." Tom nods to someone unseen.

Rope slides around Eliot's neck and binds him to the grid, putting him in a perpetual chokehold. He opens his mouth to protest, and a rag is immediately wrapped in it and tied around the back of his head.

"Don't want to give the kids nightmares from all of your screaming," adds Tom, before he turns back to his flock and opens his arms. "You are about to witness a miracle, friends," he calls to them. "Angels have been among us all along. They are inside every one of us and all it takes is an act of sacrifice to bring them out. All it takes is supplication. We give ourselves to God..."

"…And he will remake us in the image of his Angels," the crowd spoke as thought they'd recited the words before. As if they had practiced them as part of their daily Sunday practice at church.

With a sudden jerk, Eliot feels the metal grate and himself hoisted into the air. Gravity pulls against him, the ropes cutting into his skin with each sudden pull. Five feet off the ground. Then ten feet. Then fifteen.

He searches the crowd for help. Surely one of these people has some level of humanity. One of them could see that this was wrong. But every set of eyes below has some form of horrified obsession or expression of reverence. They are captivated. For them, this is a magic show, and he is the trick.

One more heave and the grate teeters back and forth from its new perch. A lackey below ties off the rope and joins some other men gathering chopped wood, stacking it into a pyre.

Eliot doesn't want to die this way. He doesn't want to die *at all*.

But what has he accomplished driving out here into the Vast at Death's request? To save humanity? How has he saved anything by visiting Diablo, a creative and powerful tour-de-force of his own right? How has he done anything but prolong what is likely to be the long-term death of Milliner's? Sure, maybe Nelly and Lucas will be able to musical chairs the Ashen away from it for a little while, but they'll get tired. Eventually, they'll let some slip through the cracks. They'll be overwhelmed. And the restaurant will suffer for it.

And Clive…

He hadn't even gotten the chance to apologize to him let alone say goodbye. The man who saw Eliot's drive, his vision, and helped nurture the spark. Clive was the one who let him have a chance and without him, Eliot never would have had as many opportunities as he'd had, never would have started Tempo, never would have met Alexis and then Harvey…and maybe that doesn't matter. They are gone, too, like he will be soon.

As tears well in his eyes, his entire body goes lax, dead weight pulling him down. The rope tightens against him. His head sags forward.

Nothing. He can do *nothing*. Nothing about losing Clive. Nothing about the Ash. Nothing about Milliner's or Flounder or Les Contemplations or Tempo or The Agave Tap. They are all good as dead and will be forgotten in a short time. No legacies for any of them.

"See folks!" Tom shouts out from below. "That's a man who has accepted his fate! That's a man who is ready to leave this capricious world behind and embrace the golden fields of Heaven."

Wood smoke rises from directly beneath him, smoldering against his nostrils. He can't cough. Can't move his head to avoid it. He can't breathe.

At least, maybe he will die from asphyxiation before he is burned alive. Or maybe he won't feel anything since his body is numb. Maybe he can slip out of the world quietly as though he isn't even—

An explosion thunders in his eardrums as a plume of fire erupts at the edge of his vision followed by the shriek of metal banging down onto asphalt. People scream, duck, and splinter from the crowd, rushing behind nearby vehicles for cover. One of the vans at the edge of the gathering is wreathed in flame, smoke wafting into the night sky.

How? Who?

It doesn't matter. He's choking on the smoke as it grows thicker beneath him, choking on the rope as it tightens from the pressure under his sagging chin. This is it. *No one* is going to come for him.

Flapping wings. Eliot can barely discern them from the darkness as they shine against the firelight from below. The sheen of black feathers ripples back and forth as they clear the smoke from in front of him, gusting it off with each rise and fall of their wings.

A crow.

No.

Death.

And she was…saving him?

A second explosion. Eliot's ears ring and his entire head threatens to cave beneath the percussive force. A second van careens across the roadway as it tumbles like a toy into the dirt, its undercarriage burning.

What the hell is going on?

In a ring of supporters below, he sees Tom pointing his flock toward the vans while keeping an eye on the burning pyre.

It's getting smokier now. The bird promptly lands on the grate over his head and keeps flapping.

Faintly somewhere in his subconscious, he hears Alexis's voice saying something. It's hard to tell what. The ringing in his ears is sharper than ever with his own pulse getting louder and louder, a drum beating inside his head.

And something faint. Alexis's voice is transforming, pitching up and down and up and down…

Sirens.

They're distant but they are enough to spur Tom and his entire posse into a panic. Women and children flee guided by their husbands to whatever nearest vehicle they can climb in; people jumping in the backs of trucks before they peel out. Sheltered by three of his devotees, Tom is ushered into the back of the only remaining van as though he's the president avoiding an assassin. Tires squeal as they cut the wheel and back up, too fast, right into the canal…

Metal and rubber screech as the vehicle's back half careens off and the backdoors smash onto broken asphalt. The front wheels spin futilely in place before the entire vehicle spins on its axis, the windshield dropping toward the blackness and ending up on its side. Eliot can see Tom through the passenger door window, gesticulating wildly as he stares at Eliot.

The sirens get louder.

The pounding in his head engulfs them.

Darkness encroaches the edges of his vision.

"Don't let go," he hears Alexis order.

He sees a lone figure standing on the pavement below, shortly before he blacks out.

22
I WANT TO BREAK FREE

For all of Terry's faults, he had never been much of an instigator as an adult until he met Eliot Lamb. One of the more popular kids in his class, Terry was indeed a joker and played the occasional prank on his friends, his sister, or cousins when he knew he could avoid any kind of reprimanding or fallout from it. Throughout trade school, he avoided gangs, he avoided speeding over the limit, parking in places where he might get towed, avoided crowded spaces after a certain time of night because, his Grandmama told him that there were "devils everywhere" and he ought not to get caught up with them because she'd find out and she'd make him pay.

Truth be told, when he heard her voice convincing him to assault a police officer because Eliot could make a good coleslaw, he hadn't known exactly what to believe. But it had sounded like her, the woman he'd grown up with who gave what for. The woman who would sit on her porch with her best girlfriends and make fun of every yuppie outfit that came and went on a sunny Sunday, who made the best iced tea he'd ever had, even if it was from a powder, and who he once watched chase a door-to-door insurance salesman off the property with her yappy Yorkie, Archibald.

Since that day in the apartment, he'd nearly been eaten by alligators, dropped out of an open window by religious zealots, lured a horde of Ashen away with a method akin to musical chairs, and now, he'd blown up two vans using an aerosol can and a discarded matchbook from under the seat of the van he'd followed them in.

He'd hoped that the explosions would lure away Tom and his cronies so that he could get in and help Eliot down, but instead, it had spread pure panic. He'd hidden to avoid being inadvertently driven over, and once he showed himself, realized his error. The van with Tom and his entourage was now perilously wedged in the middle of the canal between him and the pyre. The resulting tremors from the explosions were enough to open a transverse canal, one that separated him from the section of road where they'd tied up Eliot. The pyre had also fallen, flaming logs cascading into the black abyss past the van, a few charred ones bouncing off the metal doors.

Terry runs from his hiding spot stopping within a few feet of the canal and the van. He glances up at the grating and Eliot tethered onto it, stretched out like he's been crucified, his eyes closed.

He puts his hands around his mouth and shouts Eliot's name, but his friend doesn't respond.

"Shit. Shit, shit, shit, SHIT!"

Terry knows in order to reach the rope holding up Eliot, he needs to get to the other side of the canal. And the only way across the canal is to cross the van. The van that looks like it could slip into the void at any moment.

But as he inches closer to the precipice, the van shifts and the left front wheel drops off the pavement in front of him. It turns the van into a slide.

He can't see anything down there, just the primordial darkness that stares back up at him, an invisible thing that seems to touch all along his skin like daddy long-legs as they creep toward his face. He goes rigid. He can't think. Panic envelopes him.

He's once more that young man standing on the street corner holding his crying sister as they wait for the police to come. He's staring at the spot where his Grandmama dropped through the street and smelling the food from the restaurant around the corner. It's his grandmama's neighbor, Josephine, who eventually comes when they don't get home before seven-thirty. She calls in her pastor. She calls in the other neighbors. Terry doesn't eat dinner. His sister falls asleep on Josephine's couch. There are candlelight vigils. There's even a funeral with a box filled with Grandmama's prized possessions that goes into the ground in the church's graveyard.

"Get chur head outta your ass, Terry."

The voice startles him. He blinks and looks across the chasm at the figure standing next to the ruined pyre. In her long fuchsia and black dress, and her billowing midnight wrap, Grandmama Jean is the picture of elegance, of class, of lip. His mouth drops open. "What the hell…"

"Five cents in the swear jar."

"I'm hallucinating," he tells himself. "Grandmama, you can't be here."

"And you can't be standing there watching that poor fella die," she answers, jutting her thumb up in Eliot's direction. "Time's ticking, dear."

"But…" Terry stares down at the gap in the street. "That's not safe." That's right. He realizes. It's not safe. "What were you always telling me? Don't not be safe. Right?"

"Well, now I'm telling you to take a risk!" she shouts. "You didn't come all this way to stand there with your hands in your pockets and watch it all end here, did ya?"

No. He didn't. Terry spies the flaming cars behind him and the approaching blue and red lights in the distance. They were coming.

"They're almost here!" he yells. "They'll have a ladder or something. They can help."

"You think he's got that much time?" Grandmama Jean asks.

He focuses on Eliot. He can't even tell if his friend is breathing. What he does notice is a strange singeing in Eliot's clothes that wasn't there before, like embers burning in places along his legs. And then he notices it's also along his arms, on his flesh.

He's burning. Not from the pyre, which is barely a smoldering pile right now. He's burning from *inside*.

Terry panics.

"He's gonna die here, Terrance." Grandmama Jean opens her arms. "Unless you save him."

"That's a ten-foot-wide hole, Grandmama Jean. Don't tell me I've got this."

"Don't be so dramatic," she scoffs. "It's eight and a half feet and there's a bridge for you to find your way across."

Terry's eyes widen. "I ain't exactly a skinny dude. If I step on that thing, it's gonna fall!"

"Then you're gonna have to run fast, sugar."

Terry closes his eyes. One wrong move and he would end up dead at the bottom of a dark chasm with a van full of extremists. He needed to figure out how to do this safely, how to…

The music catches him off guard. He opens his eyes, searching for a source but can't seem to find it anywhere. It seems like it's coming from all around him. And it calms him instantly.

"There," Grandmama Jean smiles. "Go with the 'Orinoco Flow,' baby."

Terry takes the deepest breath he's ever taken in his life and runs at the van.

Several things happen all at once. As the sole of Terry's shoe connects with the front bumper of the van and plants, the back bumper scrapes along the far side of the canal and the entire vehicle pivots. Terry stamps a boot up onto the passenger side door and departs moments before the door pops open and swings out to the right. This movement sends the weight in the van off balance and tips the vehicle back toward the front.

Tom subsequently opens the sliding back door, gliding Terry along as if he's riding on a huge skateboard toward the bumper. When the door catches on the end of the slider, Terry leaps the remaining few feet onto the pavement. This last movement once again tilts the van back and as if in a game of horrific teeter-totter gone wrong, the van dumps down into the void, the screams of its occupants fading into silence.

Gasping, Terry lays on the asphalt stunned as the musicality of Enya fades into the background of his head, until all he can hear are the sounds of the fire crackling and the loudening police sirens. He searches for Grandmama Jean but finds her nowhere.

Dusting himself off, he runs to the tied off rope and unhooks it. The weight of the grating is enormous and almost pulls Terry off his feet as it hitches down a little. He hooks his foot onto the metal railway from the roadside, and bit by bit, guides the metal grate down toward the pavement.

As soon as it touches the ground, Terry scrabbles at the knots holding his friend to the crucifix and pulls the gag out of his mouth. "Eliot, hang on, okay?"

Eliot collapses in his arms as he finishes untying the ropes around his middle. He carries him over to a bare spot on the pavement. His eyes are closed, and his breath comes in hitches.

"How do they do this?" Terry asks himself, starting chest compressions. He's only done a couple before Eliot coughs, then hacks and opens his eyes.

"Terry?"

"I've got you." Terry holds his hand. "You're not alone man."

They stay there until the sirens are like screams behind them and the lights reflect off every surface chaotically along with the firelight.

LEFT LOG #6

DON'T DREAM ITS OVER

It's lit up like the fourth of July as the phone call told him it would be. Left is almost giddy in his seat as he speeds toward it. Hernandez grips the "oh shit" handle above the door like her life depends on it and the Psychologist is fluttering through her papers in the back seat. "Bible salesmen!" she exclaims. "Fucking Bible salesmen!"

"What?" he grunts.

"It's how they move from city to city without noticing. Someone that represents the higher order, a priest, travels spreading the good word of their true faith."

Hernandez tries to turn in her seat but thinks better of it and grips her door handle with more force than before. "Holy shit."

Left swerves his car onto the turn for the lost highway. Moments later, the screech of several more police car tires follow suit. "So, there's no mastermind?" He yells back at her. "No psycho that we can pin this whole thing on?"

"Think of it as a conclave of psychos," the Psychologist answers just as the THUP-THUP-THUP of a helicopter buzzes over them, the blades drowning out her voice.

"What?" he snaps.

"Like when the new Pope is elected. All the cardinals go into a room and they have to vote in secret for who they want the papacy to go to?"

"What the fuck does that have to do with the True Faith nutzoids?"

"Instead of voting to make one person in charge, they decided all the priests would be and they'd stay in contact via the radio station to spread their word nationally while they organized cells in person by traveling as…"

"…Bible salesmen."

"Jesus!" Hernandez shouts, pointing at the plume of fire resonating out their front window near the broken overpass. Headlights from approaching vehicles start zinging in every direction across the darkness and Left swerves to avoid one, a pickup with a terrified-looking family inside.

"Someone decided to have fun with pyrotechnics," the Psychologist says.

"You mean blow shit up?" Left translates.

The Psychologist ignores his comment and leans between the two front seats. "They have their burnings at Lost Highways because its symbolism for—"

"Get outta here with that, will ya?" Left yells. "I'm trying to concentrate!"

Static breaks over the radio in the Camero and Left grabs his radio to answer. "What do you see?"

"Multiple outbound vehicles. We've got sight of at least three pickups."

"And at the overpass?"

"Looks like there's two vans on fire and that fell into the canal," the voice reports. The chopper beats steadily in the background.

"Anyone on the ground?"

"Two. Can't make a positive ID. And...fuck."

"What?"

"We might have one casualty."

"Who?"

"Can't tell from here."

Hernandez drops a hand on his arm. "Look out!"

Left swerves back onto the road, his back tires fishtailing a little before settling. He quickly signs off and hooks the receiver back up before setting his eyes on the scene in front of him. As the flames grow, and the night sky is soon blotted out by the aura of fire, Left narrows his gaze at the tableau before him: the destroyed pyre, the homemade iron crucifix grating, the billowing smoke from the toppled vans.

"Eliot! That's Eliot!" Hernandez shouts.

Left's sights narrow on the two figures on the other side of the canal: the plumber accomplice, Terrance Boucher, and what had been their prime suspect up until the evidence they'd found in Morning

Sun, Eliot Lamb. Lamb looks down for the count, sprawled across the asphalt. Was he dead? Had he died in Boucher's arms?

Before he can even cut the engine, Hernandez has thrown open her door and launches out of it like a shot. Left has to grab hold of the cat to keep it from leaping out after her. She's shouting Eliot's name, and the sound of the chopper and the sirens behind them devour it. Left watches as the chef gets to the canal and stands idly near it, unable to find a way across.

"You think she loves him?" he asks the Psychologist.

"I do."

"Even though he's gay?"

"What's that got to do with it?"

He purses his lips. "I guess I don't want her to get hurt. She seems like a smart lady."

"Since when do you care so much?"

Left doesn't have an answer for that.

...

It takes another half an hour before the helicopter can evacuate the plumber and the chef from their little island, another fifteen to twenty before they land at the closest hospital, another ten before they've put Lamb in the burn unit and have assessed Boucher for his injuries. A handful of bumps and bruises, a few cuts, but nothing that would require him to stay in the ER.

Left brings the Psychologist with him to interview the plumber who gives them a name, gives them a town and a sort of address where they can start to peel back the layers of the True Faith religion. When Boucher asks if there's anything else, the Psychologist clears her throat and gives Left a look that makes him sigh. He tells Boucher his charges have been dropped, and they're letting him off with a warning due to his help with their case.

As they leave the room, the Psychologist gives Left a pat on the back. "Cheer up. You'll get to interrogate all those True Faith followers at the local station later to make up for your kindness here."

"Kindness," he sneers. They start walking back toward the waiting room. "I'm not sure what you mean."

"We both know that you view being kind as some sort of weakness. I'm sure it stems from something that happened in your childhood. Maybe you were bullied. Maybe you watched someone else suffer for their selflessness…"

"Don't analyze me," he huffs.

"Whatever the reason, you should know that what you did in there was the right call. It would have been a waste of your time to arrest him, a waste of taxpayer's money to send him to prison for such a petty crime, a waste of his own life and potential…" The Psychologist pushes through the doors in front of them. "My assumption is that you'll do the same for Lamb."

Left's jaw sets. "You want me not to? He was the reason your girlfriend died."

The Psychologist stares through him. "*He* wasn't the reason. She was. She followed a lead that was wrong. She made her own mess. But she knew that was a risk. All of you law enforcement types do."

"True," he answered.

"Besides, you were as much in love with her as I was."

The statement catches him off guard. "Which means you…weren't?"

"We had a transactional relationship. Nothing more. Nothing less. It worked for us. That's all that matters. I suppose you were more in love with her, or at least, you thought you were."

Left is about to answer before glancing around the corner and noticing that Hernandez wasn't where they'd left her, the still full paper cup of bad hospital coffee sitting on the table in front of her seat along with the copy of National Geographic she'd been pretending to leaf through. He turns and pushes back through the doors they've just come from, eyeing the signs on the walls to see if he can find where in this complicated labyrinth the burn unit is.

"You can't blame her," says the Psychologist, on his heels.

"I don't."

"Then why do you always seem so agitated by her devotion to him? After all, they're co-workers. They're friends. He's her mentor for Christ's sake."

"I don't know." He doesn't want to talk about this, but the Psychologist is like a dog playing an endless game of fetch. She is going to rip the bone right out of his hand if he doesn't throw it for her.

"Are you jealous?"

He stops and glares at her. "Of *him*?"

"Of their chemistry. Of their friendship."

"What the hell are you saying?" he asks flippantly. God, he can't wait until she gets on her plane back to Rust City.

The Psychologist stops him with a touch to his elbow, and he turns to look at her. "You are the loneliest person I've ever met, agent. And I get paid by lonely people nightly to insinuate a fantasy, to make them feel like they belong somewhere. You see what I'm getting at?"

"You telling me I need to make an appointment?" he comments dryly.

"You? No. But maybe you should tell someone what it would take to thaw that icy exterior of yours."

He rolls his eyes and continues. "Good whiskey and possibly a flamethrower."

"Maybe you should tell Meena."

Left rounds on the Psychologist, his eyes wide. "You are not a matchmaker, understand? Stop fluttering around like fucking Euclid—"

"Cupid."

"Whoever!" He waved his arms in annoyance. "You're here to organize the facts of the case, put it all together in a neat little report, and then shove off back to your red light-swathed city."

"Aw," she says as a smile curls on her face. "You're that excited to see me go?"

"Sometimes I go to sleep wishing upon a fucking star that you'd just vanish." The next intersection they come to in the hall points toward the burn unit and Left bee lines for it.

"Well, I thought you'd like to know that I requested a sabbatical from my program."

Left freezes in place. "For what?"

"Being able to study the Ashen and their behavior in the Vast is something no one else has had the opportunity to do. Any research I bring back will have medical and psychological importance. And what better way to continue that study than to ride along with—"

He shakes his head. "No!"

"Who better to protect me from all the dangers of the Vast than an agent of the Federal Bureau of Investigation? Not to mention I can provide more insight into your case with the True Faith religion. You'll need an analyst and a profiler, and I can be your dime-store option without having to call in a specialist from Washington."

Like always, the Psychologist makes a compelling argument. Yes, it would be good for the case. It would avoid a lot of phone calls to and from the bureau, it would avoid some of the waiting, and…

"I think you need company."

He keeps moving even though the words stick. They do more than stick. They seep into his skin beyond his clothing. There's something cloying in them that makes him want to roll his shoulders back, makes him want to bust free of the hospital and drink in the cold once-desert air. But there's also something in them that he refuses to ignore. He doesn't want it to be as lame as tenderness, as care. After all, she's an intellectual. Maybe all she wants is to diagnose him. Fix him.

Or maybe she's just as lonely as he is.

All these thoughts flee as he rounds the corner into the burn unit waiting area and finds Hernandez perched outside of a patient room, tapping her shoe wildly. Left glances back over his shoulder to tell the Psychologist to beat it but she's already gone. Probably went back to the waiting room for that tar they were calling coffee, he surmises. After all, they'd all been awake for over twenty-four hours.

Left joins Hernandez outside the door. "What's the prognosis?" he asks.

She sniffs and swallows. Tear trails are drying on her cheeks and her eyes are red. "Not good."

"Think he'll make it through the night?"

She doesn't say anything. She doesn't even look at him.

"Listen…" Left feels the word drop from his mouth before he's even understood what the rest of the thought is. His lips keep moving regardless. "I'm going to have to interview him. He's got valuable information about the True Faith cult and what they might be planning next. After that, well…he's not a suspect anymore is what I'm getting at."

Hernandez shudders. "What about all that shit you've been spouting off since Getty? Thought you were going to arrest him anyway?"

One of his eyebrows arches. "What's the point if he's going to croak?"

She glares at him.

"Sorry." He shifts in place a little. "Have they told you anything yet?"

"Nothing definitive. But he's burning up from the inside, losing the battle. They say he's been talking to himself a lot. They're going to keep him in that bed until he—" Her voice fades.

"I'm sorry."

She loosens her jaw, straightens her posture. "He'd hate this. This wasn't what he wanted."

Left deflates and stares down at his feet. "Sometimes we just don't get what we want, Hernandez. Even in death."

...

Hours pass. Left leaves with the Psychologist for the police station, heralded there via his superiors to dig into the perpetrators who were arrested fleeing from the Lost Highway. After all of Eliot's burns are treated and covered, Meena is allowed in, though she has to put on scrubs and a facemask.

Eliot has been taken off his respirator, an IV nestled in his arm providing him with fluids. His skin is pockmarked with irregular burns, taped over with cotton and pads to protect them. The most prominent ones are close to his face. There's a large one taped to his neck just below his right ear and another along his jaw on the left side.

When she reaches his bedside, his eyes flutter open and then narrow. "Meena?"

"I'm here, you jerk," she whispers. "Can't get rid of me that easily."

He coughs or maybe it's a laugh. She can't tell where one begins and the other ends. "Is this…where I think it is?"

"We're just outside of Clark County. Biggest General Hospital they have. Pretty fantastic burn unit apparently."

"Yeah, the drugs are pretty fabulous," he clucks.

"They'd have to be, huh?" she chuckles.

"It's coming," he says, his smile vanishing. "I can tell."

She reaches over and takes his hand in her gloved one. "You're not alone. I'm here with you until the end, okay?"

"They've got you all dressed up like Doctor Frankenstein," he mumbles.

"They don't want to risk you getting infected."

"Like it matters." He rolls his eyes. "I'm going to die here in this bed." A second later, his face contorts in sadness. "This isn't where I…"

"I know."

"If this is…it… I want to go my own way, Meena. Not filled with needles and tubes."

"I know." There's resignation in her tone when she doesn't want there to be. But she doesn't want to lie to him either.

His face scrunches up in pain.

"What is it?"

"My eyes. The light in here is so bright…"

She glances at it. Only one bank of lights is on. Granted, it's the one over his bed. She moves to the wall and shuts them off, plunging the room into darkness. "Better?"

"Mmmhmm." She can tell it's not.

"Try to get some rest, okay?"

He nods and she leaves the room.

Outside is the man she saw with Eliot at the overpass, the one who's name she found out was Terry.

"How's he doing?" Terry asks.

"Irritable. Which means there's still plenty of Eliot in there," she says.

He laughs and that smile withers into a set jaw. "He saved my life. You know that?"

She shakes her head. "But I can believe it."

"After what they did to him... I'll bet he's pissed off he's still here only to be in that little room."

"Yup."

He nods. "We should get him out of here."

Meena's mouth falls open for only a second before she regains her composure. "There's no way they'll let him go anywhere. Not when he's at risk of—"

"We tell them that we're taking him out to the Vast then. Better than them just disposing of him out their back door the moment they see there's no one home upstairs, if you catch my drift."

Meena swallows. It was what Eliot wanted. It was what he deserved. But she isn't sure she is ready to see him go when it finally happens no matter where he is.

The problem was that the fine law enforcement of Clark County didn't want any more Ashen wandering in their neighborhoods, particularly near Boulder City and Henderson. So, they likely weren't going to allow them to just take Eliot out without some kind of authoritative supervision. Which meant…

"Okay," she says. "We've got a motel room in Cal-Nev-Ari. We could take him back there."

"Aren't you staying with that asshole federal agent there? I don't think he's going to be so keen on letting us stay there."

Meena sighs. While there was a strong possibility Left would help sign Eliot out of the hospital, he most definitely wouldn't like the idea of having to sleep in the same room with him, knowing that there was a possibility of all of them being incinerated.

"What else can we do? We need a vehicle."

Terry scratches his chin. "I have a van. It's just off the overpass back where you guys found us. If I can get to it, we can get him out of here."

"And go where?"

"Eliot was trying to get to Montana for his last restaurant to visit, but I don't think he's going to make it that far." Terry shakes his head.

She agrees. "That's probably an eight or nine hour drive non-stop…"

He lifts his head. "My sister though… She lives in Rachel."

"Do you think she'd be okay with us crashing?"

Terry puts his hands in his pockets. "I'm not even sure she'd be okay with *me* crashing let alone us, but…"

Meena closes her eyes. "We're going to lose him one way or another. Maybe it's cruel to even be plotting something like this. Maybe we should just spend what time we can with him here…"

"Nah." Terry turns on his heel. "She'll have to be okay with it. She'll have to be…" He vanished around the corner.

Meena glances in the room at Eliot once more, watching the slow rise and fall of his chest before she walks to the nearest nurse station. "Is there a public telephone anywhere here?"

An older woman with bright pink lipstick gestures toward a wooden wall mount a few feet away near some chairs with a payphone nestled within it. She slides out the chair there and plops herself down before fishing some quarters out of her bag.

The phone book is a sea of names and numbers that she almost goes cross-eyed looking at before she finds the listing for the Clark County Sherrif's station and dials the number. All she had to do was get Left on board…which was easier said than done.

"Clark County Sherriff's Station. How can I direct your call?"

Meena's thoughts spiraled.

Only one person she knew had the wherewithal to convince Left and do it well.

"Do you have a visiting psychologist there at the station helping on the True Faith case? I need to speak with her now."

23
SEND ME AN ANGEL

Eliot closed his eyes in a stuffy, too hot hospital room feeling as though he'd climbed out of a volcano. He barely woke when several arms lifted him from that stiff hospital bed onto a gurney, and didn't at all when he was transferred into an even lumpier passenger seat of Terry's van.

He opened his eyes occasionally and took in the blue, the paleness of the desert expanse, and the telephone poles before sinking into his mire of medication and sleep once more.

He dreamed of a small café that used to be right around the corner from his apartment in Getty. A cozy-looking little room tucked in between an antiques store and a boutique clothing shop. The space was crowded with shelves of used books, the floor comprised of wide lacquered black boards. Worn-in leather and suede chairs dotted the place along with strange yellow and red art to warm the cream-colored walls.

He'd go there for hot cider in the fall, to watch the curled brown leaves skip along the avenues, to find some obscure cooking book from the forties or fifties and peruse its yellowed pages. He dreamed of laying back in a mossy green club chair, the aroma of a freshly baked cinnamon scone tainting the air as he lost himself in the words of a recipe for—

A car door slams, and Eliot opens his eyes.

Cool, white light invades, the searing of orange and blue stinging along with it. For a few minutes, all he can do is stare wordlessly. He feels himself drop away, awe snuffing out any thoughts of pain or discomfort. He needs to know what lies within the light, needs to… His fingers fumble with a door handle that he's vaguely aware is there and he feels it and himself release at the same time.

He drops out, his feet barely catching on the pavement as he stumbles over them. There is something so hypnotic about the way the light flickers, how it plays across the wet pavement beneath him. Is there something within? A message he's missing?

Plodding toward the large light, Eliot stops and cranes his head back to take in its full majesty.

Someone grabs him suddenly, pulls him. There's a horn honking erratically. A face in his yelling, another one behind it with fear carved in it. He's dazed, blinking rapidly, trying to figure out where he is, and what happened. Rain has soaked him, and his feet are dirty.

"I don't know," he mumbles. "I don't remember."

The angry face…Left. Meena—that's right—Meena guides him back to the van. He's seat belted back into the passenger seat and he gazes back out at the gas station neon across the street.

"We still need to pay for gas," Meena reminds Terry as she finishes buckling Eliot in. She stands outside his door as Terry goes to pay the attendant. Somewhere out of sight, he hears Left frothing at the mouth.

"Where are we? How'd we get here?" he asks.

"We're going to see Terry's sister in Rachel," she explains as if he should know better. When he doesn't answer, she touches his arm. "We couldn't just leave you there."

He nods, licks his lips. "I'm so hungry."

Meena looks over her shoulder and his gaze follows hers to the yellow light emanating from the dingy little store, scans the letter board next to the ice machine where it advertises for a full-service mechanic, and shows the current price of an oil change. There wasn't a convenience store there.

"We'll find something when we get there, okay? We're almost there."

He feels like a child nodding back to her, accepting his role of passive observer and patient all too easily. He's too tired to put up a fight. By the time Terry has returned from paying for gas, he's already asleep again.

The whir of an engine becomes the sound of water boiling on his stovetop in his backstreet apartment. Eliot pours himself a mugful and dips a teabag of lemon ginger into it. Tears For Fears plays on the radio behind him barely at a volume where he can hear the words, but just so he has something other than silence.

It's one in the morning. He hasn't slept well since Alexis's smear campaign against him. Business for the restaurant has been at an all-time low. Last night, they'd barely seated fifty tables, where as a typical Friday evening would have had them sitting close to two hundred.

All the calls he's made to her have gone unanswered. He even tried to stop by her apartment only for her to ignore him. It was over. He sits at his kitchen island staring into the steam of his tea and staring at the photo he still has on his fridge of him and Harvey. He is too exhausted to cry. He is too exhausted to be upset at all.

Even as he allows fatigue to ooze over him and thinks about the chilliness of the bed waiting for him, a knock on his window startles him. He looks up and all sadness grinds into anger as he sees Alexis, hair plastered to her face with her knuckles about to rap on his window again.

All he can do is regard her with loathing. A tiny pinprick inside wants to open the window and let her in if only to tell her his thoughts. How he hates her. How he hates himself. How he wishes she understood the years of work, of dedication to craft ruined because of her, the trickle-down effect of pain that she'd caused because of her refusal to understand…

She knocks again and waves her hand as if she suddenly somehow understands how he might be mad. Like the teenager who's trying to sneak in after curfew but assumes their parent is only mildly upset. They'll get over it.

Eliot picks up his tea and shuts off the overhead light on the stove: the only light on in the room. He makes for the hallway.

More frantic knocking.

He turns back.

Alexis's eyes have widened and she's shouting, "Come on, Eliot. Please!"

If he doesn't let her in, she's going to keep banging on the glass, keep screaming, probably make one of his neighbors file a complaint. He doesn't think she'll go so far as to smash anything, but he's not completely convinced she won't either. He sets the tea on the island, crosses over to the window, and unlocks it.

She opens it and slides over his counter inside before sealing out the sound of the storm. Her ragged breaths are the only thing that can be heard in the space. Alexis peels off her jacket and says, "Thought you were just going to leave me out there…"

"Just say what you want." The words rumble out of him before he can keep them. It feels like he's letting loose a pocket of steam inside, enough to relieve pressure if only for a few minutes.

Alexis holds her breath and narrows her gaze at him. "Give me a moment to catch my breath?"

He shakes his head. "I don't believe this…" Picks up the tea again and walks to the hallway.

"I've been thinking about you, Eliot…" she calls after him.

"Did it make you feel better?" he asks over his shoulder. "I hope so. I seriously fucking hope so."

"No," she says following him into the living room. "No. It didn't."

"You think I'm some kind of monster?" He slumps into the chair beneath his floor lamp and sets his tea down on the coffee table. "You think I didn't care about Harvey. I really thought of all the people who knew me, you knew me best. So, to get ambushed by…" He takes a reflexive breath, "…*that* reporter. That news story…"

"Jesus, Eliot." Alexis practically flops into the chair opposite him and scoffs. "Everyone knew you were gay. It's not exactly a big secret."

"You know what, Alexis? It was. It might have been obvious to you, but to my neighbors, it wasn't. To the guy who delivered my mail, it wasn't. To critics and diners and chefs that I've known socially for decades, it never was. And you decided you'd pull it out and attach it to a flagpole and fly it around because…" He massaged the knuckles of one hand with the other. "…I don't know. Because you assumed something about me that wasn't true?"

"You didn't even let me know Harvey was dead, Eliot. And because you couldn't find out how to tell me, he's gone forever. We can't even bury him."

He stands up and closes his eyes. "Get out, Alexis. We've already had this argument and it's clear nothing has changed. I don't want to do this again."

"Listen, for Chrissake!" she shouts. The glass in his cabinet vibrates under the sound of her voice.

Eliot finds himself lowering back into his chair hesitantly, not because he cares about what she's going to say but because he realizes now that she's drunk. How he didn't catch it before he's not sure. But the fact that she staggered her way along the backstreet mere feet away from a canal and climbed all the way up to his apartment in this state means she *is* crazy. It used to be a quality he admired about her: her willingness to think outside of the box, her bravado, her fearlessness of the world and what it might hold…

No. It is just as much stupidity as it is boldness.

"I may have gone too far," she admits, and Eliot can't even look at her as the words pass her lips. "All I was feeling was betrayal. All I was feeling was hurt. Harvey was such a bright spot in my life, such an incredible friend. I leaned on him over and over and over and for him to just be gone…"

Eliot doesn't say anything. He wishes this was the conversation they'd had months ago instead of what had happened. He wishes there was a part of him that cared about the things she was saying.

No. He catches himself.

He does. He doesn't want to.

But he does.

Alexis kicks off her shoes and curls her legs up into the chair. "I've never lost anyone before. Never let anyone really get close so I could feel like I lost them."

"Grief is a polarizing thing," he allows as he picks up his tea and makes himself take a sip.

"You say that like you know it well." She puts her hands together and lays her head down on them as a makeshift pillow. Her body is contorted strangely in the chair, a way that could never be comfortable unless someone were numbed by a cloud of alcohol.

"Not well. Never well."

"Sometimes, I think I actually do remember it." She stares at a spot on the cabinet behind him, maybe at her own reflection in the glass. "Like it's always been there like a stagehand that's painted the scenery, made the set, and the props… I interact with it without ever seeing it and its influence is always there."

He isn't sure how to respond to that, but it feels cyclic, like he's peering into the churning abyss that motivates Alexis, the one he's recognized for a while but now it's here, gaping like a great eye at him from across the table. This kind of vulnerability wasn't typical. It wasn't the woman he'd worked beside day in and day out for years.

Her eyes flicker to him. "Is it there all the time and we just refuse to see it?"

Eliot takes a deep breath and holds it before replying, "I don't know."

They sit in silence for a few more minutes until Alexis yawns and says, "I'm kinda fucked up right now."

"I can see that."

"Do you mind if I crash here?"

Better than thinking about her getting down those stairs in a drunken stupor. Better than him worrying about her staggering along the alley way and dropping into the canal. Or driving home. Had she driven? Had she been smart enough to take a cab? Had she walked the whole way? It was a long way to the nearest—

"Eliot?"

He stands up, walks to the closet in the hall, and pulls out a couple blankets and a spare pillow. Returning to the living room, he goes to the couch behind her and lays everything out. When he goes back to her chair, her eyes are closed, and her left knee is rocking back and forth. "Alexis?"

She hums.

"Alexis." He touches her arm and her eyes snap open.

"You're on the couch. Good night."

The empty bed welcomes him. He shuts the door, the first time he's done that since he's moved in, and stares out at the rain pattering on the glass.

He opens his eyes when he feels an arm reaching around to hold him in the bed and he stiffens.

"Alexis."

"My head is killing me," she mumbles.

"How did you get in here? I thought I locked my—"

"Maybe I can walk through walls. Maybe I was here the whole time."

Every muscle is a live wire. He's afraid to move, his skin crawling. "This isn't okay…"

"Can't we pretend? Like everything is how it used to be? Just for a few hours."

His stomach is twisting in knots. But it's been so long since he's been held, so long since anyone has treated him like a person, and he finds his eyes closing in spite of the sudden swath of anger as it's dredged in sorrowful longing. He nods against the pillow and feels her forehead curl further in to touch his back, her knees to shape along with his. The cat climbs up and settles in in front of him, pinning him there in a three-layered spoon.

In the morning, Alexis is gone. The blankets are folded on the couch. There's no note. There's nothing to show that she was even there other than a few strands of her hair on his pillow.

They never talk again.

24
JUST LIKE HEAVEN

At first, he thinks he's in the ocean. The crash of waves all around him with every movement and the cold swallowing him from head to toe. It makes him wonder if he's drowning, if he's become something other than human: stone that's been worn down into particles of sand that fling and twist with every turbulent eddy. If this was how he died, it wouldn't be so bad.

And the moment the thought intrudes, he awakens. There's a hand clasping his limply, a soft amber light emanating from a room nearby, and—

Everything is cool. He stares down at himself, at the aqua-colored bathtub he's lying in, at the clumps of ice floating in the water around him, at the charring of his fingertips. He flinches and instantly remembers Justin's mother from before the bank explosion in Getty.

He turns his head and sees Meena asleep on the floor, her back propped up against the wall and head resting on the closed toilet lid. Empty plastic bags labeled "Crushed Ice" litter the floor.

He squeezes her hand gently and she sits up straight, picking sleepers from her eyes before she sees him. "Oh!"

"What happened?" Terry says from the other room.

"He's awake." She kneels closer to the tub. "How are you feeling?"

"Like a negroni."

Terry appears in the door, sweat encircling his armpits and the neck of his T-shirt. "You were burning up. We had to do something to cool you down. Unfortunately, I think we took all the ice from the machine out front."

Eliot adjusts his leg and a chunk of ice bumps off the edge of the tub. "I'm actually starting to get a little cold."

They pull him from the tub and wrap him in towels. His pain meds have worn off. Movement of any kind hurts. Each and every muscle feels like it's been pulled too far and for too long. Even the muscles in his chest ache. Every breath like trying to pull air through a sieve.

They take him out to the room. It was not unlike the one he and Terry stayed at in Las Vegas, though a little nicer and without the loud neighbors. Curled on the bed near the end is Apple. The sight makes Eliot tear up immediately as he shuffles over to her and pets her head. The cat trills and shoves her head further into his hand.

"You...brought her this whole way?"

Meena sits on the bed next to the cat. "I wasn't going to leave her alone. And I wasn't not going to come after you."

Choked up, Eliot takes a few moments with his cat, lost in the loveliness of her purr. Reality catches up with him, the pain edging back into his focus along with his surroundings. Outside, the sky is a turquoise, fading toward black on the horizon.

"What time is it?"

"Almost seven o'clock."

He'd been out of it for over twenty-four hours. He doesn't like the shiftless haze he's been in for so long on those meds, even if they had dulled the pain. "Did you get in contact with your sister?" he asks, trying to ignore his own discomfort.

Terry cocks his head and Meena chimes in with, "I told him."

"Yeah. I talked to her about half an hour ago. I'm going to go check in with her in the morning. It felt really good hearing her voice."

"Good. I'm glad to hear it." Laughter caught him off guard from outside. "Who's that?"

"That fed and the psychiatrist."

"Psychologist," Meena corrects.

Terry shrugs. "If we hadn't had his say-so, you would still be back at that hospital."

"I was pretty sure he wanted to lock me up and throw away the key." From where he stood, Eliot could just barely make out the light of a campfire and something else that takes him completely by surprise: stars. "Holy shit."

"We should go out," suggests Meena, and with Terry's help, they get Eliot into clothes: a T-shirt, a pair of jeans that Meena picked up for him at a nearby thrift store, and a pair of worn canvas Sperry's.

It's the first time he's felt like himself in a week and it puts a smile on his face if only for a few moments.

Terry grabs hold of a backpack by his bedside before they open the hotel room door.

Eliot hobbles outside, embracing the fact that he's going to hurt no matter how fast or how slow he moves. They are in a small motor inn, the surrounding landscape punctuated by sand, saguaros, and little else. Eliot can hear the sound of cars on the road nearby. There are only a handful of vehicles in the lot along with Terry's van and what Eliot assumes is the agent's Camaro next to it.

The campfire is surrounded by a handful of Adirondak chairs, clearly a promotion from the manager to try and get people to do something other than vanish into their hotel rooms for the night. Tonight, the various people staying at the inn are perched on their cars with cheap telescopes that look like they were purchased at a nearby tchotchke store. Excited children beam as their parents point out constellations. Even who he assumes are the managers of the inn have pulled out their beach chairs and set them up in front of their office to gaze up at the heavens.

A person peers around in their Adirondak chair to look at him and says, "He lives."

It takes Eliot a moment but—yes—he does know him: Left.

"For now," he answers back.

The woman that pokes her head up from the chair next to Left he is sure he doesn't know but he assumes this is the psychologist Terry had spoken of.

Terry helps Eliot to a seat opposite her and takes the one on his right while Meena grabs the one on his left.

They sit in silence for a few moments.

"Well, what an awkward little gathering," the Psychologist breaks the ice after a few moments.

"Well, let's make it a little less awkward," answers Terry, as he unzips his backpack and pulls out a box of graham crackers, a bag of marshmallows, and bars of chocolate.

Eliot smiles. "I haven't had one of these in…" He almost doesn't remember but it comes back to him like the idea of riding a bike. Clive. Clive who had bought the cheapest versions of each of those three things and made him schlep firewood out to a cabin he'd rented. They were out there cooking a private meal for Fortune 500 clients, people who were out there for the prestige of social status, who would tell you they could taste the difference between the grass-fed and the grain-fed beef and then hours later forget what they'd eaten entirely.

"There is nothing so utterly perfect as a s'more. It's gooey. It's decadent. It turns every one of us back into a kid for a few minutes. It's a time machine," Clive had said before he stuffed the last bit of his third one into his mouth.

The memory brought a different kind of warmth to Eliot's chest: nostalgia. That had been in the early days when he had been Clive's sous chef, his right hand and Eliot had looked up to him as though he were the dad he'd never had. That was almost thirty years ago now.

Those feelings about Clive, about how he'd never had a chance to thank him, never had a chance to fix what had been broken… How he had never spoken to Harvey again before his death. How he had never fixed things with Alexis.

His life had never been neat. Bridges were seldom rebuilt after they were burnt and that was true of a lot of people not just himself. And in the wake of mourning over those bridges new ones had been built. He glanced over at Terry waving a bag of marshmallows at him with a goofy grin on his face—a perfect stranger who had taken care of him out of the goodness of his heart, who had nearly died for him; at Meena who had raced across the country trying to make sure he was alright and that he wasn't alone before he died…

Even though he had lost those others that had meant so much to him, that void had been filled. He wasn't alone. And the goodness of those he'd left behind was still with him in those lovely memories.

Terry passed the s'mores ingredients around and they all dipped in to collect. Left was particularly quiet as he plucked his graham crackers from the package and stared at them. He shared a look with the Psychologist before muttering, "Why the hell not…" and proceeded to put a s'more together.

"How do we cook them?" the Psychologist asks.

"Ed and Dolores, the managers, had these sitting around in their room. Said no one has used them in years." Meena points to a pile of pie irons sitting next to the fire.

Each person took one up, opened the cast iron plates, and layered their s'more inside. Terry made one up for Eliot, as his mobility had only gotten worse since they'd stepped outside. Then, each one was poked into the flames of the fire pit to melt.

Terry reached back into his bag and pulled out a bottle of coffee whiskey. "I also brought this."

After searching in vain for enough cups for everyone, Left finds one dingy-looking enamel mug from under the seat in the Camaro that he washes out and they take turns filling and passing around.

"Anyone remember the last time they saw stars?" the Psychologist asks passing the cup along to Left.

"I think I was on a case in Boston. Ended up on the roof of this warehouse trying to talk a guy off the ledge. Drug dealing prick who murdered one of his clients. Fucking sky clears and there they are, bright as can be. Guy immediately surrenders, blubbering because he hasn't seen them since his girlfriend's death or something like that."

Everyone stares at him for a moment.

"That's…heartwarming?" the Psychologist comments.

"Made my night a lot easier. I got to leave early and go home to—" he stops himself midsentence and stares into the flames for a while. "I took my daughter to our small park down the street. It was the best spot to see the stars without any light pollution. I pushed her on the swing while we looked at them. Anyway…" He takes a large slug of the coffee whiskey and passes it around the edge of the campfire to Meena.

"I was seventeen and I was working at this little French restaurant in this tourist trap town on the coast. You know they made me learn French for that place? I had to put on an accent every time I took someone's order."

Eliot shifted in his chair. "Sounds like every other French restaurant in the U.S. trying to sell an inauthentic experience."

"Well, I got sick of it. I dropped the accent. The owner noticed and fired me right in the middle of service. At the time, I was afraid. I needed the job to help my parents pay bills. But I didn't want to pretend to be something I wasn't. In the back alley, all I could see was this thin line of stars in between the buildings. But that's all I needed. The nearest sidewalk was crowded with people all staring up at the sky. Kind of felt like we were waiting for a parade to start or something." She drinks.

Eliot accepts the bottle from her and peers through its brown glass at the fire on the other side. "We'd just finished our dinner service at Tempo. I think it was a rough one. Someone was sick. We'd really hustled that night. I was going to take the team out for a drink and Alexis noticed the stars. We ended up drinking on the roof of the restaurant passing around a bottle of bourbon..." He paused and looked around him. "Kind of like this."

Meena reaches over and takes his hand in hers.

Terry helps Eliot take a swig before he accepts it.

"I had a job working for my uncle's plumbing company back then," he says hesitantly. "We were at one of his client's houses really late. It was an apartment building, one of the nicer ones that used to be up in Elm Grove about ten blocks from his house. We had this stubborn sink with a block and we had to take the whole thing apart. Anyway, I remembered I was under the sink cutting out the old pipe so we could do a whole new install. Uncle John said to take a break and come over to the window, but I was this stubborn little shit. I wanted to go home and relax, maybe smoke a little. I mean: stars were stars. Sure, we didn't see them often, but I also didn't really care about pretty sunsets or rainbows either.

"Uncle John pulled me by my legs out from under that sink and made me come over to the window to see. Told me to always take time for stars. Always take time for the things that the world shows us because someday, we might not be as lucky. It took me a while before I understood what he meant. Now, I pay attention. I try to." Terry looked over at Eliot. "I was sliding back into it again when I met you. You pulled me out from under the sink, man."

Left squinted.

"Metaphorically speaking," Terry added with a laugh.

Eliot gave a tight smile. "Likewise, Terry."

The pie irons gradually came out of the blaze and each one opened to a gooey melted swirl of chocolate and charred marshmallow over graham cracker. As Eliot took small bites from his, he thought of Alexis with the crystalline sparkle of stars in her gaze. Alexis laughing as she stumbles over her own shoes, a little drunk but not enough to fall on her ass. Eliot thinks about her in his apartment sitting across from him wasted, offering her a measly version of an apology. No, not an apology. An excuse.

No.

An *apology*.

Because after everything that Death has told him, everything he's let fester for years and years, he understands that she was trying. Alexis wasn't good at apologies. Never had been. But she had tried. And she had regretted what she'd done though she never said it out loud.

"I mean sugar is great and all but I'm starving!" says Left, from across the fire standing up. "I'm going to go find us some grub." He trudges across the sand toward the hotel room adjacent to the one he, Terry, and Meena were staying in but stops a few feet away before turning back to the gathering. "Anyone want to come with?" The question seems tentative.

The Psychologist leaps up from her seat. "I saw a diner a few miles back. Let's go!"

Eliot catches the relief in Left's eyes seconds before he clears his voice and says, "Fine. I guess you can come."

"Bring something back for us!" Meena shouts. She leans in toward Eliot. "I'll bet your hungrier than ever."

He hadn't eaten in over a day. Strangely though, he wasn't hungry now.

The two of them return to their room to get Left's keys and then climb into the Camaro. Its engine gutters as it slowly rolls out of the lot.

Meena rubs her arms, and Eliot watches the goosebumps rise on her skin.

"Are you cold?" he asks.

She nods.

He's not. Even out here in what seems to be a considerably blustery night, the campfire churning and sending ashes up into the cobalt. For a moment, he's envious. And that thought leaves him. All emotion melts away. "You should go get a jacket," he tells her.

She squeezes his hand and says, "I'll be right back," before she gets up and jogs to the room across from them.

It's just him and Terry.

Terry stretches his arms up and crosses them behind his head. "Nice night."

"It is," he agrees.

"Once we get some cash from my sister, we can get on the road to Montana."

"Terry…" Eliot takes a slow, rattling breath. "We both know I'm not going to make it to Montana."

Terry looks at him. "Don't say that, man."

"We can't ignore it. It's…bad." He shudders. "I don't want you to drag you any further knowing that I could go at any time. It's not safe."

Terry's face hardens. "Screw not safe. I made you a promise. Come on. Let's go all the way. You've just got to hold on a little longer."

Eliot closes his eyes. "I'm so tired, Terry."

"I'm gonna get you there no matter what." Terry stands up from his chair. "The doctor gave us some Caxaline to take with us. Should have given it to you as soon as you woke up. I'll go get it."

Eliot wants to tell Terry it doesn't matter. He wants to put up his hand and tell him to come back but the numbness spreads, envelopes him again and takes his voice.

Terry jogs toward the room and vanishes inside.

Watching the fire, Eliot notes how its tendrils slow, licking the logs and stroking the kindling almost tenderly as they burn. The flames crawl and the cinders glow and all of time stops in those moments the longer he stares.

Alexis's hand slides over the back of his hand, fingers wrapping between his. He wants to look over at her but can't.

I failed, he thinks.

"What makes you say that?" Death asks in Alexis's voice.

The whole point of this trip was to inspire four chefs. I only got to two. I didn't do what you wanted.

"You're wrong."

How?

"How many people are here because of you?" Alexis asks. "How many people came with you or followed you to be sitting right here under these stars?"

That's not just because of me, he thinks. *You straight up lied to one of them to get them to come with me and you killed a federal agent to goad the other one into pursuing me.*

"Eh, the details don't matter." She gives his hand a squeeze. "What does matter is that each and every one of them is changed because of you. And you helped stop a fucked-up cult from sacrificing more people. So…bonus!"

Eliot wishes he could laugh. *You know what doesn't make sense?*

Death gets out of her chair and crouches down in front of him. Alexis's expression is that blend of calm happy-go-lucky that he misses most about her. It's a look he saw on her face the first moment he met her at her food truck on that backstreet in Getty all those years ago.

"What?" she asks.

You could have let me die so many times along this trip. You actively went out of your way to save me. Why would Death do that? Even if you were, as you said, sending me on some mission to stop the Ash from spreading. To reignite humanity's inspiration. I don't buy that you did all of this because you wanted us to taste better. Death is Death.

The warmth in Alexis's eyes remains.

Death takes predictably as much as it does unpredictably. So…you're not actually Death, are you?

Alexis puts her other hand around his. "All right you smart fuck. Who am I then?"

Hope.

She brings his hand up to her lips and kisses it. "I knew you'd get there." She lets him go and sits back down in the chair next to him.

Eliot notes that the fire has stopped moving entirely, sparks frozen in mid-air, smoke like a slanted column trailing into the sky. Across the horizon, he senses a flickering of light. The burning inside of him plummets into numb warmth like stepping into a heated pool.

This is it, isn't it? he thinks.

"Don't be scared."

A tear escapes the corner of his eye before sizzling down his cheek and evaporating.

I need you to do one last thing for me, he asks. *For Meena.*

He can't see her, but he knows that Alexis is smiling when she answers, "Anything for you."

…

Meena doesn't understand why her sweater isn't where she left it. It had been in her bag along with everything else she'd thrown together from their stop in Morning Sun. She searches under the bed, amidst the covers and sheets, even in the bathroom wondering if maybe she'd grabbed it to use as a pillow while keeping an eye on Eliot. Not there either.

It's not until Terry comes in that he points out it might be in the van. She goes to check, and sure enough, it's in the back folded neatly as if someone had just put it there. Weird.

Meena puts it on and slides the door to the van closed. As she starts across the lot toward the campfire, she tilts her head back and looks at the night sky again. She recognizes the constellation of Ursa Major among the glittering array; the constellation her father told her was most like her. Pulling people together. Giving people a safe place to be themselves.

When she got back to Getty, she wasn't sure what was going to be in store for her, but she knew she wouldn't compromise for other people.

"Be true to yourself," Eliot had told her once, when she was in the kitchen. "You're making this for you as much as you are for them."

She smiles as she rounds the fire toward where she'd been sitting. "I just remembered that ti—"

Her words dry in her throat when she notices Eliot's empty chair. She glances around, searching for where he could have gone but there's no one else in the lot. Meena runs back to the hotel room. "Terry, did Eliot come back in here?"

Terry's eyes round. "No! Did he wander—"

They both race back out into the lot. They question everyone there: the star-gazing families who weren't paying attention to what was going on in the lot as much as they were the light show now happening above them, the managers who shake their heads sadly, the couples who were making out, and nope, didn't even notice that any of them had gotten up and left.

Until she sees the lone figure the size of a toothpick on the horizon, silhouetted against a flare of green coming up from behind the mountains. She runs toward it screaming his name.

Terry grabs her before she can get too far. "Get in the van!" They run to it, and climb in, Terry scrambling his hands over his jeans. "Fucking keys. Where are the fucking keys?"

He climbs back out and runs into the room.

Meena's throat burns with fear, her mind skittering with images of snakes biting Eliot, scorpions stinging him, needles from cactuses jabbing him…

It feels like forever by the time Terry returns with the keys and the engine roars to life. Terry rumbles the van across the lot and straight into the desert scrub, the low plants and rocks bumping and scraping against the metal below as he races them over the land toward the departing figure. It's minutes before they finally catch up.

Terry pulls the van up alongside Eliot and rolls down his window, now driving at a snail's pace. "Eliot! Wake up!"

Meena can't see with Terry's body blocking her view. She throws open her door and climbs out, carefully picking her way around the rear of the van through the succulents. As she rounds the van, she sees Eliot blunder through a patch of long billowing grass and calls to him.

He doesn't turn.

She barely registers that Terry has stopped the van as she catches up with Eliot. She grabs his arm. "Eliot. El?"

He pulls against her.

"Eliot, you need to stop. You need to—" She trips and lets him go to make sure she doesn't fall. When she glances up, she sees he hasn't stopped. He hasn't registered her at all.

Terry's door opens behind her. "Meena!"

"He's not stopping. I can't get him to stop!" Meena tugs on Eliot's hand and something falls away into her palm. She shrieks, flinging her hand away before looking at it. Black ash streaks over her fingers.

"What happened?" Terry bumps his shoulder into hers.

Meena can't say anything. Her eyes are locked on the parts of Eliot's charred hand that are now missing, the bits of his fingers that have fallen into the headlight-streaked grass at her feet. "He's…" she tries. "He's…"

Terry pushes through the grass, barreling toward him. "No! No!"

"Terry, come back!"

Through a veil of tears, Meena watches Terry catch up to Eliot, watches him put both arms on his shoulders, watches him stare into his face and say his name. Over and over and over.

A heaviness lifts from Terry after a moment. His arms fall to his sides as he steps aside. His former friend pushes past, fumbling further into the desert.

Meena makes her way over to Terry, recognizes the emptiness in his gaze, and puts her arms around them.

The two new friends hold each other in the dark and cry.

APOTHEOSIS

"UNFINALIZED" DRAFT OF LAST OBSERVATION

We follow the Ashen that used to be Eliot Lamb across the desert.

I know it was not a good idea. Even tried to explain why. Once an Ashen becomes an Ashen, they are undeniably not the person they once were. Whether there's a piece of them still trapped inside unable to communicate or not is irrelevant. From the outside, they are nothing but wandering bodies without souls and all outward attempts at communicating with them have failed so far.

The Agent[1] agreed with my sentiment but chose to humor its heartbroken colleagues instead. He's gotten soft with one of them which is to his betterment. And as much as I knew this was damaging psychologically as much as it was physically for everyone in our little party, I decided to tag along to ensure that I witness whatever I can from this observation.

For the group's sake, we maintain a distance of at least a hundred feet from the Ashen at all times. We don't want to influence its path, and we don't want to alter the environment, animal or otherwise, around it as it travels.

[1] The Agent is a member of the Federal Bureau of Investigation. As he has agreed to help me in my studies on Ashen behavior, I have agreed to keep his identity anonymous.

The first day sees a lot of reticence from the Ashen's once friends. They insist "he could snap out of it at any moment." By the second day, they have accepted the change and by the third, we are all exhausted.

The Agent frequently leaves to find sustenance for the group in whatever small town or settlement he can find close enough, not to mention to check in with his superiors about his ongoing investigation about the True Faith religion[1].

On the fourth day at around the twentieth hour, we've made camp in a small valley and are finishing the remains of the chef's campfire foil packet dinners: potatoes, corn, salt, pepper, and jicama with a hot sauce that still smolders on my tongue. As the subject used to be a chef, I feel as though it's important to document the meal we ate just before *it* finally happened.

The plumber had pointed out a greenness on the horizon shortly before dinner. I haven't paid attention to celestial diversions such as weather, solar storms, temperature, etc. in my earlier observations of Ashen behavior, mainly due to the fact that it was almost always the same, raining and fairly temperate.

But out here where the rain has petered off and the sand still holds sway, there is an extraterrestrial quality about the skies that I just can't put my finger on. Perhaps it's the fact that we are only miles away from that strange Area 51 that seems to captivate even the least delusional of people in these parts. At nearly every gas station we've

---

[1] The True Faith Religion is the subject of an ongoing FBI investigation that I am currently assisting on. I cannot discuss matters of the case in this study as per my agreement with the Bureau but, I would like to revisit the matter for a future study.

stopped, there's a small gift shop attached with alien-themed tchotchkes of every variety.

Post dinner, the sky opens up, the clouds pulling apart like whisked cream to reveal color. Shimmering streaks of pinks and greens like tourmaline rippling in ribbons through the air. We're all stunned in our seats, unable to look away because color like this hasn't occurred on the east coast of the United States in years. We don't get glorious sunrises or majestic sunsets. We can barely distinguish morning from afternoon from night in our envelope of blue darkness where we reside.

This is extraordinary. This is noteworthy.

I manage to tear my eyes away from it for long enough to notice that our Ashen has stopped. He—It never stops. It's been going for four days, never showing any signs of tire. It's lifted its head to the sky like the rest of us taking in the glow.

The plumber taps my shoulder and points out something to our far right, something else standing rigid along the ridge. Another Ashen. And there just to the left…another.

Soon enough, we can spot at least a dozen or more, all craning their necks up to the aurora.

I scramble to the Agent's car and find my camcorder, my tape recorder. I need to document this as clearly as I can[1].

By the time I have hit the record button, the Ashen have changed in formation. They have their hands raised over their heads

---

[1] This journal entry, while important, is biased by my own thoughts and feelings after said event. The audio and the video will serve as better representation of what happened and I'll be able to edit these thoughts later to make a more accurate description for my study.

as though reaching for the light. This is a tremendous sight. Not once have the Ashen ever portrayed a human level of cognizance after their full conversion. They can't negotiate rough terrain, they don't recognize people they used to know, they can't communicate vocally or through any kind of hand signals, and they don't seem to even recognize when they are in the company of others.

It's like seeing a moving painting. The colors, the textures, the splendor of the mountains rising like dark tidal waves beneath the sky. Sitting here reviewing the video footage, I remember that I was afraid to breathe, afraid that even my smallest movements would upset the utter majesty of whatever cosmic fuckery was happening in front of me. I ended up setting the camcorder down on a rock to make sure it stayed still.

"There's more," says the chef, and there are. More Ashen appearing from near and far out of the darkness as if they have melded out of it somehow. There must be close to fifty of them, and I almost lose sight of our Ashen, but managed to find him. Eliot was bald, which helps to pinpoint him among the others, though some are missing patches of hair where the environment and the Ash itself have been unkind to them.

"What the hell are they doing?" the Agent murmurs just loud enough for the camera to pick up and I shush him.

The vibrancy in the sky intensifies; becomes an overwhelming blanket of magenta, of lime green, of pearlescent refraction. At first, I think I see particles of gold within and wonder if anyone who's seen the Aurora Borealis has ever seen that shade. But soon enough, I realize it's coming from the Ashen themselves as pieces of them begin to spark off as if carried on a breeze.

Eliot, or what was once Eliot, is warmed by fractals of embers floating off of him, floating off the bodies of every creature surrounding him. There's no fear in any of their faces, no recognition of pain, only a kind of serene stupor that holds them all in place like melted wax holding guttering candles against a strong wind. Pieces of them disintegrate hot and bright and shift amongst the aurora and all of us watch because…what else can we do?

There are no explosions. There are no bodies bursting into fiery columns. Nothing graphic. Nothing gory. There is only solid and then infinite.

Each one fades at their own speed: some are sonatas meeting out over the gradual scale of the aurora's congruence while others fizzle up and depart in brighter orange spurs like sparklers, the crash of cymbals against the rising symphony of light.

And just when we're all enraptured, it fades and coolness folds down over us and we're once again simple creatures in the desert night.

I don't remember who cried first: maybe the sous chef. What I do remember is that no one says another word for the rest of the evening. What can be said? To make any kind of noise after such a show except for an ovation seems unworthy, and an applause itself is superficial. To ask why or how feels intrusive and callous.

So, no one does then. And I won't now. Not even for scientific pontification.

The Ash steals our sensations and emotions from us and makes us forget what it is to be human. If what we witnessed doesn't evoke a completely human reaction of awe from anyone, then I fear for us as a species. But judging by how the Ashen also stopped in reverence beneath those Northern Lights, maybe all isn't lost. Maybe where the soul goes isn't important. Maybe what's important is how the soul endures when it's at home in the human body.

How souls communicate with one another. How souls coexist. How we inspire one another. And how above all else, we hope in even the darkest darkness that there will be light.

25

BACK TO LIFE

Meena turns on the lights, and beholds the kitchen she remembers.

Well, sort of.

It had been in the hands of the new owner for almost two months, and they'd already begun renovations. They'd taken out the old appliances and demoed a hole in the wall between the kitchen and the bar, sold a chunk of the tables and chairs in the dining room, and had started pulling up the floor.

Tempo looks ugly, hardly the same place that she'd last worked professionally, the place where she finally got to create in her own space, a place where she was finally the one who got to nurture and care for her own creativity.

But, Tempo was gone. Eliot was gone. And that was okay.

About a week after she'd returned to Getty with Terry, she received a telegram from The Green Room Bank and Trust, the one that had been targeted in the Arts District…Eliot's bank. They'd moved into a temporary location, and in going over notes, asked for her to contact one of their financial advisors. Apparently, in Eliot's last will and testament, he'd left her whatever was left of his finances, a list of his restaurant contacts, and a note.

At first, she'd stared dumbfounded at the clerk like they must have been mistaken. Eliot had been fatalistic when he'd shut down Tempo and the idea of anyone resuscitating it seemed like a dishonor. After all, he'd been a legend even after the scandal Alexis had caused. Wasn't it just better to leave the ashes where they lay so to speak?

The note, however, changed her mind. It read: "Do what you best: be you and bring it back to life."

Meena steps into the kitchen further and lets the door clank shut behind her. She runs her hand along the kitchen counter tops, stares at the old television set still mounted up in the corner, at the empty first aid box remounted on the wall…

She'd met up with Terry a day after receiving the inheritance. They sipped coffee at a little shop around the corner from the arts district, a place with lots of old books and comfy chairs, a place that smelled earthy and reminded her of her father's old office. Terry had been supportive. He told her to do it. He told her that he believed in her and held her hand. And something kicked up in her chest at his smile. It was such a nice one.

Meena takes a deep breath in the old kitchen and sighs.

"What are you going to call it?" Terry had asked before they left the café.

"Ursa Major," she'd said. "For my dad."

They'd hugged and lingered and hugged again, and ultimately, Terry had walked her home. They'd held hands.

Just thinking about it makes Meena smile.

This is only the beginning, she thinks to herself as she turns on the lights for the dining room. *Time to make this place shine.*

…

Left white-knuckles the steering wheel as he sits in the Camero and stares at the fat rolls of rain cascading down its windshield. *This is a mistake,* he thinks as he eyes the keys dangling in the ignition. He can still leave, preserve some of his iron will until the next opportunity presented itself. But when would that be? Months from now? Years? He might not come back to this city ever again if he can help it.

"Well?" The Psychologist asks from the passenger seat.

He bites his lip. "Gimme a minute."

"If I give you any more minutes, you'll sit here all morning."

The comment bristles against him. He sighs heavily and yanks open the car door. The rain pelts against his jacket as he slides out into it. He reaches back in to grab the small bouquet on the dash, but the Psychologist has already got it. They leave the pavement walkway for the lush grass. Rows and rows of headstones whisper by them as they make their way toward the back, climbing the hill past ancient oaks almost as big around as his car.

In the back, closer to the trees where a view looks out over gray-green fields, he stops and stares at the small marker on the ground furthest away. Getting any closer feels like inciting a curse. Had she counted how long it had been since he'd last visited? If he went over there, would she reach up and pull him down to be with her for good? He swallows.

The Psychologist puts her arm around him and pushes him along. He lets her guide him, their shoes squelching in the grass until they stop directly in front of her grave.

Left's cheeks prickle. He feels sick to his stomach as his eyes trace the name on her grave marker.

"You gonna say something?" the Psychologist asks.

"Aren't we…uh…aren't we standing on her?"

The Psychologist looks down and after a moment, shifts Left over. "Better?"

He nods and clears his throat. He opens his mouth.

Silence. There's just utter silence all around. A raven sits in the tree overlooking row F and Left fixates on it. It's huge. Since when were ravens so huge?

The Psychologist sighs.

"Can you go somewhere?" he asks her. "Just for a few minutes."

She nods and starts walking away.

"Don't leave though."

Her smile assures him she won't.

Once she's out of sight, Left crouches so that he's closer to the grave and sniffs. "Hey. It's me, sweetheart. I'm…um…I'm an asshole." His voice trembles as he admits it. "I didn't deserve you. I was too selfish to have kids. I always knew that. But it doesn't make what I've done right. It doesn't make me not coming here right. So, I'm sorry."

The raven caws and takes flight, flapping once before gliding off toward the woods.

"I just wanted you to know that. I'm trying to let people in. Maybe it'll make me get here in time for your birthday next year. Anyway…" He sets the flowers down. "I don't know what they are but they're pink. Like that tutu you used to wear. Thought of you when I picked them out."

He glances right and left. The Psychologist is out of sight. There is only the dead and him.

"I love you. And I miss you. And I hope you're up there dancing with yourself or whoever else you can find. I'll see you soon, baby."

Left doesn't even realize he's crying as he leaves the marker behind, leaves the squishy grass and the too-pink flowers. His shoes clop on the walkway as he searches for the Psychologist, and when he finds her, they return to the car and get in.

He keeps his eyes on the sky, wanting to avoid eye contact for as long as he can. "Here comes the fucking rain again."

"How'd it go?" she asks.

He grinds his teeth, his hands gripping the steering wheel just as hard now as before he had even left the car. His throat is tight, and he can't make a sound. "Not good," he croaks.

She puts her hand on his, the coolness of her palm softening his grip. "Not good is okay. It's all okay. Let's get out of here."

Left eagerly starts the car, puts it in gear, and they flee the cemetery as thunder howls above them and the rain comes down harder.

...

Terry stands in the restaurant entrance hypnotized by the smells of decadent dishes. He isn't sure what it is, but he wants it, needs it. The host shows him to a vacant seat at a table along the left side of the room and Terry plops into the seat there, his eyes pulled in a thousand different directions. It's a dark little place, the walls a warm gray and lit by small sconces in each corner of the room. Each table ripples with whispers of eagerness, of joyful surprise. The sounds of clinking knives and forks and full mouths talking all around him.

And from the kitchen doors, Meena appears in her chef's tunic, her smile ebullient. It lifts Terry onto a new plane, his chest fluttering with excitement. Nothing makes him happier than seeing her in the environment where she can do what she loves.

"Hey, baby," he says when she gets closer. "This place is hopping!"

"So far so good," she agrees and kisses him.

"You know he'd be proud of you."

Meena nods, sadness contorting her features for only a moment. "I do."

Terry holds her hand and picks up the menu. "What should I get first?"

"First?" she laughs, wiping a stray tear away.

"I intend to try everything on this menu." He looks closer at the prices and flinches. "Eventually."

"This one is on me, Ter-Bear." Terry is smitten with the nickname. She only uses it occasionally, but it makes him beam with pride. Meena disappears into the kitchen.

Terry sips his wine and watches the room as he waits for his dinner. He tries to imagine Eliot in a place like this, shouting orders, knocking out amazing dish after amazing dish, time and time again. He thinks about their time in the van traveling across the country, about their various food excursions in random diners, gas stations, and eateries. He thinks about telling the entire story to his sister who let them stay at her home after they got back from the desert.

At first, Terry had suspected Rosanna wouldn't even talk to him. He thought she'd tell him to leave as soon as they were collected. She didn't. In fact, the first thing she did was pull him in for the longest hug he'd *ever* had. Minutes. Damn near a whole hour. They sat next to each other on the couch holding one another while he told her all about his trip across the country, about how he'd lost his friend the night before, about how sorry he was for not keeping in touch. And she said almost the same. She talked about how sorry she was for not reaching out, how sorry she was for not sending photos or inviting him to stay with them, for thinking that he was angry with her because it was her graduation celebration that led to Grandmama Jean's death.

But he wasn't mad.

She wasn't mad.

And everything was so much better now that they had talked.

He already had plans to drive back out to visit her at Christmas. He wanted to bring Meena along. Plus, they had to check in on Apple, who had fallen in love with his nephew almost immediately upon meeting him.

The server arrived with a plate of glistening noodles bathed in a creamy white sauce. The smell was incredible, and the taste punched him in the face. Bright acidity from lemon and sharp saltiness from the Parmesan. He scanned the menu for the name of the dish and faltered when he noticed the dedication to Eliot on the menu.

It was the closest thing he would ever get to eating something that Eliot had ever made. And it was made by the person he connected him to. He ate the whole thing and tried not to laugh with every bite as he remembered his friend for who he was and not who he became.

Not a man. Not a chef.

Just a wandering soul like the rest of them.

ACKNOWLEDGEMENTS

Where The Soul Goes wouldn't be what it is today without Kristina Osborn of Truborn Press. I came to her with a crazy pitch after Author-Con. She took a chance on my idea and signed me on after only reading the first few chapters. That's a chance that the average horror author doesn't often get and I'm so grateful to have had that to prove that this weird sad tale had legs.

More over, all of Kristina's work with the book for Truborn has been amazing and wonderful. Thank you so much for your attention to detail, your care for the story and for the entire process of putting it out.

Thank you to Erin Al-Mehairi for editing the story. Your insight was crucial in making sure that elements in the story felt cohesive and that Eliot's cat got the ending she deserved!

Thanks to my early readers and the authors who provided such beautiful blurbs. It is always a strange and nerve-wracking time when one has to ask their heroes and friends to read their work and endorse it. I appreciate you all.

Thank you to the creator of the cover art, Seanen Middleton for optioning the rights for us to use your brilliant photography work.

Where The Soul Goes was part of my journey of self-discovery about coming out as asexual. About understanding it. About what I was afraid of losing and missing but also the freedom of knowing that I was not alone anymore. That these feelings I thought made me broken are feelings others have had, will continue to have.

The book is about recognizing those who see you for who you are and love you, about making sure you give people a chance to know the real you before you discount them. And not to harden your heart against all opportunities for that love to be shown to you.

I am, have always been, will always be one who shows my love through what I write, through the things I create, through the gifts I give and the words I say. And I am so fortunate to have the friends and family I do who support me.

A few more thank yous:

Thank you to Anthony Bourdain, who sadly will never read this.

Thank you to my family for fostering a love of cooking and introducing me to weird food at a young age, even if I didn't eat all of it.

Thank you to my partner in crime for what you've taught me in the kitchen. For always being up for making something new and unexpected in the kitchen. For embarking on culinary adventures with me. For loving me for who I am.

And thank you for picking up my book, for reading a voice that isn't considered a part of the typical mainstream. For choosing to listen to a queer voice, a woman's voice, a neurodivergent voice, an indie voice. Please read more of our voices.

ABOUT THE
AUTHOR

Katherine Silva is an ace Maine horror author, a connoisseur of coffee, and victim of cat shenanigans. Her favorite flavors of the genre mix grief and existentialism which she combines with her love of the New England wilderness in her works. She is a three-time Maine Literary Award finalist for speculative fiction. Katherine is also editor-in-chief of *Strange Wilds Press*.

A NOTE FROM
THE PUBLISHER

We want to thank our readers for their support and enthusiasm. Your passion for stories fuels our commitment to bring you the horror that is strange and horrifying in the best of ways.

We appreciate any and all reviews, so help us out by leaving your thoughts online.

Thank you again for spending your time with us and remember to…

Follow us everywhere on social media!
@trubornpress

Subscribe to our substack to keep up on news, updates
and receive free short stories!

CONTENT NOTES

Acephobia

Attempted Murder/Murder

Blood/Bones

Burn Victims

Car Accident

Child Death

Conversion Therapy

Cults

Death

Depression

Drowning

Fire

Gun Violence

Hallucinations

Homophobia

Hospitalization

Hostages/Kidnapping

Profanity

Terminal Illness

Terrorism

Violence

Religious Ideology

www.ingramcontent.com/pod-product-compliance
Lightning Source LLC
Chambersburg PA
CBHW020325010826

48973CB00005B/1131